I0700646

Also by the Author

The Erin O'Reilly Mysteries
Black Velvet
Irish Car Bomb
White Russian
Double Scotch
Manhattan
Black Magic
Death By Chocolate
Massacre
Flashback
First Love
High Stakes
Aquarium
The Devil You Know
Hair of the Dog
Punch Drunk
Bossa Nova
Blackout
and more…

Fathers
A Modern Christmas Story

The Clarion Chronicles
Ember of Dreams

Angel Face

The Erin O'Reilly Mysteries
Book Eighteen

Steven Henry

Clickworks Press • Baltimore, MD

First publication: Clickworks Press, 2022
Release: CWP-EOR18-INT-P.IS-2.0

Sign up for updates, deals, and exclusive sneak peeks at clickworkspress.com/join.

Ebook ISBN: 978-1-943383-99-3
Paperback ISBN: 979-8-88900-000-6
Hardcover ISBN: 979-8-88900-001-3

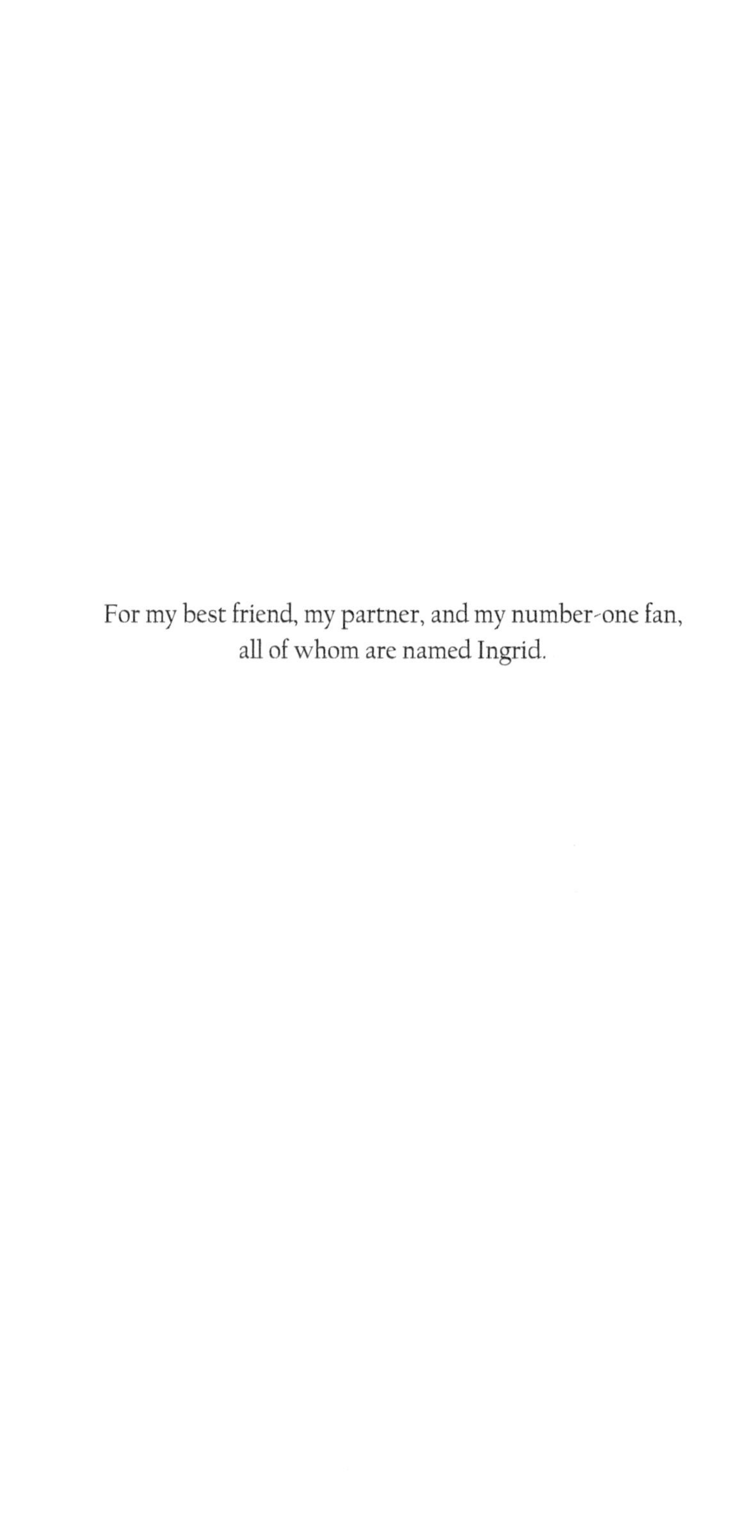

For my best friend, my partner, and my number-one fan,
all of whom are named Ingrid.

Angel Face

Combine 1 oz. No. 3 gin, 1 oz. applejack, and 1 oz. apricot liqueur with ice in a mixing glass. Stir until well chilled. Strain into a cocktail glass. Garnish with an orange peel and serve.

Chapter 1

Even if you were wearing a bulletproof vest, getting shot hurt. The bullet's energy, instead of traveling through your body, expended itself on the Kevlar weave of your body armor. The feeling was about the same as taking a full-force swing from a baseball bat. Paradoxically, wearing armor made you more likely to get knocked over, since the bullet wouldn't keep going. You might crack ribs, and you'd have one hell of a bruise.

The pain from a Taser was worse, but also more temporary. It was a deep, intense burning sensation that radiated out from the electrodes. Your muscles locked up and you couldn't move as long as the juice was flowing. But at least once it was over, you could get up and get on with your business. The only souvenirs you'd carry would be a couple of little punctures and contact burns that would itch as they healed.

Even taking a punch was no picnic, not if the guy hitting you knew how to do it. A professional boxer's fist could shatter your jaw or knock you unconscious. Brain trauma could mess with just about everything upstairs, including motor functions, short-term and long-term memory, sensory input, and cognitive capacity. Concussions played hell with your faculties. You might get full use of your brain back, but you might not.

Erin O'Reilly had been punched in the head by a professional boxer. She'd also taken a Taser jolt, and had even been shot a couple of times. She liked to think she was tough, but she had no desire whatsoever to repeat any of those experiences. Still, given the choice, she might pick any of the three over the torture she was currently undergoing.

She tried not to squirm, not to give anything away. She was a trained police detective, experienced in interrogations. She looked down and to one side of the couch where she sat. Her partner Rolf sat bolt upright at her elbow, stern and serious. He returned her look and cocked his head questioningly. At a single word from her, he was ready to spring into action. He'd fight to the death to protect her. But he was no help here.

Erin sighed inwardly and forced herself to turn away from her K-9, back toward the matter at hand. If she could handle a high-speed car chase, an unexploded bomb, or an armed felon, she could deal with this.

"Now, here's Erin on her first day back from the hospital," Mary O'Reilly said, pointing to the photo album on the coffee table. "Look at that face. A perfect little angel. Isn't she just adorable?"

"Aye, she's a fine wee bairn," Morton Carlyle agreed. He was sandwiched between Erin and her mom on his living-room couch, upstairs from his pub. On the table in front of him, Erin's whole childhood was piled into three hefty albums. The three of them were currently looking at baby pictures.

"Her brother was so sweet," Mary went on, flipping the page to show a very young Sean O'Reilly Junior holding baby Erin. "I swear, you could tell even at that age, Junior was going to be a doctor. I'm only surprised he didn't go into obstetrics."

Erin tried not to wince at the picture. In it, her face was scrunched up as if she was about to sneeze, scream, or possibly fill her diaper. Her eyes were squinting and her tiny mouth was open.

It wasn't that the pictures were so bad, all things considered. No, Mary O'Reilly's complete lack of subtlety was the really painful thing. Erin's mother had come down to the city, ostensibly to visit her grandchildren, Sean Junior and Michelle's two kids. But the O'Reilly matriarch had come to Manhattan armed with the albums, and Erin knew why.

Erin was thirty-six years old, never married, no kids. She'd been seeing Carlyle since New Year's, over nine months now, and had been living with him for almost half that time. In Mary's books, that meant it was time to start thinking marriage and children, the more and the sooner the better.

Accordingly, Erin's mom was mounting a full-court press. She probably thought she was being delicate and polite. And Erin supposed, compared to Carlyle's business associates, she was. But then, those associates were the O'Malley Irish Mob, a motley crew of murderous thugs, racketeers, and smugglers. Their idea of subtlety involved back alleys and tire irons. It was a low bar to clear.

The worst part of it was, Erin didn't need to be convinced. She liked kids, adored her niece and nephew, and was completely on board with the idea of having her own one of these days. But not yet, and she couldn't explain her hesitation to her mom. Mary O'Reilly thought Carlyle was an ordinary publican, a well-to-do gentleman who'd made his money as a successful small-business owner. But Carlyle had two secrets.

The first secret, widely known in the New York underworld, was that the Barley Corner, in addition to being a thriving watering hole for blue-collar Irishmen, was also a front for the O'Malleys, a money-laundering operation, and a haven for sports bookies. The second, known to fewer than ten people, was that Carlyle had turned informant and was compiling information to use against his boss Evan O'Malley. He'd made the choice out of love for Erin, desperation after a near-fatal shooting, and the long-shot hope of personal redemption.

Mary O'Reilly could probably forgive Carlyle his shady past. But she didn't know how much danger he and Erin were currently in. Until they'd brought down the O'Malleys and could go for a drive without needing to check the underside of Carlyle's Mercedes for car bombs, marriage and children were off the table. And they couldn't tell her this, because Mary was a generous, loving, open-hearted woman who didn't know how to keep her mouth shut.

So Erin was doomed to suffer through an interminable morning of thinly-veiled hints about the joys of motherhood, her mom thinking Erin was dragging her feet while her biological clock ticked down toward zero.

Erin glanced at the living-room clock and unclenched her jaw. She slipped her hand out of Carlyle's and stood. Carlyle, ever the gentleman, also got to his feet.

"Sorry, Mom," she lied, following it up with the truth. "I have an appointment. Work."

"I thought you were off duty today," Mary said.

"I am. But I need to be in court. There's an arraignment, a Mafia guy, and I was one of the arresting officers."

"Mattie Madonna's lad?" Carlyle said. "Alfredo?"

"You know a Mafia goon?" Mary asked.

"I knew his father, some years back," Carlyle said smoothly. "I'd hardly call us friends, but we were acquainted with some of the same people. I'd heard the lad was in a wee bit of trouble."

"Parole violation," Erin said. "I promised his dad I'd look in on him, see what I could do for him. Sorry to run out on you like this."

"And we haven't even gotten to her grade-school pictures yet," Mary said, pouting a little.

"I'm going nowhere, Mrs. O'Reilly," Carlyle said. "I'd be happy to see more of what Erin was like as a wee lass."

Erin shot him a grateful look and made for the exit. Rolf bounded alongside, tail wagging. The German Shepherd didn't understand why humans made such a point of sitting indoors all the time when they could be running around outdoors. The world was full of bad guys to chase, smells to investigate, and rubber toys to chew on. It was time to get out there and patrol their territory.

"Sorry, kiddo," she told him at the top of the stairs. "We can't have you in the courtroom. The lawyers would call it intimidation. Bleib."

Rolf froze, one paw raised. He couldn't believe it. His partner was going on adventures and he couldn't come. He gave it a moment, seeing if the instructions changed, but Erin turned away. Rolf was a good boy, so he stayed put, as instructed, but he gave her a reproachful stare as only a dog could. His intense brown eyes bored holes in Erin's back as she fled down the stairs and out of the apartment.

*   *   *

Erin didn't like going to court. As far as she was concerned, her role in the legal system was to collect evidence, arrest the perps, and hand them over to the District Attorney. After that, they became his problem. Erin distrusted lawyers, even prosecutors, and found courtroom proceedings incredibly boring. She also knew that sometimes guilty guys got off the hook, and there was nothing she could do about it, which was doubly infuriating. Being a detective had enough frustrations without that, so she steered clear of trials unless called on to testify.

But today was different. It wasn't just an excuse to get away from her mother's baby blitz. She'd made a promise to a dying man that she'd try to help his son. Matthew Madonna might have been a drug-dealing Mafioso, who'd gone down in a hail of bullets in a seedy bar. But Erin had held Mattie's hand as he died. If they hadn't been friends, they'd shared an enemy: Vincenzo Moreno, new don of the Lucarelli Family. Vinnie had been behind Madonna's murder, along with several others, but Erin hadn't been able to prove it. Vinnie's nickname was "The Oil Man," and he'd proved as slippery as ever. Vinnie had slithered out of trouble and Mattie's son Alfie had ended up fatherless and incarcerated.

Erin parked her Charger in one of the police spaces at the courthouse. She went through the front doors and the security checkpoint, where she showed her gold shield and handed over both her sidearm and her backup ankle gun. It struck her as a little silly that she, a decorated NYPD detective, wasn't allowed to bring a gun into court, but the men hired by the US Marshals to provide security were. She submitted as gracefully as she could. However, being unarmed left her very nervous these days, particularly without her dog.

The day's proceedings were ludicrous. An arraignment wasn't a trial. A jury wasn't going to be there. All it consisted of was the formal reading of the charges against the defendant and that defendant entering his plea. The whole thing would only take a few minutes.

Alfredo Madonna should have been arraigned within twenty-four hours of being charged. That was the rules. However, in Madonna's case, there'd been a delay. The kid had been hospitalized. It seemed Madonna had eaten something that had disagreed with him, badly enough that he'd needed to have his stomach pumped. Erin had been distracted at the time, dealing with a budding serial killer, and he hadn't technically been her prisoner, so she'd only gotten the information at second hand, days later.

That was why Erin was here now. She wanted to see Alfredo Madonna, and hopefully find out what had happened to him. She suspected Vinnie's hand, but then, she suspected Vinnie of everything connected with the Lucarellis. The bastard had somehow managed to have a man killed in the middle of Erin's own beloved Eightball, right there in the holding cells. If he could do that, he could definitely have slipped Alfie something nasty to go with his supper. The only surprise was that the kid was still breathing.

Erin was gratified to see a grim-looking Deputy Marshal outside the courtroom, keeping an eye on the corridor. He gave her a cool once-over, examined her credentials, and stepped aside.

The courtroom was nearly empty. Arraignments were public, so in theory anybody could show up, but except in high-profile cases they were not well-attended functions. There'd be the judge, the court recorder, the prosecutor, the defendant, and the defendant's legal team. Erin had arrived a little early, so the only people in the room yet were the bailiff and the prosecutor.

Erin eyed the young man at the front of the room. The DA's guy was just a kid, probably some wet-behind-the-ears law-school graduate on his first case. It ought to be a slam-dunk. Alfie Madonna was on parole, prohibited from associating with known felons and from carrying firearms. He'd been found in the presence of several men with long criminal records, some of them freshly dead, in close proximity to a revolver, recently fired, covered with his fingerprints. Though Alfie's dad had sworn to Erin in his dying declaration that he'd been the one to kill all the other men who'd died in that room, Alfie had still been charged with second-degree murder in addition to the weapons and parole violations. He was looking at a big pile of years.

Erin sat a few rows back and settled in as well as she could. She didn't have to wait long; only a few minutes later, the doors swung open and Alfie Madonna walked in, flanked by his lawyer on one side and a square-jawed Deputy on the other. Erin recognized the lawyer; Kingston Schultz, an attorney of Jamaican extraction who'd been representing Alfie and his dad for years. The lawyer had his arm around his client, helping him down the aisle.

Alfie looked rough. He was pale and hollow-eyed, like a man who'd seen a ghost. But he walked with slow, deliberate purpose, hardly leaning on his lawyer. He looked straight ahead, not seeming to notice Erin. The expression on his young face was cold and determined.

Once the defendant and his lawyer were seated, the bailiff stepped to the door behind the lectern. A moment later, the judge emerged. He was a gray-haired man, magisterial in his black robe. The few people in the room got to their feet when he entered, then sat right back down again.

The judge droned out the necessary legal boilerplate. Before he'd finished his first sentence, Erin could already feel her eyes starting to glaze over. After he'd finished, the prosecutor got up and read the charges. Erin already knew what these were, so she let them slide past her ears. She was watching Alfie. The kid was obviously still very weak, but he was showing some grit, refusing to so much as slouch in his chair. Erin really wanted to go right up to him and start asking questions, but she didn't want to get tackled by the bailiff, so she resisted the impulse.

"Mr. Madonna," the judge said. "You've heard the state's charges. How do you plead?"

"Your Honor," Schultz said, speaking on Alfie's behalf. "The defense moves that the charge of murder be dropped. The State's case is weak, undermined by the confession of Matthew Madonna. The state has produced no conclusive evidence that my client fired any shots during the fracas at Lucia's Bar."

The judge turned his eyes on the prosecutor.

"Your Honor," the kid said. "The State agrees to drop the charge of second-degree murder."

Erin was suddenly wide awake, sitting forward on the edge of her bench. Just like that, they were throwing away the most serious charge? Without even trying for a plea bargain? She didn't think the case was weak at all. Men had gone to prison on shakier evidence. What was going on here?

"To the remaining charges," Schultz said, "my client pleads nolo contendere."

Erin didn't know Latin, but she knew that phrase. It meant "no contest," and it was a lawyerly way of admitting guilt without explicitly admitting it. This case wouldn't go to trial. Now all that was left was for the judge to set bail prior to sentencing.

"Very well," the judge said. "Defendant is released on recognizance, to appear for sentencing two weeks from today." He banged his gavel on the lectern, stood up, and left the room.

Erin was stunned. The judge hadn't thrown Alfie back in a cell, hadn't even bothered to set bail. That was beyond absurd. Alfie Madonna was a repeat offender, a career criminal. If the murder charge had remained in effect, he might have been held without bail at all, or the judge might have set a prohibitively high bond. But now Alfie could just walk out of the courthouse and go home to await his sentencing—assuming he didn't make a run for it and flee the state, or maybe the country.

Somebody had put a thumb on the scales of justice, Erin was sure of it. What she didn't know was who and why. But she intended to find out.

Chapter 2

Erin caught up with Alfie and his lawyer before they'd gotten halfway to the courthouse exit. The kid was moving slowly and was obviously in serious discomfort. He was leaning on Schultz more heavily than he had in the courtroom.

"Mr. Madonna," she called, coming up behind.

Kingston Schultz interposed himself between them. "My client has no comment on the—Detective O'Reilly! What an unexpected pleasure."

"It's okay, King," Alfie said. "She's stand-up."

"How are you feeling?" Erin asked him.

"I'll live," he said. "At least a little longer. I'm glad I ran into you."

"Did the folks at the hospital know what got you?"

"Strychnine," Schultz said, his dark eyes flashing angrily. "The poor boy went into convulsions in his cell. By the time they got him to the hospital, his back was bent so badly he nearly snapped himself in two. He could scarcely breathe. They treated him with activated charcoal, anticonvulsants, and muscle relaxants, and kept him isolated in darkness for several days. The slightest exposure to light or disturbance of his body caused additional seizures."

Erin grimaced. "That sounds rough. Are you okay to be up and around?"

"Yeah," Alfie said.

"Do you have any idea how you were poisoned?"

"Supper," he said. "But before you ask, I got no idea who gave it to me. I was taking a nap when they shoved a fast food bag through the slot. Burger and fries. The burger tasted a little funny. Bitter. But that's not the point."

"What is the point, Alfie?"

"We both know who did it," he said grimly. "And don't worry, I remember our talk. You don't gotta worry about nothing. Thanks for getting me out."

Erin blinked. "Alfie, that wasn't me," she said, nodding back toward the courtroom. Alfie had promised her, when he'd first been arrested, that if she got him out of jail, she wouldn't have to take down Vinnie Moreno through legal means. Alfie would handle the slick don himself.

He gave her a knowing look. "Of course it wasn't," he said, doing everything short of laying a finger alongside his nose and winking. "Glad you're in the neighborhood. I won't forget it and you won't be sorry."

"You really ought to get some rest, Mr. Madonna," Schultz said. "You're only up and about as of today. You need a good lie-down in a dark room. We'll take my car."

"King's right," Alfie said. "We shouldn't be talking. Be seeing you, Detective."

He touched his forehead respectfully and turned away, leaving Erin as mystified as before. She watched him go, wondering how much of her street rep was built on people giving her credit for other folks' actions. Then, shaking her head, she followed to the security checkpoint.

Alfie and Schultz breezed through security. Erin was

delayed a few moments, getting her guns back. She clipped her trusty Glock to her belt and strapped her snub-nosed .38 in its ankle holster. She pulled down her jacket over the waist gun. It was a chilly September day and she didn't want a draft under her coat. Then she nodded politely to the guards and made her way outside.

Schultz spoke briefly to Alfie and walked away. The young Mafioso sat down on the courthouse steps and dangled his hands between his knees. Erin caught up with him and stood beside him.

"Lawyer ditched you, huh?" she said.

"He's just going to get the car," Alfie said. "I'm feeling pretty lousy. King tried to push back the arraignment a couple more days, but the judge said no way. I think they just wanted to clear me off the books. Y'know, if the Family ran the courts, they'd run a lot smoother."

"Yeah, and your guys would never end up in the system," she said with a wry smile.

"How's that different from what we got now?" he replied. "If you got the right connections, you can get away with anything. If you don't, you can't get away with nothing. That's how it always is. Only difference is who's calling the shots. Thanks again."

"Look," she said. "I don't know what happened in there, but I swear, I had no idea it was going to happen."

"Then why were you there?"

"Because of your dad."

"You didn't hardly know him."

She shrugged. "I was there when he died. And I don't think you're such a bad guy, Alfie. Who knows? If you keep your nose clean and stay out of trouble this time, you might be able to make something of yourself."

He shook his head. "It's a little late to be going straight.

Besides, I got a job to do."

"If you're thinking about revenge, don't," she warned him. "That's a rough, one-way road."

"You think I care?" His eyes were windows into bitterness, anger, and pain. "They killed my dad. What would you do if it was your old man?"

Erin thought of her father, of his bushy gray mustache and his serious, proud eyes. She heard in her head the way he always called her "kiddo" and remembered the smell of his shaving cream when he'd bent down to kiss her forehead on the way to work when she was a girl.

"I'd feel the same as you," she said. "But—"

Her attention was caught by a blur of navy blue in the corner of her eye. She'd already subconsciously pegged the approaching man as a uniformed cop before she'd really registered him. If you spent enough time on the streets, you learned to spot NYPD blue. The cop was making straight for the two of them, walking purposefully.

"Everything's fine, Officer," she said, thinking he'd noticed Alfie's obvious pain.

The uniform didn't say anything. He wasn't even looking at Erin. And his body language was all wrong.

Erin would have time later to think about what tipped her off. It could've been any number of little things, all of them swimming under the surface. Maybe it was the stiff way the man moved. When your adrenal glands kicked into overdrive, fine-motor control went out the window and people started moving in large, jerky motions. Or maybe it was the sheen of sweat on the guy's face on a day when it was forty and overcast. Or the sloppy way the man had fastened his equipment belt. Or the non-regulation turtleneck peeking over the top of the police windbreaker. Whatever it was, all the signals combined into a big, bright red flag in Erin's brain.

"NYPD!" she shouted, and knew she'd been right. The man flinched back and his eyes flashed quickly around. He reacted not like a cop, but a perp. It was only for an instant, and the man recovered fast, but to Erin's streetwise eyes, it couldn't have been more obvious. This guy was no policeman.

Erin went for her gun. The counterfeit cop grabbed for his own weapon. She got her hand under her jacket and snatched at her Glock. But it snagged on the lining of her coat for a critical instant. She saw the man's hand come up, a pistol in it, a Glock just like hers, and knew she didn't have time to take him down.

"Gun!" she yelled. She wasn't wearing her body armor. Every instinct screamed at her to take cover, but she was halfway down the courthouse steps. They were totally exposed. The fake cop was at the bottom of the stairs, less than fifteen yards away. That was about the standard range for police gunfights, and a lot closer than she ever wanted to be to an armed opponent.

The man started shooting, holding his gun one-handed. He'd been aiming at Alfie, but Erin had distracted him and his aim had followed his attention. The first bullet caromed off the concrete directly between her and Alfie, spraying chips in all directions. The second and third marched closer to Erin, blasting chunks out of the steps.

Alfie yelped in surprise and did the only sensible thing he could, which was to flop over on his side and curl up as small as he was able. Erin dodged away from him, hearing a bullet whine past her ear with a high-pitched zip that set her teeth on edge. She twisted her wrist savagely and finally cleared her sidearm, bringing it on line and wrapping her left hand around her right.

She didn't have a clear shot. Her background was full of pedestrians, the street jammed with cars. She hesitated an instant.

The gunman, under no such compunctions, fired two more times.. Her opponent's second bullet dug a hot furrow along her jaw, just under her ear. It felt like taking a lash from a bullwhip. Her whole body jerked to one side. She stepped wrong on the stairs and felt her ankle twist under her. Then she was tumbling down the steps, bumping and rolling, and ducked her head under her arms.She fell all the way to the bottom of the courthouse steps, landing with a shock that rattled her teeth. She rolled over onto her back and tightened her abdominal muscles, sitting up and raising her Glock between her feet.

"Police!" someone shouted from the top of the stairs. That would be the cops—the *real* cops, courthouse police. Three of them were running down the steps, guns drawn.

Erin paid no attention to them. She saw the fake cop fleeing across the street. She took aim at his retreating back, but he was surrounded by a cluster of startled, staring New Yorkers. If she missed, or even if she hit but got unlucky with the overpenetration, she could easily kill a bystander.

"Freeze!" Erin rasped out, but of course the would-be assassin paid no attention. In another moment, the man was out of her line of sight.

There was no question of giving chase. Erin knew that as soon as she scrambled to her feet. Her ankle screamed in protest and tried to buckle. She winced and tested it. Not broken, but probably sprained. She'd be running again, just not today. Something warm and wet was oozing down the left side of her neck. She brushed at it distractedly and saw blood on her fingertips.

"Drop it!" a man shouted from a few steps above her. "Show me your hands, lady!"

"Take it easy, guys," she said dully, dropping the Glock and raising her hands. "I'm one of you. O'Reilly, Major Crimes. We've got a shooter on foot, making a run for it. He's dressed in a Patrol uniform."

"Let's see your ID," one of the cops said, approaching her

carefully.

Erin slowly used one hand to pull up her coat to show the gold shield at her belt.

"Okay," the man said, lowering his gun. "You said you got shot at by another cop?"

"No, a guy dressed as a cop, in a NYPD windbreaker," she said. "Call it in now. I want a BOLO on a lone man in NYPD uniform, lightly built, about five-foot ten. Armed and dangerous."

A black Audi had pulled up to the curb. Kingston Schultz got out of it. The lawyer stared at Erin and his client, who was still curled into a fetal ball on the steps. Then he hurried toward them.

"Detective!" he exclaimed. "What in God's name happened?"

"Someone just tried to take out your client," Erin said. "And me along with him. I don't think Alfie's been hit."

Alfie cautiously raised his head. "Is it over?" he asked.

"Are you hurt, boy?" Schultz's concern came across like anger.

"I... no," Alfie said, patting himself on the chest. "No. I'm fine."

"You need to get him off the street," Erin said to Schultz. "We can go to the Eightball. That's Precinct 8, my station house. We can keep him safe."

"And you think he'll be safe there, do you?" Schultz was definitely angry now. "Detective, my client has narrowly escaped murder in a police station once. Now a second time, on the very steps of your city courthouse. You will forgive my skepticism when you guarantee his safety."

Erin swallowed a retort, realizing he had a point. "What do you suggest?" she asked, trying to keep her own voice calm and level, though her heart was hammering and her hands were shaking.

"You've been shot, ma'am," one of the cops said. "We need to get you to a hospital."

"I'm fine," she said brusquely. "Forget about it. Where are you taking Mr. Madonna, Mr. Schultz?"

"I do not think I will tell you," Schultz said stiffly.

"King, she saved my life," Alfie said quietly.

Schultz's face softened. "I see," he said. "Forgive me, Detective. We are all a little upset."

"Forget about it," she said again. She stepped away from the courthouse cops and lowered her voice for Schultz's ears alone. "Look, do you think it's a coincidence, your client getting off the hook and a guy waiting right outside to waste him?"

"I am a lawyer, not a fool," Schultz said, his eyes showing a glimmer of dark amusement.

"So somebody's gunning for him," she went on. "I can help him, but only if you and he will let me. If you can give me a couple hours, I can arrange a safe house for him. Can you look after him until then?"

He nodded. "I think it will take his enemies some time to regroup for another attempt," he said. "In the meantime, I will take him to my office. The building is quite secure."

"Okay," she said. "I remember it. I'll get there as soon as I can. It'll be me, in person, and maybe one or two others. If I'm not there, you don't let anyone else in. You copy?"

"I copy, Detective. And I thank you. Not everyone in your occupation would take so much trouble over a boy like Alfredo."

"Maybe I just don't like guys getting murdered in my city," Erin growled.

A police sergeant was approaching Erin with the businesslike air of an officer wanting to know what was going on. Erin sighed inwardly. Her immediate future was definitely going to include at least one official statement and a use-of-force report, with all the other paperwork that accompanied it. Now that the shooting had stopped, every muscle in her body was aching, reminding her that she'd just fallen halfway down a concrete stairway. And in spite of the way she'd brushed off the other cop, she should probably get her neck looked at and make sure she didn't bleed to death or get an infection. So much for a quiet day off. She'd have to call Carlyle and make sure he took her mom out to lunch or something. It didn't look like she'd have much time for family.

Chapter 3

"I think we need to go over the concept of a day off again, O'Reilly," Lieutenant Webb said.

Erin smiled wearily at her commanding officer from her perch on the back of the ambulance. "I'll just tell the bad guys to only shoot at me when I'm on the clock, sir," she said.

"I swear, it's a miracle you're still alive," he said, shaking his head. "So now we've got hitmen running around New York dressed like our guys."

"That's a class E felony," she said. "First-degree criminal impersonation."

"Somehow, I doubt if that bothered him, given that he was trying to commit murder," Webb said dryly. "Who was the target?"

"Alfredo Madonna," Erin said without hesitation. "The gunman only shot at me because I intervened. Nobody even knew I was going to be there, so there's no way they could've set it up to hit me."

"That's some relief," Webb said. "Close call, though. How's the neck?"

"Just a graze," she said, touching the butterfly bandage gingerly. "I didn't even need stitches."

"Why go to all this trouble to take out this kid?" Webb asked. "Who is he? I know his dad was a big mover in the Family, but Alfredo's a nobody."

Erin glanced around. The paramedics were packing up their gear, having tended to her and determined she didn't need to go to the hospital. Half a dozen uniformed cops were guarding a perimeter around the courthouse, but there wasn't much point. The only evidence the shooter had left at the scene was a handful of cartridge cases, and they'd already scooped up the spent brass and packed it in evidence bags.

"Vinnie Moreno," she said quietly. "He's old-school Mafia. You remember at the beginning of Godfather II, when that Sicilian guy kills Vito's dad and wants to kill him, too, even though he's just twelve years old?"

"This isn't a movie, O'Reilly," Webb said. "But I see what you mean. You think the Oil Man's worried about revenge for what happened to Madonna's dad?"

"I'd be worried if I was him," Erin said. "Alfie basically told me he was going after Vinnie."

"You think he'll succeed?"

She shrugged, then winced as the motion pulled at the bandage on her neck. "I think Alfie's young and pissed off, thinks he's got nothing to lose."

"Can you flip him?"

"I tried back when we first busted him. He said he couldn't give us Vinnie. He didn't know anything incriminating enough."

"Maybe we can use him to land some smaller fish," Webb said. "Hurt the Lucarellis without decapitating them. Madonna might go for that. I think it's worth a try. The kid seems to have a soft spot for you. See what you can do."

"Copy that, sir. He could use witness protection anyway. I told him I'd set something up."

"Only if he cooperates. We're not running a criminal charity. Now, about this gunman."

Erin had already been searching her memory for details. She shook her head. "I don't have much. It happened fast. Young, skinny, dark hair, probably Italian. I could pick him out of a lineup, maybe, but we'd need a suspect."

"Try looking through mug shots of Lucarelli foot soldiers," Webb suggested. "Otherwise, I don't think there's much we can do." His phone buzzed, interrupting his train of thought. He pulled it out and looked irritably down at the screen. He put the call through with a grumpy swipe of his thumb and brought the phone to his ear.

"First O'Reilly, now you, Neshenko?" he said. "You're just lucky I'm in town at all. I was thinking of getting out of here for a while. O'Reilly got shot at. That's why she called. What's your excuse?"

Erin was close enough to hear Vic Neshenko's reply. The big Russian didn't sound particularly upset or excited, but he didn't sound apologetic, either.

"I was visiting Mom down in Little Odessa," Vic said. "Heard a call on the police band while I was driving there."

"You listen to cop frequencies on your downtime?" Webb asked.

"It beats talk radio," Vic replied. "Anyway, I just wanted to let you know I'm in position, since I was already on Long Island. I'm almost at the scene."

"What scene?" Webb asked. "I'm at the courthouse with O'Reilly. In Manhattan."

There was a short, confused pause.

"They didn't call you yet?" Vic asked.

"Neshenko, why don't you assume, just for a moment, that I don't know what the hell you're talking about, and explain yourself," Webb suggested.

"Oh. Sure. Okay." Vic paused again. "I just assumed they would've called you first, but I guess it's a fresh one. We got a homicide."

"In Brooklyn?"

"Yes, sir."

"Neshenko, there's hundreds of homicides in New York. We don't get called to every one of them. That's why there are Homicide detectives. We're Major Crimes. Why would they call us?"

"It's a messy one. Blood all over the walls. Might be a hate crime, or..."

"Or what?" Webb asked softly.

"You don't like us using the word," Vic said.

"Don't spare my delicate feelings," Webb said.

"Have it your way, sir," Vic said. "Could be part of a series."

Webb took the phone away from his ear and looked at it. "I've got another call coming in, Neshenko," he said. "Probably Dispatch."

"I'll be at the scene, helping out, just in case." Vic hung up.

"Webb," Webb said in response to the second call.

"Lieutenant, this is Dispatch," was the predictable response.

Erin didn't wait to hear the rest. She hopped down from the back of the ambulance. "I'll swing by home to grab Rolf," she told Webb. "Text me the address. I'll meet you there."

*   *   *

Carlyle and Erin's mom were sitting in a booth in the Barley Corner's main room when Erin hurried in. They had Irish stew in front of them and looked to be having a good, deep conversation. The baby pictures had been put away, thank goodness.

"Hey Mom," Erin said. "Don't get up," she added to Carlyle. "I'm in a hurry. Work."

"Oh my goodness!" Mary cried, putting a hand to her mouth. "What on Earth happened, Erin? Your face!"

Carlyle was also alarmed, but he covered it better. He'd seen Erin in worse condition plenty of times. "Anything to be concerned about, darling?" he asked.

"No," she said hastily. "Someone tried to pop Alfie at the courthouse. I got in the way. Everybody's fine."

"Your neck," Mary insisted. "Let me take a look at it."

"The medics already patched me up, Mom," Erin said impatiently. "Look, I need to get down to Brooklyn. We just caught a body."

"It's your day off," Mary pouted. "We're supposed to have dinner with Junior and Shelley tonight, as a family."

"Someone forgot to tell the perps," Erin said. "I should still be able to make dinner. If anything comes up, I'll let you know. Love you."

She gave her mother a quick kiss on the cheek. Then she nodded to Carlyle and hurried upstairs before the smell of the stew could tempt her into stopping to eat. Her stomach was growling and she'd have to grab lunch on the go.

Rolf let her know that he forgave her for leaving him behind, but did not intend being abandoned again. He stuck very close beside her, sniffing at her anxiously and licking her hand. He could tell she'd been hurt. She smelled like blood and adrenaline. If he'd been there, he would have stopped the bad guy. He didn't understand why he'd been benched.

Erin ached all over from her tumble down the steps. Her head throbbed dully and insistently, a souvenir of the nasty concussion she'd gotten a few months back. A quick glance in the bathroom mirror showed a scrape on her cheek where she'd caught the rough edge of a slab of concrete. She was neither looking nor feeling her best, but with Rolf in hand, she did feel better than before.

"Sorry, kiddo," she told him. "I should've brought you. Maybe then that scumbag wouldn't have gotten away."

Rolf nosed her. There was no maybe about it. The human hadn't been born who could outrun him.

*   *   *

Erin had been living in Manhattan over a year now, but Long Island still felt like home. No matter what happened, she always felt like a blue-collar cop from Queens. She liked crossing the East River and seeing the familiar small houses and apartments of her own people. Brooklyn wasn't Queens, not quite, but it was the next best thing.

However, she felt an unpleasant shiver down her spine when she got to the crime scene. The address Webb had sent her was a brownstone on President Street, just a couple of blocks from Carroll Park. That meant Vinnie Moreno's place was right down the street, almost within shouting distance. The last time she'd been there, Erin had been contemplating homicide.

She pushed the memories firmly out of her mind. This was just another murder site, nothing more. It had nothing to do with the Oil Man or his Lucarelli associates. She parked her Charger next to an NYPD blue-and-white and unloaded Rolf. She saw the familiar shape of Vic's unmarked Taurus a couple of spaces from her. A pair of uniforms were at the top of the brownstone's stairs, guarding the door. She showed them her gold shield.

"Upstairs, Detective," one of them said, stepping aside.

Like many New York brownstones, this one had originally been built for one family, but the skyrocketing cost of real estate had resulted in it being parceled out into apartment units, one per floor. Erin jogged up the stairs to the third story, Rolf loping easily beside her.

The door to the top-floor apartment stood open. Webb and Vic were in the living room. Webb had an unlit cigarette in his hand. He was rubbing it as if he could absorb the nicotine through his fingertips. Vic was chewing a toothpick. Both men looked unhappy.

"Bad one?" Erin guessed.

"Yeah," Vic said. "Pretty goddamn bad. What happened to you?"

"Never mind me. What happened?"

He shook his head. "Knife," he said. "I'd bet my shield on it. Victim's a woman. Hell, a girl, more like. She's... shit, she's cut to pieces."

"Neshenko's exaggerating," Webb said, but his eyes were hollow and haunted. "She's still in one piece. Looks like a whole lot of stab wounds to me. Nothing too freakish; just a psycho with a knife. I see why they called us. Levine's on the way. Maybe she can tell us... I don't know, something. Better keep your K-9 out here and watch your step. There's... evidence all over the bedroom."

Erin looked down at Rolf. The Shepherd looked back at her.

"Sitz," she told him. "Bleib."

Rolf sat, curled his tail around his hind legs, and awaited further instructions. His nostrils twitched but he didn't move.

Erin could smell it too; the coppery reek of blood, laid over that undefinable smell of death that every veteran cop learned to recognize. She didn't want to go into the bedroom, didn't want to add more fuel to her all-too-frequent nightmares, but that was the Job. She swallowed and walked to the doorway.

She'd seen worse deaths, but not very many. Her stomach gave a lurch at the sight in front of her. The slim hope she held onto was that the young woman on the bed had died before the killer had really gone to work on her.

"See the writing?" Vic asked from behind her. He spoke quietly, but Erin jumped at the sound of his voice.

"Yeah," she said. It was hard to miss the bloody letters scrawled on the white plaster.

"You know what it means?"

"Yeah," she said again. It was one word, written in red, four letters long. It wasn't in English, but police officers gained a smattering of other languages in the course of their work, and Erin knew enough vulgar Italian to translate. She turned to face Vic, mainly so she wouldn't have to keep looking at the sight in front of her.

"Puta is Italian," she said. "It means 'whore.'"

Chapter 4

"Was she?" Vic asked.

"Was she what?" Erin replied. They'd moved back to the living room to await the Medical Examiner. Rolf was watching Erin intently. Webb, at the window, was still fingering his cigarette and staring out at the street.

"A whore," Vic said. "A hooker. A pro. A streetwalker. A…"

"I know what a whore is," Erin snapped.

"Because if she was, one of her johns might've done her," he said.

"The apartment is registered to Isabella Romano," Webb said.

"Like the cheese?" Vic asked.

"Yes," Webb said. "Like the cheese. You do know cheeses, like surnames, often originate in the names of places?"

"I was just asking," Vic said in wounded tones.

"Run the name, please," Webb told him.

"On it." Vic started for the door.

"Criminal record, known associates, spouses," Webb said.

"Sheesh!" Vic said. "I know how to run a name. Is everyone in a bad mood today?"

"I got shot in the neck," Erin said. "What's your excuse, sir?"

"I have to put up with you two," Webb said. "What's yours, Neshenko?"

"Generational trauma from being Russian," Vic said. "We inherit our bad moods."

"How did we hear about this body?" Erin asked Webb.

"Neshenko called," Webb said. "You heard him. Then Dispatch hit us up."

"That wasn't what I meant," she said. "Who called it in? This is the only apartment on this floor, and it's the top one. Did she scream? The blood still looks fresh."

"Agreed," Webb said. "I don't think this crime scene is more than an hour old. Our friend Anonymous called it in. Female voice, wouldn't identify herself. All she said was she'd heard some sort of fight going on. A Patrol unit responded, found the door ajar, and made entry. They found the victim like this. They didn't bother calling a bus, for obvious reasons."

"Sounds like somebody who was pretty close by," Erin said. "Do we know who else lives in this building?"

"Good place to start," Webb said. "Take a walk downstairs, knock on all the doors."

Erin took Rolf down to the second floor. The name on the door read TOMMASINO. Erin knocked and waited.

After a couple of moments, a woman's voice, tense and cautious, emanated from behind the door.

"What do you want? Who are you?"

Erin held up her shield in front of the peephole. "Ma'am, my name is Detective O'Reilly. I'm with the NYPD. May I come in?"

There was another brief pause. "Why?" the woman asked.

The hairs on the back of Erin's neck tingled. That didn't sound like an innocent bystander. It sounded like a scared woman with something to hide. A very scared woman.

"Ma'am?" Erin said, dropping a hand to the butt of her Glock. "Are you alone in there?"

"Yes," the woman said. "Please, leave me alone. I don't want to get in trouble."

"You're not in any trouble, ma'am," Erin said. "I need to talk about your upstairs neighbor. Isabella Romano. Please, open the door at least, so we can talk face to face. I don't have to come in."

After another long moment, Erin heard the chain lock engage and the bolts click open. The door had three locks. All of them had been locked. That struck her as a little odd. Sure, this neighborhood had a Mafia don living two blocks down, but that meant street crime was actually less of a problem here. Mafiosi took a dim view of their friends and family being attacked by two-bit thugs, and their displeasure could be violent. Petty criminals quickly learned to avoid areas like this one.

The door opened a couple of inches to reveal the round, olive-skinned face of a woman in her thirties. It was a pretty face, with big, luminous brown eyes framed by glossy, thick black hair. But those eyes were deeply frightened.

"I hardly know Isabella," the woman said. "I don't think I can help you, Detective."

"What's your name, ma'am?" Erin asked.

"Teresa. Teresa Tommasino."

"Does anyone else live here, in your apartment?"

"No. I'm not... I'm alone." Teresa's eyes strayed to Rolf, who was watching Erin for guidance. "What's that?"

"This is Rolf," Erin said. "He's a police K-9. Don't worry, he's perfectly safe. Have you been in your apartment all day?"

"No. I... I went out shopping. For groceries."

"When was that?"

"I don't know. I suppose... ten o'clock?"

"When did you get back?"

"About forty minutes later."

"Did you hear anything from the upstairs apartment?"

"No." Teresa met Erin's eyes, but there was a shifty quality in them. She wasn't lying, not exactly, but Erin didn't think she was telling the whole truth, either.

"Did you see anyone unusual hanging around the building? Anyone who didn't belong?"

Erin was looking for it, so she spotted the slight hesitation before Teresa said, "Nobody out of the ordinary."

Erin remembered learning, when she'd first started getting to know Carlyle, the way he danced around the truth, never telling an outright lie, letting her assumptions lead her in the wrong direction. There were two ways she could handle this woman. She could do what Vic would do, call out her bullshit for what it was and try to intimidate the truth out of her. But Teresa was already spooked. Scaring her more might just make her clam up, or worse, say what she thought Erin wanted to hear. That could give her a false lead, waste time, and derail the whole investigation. The other option was to play nice, to be gentle.

"What do you do for a living, Teresa?" Erin asked, deliberately going to a first-name basis.

"I teach grade school. Third grade. There's no class today. Administrative holiday."

"Yeah, I know," Erin said. "My niece is in the third grade. My parents came down to visit the grandkids."

That won her a hesitant smile. Anything that built rapport was useful in an interview, and Erin wasn't above using a family reference to forge a connection.

"Do you know what Isabella does?" Erin asked.

The smile vanished. "I don't know anything about her," Teresa said. "I'm sorry I can't help you, Detective. Goodbye."

The door clicked shut in Erin's face. She heard the three deadbolts slam home, one after the other. Erin stared at the door. She knocked a couple of times, expecting no further answer and getting none. Rolf watched her expectantly.

Erin sighed and turned away. Teresa wasn't a suspect. Erin had no probable cause to kick down her door, and if she did, she'd probably frighten the poor woman to death. There was no law that forced civilians to talk to cops.

But it was frustrating. Teresa knew something, it was obvious. Maybe she even knew who the killer was, had seen their face. But if so, why stonewall the cops? Teresa was no hardened gang member. She was a grade-school teacher, for God's sake! She looked to be just about the least dangerous person Erin had seen in the course of her job in a very long time.

Rolf lowered his snout and snuffled at the landing, nostrils flaring. Erin looked down and saw what the K-9 had smelled. A couple of fat, dark drops of liquid had landed on the woodwork. They were still slightly moist. If that wasn't blood, Erin would turn in her gold shield.

"Rolf, *such!*" she said, giving his German "search" command.

That was all the dog had been waiting for. The scent was fresh and the direction was plain. For a trained search dog, a blood trail might as well be lined with neon lights. He followed the blood to Teresa's door, paused a moment, then forged ahead, down the stairs and out the front door of the brownstone.

Vic was just getting out of his Taurus. They went straight past him, along the sidewalk. Erin could see the occasional small spot of blood, but she wouldn't have been able to track them on her own. She kept her head down, watching her dog.

Vic fell in step beside her. "What're we following?" he asked.

Erin pointed. "Blood."

He squinted. "I don't see it."

"I'm guessing it's the victim's," Erin said. "And the killer got it on him."

"He must've been a mess," Vic agreed. "All that spatter in there. Where do you think he's going?"

Erin didn't need to speculate. Rolf came to a halt at the curb next to a fire hydrant. The Shepherd sniffed vigorously around it, tail waving uncertainly.

Vic snickered. "Tell your mutt he's on the clock. He can take a potty break later."

"He's lost the scent," Erin said. Rolf knew better than to be distracted by the smells of other dogs when he was working.

"So where'd the guy go?"

"Car," Erin said.

"Great," Vic said. "Waste of time. Our boy gets in a car and drives away. Fantastic. I don't think we needed a K-9 to tell us that."

"It tells us one thing," Erin said.

"Yeah? What's that?"

She pointed to the hydrant. "What's that tell you?"

"You want me to sniff it?"

"I want you to use your brain, not your nose."

Then Vic got it. "This is a no-parking zone," he said. "You can't park next to a hydrant."

"Our guy was illegally parked," she agreed. "Either that, or he had an accomplice who picked him up here. But that doesn't make sense. He wouldn't walk down the street covered with blood if he didn't have to. He'd have had his ride scoop him up in front of the house."

"Stupid thing to do," Vic said. "Why park at a hydrant when you're planning to carve a girl up? Suppose he'd stepped outside and one of ours was standing right there, writing him a ticket? Our traffic cop sees him covered with blood, maybe still holding the knife. Little awkward, don't you think?"

"Maybe it wasn't planned," Erin said thoughtfully. "Maybe our killer is just the kind of guy who does this sort of thing, breaks laws because he can. We'll need to try the houses along the street, see if anyone saw a bloodstained psycho get into a car."

"Nobody saw nothin'," Vic predicted.

"Probably," she agreed. "But it doesn't hurt to try."

*   *   *

The initial canvas of the neighborhood turned up nothing. Most of the doorbells went unanswered. That wasn't terribly surprising; it was the middle of a weekday and most people were at work. The couple of stay-at-home moms they did manage to roust were terse and uncooperative. Yes, they'd been home all morning. No, they hadn't seen or heard anything. Yes, they'd think they would've noticed a blood-soaked man walking down the street, but they were doing laundry or watching TV or taking care of their kids.

Demoralized, but hardly surprised, Erin and Vic detailed two of the Patrol cops to keep knocking on doors. It was just possible they might get lucky. Then the detectives went back to check in with Webb.

"Shit," Erin said as they climbed the front steps.

"What?" Vic asked.

"I need to call the Marshals."

"What for?"

"I need to set up protection for a guy. He might be going into WitSec."

"Anybody I know?"

"Alfie Madonna. Mattie Madonna's kid. A hitman tried to whack him outside the courthouse. That's how I got shot. I almost forgot."

Vic stopped, his hand resting on the brownstone's doorknob. "You got shot, and you *almost forgot about it?!* Christ, Erin, I knew you were tough, but you're something else."

"There's been kind of a lot going on this morning," she said. "I'm stretched a little thin right now, okay? Go on in and talk to the Lieutenant. I won't be long."

Witness Protection was a Federal thing, under the jurisdiction of the US Marshals. Erin hadn't needed to contact them before, but she knew how it was done. She put in a call to the Southern District Marshals Office. The first person she got was a receptionist, who transferred her to three petty bureaucrats in succession. Erin knew how the Feds operated, so she persevered, finally ending up with someone who might actually have the knowledge and authority to do something useful.

"Deputy Marshal Headley," the man on the other end of the line said. "I understand you've got someone in need of our services."

"That's right," Erin said. "Low-level Mafia soldier. His old Family is out to get him. They've already made one play to take him out."

"Alfredo Madonna?"

"How do you know that?" Erin asked sharply.

"Relax, Detective," Headley said. "I was at the courthouse this morning on other business. I missed the excitement, but I heard what happened. So Madonna wants to flip?"

"He's asked for protection," Erin said, choosing her words carefully.

"Okay," Headley said. "Where is he right now?"

"At a fairly secure location, but it's temporary," she said. "He's feeling a little paranoid right now, so he's waiting to see me personally before he moves."

"I copy. Is he ready for WitSec? Does he understand what it means?"

"He hates the Lucarelli boss. He'll do anything he can to bring the guy down."

"I meant, does he understand the changes he'll have to make in his life? He'll need to sever all his ties. Every one of them. His friends can't know where he's going, can't get in touch with him. His family won't know his contact info. He'll have a new name, new identity, the works. And he can't circle back into his old life. If he does, he'll forfeit protection."

"They killed his dad," Erin said. "It's because of his family that he wants revenge. He'll be on board."

"Understood. Clearly, there's an established danger to his life."

Erin touched the bandage on her neck. "Yeah, you could say that."

"I can set up a temporary detail for him while we build him a new identity. The permanent placement will take a little longer, but he'll be okay for a few days. You said he'll only talk to you?"

"That's right."

"I'll call you back when we're ready to move him," Headley said. "You can rendezvous with my people and me. Then we'll go get him together. What's his current location?"

"It's better if as few people as possible know that, Marshal," Erin said. "No offense."

"None taken." Headley actually sounded pleased. "Glad to hear both of you are taking this seriously. I'll be in touch."

With that taken care of, Erin hung up. She was just in time to see the Medical Examiner's van arrive and Sarah Levine get out. Dr. Levine was already wearing her lab coat and gloves; Erin had only seen the other woman in different clothing once, on

New Year's. Otherwise, she'd have thought Levine slept in her lab gear.

"Hey, Doc," Erin called, waving her over.

"Where's the dead guy?" Levine asked, never one for small talk.

"Girl," Erin corrected. "She's upstairs."

Rolf snuffled at the hem of Levine's coat as they went in. Levine always smelled very interesting, a mix of chemicals, blood, and tissue samples. The Shepherd would have no trouble at all tracking Levine if she ever got lost.

In the Romano apartment, Levine immediately peeled off and disappeared into the bedroom to begin her preliminary examination. Vic, Webb, Erin, and Rolf stayed in the living room, out of the ME's way.

"I was just telling the boss about Romano," Vic said.

"What is there to tell?" Erin asked.

"She wasn't a hooker," he said. "At least, not as far as the Vice squad knows. But she was a wild child, that's for sure. Only nineteen years old and she's got a jacket thicker than some heavy hitters I know. Nothing too major, but she got in a lot of trouble. Long juvie record."

"What for?"

"Drugs, disorderly conduct, shit like that." Vic shrugged. "She hung out with a bunch of street hoods. She kept getting busted at parties where there was lots of underage drinking and drugs. Never did any serious time, though."

"Known associates?" Webb asked.

"I've got a list as long as your arm," Vic said. "Take your pick. Young punks, mostly."

"What about family?" Erin asked. "Nineteen is a little young to have her own apartment in this neighborhood. Either she had one hell of a nice entry-level job, or somebody else was paying her rent."

"Next of kin we have on file is a mom and dad," Vic said. "They're local, less than a mile from here. Two siblings, no spouse, no kids."

"Good," Webb said. "O'Reilly, you can do the notification."

Erin winced. "Sir," she said. "I have something else going on, something important."

"More important than a major homicide?"

"I don't know. But I may have to leave on short notice."

"Then you'd better get going now," Webb said. "Get the notification out of the way before you get interrupted. We'll keep you posted on what Levine finds out."

Chapter 5

"I wasn't trying to weasel out of it," Erin told Rolf once they were back in her Charger.

Rolf wagged his tail. He didn't think she was a weasel.

"It's just that I might get a call from the Marshals any time," she explained. "I shouldn't be in the middle of something delicate."

Rolf stuck his head through the hole between the front seats to see where they were going. Maybe there'd be bad guys to chase when they got there.

"Okay, I hate doing family notifications," she said. "They're miserable."

Rolf nosed her ear.

"Thanks, kiddo," she said, rubbing his neck. "I know you've got my back."

The Romano family lived in a small, very ordinary-looking house in a quiet middle-class Brooklyn neighborhood. Erin left Rolf in the car; the K-9's presence might not be appreciated. She took a second to check herself in the rear-view mirror. She still looked like a mess. She did what she could with her hair and got a tissue to wipe the most obvious smudges off her face. Then she got out and walked up to the front door.

A middle-aged woman with a Mediterranean complexion answered the door. She was good-looking in a stout, sturdy way, her hair obviously dyed and carefully styled.

"We ain't interested," she said in a strong Brooklyn accent. "No matter what you're selling."

Erin held up her gold shield. "Ma'am, my name is Erin O'Reilly. I'm a detective with the NYPD. Are you Ms. Romano?"

"Yeah, that's me," the woman said. "Luisa Romano. What's the matter? Don't tell me Bella got herself in trouble again. I told her not to run around with those no-account boys."

"This is about Isabella," Erin said. "May I come in, ma'am? We should sit down."

Luisa considered her. "Okay, sure," she said. "You want me to put some coffee on?"

"I don't need any, thanks," Erin said as she stepped inside. The house was clean and well-kept, but a little cluttered with old furniture. The walls were covered with pictures, mostly black-and-white photographs but with a few prints of landscape paintings interspersed. Luisa led her to the living room and indicated a well-worn couch. Erin dutifully took a seat. Luisa sat down in an overstuffed armchair.

"Is your husband home?" Erin asked.

"Nah, he's at work."

"What kind of work does he do?"

"Sanitation."

That sparked something in Erin. "Garbage collection?" she asked, trying to disguise her interest.

"If you want to call it that. It's good honest work. You got a problem with that?"

"No," Erin said hastily. But she was thinking about the Mob. The O'Malleys and the Lucarellis had fought over the garbage rackets on Long Island back in the Nineties. Carlyle was suspected of building bombs that had destroyed several rival garbage trucks, though he'd always been careful to construct the devices so that nobody was killed or injured. The Lucarellis had won that round, in spite of Carlyle's efforts, but were in the process of getting out of the labor rackets.

"So what's Bella's problem?" Luisa asked.

"Ma'am, I'm sorry to be the one to tell you this," Erin said. "Isabella was found in her apartment earlier today. It appears she's been murdered."

Erin had seen many reactions to the news of the sudden death of a family member. The most common responses were shock, followed by tears. However, there was a wide range of emotions that might be on display. Luisa Romano managed to surprise her.

"I told her this was gonna happen," Luisa said, shaking her head. "How many times did I say it? 'Bella, if you keep stepping out with those no-good kids down the street, you're going to end up strangled in a back alley one of these days.' Who did it? Was it one of her old boyfriends? Or the new one, the pretty one?"

Erin was momentarily baffled. The woman was treating news of her daughter's death like the girl needed to be grounded. "Ma'am," she said gently, thinking she might not have gotten through the first time. "Isabella is dead."

"I know that," Luisa retorted. "I heard you just fine the first time. This is her father's fault, you know. I told Gio he was too soft on her. I swear, he let her get away with everything. If he'd have stepped in and put his foot down the first time she skipped school, this wouldn't have never happened."

"The boyfriends you mentioned," Erin said. "Could you tell me their names?"

"Who can keep track of all those boys?" Luisa replied, throwing her hands in the air. "They was always coming and going, all hours of the day or night. I told her, I said, 'Bella, nobody respects the town bicycle, if you know what I mean.' She just laughed. Laughed at her own mother, for thinking about her reputation!"

"You said something about a new boyfriend," Erin persisted. "A pretty one?"

"Yeah," Luisa said. "He came by the house a couple weeks ago, said he wanted to pay his respects. All dressed up nice. Suit, tie, even a hat. Looked like he stepped right outta one of them old movies. Brought me flowers, if you believe it! Said he wanted to do things right, meet the parents. With all respect. Nice manners, that boy. And good looking, my God! If I was Bella's age, he'd make me go all weak in the knees too. Gio didn't never look that good, not even when we was married."

"What's his name?" Erin asked. "If he introduced himself, you must have heard it."

"Yeah, it's right on the tip of my tongue," Lu said. "It might've been Angelo. Bella called him Angel, see? Like a nickname. God only knows how a girl like her ran into a guy like him. Most of the boys she hung out with was trash, just plain trash like you throw in the gutter."

"Did you get a last name?"

"Yeah, he said it, but I don't remember. Maybe it'll come back to me."

"Had Isabella been living on her own long?" Erin asked.

"Since she graduated high school in June," Luisa said. "We had a huge fight when I caught a boy sneaking out of her bedroom the morning after graduation. I found him tiptoeing down the stairs with his shoes in his hand and this big shit-eating grin on his face. Under my own roof! And when I told Bella that, she said fine, she wouldn't stay under my roof, she'd get her own place. I told her she'd be back in a week. But I guess she made it work, though Lord knows where she got the money."

"Did you have much contact with her after she moved out?"

"Not a lot. But she'd come by now and again." Luisa paused and an odd look came into her face. "She's really gone?"

Erin nodded. "Yes, I'm afraid so. Do you know why anybody might want to hurt her?"

Luisa shook her head. "She was a stupid girl, stubborn, like she wanted to make every mistake there was, but she didn't have a mean bone in her body. She never hurt nobody. All the boys loved her, and I know why, but they wouldn't never hurt her."

Tears welled up in Luisa's eyes. "Oh my God, the last thing I said to her was a scolding. I shoulda told her I loved her. I don't remember the last time I told her that. Lord knows, she didn't make it easy on me. It was Gio she really loved. She'd bat her eyes at him and he'd let her get away with murder! God, he's coming home this evening. What am I gonna tell him?"

"Tell him we're doing everything we can to find out what happened to her," Erin said. She handed the other woman one of her cards. "If you think of anything, like the boyfriend's name, give me a call. There's a number there for family assistance, too. They'll help you with what you need to do."

"I loved that stupid, stubborn girl," Luisa said, staring at her hands. "God help me, but I loved her."

*   *   *

Erin had just gotten back in the Charger, and was dealing with Rolf's inquisitive nose, when her phone rang. She didn't recognize the number.

"O'Reilly," she said.

"This is Deputy Marshal Headley," the man on the other end said. "Are you ready to go get your boy?"

"If you are," she said. "It'll take me a little while to get there, though. I'm on Long Island right now."

"Not a problem," Headley said. "Just swing by Union Square Park and call me at this number."

"Copy that. See you there."

Erin hung up and immediately called Webb.

"Get anything from the family?" Webb asked by way of greeting.

"Apparently our victim went through a lot of boyfriends," Erin said. "Could be jealousy as a motive. Unfortunately, Romano's mom didn't remember any of their names. Just one partial, somebody named Angel or Angelo or something like that. No last name."

"Helpful," Webb said dryly. "We'll run Angelo through the system. I'm guessing we get about five hundred hits."

"Now I need to head back to Manhattan," she said.

"For what? Grocery shopping?"

"No, sir. Meeting some Feds."

"What about?"

"Something I probably shouldn't discuss on the phone."

"I see. Any idea how long it'll take?"

"Probably a couple of hours. You want me to come back here after?"

"No. CSU will be all over the place, collecting evidence. You'll just get in the way. Come to the Eightball. We'll regroup there and see where we stand."

"Copy that. O'Reilly out."

And then it was time for another drive across the East River.

"Why Union Square Park?" she asked Rolf.

The Shepherd didn't have an opinion on that, but he loved being in the car with her.

"Security precaution," she said, answering her own question. "If anybody suspects Alfie is talking to the Feds, they might tail the Marshals from their office. If they're offsite to start with, then maybe the bad guys won't tumble to what we're doing. This damn cloak-and-dagger stuff is driving me nuts. Remember when we were just cops, wearing uniforms?"

Rolf had no idea what she was talking about, but she was talking to him, and he always liked that. He panted at her and wagged his tail to let her know he was on board with her plan, whatever it was.

They arrived at the park about half an hour later. Erin parked and looked around for a guy who resembled her mental image of a US Marshal. This image was colored by movies like *Tombstone* and pretty much matched the actor Sam Elliott, mustache and all. Not seeing a gunslinger straight out of a Western, she called Headley's number.

"I'm here," she said. "Black Charger, parked on East 14th."

"I see you," Headley said. "I'll come to you."

A minute later, a tall, slender, gray-haired man in a dark suit approached the Charger. He held up a hand to reveal a Marshal's star in his palm. Erin unlocked the passenger door and he got in.

"Good to meet you in person, Detective," he said. "Mark Headley."

"Erin O'Reilly," she said, shaking hands. "This is Rolf."

Headley offered his hand to Rolf, who gave it a businesslike sniff. "Beautiful dog," he said. "I've got a mastiff at home. Hundred and fifty pounds, thinks he's a lapdog. Looks mean, but he's a marshmallow. Unusual, for a detective to have a dog on duty. Never heard of it before."

"We're unique," Erin said.

He smiled thinly. "I think I might have heard of you. Where are we going?"

"Is it just you?" Erin asked. "I thought we had a security detail."

"We've got another car," Headley said, pointing over his shoulder with his thumb. "Two of my guys will follow us."

"Got it. We're going to a law office."

"The kid's lawyer?"

"Yeah."

"That's not particularly safe," Headley observed. "The bad guys might guess he's there."

"They whiffed at the courthouse," Erin said. "I don't think they'd be able to set up a second try too fast. These are mobsters, not Navy SEALs."

"I can see why you want him moved ASAP," Headley said.

The Manhattan office building containing the office of Kingston Schultz looked quiet enough. But Erin was taking no chances. Before getting out of the Charger, she strapped on her vest. Then she put Rolf into his own body armor. As she did so, she saw a black Lincoln Towncar pull up behind her. A pair of serious-looking young men climbed out and took up positions on either side of the front door, scanning the street for potential threats. Both were wearing Kevlar under their suit coats, and Erin caught a glimpse of a shoulder holster on one of them. One of the men handed a spare vest to Headley, who tucked it under his left arm.

"You and I will go in," Headley explained. "Boone and Calley will stay out here, in case of ambushes. This is the choke point. If anything happens, it'll happen right here."

"Copy that," Erin said.

"Is your dog trained in explosives detection?"

"Yeah."

"Good."

Erin and Headley got into the elevator, Erin fighting down the nervousness that always accompanied entering the little metal box. She reminded herself that nobody was lying in wait for her, that people rode elevators all the time. But she was gratified to see Headley unfasten the safety strap on his sidearm, recognizing that she wasn't the only one on edge.

"What're you carrying?" she asked as the car hummed up into the heart of the building.

".357 Smith and Wesson wheelgun," Headley said.

"Old-school," Erin said. "You like revolvers?"

"Six shots has always been plenty for me," Headley said. "I like the Mag's stopping power. That a Glock you're wearing?"

"Yeah. Department issue."

He nodded. "Solid gun. Ever been in a gunfight before this morning?"

"A couple times. You?"

He nodded again. There didn't seem to be anything else that needed to be said.

The elevator slowed and stopped. The doors slid open. Erin tensed, but all she saw was a suite of offices labeled SCHULTZ AND BECKER, ATTORNEYS AT LAW. They walked quickly to the entrance and found the door locked.

A young woman was at the reception desk. Erin recognized her as Aayla Schultz, Kingston's daughter. Erin held up her shield and waved through the glass, seeing recognition in the other woman's eyes. Aayla stood up and walked to the door, unlocking it.

"Hello, Ms. O'Reilly," Aayla said in her distinctive West Indies accent. "I am pleased to see you again."

"Where are your dad and Alfie?" Erin asked.

"In back. I will take you there."

"I'll stay here," Headley said. "This is for the principal." He handed the spare vest to Erin before setting himself behind the desk where he could keep an eye on the door and take cover if necessary. The whole thing would have struck Erin as unnecessarily cautious and even paranoid, if she hadn't been swapping bullets with a hitman earlier that day. As it was, she was glad Marshal Headley was with her. He had the calm confidence that came with long experience and she had the instinctive sense she could count on him.

Alfie and his lawyer were in Schultz's office. Schultz was sitting at his desk, working at his computer. Alfie was walking back and forth, wearing down paths in the carpet and fidgeting. When he saw Erin and Aayla, he started. Then he smiled.

"I was starting to think you weren't coming," he said. "Like maybe you forgot about me."

"It just took a little while to set things up," Erin said. "We're going to the safe house now. I've got some Marshals here to help."

"Cool."

"Put this on." Erin handed over the Kevlar vest. "Don't worry, we don't know of any immediate threat. It's just standard procedure."

"Can I have a gun, too?"

Erin gave him a look. "Alfie, you're a convicted felon awaiting trial on an illegal weapons charge. What makes you think any cop on Earth is going to give you a gun?"

He shrugged. "It's illegal for me to be wearing a bulletproof vest, too. Just thought I'd ask. Where are we going?"

"I told you that. A Federal safe house. Get that vest on. We need to keep moving."

Alfie fastened the Velcro straps around himself. "I still think I should have a gun," he muttered. "Dad always gave me a gun."

"Mr. Madonna," Schultz said warningly. Then he turned to Erin. "What my client just said was meant jocularly, and is in no way, shape, or form a confession to any wrongdoing."

"I know," she said impatiently. "And I don't care right now. What I care about is getting under cover before someone takes another shot at your client."

"I do appreciate this, Detective," Schultz said. "You are doing Mr. Madonna a great service."

"I'm just trying to keep everybody alive," Erin said. "All set there?"

"I think so," Alfie said. "Never worn one of these before. They're heavier than they look."

"You want them heavy. That's the stuff that stops the bullets. Let's move."

In the reception area, Headley and Alfie gave one another a quick once-over. Headley didn't seem impressed. He just nodded curtly and said to Erin, "I've got the principal. You take point."

Erin accordingly led the way to the elevator with Rolf beside her, making sure the car was empty before getting in and waving Headley and Alfie to join them. Headley touched the side of his head before pushing the button for the lobby, and Erin saw he was wearing an earpiece.

"Everything clear?" he asked. Calley or Boone must have answered in the affirmative, because Headley pressed the button.

The ride down was uneventful. When they got to the bottom, Erin and Rolf took the lead once more, crossing the lobby and exiting the building. The two other Marshals were right where they had been, armed and impassive. One of them walked quickly to the Towncar, got in, and started the engine.

"Where are we going?" Erin asked Headley.

"Boone and I will take the principal in our car," Headley said. "Calley will ride with you. He'll give you directions."

"Wait a second," Alfie said. "I'm riding with her."

"No, you're not," Headley said. "Because there's a dog in her car. And you get two Marshals on you at all times, so that means our car. And we're not discussing this here. Move."

Alfie gave Erin a helpless look as the Marshal hustled him to the Towncar. Erin replied with what she hoped was a reassuring smile. Then she loaded Rolf into his compartment and got behind the wheel of her Charger. Calley took the shotgun seat and the little caravan started rolling.

"Okay," Erin said to Calley. "Where's this safe house?"

"Follow the Lincoln," Calley said. He placed his phone on the dash. "Directions are here, in case we get separated. Try not to."

"Copy that." Erin steered into the Manhattan traffic, sticking close behind the Towncar. "Do you do this kind of detail often?"

"All the time," Calley said. "It's better than prisoner transport. At least the guys we're protecting here want to go where we're going, most of the time."

"What's it like being a Marshal?"

"A lot like any other cop, most of the time. I guess we move around more. We can cross state lines, so we can chase the fugitives you guys don't nail. Speaking of being chased, I think someone's tailing us."

Chapter 6

"Which one?" Erin asked. She checked her mirrors. They were driving in Manhattan in the middle of the day, so she saw about fifty cars.

"Gray minivan, next lane over, two cars back," Calley said. He pressed his earpiece. "Calley here. We've got a possible tail on us. Gray van, five o' clock."

"You sure?" Erin asked. Her nerves were jangling. She fought the urge to floor the pedal. They were in heavy downtown traffic. Whatever this was, she thought, it wouldn't turn into any sort of high-speed insanity. This would be more like one of those slow-motion nightmares where she was caught in quicksand.

"Pretty sure," Calley said in answer to something Headley had said. His voice was perfectly calm. He paused a moment, listening to his earpiece. Erin kept driving, but now she was thinking tactically, looking for choke points and escape routes.

"Boss says keep going for now," Calley reported. "But keep your eyes open. You want to call for NYPD backup?"

Erin considered it briefly. "No," she said. "The whole point is to keep this low-profile. If we get a bunch of blue-and-whites screening us, we might as well put up signs saying where we're going. Let's just ditch this loser."

"Copy that," Calley said. "Can I grab your phone?"

"Sure." Erin unlocked it and handed it over with one hand, keeping the other on the steering wheel. Calley quickly dialed and set the phone on the dash next to his own.

"Headley," came the answer.

"Hey, boss," Calley said. "Got you on speaker. O'Reilly says to keep it a private party for now. Wants us to be discreet, but thinks we ought to shake off our shadow."

"I agree," Headley said. "Get on 5th Avenue and head south."

"Copy that," Erin said.

"Try to put some cars between you and him," Headley said. "Then see if we can skate through the tail end of a traffic light. You think they've set up a revolving tail?"

"I doubt it," Erin said. "If they'd known our guy was in the law office, and if they had enough guys for that, they'd have just busted in and shot up the place."

"Good point," Headley said. "So this fellow's just a scout?"

"Probably," Calley said.

"Assuming he's got anything to do with us at all," Erin said. "And we're not just being paranoid."

"There's no such thing as paranoia on a Mob witness detail," Headley said.

In the background, Erin faintly heard Alfie's voice. "You know, guys," the mobster said. "I could just get out and make a run for it. You don't gotta do this."

His words were followed by the quiet but distinctive sound of the Towncar's locks engaging. Headley was clearly taking no chances with his protectee.

The Towncar slid between a flatbed truck and a sedan, drawing an irritated honk from the truck driver. Erin gauged the distance, figured she had room, and followed. It was a near thing. The truck swerved half out of its lane and the driver really laid on the horn. Erin didn't even bother checking the rearview, knowing perfectly well the man would be giving her the one-finger salute. Headley's car changed lanes again, and again Erin followed suit, sticking as close as she could.

Up ahead, the streetlight turned yellow. There wasn't time to get through before it turned red. Erin *knew* there wasn't time. Headley's car accelerated. Erin set her jaw and did the same. The light flicked red. The Towncar entered the intersection half a beat later. Then Erin blew through it, blatantly running the red. Horns erupted from the cross-street. She just kept going, looking straight ahead, gripping the wheel tightly.

"We've got a traffic cam on that intersection," she said. "They're going to mail me a ticket. Can I expense it to the Marshals?"

Calley laughed quietly. "Like you've never run a red—holy shit!"

Brakes squealed, more horns sounded. Erin's eyes flicked to her mirror just in time to see the gray van slalom straight through the cross traffic. Its driver knew his business. He handled the van like a stunt driver, whipping around the oncoming cars. A taxi lurched out of the way, but the cabbie misjudged the distances and plowed into another car right in the middle of the intersection. Metal shrieked against metal.

The van kept coming, ignoring the chaos in its wake. It very nearly made it through unscathed. Then a yellow delivery truck clipped it on the rear fender. There was another crash as the delivery truck sheared off the bumper. The silver metal bar skittered across the pavement.

The gray van wavered but carried on. It was closing in on them now, with nothing but open road separating them thanks to the traffic light.

"They're definitely following us," Calley said. He reached under his coat and drew his gun, a Glock 18 just like Erin's. "How do you want to handle this?"

"Keep going, Headley," Erin said into the phone. "I'll take care of these guys."

"How?" Headley asked.

"Like a cop," Erin said grimly. It was time to shut this shit down before someone got hurt. She checked her mirror again. The van was pulling alongside, coming up on her left. She could see two men in the front seat. The guy in the passenger seat was wearing sunglasses. He was hoisting something that looked disturbingly like a sawed-off shotgun.

"Get ready to duck," Calley said. He twisted in his seat, raising his pistol in both hands.

"Hold on," Erin said. "Rolf, *platz!*"

The K-9 immediately plopped down flat on his belly and planted his chin between his paws. Erin waited a second longer, letting the van come nearly level with her. Its passenger window was rolled down. She realized she'd misjudged these guys. They weren't just scouts, and they were absolutely willing to take on the Marshals, on a busy city street, no less. She couldn't let this turn into a gunfight, not here. There were way too many civilians around, too much chance of the wrong people getting hit.

She stomped on the brake. The Charger fell back instantly, the van hurtling ahead. Erin caught a passing image of the gunman in the passenger seat, the big black barrel of his shotgun pointing toward her, and then she was behind the van and just to one side of it, out of his line of fire.

Erin goosed the accelerator. The Charger's eight-cylinder engine roared, easily catching up to the van. She set the nose of her car against the right rear wheel well of the van, nudging it almost gently. Then she twisted the steering wheel and angled in.

It was a classic police technique called the PIT maneuver. It was also risky as hell. There was an excellent chance for the cars to barrel into the other traffic, causing a chain-reaction. But she didn't see a choice. It was that or start shooting.

Erin had never done a PIT for real, and hadn't practiced it in months, but just like riding a bicycle, it wasn't something you forgot how to do. She caught the van in the sweet spot just as the other driver started to slow down to match her unexpected change in speed. The van spun out in a majestic arc, going completely around. The front of the vehicle whirled past, and Erin saw the driver frantically cranking his own wheel, trying to regain control.

It would have made two full rotations and gone up onto the sidewalk if it weren't for the lamp post on the curb. Erin had seen it and aimed for it, not wanting to ram the van into pedestrian traffic. She followed the van in, nosing it into the lamp. The van slammed into the post broadside, crunching into the sturdy metal base. It came to a very abrupt stop. The men inside were tossed sideways like ragdolls. Some part of Erin's brain noted that the dumb bastards hadn't been wearing their seatbelts.

She came to a stop less than ten feet from the crashed vehicle, flicking on her flashers and shoving the gearshift into park. Then she was out the driver's side and Calley was exiting the other door. Both of them had their guns ready.

"NYPD!" Erin shouted. "Show me your hands!"

Calley was already at the passenger door of the van and had his Glock right in the gunman's face. But the driver, on the other side of the van, had somehow retained enough of his faculties to fumble for the door handle, and had been lucky enough not to crumple his door against the post. He got the door open and tumbled out the far side of the van, hitting the ground running.

Erin could see the fleeing man, but the sidewalk was full of startled New Yorkers. There was no way she was going to start shooting into a crowd. She dropped a hand to her belt and popped the release on the Charger's rear compartment.

An instant later, Rolf exploded out of the car, ninety pounds of fur and fangs. The Shepherd was at Erin's side in two running strides.

"Fass!" she snapped.

That was all the K-9 needed to hear. He could see a lot of people in front of him, but only one of them was running away. That man was violating a basic rule of self-preservation: never run from a police officer or a dog. They would always, always chase you.

On a straightaway, over flat ground, no human being on Earth could outrun a German Shepherd. Rolf caught the running man before he'd gotten more than twenty yards, threading his way through the bystanders like they weren't even there. He coiled, sprang, and snapped, and then the man was on the ground screaming and the chase was over.

Erin took a second to make sure Calley had his man under control. That guy had hit his head on the windshield and had been momentarily stunned. Calley reached into the car, grabbed the shotgun by the barrel, and pulled it out of reach. His target was no threat, didn't even seem to be aware of what was going on, so Erin left Calley to it and ran after her dog.

Rolf had the perp's right arm in his teeth. He stood proudly over his prey, tail whipping enthusiastically back and forth, ears perked to full upright position. He hadn't really hurt the man, just bitten down hard enough to bruise the flesh and immobilize the limb. It was a flawless takedown.

"You're under arrest," Erin said to the driver. She was breathing hard from the adrenaline rush.

"I didn't do nothing," the man on the sidewalk predictably said.

"You caused an accident," she retorted. "The charge is reckless endangerment and fleeing the scene of an accident. Not to mention your buddy's illegal firearm. You have the right to remain silent, so why don't you shut the hell up?"

Down the street, Headley's Towncar turned a corner and disappeared from view. Erin figured she'd connect with him and Alfie later. In the meantime, it was a safe bet nobody else was following them.

*   *   *

The two guys from the van were obviously Mafia goons, from their sullen, sneering faces right down to their alligator-skin shoes. The driver had a license which listed him as Kevin Pileggi. The gunman had no ID on him. He not only refused to identify himself, he didn't say a single word. With two suspects in custody and no good way to hold or transport them, Erin had to call for backup after all.

It took very little time for a pair of squad cars to roll up. They'd already been on their way to the scene of the dual accident even before Dispatch relayed her request. Soon the pair of thugs was securely tucked away in the back of one of the blue-and-whites and on their way to the Eightball. Erin had to go that way too, since she needed to process the prisoners and fill out the accident and arrest reports.

She was stretched way too thin. At current count, she had three places she urgently needed to be: taking care of the two losers she'd just arrested; with her squad handling Isabella Romano's murder; and at the Marshals' safe house, looking after

Alfie. There was an engineer's saying that went, *"Everybody wants it fast, they want it good, and they want it cheap. Pick two."* Erin didn't even have that luxury. She'd have to make do with one. But which one?

Vic and Lieutenant Webb ought to have a handle on the murder, at least until they got Levine's report and CSU's evidence. And Headley seemed pretty competent, so he should be able to manage Alfie Madonna for a little while. That left the two mopes in the back of the Patrol car.

"I shouldn't drag you into this mess," she said to Calley. "We can swing by the safe house if you want, or I can drop you somewhere else."

"Just pull over anywhere," he said. "I'll take a cab and expense it. I can text you the address of the safe house."

"Better just show me on your phone," she said. "Don't send it to me. That'd leave an electronic trail."

"Wow." Calley smiled slightly. "You *are* paranoid."

She didn't return the smile. "The guy you've got almost died in police custody," she said. "Another man connected to this case did die. In a holding cell. The people we're after are extremely dangerous and they know their way around the Department."

"Are you saying what I think you're saying?" Calley had been amused. Now he looked alarmed.

"Yeah."

"That changes things."

"Why did you think I brought the Marshals in on this?"

"Because witness protection is what we do?"

"Because I trust you more than I trust my own people right now. And I shouldn't even be talking about this in my car."

He blinked. "You mean—" he began. Then he bit off what he'd been about to say and chewed on it for a while.

After a couple of minutes, he said, "Why don't you stop here."

Erin pulled over and stopped. Calley unfastened his seatbelt. Then he showed Erin his phone's screen. She memorized the address on it.

"Got it?" he asked.

"Got it. Thanks for the help. Try to keep Alfie alive until I get there."

"My pleasure. We'll do what we can." He got out of the car and she drove away.

Chapter 7

Back in the Precinct 8 parking garage, Erin let Rolf out of his compartment. Then she did a quick walk-around of her Charger. She grimaced. A PIT maneuver was relatively low-impact compared to, say, ramming another vehicle head-on, but it still involved making hard contact with another car at speed. The Charger sported a bright, shiny gouge and a significant dent right next to the left headlight. She'd need to put in a maintenance request to the motor pool, which meant even more paperwork.

"What was I supposed to do?" she asked Rolf. "That guy was playing demolition derby on Fifth Avenue! If I hadn't stopped him, he'd have wiped out some pedestrians or something."

Rolf cocked his head. Chasing down bad guys was the right thing to do in his book; the *only* thing to do. He saw no problem here.

She ruffled his fur and led him inside. The Patrol officers who'd transported the suspects were at the front desk, getting the initial processing done. Erin thanked them for their help and took over.

"Lawyer," Pileggi said as they were getting him set up for his mugshot.

"That's all you've got to say for yourself?" Erin asked.

"Phone call," he added.

She rolled her eyes. "Not your first dance, is it? How about your friend Silent Bob?"

Pileggi smirked. His comrade's expression didn't even change.

Since Pileggi had lawyered up, Erin couldn't legally question him without counsel present. She got him his phone call. He called a Manhattan number which Erin mentally noted, though she was sure it wouldn't lead anywhere useful. The conversation lasted less than thirty seconds and basically consisted of Pileggi saying he'd been scooped up by the police. Then he went into a holding cell with the resigned, bored attitude of a man who'd done it many times before.

Since the other guy hadn't asked for a lawyer, Erin could freely interrogate him, assuming he even spoke English. She left Rolf in the observation gallery and went into the interrogation room. The man watched her with dark, cautious eyes.

"You're screwed, buddy," Erin said.

He made no reply.

"You attacked an NYPD detective," she went on. "With an illegally modified shotgun, while driving recklessly and causing a major accident. We'll know who you are in a matter of minutes, since I'll bet a week's pay we've got your prints on file. If you're on parole, which I'll make another bet you are, and your friend Pileggi's also a convicted felon, which he is, then you're looking at three major violations, minimum. You're going back inside. And you know that already. So lose the stupid old-fashioned Mafia *omerta* bullshit and tell me who sent you after Alfie Madonna."

At that name, the man's eyes flickered slightly. But his face remained impassive.

Erin leaned forward. "Think, buddy," she said. "He's the second witness guys like you have tried to make disappear. This was your bunch's second try at Alfie. You won't get a third. We've got him squared away by now, safe and sound. You've screwed up, and you've been caught, which makes you both useless and a danger to the guys you work for. You can talk to me now, or you can wait for them to make their move. Once you hit genpop at Riker's Island, someone may find a way to stop you talking for good."

"What's your name?" the man asked. His voice was soft, but there was a nasty edge to it that Erin didn't care for.

"Detective O'Reilly," she said. "Major Crimes. Now what's yours?"

"Nicky Spillano," he replied. "I thought it was you. Why didn't you keep your nose out of this?"

"Out of what?" she retorted.

"Why don't you ask the guy we both work for?" Spillano suggested. "You should've let us take care of our business. Now get me out of here. I got nothing more to say."

When Erin got back from Holding and went to retrieve Rolf, Lieutenant Webb and Vic were waiting for her in the observation room. Vic was holding Rolf's leash and rubbing him between the ears.

"Heard you brought us some fresh perps," Vic said. "We had to come see what was going on."

"You catch any of that?" Erin asked.

"Just the tail end," Vic said. "Something about being partners in crime, I think."

"Who did he mean?" Webb asked. "Who's the guy you both work for?"

"I think he meant Vinnie the Oil Man," she said. "But I don't work for him. Obviously."

"You've already got a job," Vic said.

"Why does he think you work for Vinnie?" Webb asked.

Erin glanced out into the hallway to make sure nobody was close enough to overhear. Then she closed the door firmly. "Vinnie wanted me to take out Alfie Madonna's dad."

"Mattie Madonna died without you doing anything," Webb said.

"Yeah, but Vinnie didn't know he was going to die in that ambulance."

"Wait a second," Vic said. "Let's go back to the part where Vinnie the Oil Man, Vinnie the Mafia boss, thinks you're his personal hitman."

"I'm a woman," Erin said.

"It's a goddamn gender-neutral term!" Vic snapped. "It's not my fault your sex wasn't properly represented in the field of contract killing when they made up that word! How come Vinnie's coming to you with contracts? And if he is, how come we haven't busted his sorry ass?"

"Not so loud," Erin murmured.

"Vinnie wouldn't have done it in person," Webb said. "That's not the way the Mafia do things. He'd have used an intermediary."

"It was a phone call," Erin said. "Unfamiliar voice, burner cell."

"Then how do you know it was the Oil Man?" Webb asked.

"He sent one of his personal goons to take out Mattie," Erin said. "He's the only logical choice."

"And you didn't report this at the time?" Webb asked.

"Of course I did."

"Not to me you didn't."

"No, sir. Not to you." She met his stare steadily.

"Right, the other thing." Webb sighed. "Isn't there something in the Bible about not being able to serve two masters?"

"Don't know, sir," Vic said. "I goofed off a lot in Sunday school. All I remember is something about doing unto others before they get the chance to do unto you."

Webb rubbed his temples. "So who are these guys, anyway?"

"I thought they were just trying to scope out Alfie," Erin said. "But it turns out they were ready to take a shot at him."

"How many times do I have to say this?" Vic said. "This kid doesn't matter! He's just a basement-level Mob grunt. Why go to all this trouble?"

"He's going to kill Vinnie," Erin said.

"Yeah, and I'm going to be Police Commissioner," Vic said, rolling his eyes. "Shouldn't he learn how to tie his own shoes first? Or maybe get out of diapers?"

"Take it easy, Neshenko," Webb said. "O'Reilly's got a point."

"It doesn't matter if he's able to take Vinnie out," Erin said. "All that matters is whether Vinnie thinks he'll try. If he's perceived as a threat..."

"Who cares if he actually is?" Webb finished for her. "Maybe we can use this."

"How?" Erin asked.

"To bait Vinnie out," Webb said.

"Hold on," Vic said. "If Vinnie thinks Erin's in his corner, which doesn't make any damn sense, but whatever, how come he didn't go to her on this? She could've taken the punk out, no fuss."

"He didn't know I had access until today," Erin said. "But he'll hear about me from Spillano. Then, who knows? Maybe he will."

"If he does, get it on tape," Webb said grimly.

"Yeah, then we can burn his slippery Sicilian ass," Vic said.

"Weren't you listening?" Erin shot back. "He won't give me the order himself."

"He's not gonna be happy you grabbed two of his guys," Vic said.

"I didn't know they were his guys! It's not like these punks wear name tags!"

"Okay, okay." Webb held up his hands. "We'll let that be for the moment. We have a murder to solve, remember? Let's go upstairs and discuss this like reasonable people."

"I'll make you an offer you can't refuse," Vic said, doing his best Pacino impression. It wasn't a very good one.

*   *   *

"So, back to our murder," Webb said.

"And away from O'Reilly's routine traffic bust," Vic said, grinning.

"I'm going to be finding parking tickets on my desk for the next month, aren't I," Erin said gloomily.

"Oh yeah," Vic said. "At least a month. Maybe longer. I could maybe get you one of those meter-maid reflective vests."

"Give me one of those and the next time your doc gives you your colonoscopy, he's going to wonder why the light he shines up your ass is shining right back at him."

"Isabella Romano," Webb said patiently.

"What did Levine say?" Erin asked.

"She's got our victim downstairs on the slab right now," Webb said. "But her preliminary hypothesis is death by blood loss due to a massive number of stabs and lacerations."

"I thought she might've fallen down the stairs," Vic said. "Or maybe cut herself shaving. Shows what I know."

"The weapon was not found at the scene," Webb went on. "But based on the diameter of the stab wounds, it was most likely a large kitchen knife, probably a butcher knife."

"Classic," Vic said. "We should put out a BOLO for Michael Myers."

"CSU searched the apartment and found a knife block in the kitchen. The butcher knife was missing."

"So it was probably a crime of passion," Erin said. "Not a serial killer."

Webb nodded. "A pattern killer would've brought his own weapon," he said. "I'm thinking a domestic dispute that turned ugly."

"Really, really ugly," Vic said. "We're not talking broken plates and shouting at each other."

"How about the blood trail?" Erin asked.

"It's almost certainly the victim's blood," Webb said. "CSU is running a match."

"And the trail stops at the curb outside," Erin said. "The downstairs neighbor knows something, but she's not talking."

"The large number of wounds on the victim is indicative of rage," Webb said. "And then there's the word on the wall."

"*Puta*," Erin said, remembering. "According to the victim's mother, Isabella was really into boys. She may have cheated on her boyfriend."

"And if he found out, maybe he got mad," Vic said.

"Unfortunately, she had a bunch of boyfriends, according to Ms. Romano," Erin said. "Any one of them could be our killer. And we don't have any names or descriptions, except for the last boy. Angel or Angelo, polite, well-dressed, very good-looking."

"That's not much to go on," Webb said. "Neshenko, you want to see how many Angelos are in the phone book?"

"I really, really don't, sir," Vic said.

Webb sighed. "I hate to say it, but you're right. That's just shooting in the dark. Forget I asked. There'll be hundreds of them, and without a last name, we've got no idea who we're looking for."

"Fingerprints?" Erin asked.

"They're all over the apartment," Webb said. "But it looks like the killer was smart enough or lucky enough not to leave any in blood, so any given boyfriend could just claim his prints were from a previous visit. Textbook reasonable doubt."

"We should run them anyway," Erin said. "The mom said Isabella hung out with a wild crowd. I'm guessing at least some of the boys will be in our system. Maybe we'll get lucky and find an Angelo."

"Good idea," Webb said. "Get on it."

"Anything from the uniforms who were canvassing the area?" she asked.

Webb shook his head. "If anyone heard anything, they didn't call us then and they won't admit it now."

"I have some DD-5s to fill out," she said. "Along with the accident and arrest reports."

"Fine," Webb said. "Do your paperwork. Neshenko, you run the fingerprints. I'll be looking through cold cases, seeing if we've got anything that matches this MO."

"But we agreed it wasn't a series," Erin said.

"It probably isn't," he agreed. "But we're covering all the bases, just in case."

So Erin went to work on her reports. She'd always thought essay exams in school were a stupid waste of time, until she'd joined the NYPD. Then she'd learned that some organizations really were built on a foundation of poorly-worded essays written by overworked, stressed employees. Not that penning a discussion of Nathaniel Hawthorne's view of Puritanism in early

America as depicted in *The Scarlet Letter* was the best rehearsal for filling out an arrest report, but it was better than nothing.

She was in the middle of describing how she'd disabled the suspect vehicle when her phone rang. It was an unidentified number, which meant either nothing or everything. She pushed her chair back from her desk, which attracted Rolf's attention. The Shepherd perked up. Then, seeing her raise the phone to her ear, he flopped his head back down with a sigh. He'd learned to distrust the little black boxes humans loved holding against their faces.

"O'Reilly," Erin said.

"We need to talk," said a male voice. It sounded familiar, but she couldn't immediately place it.

"What about?" she asked.

"Business," the man said. "It'll be something you want to hear. Come to Little Italy, Lucia's Bar."

Erin was startled. "Why there?" she blurted out. She knew that place. It was where Mattie Madonna had been shot.

"I'll be there for the next couple hours," the man said, ignoring her question. Then he hung up.

Erin got to her feet. "I have to go," she announced.

"What's up?" Webb asked.

"I'm not sure," Erin said. "Something with my other case, I think. I'll be at Lucia's Bar."

"Hey," Vic said. "Isn't that the place where—"

"Yeah," she said. "The meeting site is part of the message."

"You want some backup?" He was already halfway to his feet.

"Better if I go alone."

"I'm not happy about that," Vic said.

"When's the last time you were happy about anything?" Erin retorted.

"Russians don't know how to be happy," he said. "Are you at least taking the dog?"

"Of course I'm taking the dog. Rolf, *komm*."

Rolf bounded up, wagging and ready.

"Do you know who you're meeting?" Webb asked.

"I think I'll recognize him. I knew the voice."

"Take Neshenko."

"Sir..." she began.

"Don't bring him inside if you don't want to. Park him on the street, but nearby. Just in case."

"It's nice to know you care, sir," Erin said.

"I don't," Webb said. "Dry cleaning is expensive. I don't want to have to get my dress blues done for a departmental funeral."

"That's more like the Lieutenant I know," she said. "I'll call you when I get out of the meeting."

"We're going to have to get you a secretary," Vic said. "To keep track of all your social engagements."

Chapter 8

Lucia's Bar was a small, dingy joint in Little Italy. The air reeked of cigarette smoke, in blatant contradiction of the city's no-smoking policy for bars. It was early afternoon, the booths populated by aging Italian men with nothing to do and nowhere to be. Vic was outside, stewing in the passenger seat of Erin's Charger, hoping she'd get in a fight so he'd have an excuse to come storming through the door and start breaking heads.

Erin took a second in the doorway to let her eyes grow accustomed to the dim light. Rolf, at her side, sniffed the air and sneezed. A few heads turned to look at her, but since she was silhouetted against the daylight, it was doubtful anyone could make out her face. On the other hand, how many women walked into this place with a big German Shepherd?

The last time she'd been in this bar, it had been in the aftermath of a Mob shooting. She'd come in with the Street Narcotics Enforcement Unit to find a room full of blood and bodies. Only two men had survived the shootout; Lucarelli soldier Carlo Peralta and Alfie Madonna. Erin had tried to flip Carlo, but he'd chosen to stay loyal to the Lucarellis, even though Vinnie had tried to have him killed in the hospital to make sure he stayed silent. Carlo was now in the prison hospital at Riker's Island and was probably still alive.

Erin waved a hand in front of her face to drive away the cloud of smoke and memories. She could still remember the feel of Mattie Madonna's hand in hers as the ambulance tried to get him to the emergency room in time. He'd asked her to get Vinnie for him, and to look after his son. Erin was doing her best to do both those things, not because a dying mobster had said so, but because Vinnie had to be stopped, and Alfie might still be saved.

As her eyes grew acclimated, she took a look around. She still didn't know who she was looking for, but she knew what she expected to see; three guys, probably. One would be a boss, the other two would be bodyguards. The guards wouldn't be sitting with their guy. They'd be at the next table, maybe, far enough so they wouldn't listen in on what was being said, but close enough to help if things got rough.

In the left back corner she saw what she'd hoped for. An older gentleman sat alone in a booth. Two younger guys, slightly less well-dressed, were at a table across the aisle. The older man was wearing a very expensive suit. And Erin had met him before.

"Mr. Vitelli," she said, approaching the table. "Good to see you again."

Valentino Vitelli was one of Vinnie the Oil Man's lieutenants, an old-school Mafia don who was in charge of the Lucarelli heroin trade. He looked like a harmless old man, white-haired and meticulously dressed, but Erin knew he could be as ruthless as any professional killer.

He smiled at her and got slowly to his feet, his movements indicating the frailty of advancing age. He extended a hand, which she took. Instead of shaking, he raised her hand to his lips and kissed the back of it.

"Thank you for taking the time to see me, Miss O'Reilly," he said. His accent was pure Brooklyn. "I see you've brought your loyal companion."

"They say diamonds are a girl's best friend," Erin said. "But they only say that because they haven't met Rolf."

Vitelli smiled. "Please, have a seat," he said.

Erin slid into the booth across from him. "Rolf, *sitz*," she said.

The K-9 sat at the end of the table, the top half of his face showing over its edge. He could feel Erin's tension, so he was alert, but she hadn't told him to attack anybody. He kept a wary eye on the man, in case it became necessary to bite him.

"I know you're a busy woman," Vitelli said. "So I'm not going to waste your time. I understand you had some unpleasantness earlier today."

"You could call it that," Erin said. "Do you mean the guy who tried to kill me at the courthouse, or the two idiots who caused a pileup on Fifth Avenue and pulled a gun on me?"

"I apologize for all that," Vitelli said. "None of it should've happened. What can I say? Young people got no respect for their betters these days. They think they know everything, so you can't tell them nothing. You know how it is. My own boy, I try to raise him right, try to teach him respect, and he's a good boy, he really is, but he don't know how it is in the Life. He thinks it just means you do whatever you want. You and me, we know it don't work that way."

Erin nodded. "Rookie cops are the same," she said. "They think they know the whole *Patrol Guide*. They don't realize you have to learn from the streets."

Vitelli snapped his fingers and wagged one of them at her. "Exactly!" he said. "That's just what I'm trying to say. Fortunately, in addition to being morons, those guys who hassled you couldn't shoot straight, neither, so no harm done.

And I appreciate you not capping them right in their stupid faces, though God knows they deserved it."

Erin blinked. She reminded herself that her reputation in the Lucarellis was that of "Junkyard" O'Reilly, Carlyle's personal attack dog. She was a hardened cop with the street cred of a killer.

"Hell, you took out Mickey Connor. A couple young punks ain't nothing for you," Vitelli said. He chuckled dryly. "But you took them in instead. That's a courtesy, so thank you."

"I didn't know they were yours at the time," Erin said. "The first shooter was wearing an NYPD uniform, for Christ's sake! You can't have your people doing that, dressing like us. If you keep doing that, somebody's going to get hurt."

Neither of them remarked on the fact that the shooter had been attempting a hit. Somebody getting hurt had been precisely the point.

"And those other two idiots were plowing through traffic in downtown Manhattan!" she went on. "They were putting civilians at risk. No matter who they were, I had to stop them."

Vitelli put up a hand. "I get it," he said. "Nobody's mad at you. But we've still got our little problem. And both times it could've been solved, you were in the way."

"Maybe that's because nobody bothered to tell me what was going on," she said.

"It's better you don't know," Vitelli said. "You know how this works. We don't exactly spread news around. I asked you here because I've just got two questions for you."

"Those being?"

He extended his index finger. "Do you know where this punk is right now?"

Erin noted Vitelli, for all his apparent candor, was choosing his words carefully. He wasn't naming any names, nor was he going into specifics. She had to act similarly, dance around the truth. It was risky to lie to one of these guys. They hung around liars and con men all the time. A man like Vitelli was good at sniffing out the truth.

"You missed your shot," she said, truthfully enough. "He's under the protection of the US Marshals. WitSec. Your guys interrupted the handoff. The NYPD's got nothing to do with his safety anymore. That responsibility now belongs to the Federal government."

"Then that answers my second question, too," Vitelli said. "You can't get to him."

"He'll have a Marshal with him twenty-four-seven," she said. "Maybe more than one."

"Well, I guess that's all there is to say about that," Vitelli said. "It's too bad. It used to be, you could trust a kid not to run to the Feds. I appreciate you telling me in person. You're stand-up, Miss O'Reilly."

"Forget about it, Mr. Vitelli," she said, getting to her feet. "We're all just trying to make a living."

"Hey, before you go, I want you to meet somebody," Vitelli said. He waved to the table at which the two youngsters were sitting, beckoning one of them over. The kid hurried to the booth.

Vitelli smiled broadly. "This is my boy, Gabriel," he said. "Gabriel, this is Erin O'Reilly. You've heard of her."

That was a high compliment in the underworld. Erin tried her best to look like a badass dirty cop, someone not to be trifled with. She nodded to the young man as casually as she could.

"Good to meet you," she said. She offered a hand, which the kid looked at for just a second, then took. To her amusement, he kissed it just like Valentino had done. It seemed he'd absorbed his lessons in manners from his old man.

When he looked up, she caught her breath in surprise. In the dark room, she hadn't gotten a clear view of his features until now. Gabriel Vitelli was extraordinarily good-looking; movie-star handsome. His complexion was smooth, unblemished olive. His black hair was thick and wavy, stylishly cut. His eyes were a dark brown that could best be described as "smoldering." His lips were exquisitely curved, his cheekbones chiseled as if a Renaissance sculptor had carved them out of marble.

Erin wasn't one to set much store by appearances, but even so, the close proximity of this man, surely the sexiest guy she'd ever met in person, made her heart flutter just a little. His grip on her hand was firm, his own fingers warm and confident.

Jesus, she thought. *I'm probably old enough to be his mom! He can't be a day over nineteen! Get a hold of yourself, O'Reilly. You're not in high school anymore.*

"I've heard a lot about you, ma'am," Gabriel said. "Is all of it true?"

"Only the good stuff," she said with a twinkle in her eye. "So, you're learning the family business from your dad?"

"I try to help him out," Gabriel said.

"He's a good boy," Valentino said with obvious affection. He lightly cuffed Gabriel's cheek. "You don't have kids, do you, Miss O'Reilly?"

"Not yet," she said.

"Then you don't understand," he said. "I'd do anything for this boy. All right, Gabriel, go on back. We're done here."

Erin once more offered the old man her hand. This time, they shook.

"Don't worry about the rat infestation," Valentino said. "It ain't your problem, and it don't concern you no more. I promise you won't be bothered again."

"Thanks," she said, wondering exactly what that meant.

"You should come to dinner with me," he said. "My wife makes the best chicken parmesan you've ever had. Why don't you come sometime?"

"To your house?"

"Why not? Bring your guy. He's welcome too. We're all friends here, you know?"

Erin wondered. The Lucarellis and the O'Malleys had officially made peace, but they'd been killing one another only weeks earlier, and might easily do so again. Still, he'd have to be crazy to try to whack Carlyle in the presence of a police detective.

"Thanks for the invitation," she said. "I'll have to check my calendar. But I'll let you know. You have a good day, Mr. Vitelli."

"You too, Miss O'Reilly."

*   *   *

"All right," Vic said as they got out of Erin's Charger back in the Eightball's garage. "I know you don't like talking shady business in your car, because you think somebody might be listening. But now we're safe, right? So tell me what's going on."

Erin shrugged. "The Lucarellis are trying to kill Alfie Madonna."

"We knew that already."

"They want me to set him up."

Vic blinked. "They want what, now?"

"You heard me."

"They asked a police detective to help whack a guy? Tell me you got a recording."

"Of course I did." Erin had a miniature recorder sewn into the underwire of her bra, courtesy of Phil Stachowski's tech support. She'd started it running before going into Lucia's. "But

Vitelli's smart. He didn't name any names or say anything that proves anything."

"So he doesn't trust you?"

"He doesn't trust anybody. Well, maybe his son. He made a point of introducing me to the kid."

"How sweet," Vic said. "Was it Take Your Kid to Work Day for the Mafia?"

"No, he's an adult... barely. Looks like Old Man Vitelli has his son on his personal security detail, just like Mattie Madonna did. Probably because of what I just said; in the Mob, your own flesh and blood are the only guys you can really trust."

"Why'd he want you to meet his brat?"

"Networking," Erin explained. "You can't just slide into the Mob. Somebody always has to vouch for you. Vitelli's getting close to retirement age. He wants to make sure his boy knows the right people, so when Gabriel gets an important position, he'll have the right connections."

"One of which is you?"

"Apparently."

"Are you complimented or insulted?"

Erin smiled. "A little of both, I think."

"What'd you think of this Gabriel?"

"Prettiest gangster I ever met."

"Oh, God." Vic slapped his forehead. "Not again!"

Erin smacked him on the shoulder. "I didn't mean it like that! Sheesh. I can keep my pants pulled up."

"You know what the best predictor of future behavior is?" he asked with a nasty grin. "Past behavior."

"I am so very done talking about this."

"I'm just getting started."

"So, have you and Zofia picked out baby names yet?"

"We were having so much fun," Vic said. "Then you had to go and get personal on me."

"We can keep talking about this. Or do you want to go upstairs and do some more police work?"

"Yeah, that's a good idea."

Webb greeted them with a sour smile. "Glad you're back," he said. "Anything I need to worry about?"

"No, sir," Erin said.

"Good. I've got enough heartburn. Neshenko, if memory serves, you have some fingerprints to run."

"Copy that," Vic sighed. "I didn't even get to punch any mobsters."

"We're all very sorry for you," Webb said. "O'Reilly, I want you to go through our victim's financials and phone records. While you were gone, I looked over her jacket."

"Yeah, she was a wild child, right?"

"Nothing too major, but she's no stranger to the legal system. All non-violent offenses."

"Party girl," was Vic's opinion. "Harmless."

Erin settled in at her desk. Rolf planted himself a little closer than usual, resting his snout on her foot.

"If I'd wanted to be an accountant, I'd have gone to business school," she muttered under her breath. She was no good with numbers. The only member of their squad that had really known how to sift through financial records had been Kira Jones, and Kira had transferred out of Major Crimes after one gunfight too many. Now Kira was upstairs, riding a desk at Internal Affairs. They were still friends, or at least as friendly as a detective and an IAB investigator could be, but it left Erin floundering through the accounting swamp on her own.

By the end of her shift, Erin was sure of only two things; Isabella Romano had been getting a lot of money from someone other than her employer, and Erin herself could really use a double shot of good top-shelf whiskey. She logged off her computer and pushed her chair back.

Rolf was on his paws instantly, ready for adventure. When Erin didn't immediately clip his leash to his collar, he picked it up in his mouth and wagged his tail. She knelt and took it from him with a smile, scratching the base of his ears.

"I'm out," she told the room at large. "Only one thing popped for me. Our victim had some undeclared income."

"Parents?" Webb guessed.

"Maybe, but the way her mom talked, she wasn't getting much from them. I'm thinking boyfriend."

"Boyfriends," Vic corrected.

"Whatever," she said. "Anyway, nobody's made any withdrawals from her bank account since she died. I can't see anything shady at first glance."

"How about her phone?" Webb asked.

Erin shook her head. "A lot of calls, and a lot of texts with a bunch of guys, but it's all pretty innocuous. There is one thing."

"What's that?" Webb and Vic asked in unison. The way they both sat forward, immediately alert and interested, reminded her so much of Rolf that she had to bite back a laugh. Detectives always looked for what her dad called "odd socks," little details that didn't fit the established narrative. Those were the clues that could break cases.

"She has a bunch of calls to and from an unregistered number, starting about three months back," she said. "I think it's a burner phone."

The energy went out of the other detectives' faces. "We can't do anything with that," Vic said.

"It's interesting, though, isn't it?" she said. "A girl starts talking to somebody using an untraceable phone, and a couple months later she turns up dead?"

"Did you ping the phone?" Webb asked.

"I tried," she said. "It's either turned off or out of batteries."

"Or lying at the bottom of the East River alongside a butcher knife," Vic said. "So you think it's our killer?"

"There's a decent chance the phone belongs to a criminal," she said. "And that would definitely make the owner a POI."

"Add it to the board," Webb said. Erin duly went to the whiteboard and wrote down what she knew about the caller, including the phone number, as a Person of Interest.

"That's it?" Vic asked.

"It's all I have for now," Erin said. "How're the fingerprints coming?"

"Slow," he said. "CSU lifted them all over the damn apartment. There's gotta be a couple dozen sets, maybe more. I think I'll stay an hour or two, if the Department will approve my overtime."

"The NYPD will be happy to subsidize your drinking and gambling habits," Webb said with a straight face.

"Hey, I don't gamble that much," Vic said. "And I mostly drink the cheap stuff."

"You say that like it's a good thing," Erin said.

"When the city hires a crew to knock down a building, they go with the lowest bidder," Vic said. "I figure I'll handle my liver the same way."

"And it'll crumble just like Manhattan's infrastructure," she said and headed out the door.

Chapter 9

"Rough day?" the bartender asked. He'd tracked Erin's progress across the Barley Corner's main room; a straight, no-nonsense walk directly to the bar.

"You tell me, Danny," Erin said. "I've been in a car crash, shot at, met with professional criminals, dried out my eyeballs staring at bank statements, and had to watch my mom show my boyfriend a bunch of my old baby pictures."

"Glen D?" Danny suggested.

"Make it a double," she said.

"Come now, darling," Carlyle said, coming up beside her. "The pictures weren't so bad, surely. Your mum's promised to show me more at dinner."

For a moment, Erin's mind went totally blank. Then she said, "Shit!"

"Forgot about our dinner engagement?" he asked gently.

"Yeah. The car chase put it right out of my mind. We'd better get moving."

"I was beginning to wonder if something had come up. Will you be wanting to change?"

"No time." It was after six already and they were supposed to be at her brother's house by six-thirty. It would be a tight squeeze anyway. Erin looked down at herself. She had the grime and sweat of her busy day all over her. A shower and change of clothes would have been nice; hell, it would've been necessary. She cursed inwardly for letting her schedule get away from her. She could've been back half an hour earlier.

"I'll phone your brother and tell him you've been detained," he said. "They'll understand. Your da was a copper enough years. Surely you ate your share of late meals growing up."

"That's true," she said. "Okay. I'll drink my drink, then I'll get cleaned up and be back down here, ready to go. Fifteen minutes."

"Make it twenty," he said. "Don't go gulping my good whiskey, darling. That stuff's got to come all the way from Scotland, you ken. It's meant to be savored."

*   *   *

A short while later, hair still wet from her shower, wearing a clean blouse and slacks, a freshly-fed Rolf in tow, Erin joined Carlyle and Ian Thompson. Ian led the way out of the bar, scanning the street for potential threats. Finding none, the former Marine motioned them to follow. They crossed to the parking garage where Carlyle kept his gray Mercedes. Normally, Ian would have brought the car out of the garage and picked them up curbside, but that would have wasted Rolf's fine-tuned nose. Ian recognized the dog's talents and had incorporated him into his security procedures. The K-9 found no trace of explosives.

"It'd be too ironic for words if Cars Carlyle got done in by a car bomb," she said as he helped her into the back seat with a courteous hand.

"I believe our Lord and Savior once said, he that lives by the sword should be expecting to die by it," Carlyle said. "If they'd automobiles in biblical times, he'd have said the same about car bombs, I've no doubt."

Ian got behind the wheel and started the engine. The car rolled quietly and smoothly out of its parking spot and down the ramp onto the Manhattan streets.

"I met our mutual friend Valentino Vitelli today," Erin said.

"On what business?" Carlyle asked.

"He wanted to talk about Alfie Madonna. Vinnie wants Alfie dead."

"Did he ask you to kill him?"

"He danced around it, but I short-circuited the conversation. I told him the Marshals have Alfie, which they do. I could probably still get to him. Hell, I'm going to go see him later tonight, if dinner doesn't run too late. I want to make sure he's settled in okay after the unpleasantness on Fifth Avenue. But Vitelli didn't need to know that."

"Be certain you're not followed," Carlyle said. "Tailing coppers is a time-honored way of finding witnesses if they're lying low."

"I'll keep that in mind," she said dryly. "Vitelli also wanted to introduce me to his kid. Now, don't get jealous, but I have to say, he's the best-looking guy I've seen in a really long time. Maybe ever."

Carlyle was amused. "Darling, if I was worried about other lads, I'd not be the man I am, nor you the woman you are. So you've met Angel Face Vitelli, have you? I'm not surprised he made an impression. You think that sort of nickname comes about by accident?"

"Say that again," Erin said sharply.

"You think that sort of nickname—" Carlyle began, bewildered.

"No, the nickname," she interrupted.

"Angel Face," Carlyle said. "That's Gabriel Vitelli, aye? The lad you met?"

"I don't believe this," Erin said.

"What's the matter, darling?"

"You're a gambler," she said. "You're good with odds, right?"

"It's a large part of the job, aye," he said. "Gamblers don't last long in the business if they're bad at maths."

"What are the odds that I'd run into a Person of Interest from a murder in Brooklyn later the same day, in Little Italy, on something completely unrelated?"

Carlyle smiled thinly. "I'd say somewhere along the lines of winning the Irish Sweepstakes," he said. "And they discontinued that back in '87."

"The Irish what?"

"Sweepstakes," he said. "It was an Irish hospital benefit that ran some fifty years. A great deal of its money came from tickets smuggled across the Atlantic from America, from transplanted Irishmen. The ticket stubs were matched to horses that ran races in Ireland. If your horse won, you won a prize. It was quite the crooked contest. There was a great deal of counterfeiting of tickets, along with the usual corruption and rigging of bets. My point is, if you weren't running the stakes, you'd never be likely to see much return on your investment."

"Well, I think my horse may have won the race," she said. "Excuse me. I need to make a call."

"Forget something?" Vic asked when he answered his phone. "Or did you just miss me?"

"I missed you," she said. "But next time I won't. I'll just lead you a little more and empty the clip. Are you still working the prints from the Romano apartment?"

"Yeah, but that's okay. I've got a two-liter of Dew and some shitty Chinese takeout, so I'm set for a while. What's up?"

"Do you have a match with a Gabriel Vitelli?"

"How the hell did you know that?" The banter dropped out of Vic's voice and he was all business.

"Craziest coincidence," she said. "He was one of the guys I ran into in Little Italy this afternoon. Him and his dad."

"You're shitting me."

"No, I'm not. Remember I told you about meeting a real pretty boy? Vitelli's bound to be in the system. Call up his mugshot."

There was a brief pause. Then Vic said, grudgingly, "Okay, he's kinda good-looking. If you like that sort of thing."

"What's his record like?"

"He's in the Mafia, but he's young, so he hasn't had time to pile up too much crap. He busted his cherry a couple years back, did six months for a delivery truck hijacking. He's got a couple drug offenses, too. Not a user, but he had dealer weight on him. He should've done time for that, too, but I'm guessing he drew the right judge and he got off with probation both times."

"Who was the judge?" she asked.

"What's that got to do with anything?"

"Just humor me, Vic."

"Okay, okay. Just a sec. I have to log into the court records." Erin heard Vic's fingers clacking away at his keyboard. She waited.

"It's not our buddy Ferris, if that's what you're wondering," Vic said. "It's some mope named Barberis. Pasquale Barberis. That's a hell of a mouthful."

"Can you check one more thing, as long as you're looking at the court records?"

"I live to serve, o captain my captain."

"Vic, if there's a gland that secretes sarcasm, I think yours is leaking."

"What I'm leaking is none of your business, O'Reilly. What do you want?"

"Who's the judge presiding over Alfie Madonna's case?"

"Looking now." Vic's sigh was clearly audible. "Looks like it's Judge... Barberis. Erin? What in the hell is going on?"

Erin sat back in the Mercedes's comfortable upholstery. "I'm just putting pieces together, Vic. One at a time."

"You need me to do anything on Vitelli?"

"No. He'll keep until tomorrow. Thanks."

"Don't mention it."

*   *   *

Ian considered himself on duty, but the O'Reilly family was having none of it. After he'd taken five bullets trying to stop Michelle O'Reilly's abduction, he'd been brought firmly into the family as an honorary younger brother. The moment they entered Sean and Michelle's Midtown brownstone, Anna threw herself at him for a hug. He'd no sooner set the nine-year-old back on the floor than Michelle was there with a hug of her own and a kiss on the cheek.

Erin's heart warmed at the sight. Ian was doing a lot better these days. He'd healed almost completely from his bullet wounds, but the healing went deeper than that. He had a new spark in him, thanks in part to the O'Reillys, and in part to the shelter dog she'd convinced him to adopt, but she thought most of it was due to his new girlfriend. Cassie Jordan was a war widow with a young son, a rehab nurse who'd met Ian during his recuperation. Erin was fuzzy on the details, but Cassie had clearly been very good for him. Now Ian had a smile that went deeper than his mouth. He was still a traumatized, hypervigilant combat veteran, but he was moving in the right direction.

Erin watched Michelle and Sean Junior as the family assembled around the dinner table. Their relationship had been a little strained on account of the events surrounding Michelle's kidnapping. But tonight everyone seemed happy. The presence of Erin's mom and dad played into that.

"Looks like you got a little too close to something, kiddo," Sean O'Reilly Senior observed, giving the bandage on Erin's neck a pointed look.

"It barely grazed me," Erin said. "The guy was a lousy shot."

"Dodging bullets isn't a healthy hobby," Sean said.

"It's healthier than not dodging them," she replied, earning a chuckle from Carlyle and a wry twist of the mouth from Michelle.

Dinner was excellent, though Erin had no idea what she was eating. Michelle's adventures in cuisine reflected her French Canadian upbringing and were very different than the roast beef and potatoes of Erin's childhood. Shelley made complicated sauces and used spices Erin had never even heard of, but she made it work, most of the time.

After dessert, Mary and Michelle went to the kitchen to do the dishes, while Erin's brother, dad, and boyfriend retreated to the living room. Ian went with them, but only so he could play blocks with Anna and Patrick on the carpet. Ian started constructing a forward operating base, making sure he had good fields of fire between Sean Junior's easy chair, the couch, and the coffee table.

Erin went with the menfolk. She sat down on the couch between Carlyle and her dad. They had glasses of Guinness in front of them and not a photo album in sight, thank goodness.

"What's on your mind, kiddo?" Sean asked.

"What makes you think anything's on my mind?" Erin shot back.

"I'm your dad. I can read you like the *New York Times*."

She smiled. "I'm thinking about a case. Well, two cases. Except maybe they're the same case, sort of."

"You detectives," Sean said. "Always tying yourselves up in knots. This is why you should've stayed on Patrol."

"You don't mean that," Erin said.

"Of course he doesn't," Carlyle said. "He's proud of you, darling, as you well know. You're his legacy with the Department."

"That's just what I'm thinking about," she said. "Legacies. There's these two mobsters, okay? And both of them have sons who went into the family business, just like I did."

"These guys are absolutely nothing like you," Sean said.

"Whatever." Erin took a second to make sure none of the civilians in the room were paying attention. Her brother had the newspaper in front of him. Anna and Patrick were absorbed in Ian's explanation of modern military fortifications.

"Anyway," she went on. "One of the dads got killed. His son was right there, watching it happen."

"That's rough," Sean said quietly. "I can't even imagine what that'd be like."

"He took it hard," Erin agreed. "Now he's determined to get even, and the guys who killed his old man know it. So they're gunning for him, too."

"What about the other son?" her dad asked.

"His dad is with the faction that ordered the hit," she said. "So he's along for the ride, too."

"Sounds like something out of an old movie," Sean said.

"Or Shakespeare," Carlyle said. "Or perhaps Greek tragedy."

"So are these two punks going to end up killing each other?" Sean asked. "Sins of the father, and all that?"

"I hope not," Erin said. "And the other son is involved in my murder investigation. I don't know if he killed his girlfriend, but he might've."

"Busy little gangsters," Sean said.

"So I need to go check on the mobster who lost his dad," she said. "Make sure he's all tucked in at the Marshals' safe house. He had a couple close calls earlier today, so he's probably a little shaken up."

"That's where you caught the bullet?" Sean asked.

"Yeah. Shooter got away. I should've had him, but I took a bad step." Her ankle was still hurting.

"The Marshals can handle it," he said. "They have lots of experience hiding guys from the Mob."

"I know," she said. "But something's bothering me. Every time we turn around, there's more Mafia goons coming out of the woodwork. It's like they know what we're doing before we even do it."

"You think there's a mole," Sean said very quietly.

"I know there's a mole," she said. "More than one."

"You have to report that to IAB," Sean said.

"And they'll do what, exactly?" Carlyle asked in tones of profound skepticism.

"They'll investigate!"

"And it's your experience, is it, that your Internal Affairs lads are skilled at exposing the right people?"

That was a cheap shot and it momentarily silenced everyone on the couch. Carlyle's first contact with the O'Reilly clan had happened because of an IAB investigation into Sean's partner. Sean himself had also been implicated, and only Carlyle's unlikely intervention had gotten him off the hook with his job and pension intact; a favor he'd never called in. It was still a sore point with Sean, almost twenty years later.

"It's their job," Sean said when he'd recovered.

"I don't know who it is," Erin said. "I can't just tell them I suspect somebody in the Eightball. You know Lieutenant Keane."

"By reputation," Sean said. "I've never had the pleasure of meeting him face-to-face."

"You can be glad of that. I swear, he's half reptile. Cold-blooded as they come. It's better to steer clear of him when I can. And there's a chance, just a chance, IAB itself is compromised."

"Who watches the watchmen?" Carlyle quoted grimly.

"I do know one mole," she went on. "But IAB can't help with that and I don't have enough proof to stick it to him."

"Why can't they help?" Sean asked.

"Because he's an FBI agent," she said.

"Oh." Sean blinked. "Jesus, kiddo, what've you got yourself into here?"

"I ask myself the same thing every day."

"But if the Feds have a leak," Sean said, "how do you know the Marshals are okay?"

"The Marshals Service is separate from the Feebies," she said. "You know that."

"But if they've an ear in one branch of the service, who's to say the others haven't been penetrated?" Carlyle asked.

"Headley and his guys are okay," Erin said. "If they weren't, I don't think things would've gone down the way they did on Fifth Avenue. They had my back every step of the way."

"That's grand," Carlyle said.

Meanwhile, on the carpet, Anna was trying to figure out how to get inside Ian's defenses. She had a small cavalry troop of My Little Ponies and was maneuvering them around the legs of the coffee table, attempting a flanking maneuver.

"What if I come at you from this way?" she asked.

"Don't think you'll make it," Ian said. "I've got guards posted here, see?"

"But that guard works for me," Anna said, pointing to the gate to Ian's little compound. "He'll open the door."

Erin looked back at her father and boyfriend. "See why I'm worried?" she asked. "Even the kid gets it."

"Treason's the best way to get inside a place you've no business being," Carlyle agreed.

"I think I'd better get to that safe house now," Erin said. "I'm getting twitchy. Can I borrow your car?"

"Take Ian with you," he suggested.

"To a WitSec safe house?" She was shocked.

"He understands operational security," Carlyle said. "Better than your lot, I'd warrant. And he'll not talk. You can swing by later to fetch me. I understand I've some photos to examine." He winked.

"Hey, Ian?" Erin said.

"Problem?" he asked.

"No. I just need a lift. Care to give me a ride?"

"Happy to," he said. Then he turned to the kids. "Sorry. Got my orders. I'm pulling out."

Anna giggled. "I like the way you talk," she said.

"How's that?" he asked, smiling at her.

"Like you're still in a war."

His smile faded slightly. "Habits are hard to break."

Chapter 10

"Not sure about this," Ian said. He maneuvered the Mercedes through the Manhattan streets, his face calm but his eyes in constant motion.

"How do you mean?" Erin asked from the passenger seat. Rolf was in back, staring out the window and panting. He didn't care where they were going. The fact that they were in motion was the important thing.

"Marshals might not like me being there," he said.

"How come? You're a decorated Marine veteran. You've got a clean record."

"I hang out with Mob guys. Kill people sometimes."

"Ian, I hang out with Mob guys and kill people."

"You're authorized. What's my objective?"

"It wasn't my idea. I guess Carlyle wants someone backing me up, someone I trust. You're carrying, right?"

"Affirmative. Beretta 92. Expecting trouble?" Carlyle had used his connections to arrange for a concealed-carry permit for Ian. Since the former Marine had never been convicted of a felony, he could get away with it in spite of Manhattan's tough gun laws.

"These days I'm always expecting trouble," she said.

"Same." He turned at a stoplight onto a side street.

"This isn't our turn," she said.

"I know." Ian made a quick turn into an alley. He drove along it, then got out at the next street and put them back on course.

"You're trying to shake a tail," she said.

"You're not the only paranoid one," he said. "Don't think we're being followed. Better to be sure."

"And you wonder why we want you around. Just remember, you can't tell anyone about this. Don't even tell Carlyle the address. Got that?"

"Affirmative."

"I'll call the Marshals and let them know we're coming." She pulled out her phone.

"Good idea," Ian said. "Makes a blue-on-blue incident less likely."

"Blue-on-blue?"

"You'd call it friendly fire. Marines say there's no such thing."

Erin punched in Headley's number. It started ringing. She didn't start to get nervous until the third ring.

"Pick up," she muttered. That didn't mean anything. Maybe he was in the bathroom. Maybe his battery was dead.

It rang a fourth time.

She gripped the phone tightly. Headley had two other Marshals with him. They were trained, experienced, armed. And after the day's events, they were expecting trouble. They'd be fine. They had to be. They just had to...

"Headley."

The Marshal's voice in Erin's ear made her sag with relief. "This is O'Reilly," she said, forcing her mouth to work. "I'm inbound, should be there in just a couple minutes. Everything okay?"

"Yeah, we're fine." Headley sounded, if anything, a little bored. "Sent Boone out for pizza twenty minutes ago. Our subject's bitching about not having any wine. Says he might as well have stayed in jail. It's about the same, according to him. No booze and we won't let him leave. He says behind bars, at least they let you make phone calls."

"He's got a point," Erin said, smiling.

"Calley told me what happened to you," Headley said. "Think we can expect any follow-up from the opposition?"

"They're still looking for him," she said. "By the way, I've got a guy with me."

"Who?" Headley's voice had an edge to it.

"Driver and personal bodyguard," she said. "Name of Thompson. He's former Marine Corps, Scout Sniper, tough as they come. And he's rock solid."

"I don't doubt his credentials," Headley said. "But every new face we bring into this is a security risk."

"Not this guy," she said. "I won't be staying long. I just wanted—" She paused, trying to find the right words.

"I know what you wanted, O'Reilly," Headley said. "It's okay. People think WitSec is like in the movies, bad guys all over the place. What it really is, is cheap takeout, bad company, worse hours, boredom, and lousy apartments borrowed from the FBI."

"FBI? What've they got to do with anything?" she asked sharply.

"We didn't have an available safe house on such short notice," Headley explained. "So we liaised with the Feebies. Their Organized Crime Division had a place we could borrow. It's just for a couple of days—"

"Who did you talk to?" Erin interrupted. "What was his name?"

"I don't remember. Some agent or other. Why?" Headley's tone turned suddenly cautious.

"You've got to get out of there," she said. "*Now.*"

Ian, hearing her words, and especially the tone in which she said them, put his foot down. The Mercedes surged forward, laying rubber on the final turn into the apartment parking lot.

To Headley's credit, he didn't waste time asking for details, or accusing Erin of imagining things or borrowing trouble. "We need somewhere to go," he said briskly. "Best thing is probably to check into a motel under a fake name. It's shaky, but it'll buy us a couple hours while we get something else lined up."

"I'm coming in," she said. Ian stopped the Mercedes in front of the apartment's front door.

"No, wait down there," Headley said. "We'll be moving to the Lincoln out front. Keep your eyes open and cover our exit. We'll be down in minutes. Headley out."

"Trouble?" Ian asked quietly. It was rhetorical. He was already scanning the area for threats. His coat was open and he'd unfastened the safety strap on his shoulder holster.

"Maybe," Erin said. "We can't take the chance. The FBI have a dirty agent who's in bed with the Oil Man. If he's heard about this, we're made."

"Understood." Ian hadn't stopped looking around while they talked. Now, still speaking in the same calm tone, he added, "Black SUV, ten o'clock."

Erin saw the vehicle he meant. "What about it?" she asked. The sun had dropped below the skyline and the lot was shrouded in shadows. The SUV in question was parked just far enough from the nearest light to make it hard to see.

"Guy behind the wheel."

She didn't ask if he was sure. Scout Snipers were recruited for tactical proficiency, physical and mental toughness, and above all, steady hands and keen eyesight. If you pitted a cat against Ian Thompson in a nighttime staring contest, Erin would bet on Ian every time.

"What's he doing?" she asked.

"Not moving. Watching the door. Got eyes on us, too."

"Copy that," Erin said. "Anyone else in the car?"

"Not up front. Could be in back. Windows too tinted to tell."

It might be an ambush. Maybe it was a Lucarelli hit squad, just waiting for the Marshals to make a move. But that didn't make sense. Alfie might not leave the apartment for days. The Mob didn't do stakeouts like that. It was more likely that this was a getaway driver. And if that was the case, someone might already be inside.

"Shit," she said. "Wait here. Cover my back."

She opened the passenger door and got out of the Mercedes. Then she reached for the back door to let Rolf out. If she was going to play hide-and-seek with a Mob assassin, she wanted her K-9. Maybe she should call for backup. But that would directly involve the NYPD and would certainly blow Alfie's cover, if it wasn't already blown.

At that moment, Erin saw a bright flash from a second-floor window. A muffled thump accompanied it.

Shotgun, Erin thought. And she didn't think the Marshals were carrying shotguns. There were three more flashes in rapid succession, accompanied by the sharp popping sounds of pistol shots. Then the shotgun fired again. The window shattered. Shards of glass came down in a sparkling shower, raining onto the pavement.

Ian was out of the car so fast, she barely saw him move. He dropped to one knee, taking cover behind the Mercedes's engine block and pulling his Beretta. Erin's Glock was in her hand, though she didn't remember drawing it.

She yanked the car door open. Rolf hopped out onto the asphalt, tail wagging, ready to go to work.

"Stay here!" she told Ian again. Rolf's leash wasn't attached, but there was no time to link him up. She'd have to count on his training and his bond with her. "*Fuss!*" she said to the dog.

Then they did what good cops were supposed to do. They ran toward the gunfire.

*   *   *

Erin and Rolf crossed the apartment lobby in a few running strides. Erin shouldered her way through the door to the stairwell. More gunshots echoed down the concrete shaft. It sounded like at least two, maybe three shooters, but the reverberations made it hard to tell. She took the stairs two at a time. Rolf loped beside her, tongue hanging out.

Neither one of them was wearing body armor. This had just been a visit; it wasn't like they were serving a felony warrant. Erin cursed inwardly, remembering her Patrol days, when she and Rolf would put on their Kevlar as part of their everyday uniform. Maybe she ought to go back to wearing her vest all the time. If she lived through the next ten minutes, she'd consider it.

As she reached the second-floor landing, she heard more shots popping off. She put her hand on the doorknob and took a breath.

"NYPD!" she shouted. "Hands where I can—"

A heavy blow slammed into the door, knocking her backward. Startled, off-balance, she stumbled. Pain shot up her leg from her twisted ankle, which nearly buckled. Her heel slipped into empty space, a full flight of concrete stairs yawning behind her.

The door flew open and a man tumbled through. Erin saw a face, teeth clenched, eyes wide. She saw a hand clutching the grip of a sawed-off shotgun. She saw the slick stain of blood on the man's jacket.

"Fass!" she snapped reflexively, bringing her Glock in line as well as she could from her precarious position. The man kept moving, falling to the floor even as Rolf sprang at him. The Shepherd was blocking Erin's line of fire, but he did what he'd been trained to do. His jaws clamped down on the man's gun-arm. Man and dog hit the floor, Rolf on top.

"Marshals!" someone shouted from the hallway.

"NYPD!" Erin called again, recovering her balance and stepping forward. The shotgun had fallen from the downed man's hand when Rolf had grabbed him. She kicked the weapon down the stairs. She didn't worry about the guy himself. Rolf had him under control.

"Hallway clear," the unseen Marshal reported.

"Who is that?" Erin asked. She wasn't about to trust her life to a stranger's word.

"Boone. US Marshals. O'Reilly?"

"Yeah. Got one in custody here. I'm coming out. Hold your fire."

"Copy that, O'Reilly. Come ahead."

Erin stepped into the hall. Her pistol was still in one hand, but she held it up and away from her body, just in case. After a firefight, people tended to get jumpy. The smell of gunpowder filled the air. Wisps of smoke drifted through the hallway. To her right, a body lay on the floor. It was a man, a stranger dressed in street clothes, blood all over his chest. He still clutched a pistol in one hand, but he wasn't moving.

Just behind the body, Marshal Boone knelt in the doorway to Unit 208. He was covering the hall, pistol ready. His face was drawn and tense, his eyes holding a wild, fixed look Erin didn't like at all. He relaxed slightly when he saw her, but his hands were shaking.

"Just the two of them?" Erin asked.

"That's all I saw," Boone said. "Is backup on the way?"

"Not yet," she said. "I wasn't sure we wanted the extra attention."

"It's too late for that," he said. "Call an ambulance. Now."

The bottom dropped out of Erin's stomach. "Who's hit?" she asked. She'd already known they'd need to call the paramedics, for the man in the stairwell if nothing else.

"Headley. God damn it, they got Headley."

"Is he alive?"

"Yeah, I... I think so. He was a minute ago. Calley's doing first aid."

"Where's Alfie?"

Boone cocked his head. "Inside."

Erin fished out her phone and called Dispatch. "This is O'Reilly, shield four-six-four-oh," she said. "I need a bus to my location, forthwith. Better send a couple Patrol units, too. We've had an OIS, multiple casualties."

"We copy, O'Reilly," Dispatch said. "Backup and bus are en route. Patrol ETA two minutes, bus seven."

"Copy that. O'Reilly out." She hung up and turned to Boone. "I better secure the other guy. Stay there for a second."

Rolf was still on top of his target, enthusiastically gripping the limp arm. His tail was whipping fiercely back and forth and he was growling.

Erin considered the man. Rolf's jaws could crack bones like matchsticks. The pain from that bite had to be immense, but the guy wasn't twitching at all. His eyes were still open, but they had a wide, unseeing stare.

"Shit," she muttered, dropping to one knee beside him. She felt for a pulse at his neck. Nothing.

Rolf glanced at her questioningly, but held on. He wouldn't let go until she told him to.

"*Pust*," she said quietly. This guy wasn't going to get up; not now, not ever.

Rolf dropped the man's arm and stopped growling. He looked at Erin and cocked his head, waiting to be told what a good boy he was. He already knew it, of course, but he never tired of hearing it.

"*Sei brav*," she said, rubbing his head. She realized she'd forgotten his reward toy. She'd somehow left it out of her jacket pocket. How could she explain that to him?

Tires squealed outside. She heard the roar of an engine being gunned. She also heard sirens, but they were farther away.

The getaway driver. Erin hesitated just an instant, then sprinted back into the hallway. She ran to the window at the end, the one that had been shot out in the gunfight. Rolf went with her, all excitement again. Maybe there'd be more bad guys to bite.

She was just quick enough to spot the taillights of the SUV as it disappeared around the corner, accelerating as it went.

"Ian!" she called, cautiously poking her head out the window.

"Ma'am?" he predictably called back. Erin had made him promise never to call her that again, but in the heat of the moment, she let it slide.

"Put your gun away and get out of here!" she shouted. "We've got backup inbound, less than two minutes!"

"You good?" he asked. He stood up from his position behind the Mercedes, tucking his pistol back into its holster.

"I'm fine. Just go!"

"I'll leave the keys in the glove compartment," he said. After taking a moment to do just that, he jogged away into the gathering dark without another word.

Erin turned away from the window to find Boone checking the body in the hall. He'd knocked the pistol away and was in the process of standing up, shaking his head.

"He dead?" Erin asked.

"Yeah," Boone said. "Your guy in the stairs?"

"Him, too. We're clear." Erin looked more closely at Boone. The man was wearing a white shirt under a black sport coat. The shirt had blood spattered on it. "How about you?"

"What?" Boone was confused. Then he realized what she was talking about. "Oh. This isn't mine. Headley... Calley's with him. I told you that. Damn it, we'd better check on him. Christ."

Erin and Boone hurried into the apartment. The sirens were much closer now. Backup would be arriving any moment.

The apartment was every bit as seedy as Headley had suggested on the phone. The walls were covered with an ugly fake-wood veneer that hadn't even looked good in the Seventies, when it'd been new. Now it was pitted, scratched, and stained. The whole place stank of stale cigarette smoke and the other undefinable odors of cheap housing. On the way to the bedroom, Erin saw a pizza box lying on the floor. Rolf sniffed at the box with more than passing interest, but was too well trained to try to snatch a slice.

The bedroom contained a battered dresser and end table, and an old bed with a sagging mattress. Calley had Headley up on the bed. The older Marshal's coat was off. Calley was pressing a towel against Headley's upper chest. Headley was sheet white.

"Evening, Detective," Headley said in a faint, slightly watery voice. A little bubble of blood formed at the corner of his mouth and burst, spraying tiny droplets of red onto his chin.

"Jesus, boss, don't talk," Calley said. "You'll be fine, but you've got to lie quiet."

"What happened?" Erin asked.

"I'd just come back with the food," Boone said. "I ran into the others in the kitchen. Headley said we were leaving. He told Calley and me to stay with the subject while he got the car. He opened the door and..."

The man stopped talking and ran a hand through his hair. He'd looked to Erin like a tough son of a bitch when she'd first met him, but now he looked years younger and thoroughly miserable.

"They must've followed me," he said. "They were waiting in the hallway. As soon as he stepped outside, they let him have it with a shotgun. Headley's quicker than he looks. He managed to get a little cover in the doorway, but he still caught some buckshot in the chest. Calley grabbed him and pulled him inside. I returned fire and got one of them when he tried to rush the door. I fired six—no, seven times at him. Then the other guy and I shot it out. He was just down the hall a ways, using another doorway. I guess he decided to make a run for it. He went for the stairs and I gave him a couple more shots. Three, I think. I'm pretty sure I hit him."

"You did," Erin said. "He was dead when Rolf grabbed him, and I didn't fire a shot. That was excellent shooting, Marshal."

The sirens were very close outside now. She heard car doors and police officers shouting.

"So where's Alfie?" she asked.

"Bathroom," Calley said. "I told him to get in there, lock the door, and get in the tub. I figured that might give him a little more protection from stray rounds. Easy, boss, easy."

Headley moved weakly and coughed. Blood spattered from his lips. That wasn't good. It meant he'd taken at least one pellet in either the windpipe or the lung.

"How come you guys weren't wearing vests?" Erin asked. She knew there wasn't much point in asking it, and she wasn't wearing one herself, but the question just popped out.

"This was supposed to be a low-profile job," Boone said bitterly. "We were trying not to look like Marshals. Eight years I've been doing this and I never shot anybody. Now I just gunned two guys and my boss is bleeding on a goddamn flophouse mattress. What a shitshow this turned out to be."

"You got that right," Erin said. "But this wasn't your fault."

"Didn't you hear me? They followed me! I was tailed. If it isn't my fault, who the hell's is it?"

She shook her head. "You were already blown. There was a leak. Forget about that for now. We need to take care of the situation. We've got cops coming up."

Boone nodded, but he didn't look convinced. He'd done great in the heat of the moment, but now his first gunfight was over and he was feeling it.

She went to the bathroom door and knocked. "Hey, kiddo?" she called. "You can come out."

There was no response.

"Alfie?" she tried again. "The fun's over. You're safe. This is Erin O'Reilly."

Only silence answered her.

Erin frowned. "Alfie? You okay in there?"

It would be just her luck, she thought, if some freak bullet had ricocheted through the bathroom wall and punched Alfie's ticket. Or maybe the idiot kid had tripped and knocked himself out on the bathtub. Didn't people say bathrooms were the most dangerous rooms in the home? Or was that kitchens?

She pounded on the door with her fist. "Alfie! Stop screwing around and open up!"

"NYPD!" someone shouted from the hall.

"US Marshals!" Calley yelled back. "We've got a wounded man in the bedroom!"

Erin glanced at Boone, who was still having his private pity party. She knew from personal experience that a cop's first shooting left a mark. But right now she didn't have the time or spare energy to help him through it.

"Does anyone care what happens to this apartment?" she asked Calley.

"Well, the FBI, I guess," he said.

"Oh, that's fine then," she said and kicked the bathroom door in.

Like most interior doors, this one was hollow-core wood, more of an aid to privacy than a serious barrier. Erin's kick splintered the door and sent it flying open, rebounding off the wall and swinging nearly shut again. But she was already moving in. It felt very strange to do a dynamic entry without a gun in her hands, but that would definitely give Alfie the wrong idea, and the poor guy had already had more than his share of scares today.

"Happy now?" she growled. But she realized she was talking to herself. The bathroom was small, dingy, dirty—and empty. The little window stood open, letting in the cool autumn breeze. Alfie Madonna had made a run for it.

Chapter 11

Erin didn't waste time getting pissed off. The shooting had started less than five minutes ago. Assuming Alfie had gone straight out the window, that meant he'd been on the move for about four minutes. Alfie had no car and no money, as far as she knew, but a running man could cover a lot of ground in that time.

"Boone!" she snapped. Uniforms were pouring into the apartment now, but she ignored them. Calley was still tending to Headley, a pair of Patrol cops moving to help him. Boone was hunkered down, leaning against the refrigerator in the kitchen, his head in his hands. He didn't seem to hear her.

Erin grabbed him by the shoulder with one hand and knocked his hands away from his face with the other. "Marshal! I need you here. With me. You're still on the clock. Focus!"

He looked up at her with red, puffy eyes. She was looking at a man who was finally realizing what it meant to carry a gun.

"What?" he asked quietly.

"Alfie Madonna's in the wind," she said. "I need something he was wearing, or something he was the last guy to hold, and I need it right now."

"Thought he was in the bathroom," Boone said. He was acting drunk, slurring his words. Erin recognized the symptoms of mild shock.

"Forget the bathroom," she said, giving him a shake. "Alfie's clothes. *Now.*"

Boone blinked and slowly looked around the apartment. Erin was practically dancing with impatience. So was Rolf. The K-9 could feel his partner's energy, her urge to be in the chase, and he intended to be part of it.

"Front closet," Boone said at last, pointing to a sliding door beside the apartment entrance. He carefully enunciated his words, getting them out in small chunks. "Black coat. Loaner. From Headley."

"Thanks," Erin said. "You stay here. When the medics get here, have one of them take a look at you. You might be hurt and not know it."

She doubted Boone had taken any physical injury, but she also thought it'd be a good idea to have him examined by an EMT. He looked like he could use a shot of something a good deal stronger than anything they sold at the Barley Corner.

But that was up to the paramedics who'd be there in a minute. Erin dismissed the Marshal from her mind and hurried to the closet. Sure enough, a black windbreaker hung on a cheap wire hanger. She snatched it down and left the room, Rolf prancing eagerly at her hip.

"Detective O'Reilly?" a Patrol Sergeant hailed her. Erin paused. She couldn't place his face.

"Do I know you, Sarge?" she asked.

"Know your face from the news," he said. "That City Center thing last year. What're you doing here?"

She shook her head. "Can't explain. No time."

"Who's in charge?"

Erin cocked a thumb over her shoulder. "Deputy Marshal Calley. He's in the bedroom. I have to move, Sarge."

She and Rolf jogged down the stairs and out of the building, passing more cops. An Officer-Involved Shooting would bring every available officer. The parking lot was a lurid mass of blue and red flashing emergency lights and squad cars. Carlyle's Mercedes sat incongruously front and center, abandoned. There was no sign of Ian.

It had been a deliberate choice not to ask for Patrol assistance in running Alfie down. The more people who knew he was out in the open, the more likely the Oil Man was to hear about it. Erin had known one cop who'd killed for the Mob, and for every one you knew about, there was a good chance there were two you didn't, or maybe ten. She hated thinking that way, but her current situation made it the only rational way to think.

Besides, she already had the best search tool in the NYPD running beside her. She led Rolf around the building, looking up until she saw the open window that had to lead to the bathroom.

"He landed here," she said, toeing the ground. Then she held the coat in front of Rolf's snout. "*Such!*"

The scent on the jacket was fresh and sharp in the dog's nostrils. He'd done this dozens of times, both in training and for real. Following a scent was as easy and natural for him as for Erin to run toward something she could see with her eyes. They were standing on a Manhattan sidewalk. Hundreds of human beings had walked here in the past day or two. Thousands of smells were intermingled.

It made no difference. Alfie Madonna's smell was distinct from all others. Rolf zeroed it in and started moving.

"*Fuss!*" Erin said, reminding him to stay close. She still didn't have his leash or his toy. She should've retrieved the leash from the Mercedes, but hadn't wanted to take the time. She'd rely on his training and obedience to her voice.

The trail led down the street away from the apartment, then angled onto East 14th Street. Erin saw several pedestrians, all going about their own business, but decided not to bother asking them if they'd seen a young Italian guy running away. As long as Rolf had his trail, she didn't need any other directions.

"Sitrep?" a man said just behind Erin and to one side.

She spun on her heel and snatched out her Glock. Then, as she raised the pistol, her brain belatedly identified the voice.

"Jesus, Ian!" she gasped. "Don't sneak up on me like that! Not after a gunfight!"

"Sorry," he said, stepping out of the doorway of a storefront that held a dry cleaner, a nail salon, and a Yoga studio. "No excuse."

Until he moved, Erin hadn't seen him. Either he'd been waiting for her, knowing which way she'd come, or he'd followed her so closely and quietly that she hadn't had any idea he was there.

"I told you to get away!" she said in a low voice.

"Cleared the combat area," he said. "Thought I'd better hang around in case you needed support."

"There's twenty cops back there!" she said, walking quickly while she spoke. Alfie was getting farther away with every passing second. "And you thought I'd need backup?"

"All respect, cops don't always shoot the right target," he said, falling in step beside her.

She winced. Ian had been shot repeatedly by a pair of police officers who'd mistaken him for a perp that summer. He still walked with a slight limp from one of those shots.

"Besides," he added. "Mr. Carlyle would kill me if I let something happen to you. What's the situation?"

"A couple Lucarellis got into it with the Marshals," she said. "The shooters are dead, one of the Marshals is hurt pretty bad, and Alfie did a runner. We're following him."

"Understood. We expecting resistance?"

"No. Keep your gun holstered. Alfie isn't armed and he's not the enemy."

Rolf led the way to the entrance to the subway. He paused a moment and then started down the steps. Erin and Ian followed.

"Driver got away," Ian said. "I wasn't taking fire, so didn't engage. Maybe should've. Could've stopped him."

"No!" she said sharply. "You can't shoot a man who's running away, Ian. You're not a police officer. That'd be murder. You'd go to jail for that."

He nodded. "Got the license plate. Probably stolen."

"Probably, but give it to me," she said. "Maybe we'll get lucky."

"Foxtrot delta mike three four six two," Ian said, using the military alphabet to designate the letters on the plate.

"Copy that." They'd reached the bottom of the stairs and were facing the turnstiles. Erin had a Department-issued subway card. It didn't surprise her that Ian had a card of his own, even though to her knowledge he never took the subway. He was the sort of guy who was prepared for this kind of thing.

Rush hour was over and the platform was nearly deserted. A guy in a business suit stood near the tracks, holding a briefcase in one hand. Over by the far wall, a teenage girl was looking at her phone.

Rolf snuffled his way across the station. But instead of going toward the platform, as Erin expected, he angled to one side. He scratched at the door to the men's restroom and whined.

Erin glanced at Ian, who nodded. She put her shoulder against the door and shoved it open.

The smell of stale urine hit her like a physical blow. Most of the fluorescent lights actually worked, but that only showed the rest of the room in sharp, horrible detail. The tiles were cracked, several were missing, and a jagged hole gaped where the soap dispenser should have been. Half-hearted graffiti was scrawled across the sheet metal wall of the stall. The floor was stained a muddy brown color in several places. Erin hoped it was only from dirty water leaking in. One of the light bulbs buzzed, giving a hopeless, droning soundtrack to the place.

Alfie Madonna stood in the corner, facing the door, face pale, fists clenched. He didn't seem at all surprised to see Erin, Rolf, and Ian.

Rolf barked twice and nosed at Alfie, confirming his scent. Then the K-9 looked back at Erin and cocked his head, waiting for praise.

"Smartass dog," Alfie said. "I knew you'd come after me."

"Why'd you run?" Erin asked.

"I'm done with this," he said. "Your goddamn Marshals can't do shit. They were supposed to protect me!"

"They did protect you!" she retorted. "One of them took a shotgun shell for you! They killed two of your buddy Vinnie's goons. All you had to do was stay put!"

"And then what?" he shot back. "Wait for the next batch of shooters? They knew where I was! You got a rat!"

"You think I don't know that? But you know me. Look, Alfie, if I wanted you dead, you'd be dead."

"So what? You ain't the only cop in this city, and you're on the take, too! I can't trust nobody!" Up close, Erin could see the kid wasn't just angry. He was scared half out of his mind. Why else would he have fled to a New York subway bathroom, one of the most awful places within a ten-mile radius?

"You have to trust me," she said. "I can protect you."

"You can try," he said bitterly. "Since the cops got their hands on me, I've been poisoned, shot at, and had guys try to run me down. This is the fourth time somebody's tried to whack me! Sooner or later they're gonna get lucky, or your luck's gonna run out."

"Alfie, who'd you piss off?" she asked. "Seriously. Did you mouth off to somebody at Riker's? Did you screw Vinnie's daughter? Because I'm sorry, but from what I can see, you're not worth all this effort to them."

He spread his hands helplessly. "How the hell do I know? I told you before, I can't give you nothing that'll put the Oil Man away. I don't know nothing! And I ain't nobody! And it don't matter, because I'm getting out of it."

"What do you mean?"

"I'm done with your damn Marshals and your cops and your lawyers and your judges and everything. I'll take care of myself."

"Don't be an idiot, Alfie," she said. "You wouldn't last a day on the streets on your own."

"I'm better off taking my chances," he said stubbornly. "At least if I'm on my own, I don't have to worry about no goddamn rats."

"I promised your dad I'd look after you," she said. As she spoke, she felt the tremor in the floor that indicated an incoming train.

"How are you gonna feel if I get popped?"

"Pretty damn lousy. Look, Alfie, I don't want to take you in, but I will if I have to."

"What for?" he demanded. "I'm out on bail. As long as I don't leave the city, and don't commit no crimes, you can't bust me. I've got a court date. If I don't make that date, you can haul me in. Until then, get the hell out of my way!"

The train rumbled into the station. Alfie stepped forward, moving around Erin. Ian silently placed himself in the doorway, blocking Alfie's escape.

"Who's this mope?" Alfie asked, sizing Ian up. "He ain't no cop."

"His name's Ian," Erin said. "He's Cars Carlyle's top security guy."

"He don't look so tough," Alfie said. "You gonna move, buddy, or do I gotta move you?"

Ian wasn't a large man, only about five foot ten. He was very physically fit, but he was built like a runner, not a bodybuilder. But Carlyle had once described Ian to Erin as the most dangerous man in New York, and she believed him. Ian's expression didn't change. He shifted his weight slightly, getting ready.

Erin knew Ian was calm under pressure, a lethal shot with any firearm, and as tough as they came, but she'd never seen him in a hand-to-hand fight. This didn't seem like a good time to start. Knowing the guy, he'd probably break Alfie's arm at the very least.

"It's okay, Ian," she said. "If he wants to go, let him go. But it's a mistake, Alfie."

Ian, without taking his eyes off Alfie, stepped to one side, clearing the exit.

"Maybe," Alfie said. "But geez, lady. Your own guys are getting shot too. I gotta take myself out of circulation, let this all die down. I'd think you'd be glad to be rid of me."

He went quickly to the door and out onto the platform. The subway train was about to leave. He stepped aboard.

"Wait!" Erin called.

"What?" He looked back at her, his face still pale, but now showing more determination than fear.

"How can I contact you?" she asked. "If I need to?"

"Call King," he said. Then the doors slid shut. The train started rolling, disappearing into the tunnel one car at a time.

"There a point to all that?" Ian asked, coming to stand beside her.

"I don't know," Erin sighed. "But he's right. I can't protect him. Not inside the Department, and not in WitSec either. That's why I had to let him walk. How the hell do we deal with Vinnie Moreno?"

"Know one way that'd work," Ian said.

"No. You are not going to go up in some Manhattan high-rise with a rifle and blow Vinnie's head off like Lee Harvey Freaking Oswald. And that's an order."

"Just a thought," he said, and though he didn't smile, she caught a faint twinkle in his eye and knew he was yanking her around. "Now what?"

"Now we go get the Mercedes back," she said. "The crime scene's upstairs, so we shouldn't have any problem. You up for a rescue mission?"

"A Marine's always ready."

"Then let's go save my boyfriend from my mother. After that?" She scowled. "I go back to work."

Chapter 12

"Very well, darling," Carlyle said from the shotgun seat in the Mercedes. "I'm perfectly willing to play innocent in front of your relations, but we've no need for further deception. What's happened?"

"Vinnie made another play for Alfie," Erin said. She was in back with Rolf. Ian was driving. They'd swooped in on the O'Reilly household and snatched Carlyle away from Mary with a hurried apology. Carlyle had certainly played along, but Erin knew her dad, at least, suspected something. Sean had given her the sort of hard-eyed, searching stare only a retired cop could deploy.

"In spite of the Marshals?" Carlyle was startled. "That's bloody reckless of him."

"Tell me about it," she said. "One Marshal's in the hospital and two Italians are in the morgue."

"And the lad?"

"Dropped off the map. Rolf ran him down, but he wouldn't come with us. Can't say I blame him, either. We've done a pretty crummy job protecting him."

"So you've arrested two Lucarellis and killed two more, not to mention the fake copper who got away," Carlyle said thoughtfully. "That seems a bit of a high price to pay merely to dispatch one lad scarce out of his short pants."

"I know," she said. "But Alfie did promise me he'd kill Vinnie."

"Did you happen to mention that to anyone?"

"What do you mean?"

"In the old days, when they killed a lad, the Mafia would do away with his sons, just to be on the safe side," Carlyle said. "But that sort of thing's gone rather out of style. I've never known Vinnie to slay a lad on account of his parents. So unless the Oil Man knows Alfie's gunning for him, I'd not expect him to go to this much trouble."

"I didn't tell any Mob guys that Alfie was out for revenge, if that's what you're asking," Erin said, bristling slightly. "Of course not! You think I'm trying to get the kid killed?"

"I know you'd never do anything like that on purpose, darling," Carlyle said. "But something may have slipped out. There must be a reason for all this bloodshed. And I'll warrant it's not simply what happened to Alfie's da."

"Okay, then why?" she challenged. "Because there's something, sure as hell! These guys keep popping up and we keep knocking them down. They're not doing it for thrills."

"You're right," he said. "The Mafia doesn't just kill lads for fun. It's either business or it's personal, one or the other."

"I thought it was always business," she said with a wry smile. "And you weren't supposed to take it personally."

"I've no acquaintance with Alfie Madonna," Carlyle said. "Does he strike you as the sort of lad who makes enemies?"

"Not really. He's a gangster, sure, but he's not a jerk. I've known some real assholes in the Life and he's not one of them."

"Did he give you any indication he knew why these lads are so keen to put an end to him?"

"No. He's scared and confused."

"Then there's a business reason of which he's unaware. Find what that is and you'll understand what's happening."

She shrugged. "It's not supposed to be my problem anyway. It'll be a Federal case, since it was the Marshals who did the shooting. Damn it, they ran things through the FBI."

"Special Agent Giusto got wind of it?" Carlyle asked. He, like Erin, knew about Vinnie's man in the FBI. Erin had sniffed him out during a previous case, but hadn't been able to prove anything.

"I can only assume. How else would they have known where Alfie was hiding? I saw how Headley and his guys operate. They were careful. Nobody tailed them." She struck her armrest angrily. "I want this guy. I want Giusto behind bars or in the goddamn ground."

"You can't move on him yet," Carlyle said gently. "Not until our business with the O'Malleys is concluded. Besides, you said it yourself. You can walk away from this one."

"But I don't want to! Alfie belongs in jail, sure, but he doesn't deserve to die. And I promised his dad."

"A promise to a dying man is a serious thing," he agreed. "But now the lad's on the run. You can't be watching his back every minute. He'll have to look out for himself."

She sagged back in her seat. Rolf worked his snout under her hand. She stroked his head absently.

"I know," she said. "And I've got this other thing to solve. I think I've got a witness. I just need to convince her to talk to us."

"Why won't she?"

"She's scared."

"Then you've two choices, darling. Either you've got to take away her fear..."

Erin snorted. That would be almost impossible. "Or?"

"Or you've got to give her something to be more frightened of than the source of her fear."

"The NYPD's not a street gang," she said. "Not anymore. We don't beat confessions out of suspects and we don't intimidate witnesses. This lady's no mobster. She's a grade-school teacher, a civilian. I don't want her to get hurt and I don't want her more scared than she already is."

"Can you close your case without her?"

"I don't know. We might end up knowing who did it, but not being able to prove it."

"Perhaps you'd best try it without her first," he said. "Then, if all else fails, try to persuade the lass. You're rather good at getting folk to do the right thing, when once you set your mind to it."

*　　*　　*

Erin split off from Ian and Carlyle at the parking garage, leaving them to attend to Carlyle's business. She had Rolf check her Charger, just in case, then got in and drove to the Eightball. It was getting late by most people's standards, but for a New York cop, the night was just getting started.

The Eightball was humming with the usual evening activity. Erin paused in the lobby on her way up to Major Crimes to help break up a scuffle between two drunk and disorderly New Yorkers and four Patrol cops. The threat of Rolf's teeth quickly calmed things down and they continued on their way.

The Major Crimes office was dimly lit and mostly deserted. Vic Neshenko was at his desk, his face glowing blue in the light of his computer monitor. He raised his eyebrows when she and Rolf walked in.

"Decided to go back to working nights?" he asked.

"I thought I should see where we were with the Romano murder," Erin said. "Did you match all the prints in the apartment?"

"Yeah. Hell of a job. Took forever. I've been looking up all these mopes. That girl had shitty taste in boyfriends. Worse than you, even."

"Thanks." She went into the break room and got a cup of coffee. She saw a cardboard box with half a donut lying inside. Against her better judgment, she picked it up. It was so stale she thought she might be able to pound in nails with it. She tossed it to Rolf. The K-9 caught it in midair and carried it proudly to her desk, where he hunkered down and started gnawing on it.

"Here's the thing," Vic said. "They're all wiseguys."

"Really? She's a Mob groupie?"

"Okay, technically they're not all in the Mob," he admitted. "But they've all got dads or uncles who are. Gabriel Vitelli, the guy you asked me about? His dad's Valentino Vitelli. People call the old man Rudy, I've got no idea why."

"You've never heard of Rudolph Valentino?" she asked.

"Who's he? Some other Mob guy?"

"He was a pretty famous actor."

"When?"

"About a hundred years ago."

"And I'm supposed to remember that?"

"He's a cultural icon."

Vic rolled his eyes. "Whatever. Anyway, Valentino Vitelli's no cultural icon. He's into heroin in a big way for the Lucarellis."

"I know. I talked to him earlier today, remember?"

"Right. The rest of the guys this girl was running with, they're the same. One of them is Vinnie Moreno's cousin, if you believe that. Or second cousin, or cousin once removed, or something. Shit, I can never remember how that works."

"What's the cousin's name?"

"Federico Campano," Vic said. "AKA, Freddie Four Days. These nicknames. You got a Mob nickname?"

"Why would you think that?"

"You hang around Mob guys." He grinned. "You do, don't you. Okay, spill. What is it?"

"I'm not playing this game."

"Don't want to tell me? Fine, I'll guess." Vic tapped his chin. "Let's see... how about PETA O'Reilly, since you're all about animal rights? No? Okay, I got it. They call you Fetch. No? Give me something here. You know my ESU nickname, it's only fair."

"Hey, that's right," she said. "Toothpick Vic." She'd heard that from a couple of his former ESU teammates.

"C'mon, what do they call you?"

Erin held up her hands. "If I tell you, you have to promise me something."

"Yeah?"

"I know you won't shut up about it. All I'm asking is you don't spread it around the Department and don't use it when we're working. Deal?"

"Deal." He waited eagerly.

"Junkyard."

"Junkyard?"

"As in, Junkyard Dog."

He nodded. "Okay, I like it. How come you don't want me using it? Sounds kinda badass."

"Because it's a Mob nickname and we're cops."

"All right," he said in tones suggesting she was being very unreasonable. "But I'm still allowed to call you a bitch, aren't I?"

"As long as I can still call you every true and accurate name I can think of."

He grinned again. "Fair enough."

*   *   *

Erin hadn't meant to stay at the office all night; it just worked out that way. The caffeine was probably a mistake, but even without it, the residual adrenaline from the gunfight would have kept her up for hours. After that, it was just habit and stubbornness.

Rolf tapped out early, falling asleep on his blanket next to her desk. Vic headed out a little after ten, saying there was an MMA match he wanted to catch on pay-per-view.

"And don't take it personal, Erin," he said, "but I'd rather watch sweaty guys punch each other in the crotch than hang out with you and do desk work."

"Who wouldn't?" she replied.

Then she was alone in the office, trying to sort through what was left of Isabella Romano's life. She had the CSU reports, Levine's autopsy, and the results of Vic's fingerprint inspection. The girl hadn't held a job, unless she'd actually been a prostitute, as her killer had claimed. And hookers didn't file 1099s, so proof on that front would be hard to come by.

Regardless of occupation, Isabella had definitely had quite a few callers. Vic was right; according to his exhaustive print matches, Isabella had entertained a rogue's gallery of Lucarelli offspring. He'd also found a few prints belonging to women, who were likewise affiliated with the Mob.

It took time to look through the police jackets of all the young punks. Everyone had a juvenile record, everyone had known associates in the Lucarellis. Most of the boys and a couple of the girls had done time upstate after they graduated to the adult legal system. But none had anything as serious as a murder rap on their sheet. She didn't get a sense of any of them being budding serial killers.

"But I'm not a profiler," she sighed. "We'd need the FBI for that." And they weren't talking to the FBI, not about the Mafia.

Rolf lifted his head and blinked blearily at her. Then he stood up, reversed the curvature of his body, circled twice, lay back down, and went to sleep again.

Erin was getting nowhere. The hands on the clock stood at a little past three. The caffeine and adrenaline had worn off and she was starting to droop. The whiteboard showed a list of suspects twelve names long, with nothing to differentiate between them. Any of them might be guilty; none of them might be. Maybe the killer had worn gloves and simply hadn't left prints and the whole exercise was a waste of time.

Without much hope, she turned to the autopsy. Levine had done her usual thorough, professional job. Every injury was catalogued with precision, accompanied by photographs guaranteed to give sensitive people nightmares. The bloodwork was included, as were the contents of the victim's stomach.

Erin had been putting off the autopsy, which now seemed like a bad decision. It didn't make for good late-night reading. She didn't think she'd learn anything from it in any case. They'd already guessed the victim's own butcher knife had done the damage. What did it matter how many times Isabella had been stabbed and slashed? She'd have been just as dead from ten stabs as from twenty.

Erin's fatigue-fogged brain took a second to catch up on what she was reading. Then she shook herself, rubbed her eyes, and tried to focus. Levine's handwriting, fortunately, was more legible than that of many doctors, the letters small and neat. The words were clear enough:

"Victim is approximately ten weeks pregnant."

"Shit," Erin said, sitting back in her chair. They'd get DNA they could match to the father, but that would take time, assuming they even had a match on file. Maybe it didn't mean anything for the case, but she had the feeling it did. Why had the murderer written a word meaning "whore" across the wall? That would be quite a coincidence.

Erin suddenly stood up and went to the whiteboard. Before she could change her mind, she added Luisa Romano to the list of suspects. It was an awful thought, one she shied away from, but that was what it meant to be a detective. Would a woman murder her own child? She remembered her mother showing Carlyle her baby pictures. She shuddered. But honor killings were a thing that happened. Was Luisa the sort of woman who'd kill a girl rather than see her disgrace the family name?

Still turning that over in her head, Erin returned to her desk. Rolf had opened one eye when she'd gotten up, but the Shepherd had decided nothing was happening and hadn't bothered to stand.

The rest of the autopsy didn't hold any surprises, at least not on the surface. Isabella had classic defensive wounds on her arms and hands, showing she'd tried to fend off her attacker. She'd been a spunky girl; she'd probably put up the best fight she could. One of her fingers was broken, the fourth one on her left hand. Erin hoped she'd gotten in a good gouge on her killer, but a quick examination of the forensic results proved a disappointment. CSU had scraped under Isabella's fingernails and hadn't come up with any foreign tissue.

Erin paused. "If she didn't scratch him, and the finger wasn't cut, how did it get broken?" she asked Rolf.

The K-9 cocked his head sleepily and blinked at her. He was listening, but only with half an ear.

"Maybe she fell and jammed it on the floor," Erin decided. She leaned back in her chair. "When you get in bare-knuckle fights, you break fingers. A broken ring finger doesn't mean anything."

She leaned forward again. The chair tilted and almost overbalanced, but she caught herself on the edge of her desk. She checked the autopsy photos and brought up the image of Isabella's left hand.

"No rings," she said. "And no line on the skin. If our girl had on a ring, she hadn't been wearing it long. CSU didn't find any loose jewelry in the apartment. And Mom didn't say anything about her being married, or even engaged."

Rolf was a little more awake now, but he had no idea what Erin was talking about. He stared at her, letting her know he was paying attention and that he was on board with her idea, whatever it was.

"She had an engagement ring," Erin said. "And the killer took it with him. He was so pissed off, he practically ripped her finger off to get it, even though it wasn't tight. This is about jealousy."

She stood up again. This time, picking up on her renewed energy, Rolf scrambled to his paws and started wagging.

"We're going to Brooklyn," Erin announced, clipping Rolf's leash to his collar. "My mom should be happy. We're finally looking at engagement rings."

Chapter 13

The apartment building was dark and silent, which was hardly surprising. Even in New York, the city that never slept, residential areas tended to be quiet at four in the morning. Erin and Rolf climbed the stairs to Isabella's floor, stepping lightly so as not to disturb the neighbors. Erin used her flashlight to light the way.

The door to the victim's apartment was locked and the doorway covered with crisscross yellow police tape. She had Isabella's keys, which CSU had retrieved from the victim's purse. She unlocked the door and opened it, ducking under the tape. Rolf slid easily through, only having to dip his head slightly.

Once inside, Erin flicked on the light and turned off her flashlight. It made it a lot easier to see what she was doing, and as a bonus, it dispelled the creepy ambience. She examined the edge of the door and the doorframe. CSU had found no signs of forced entry. The woodwork was slightly worn with long use, but otherwise undamaged.

"Either the killer had a key, or our girl let him in, or she was an idiot who left her door unlocked," Erin told Rolf.

Rolf didn't disagree. But then, a closed door would stop him whether it was locked or not. For all his strength, agility, and training, he'd never quite figured out how to manage a doorknob.

"No signs of a struggle in the living room," Erin went on, walking through the apartment. "There definitely would've been blood if it'd happened out here. This went down in the bedroom. Time of death was mid-morning. Ten is a little late to be in bed, but our girl was a party animal. Maybe she slept late. Or maybe she invited her killer into her bedroom.

"Our anonymous caller made her call about ten-thirty. But Levine's report puts time of death half an hour earlier. Levine could be off in her measurements."

Rolf cocked his head and stared at her.

"I don't think so either," she said. "If Levine made a mistake in her examination, it'd be the first time. If she says the victim died at ten, she died at ten. Why the gap? Because our witness was scared. She wasn't sure what to do. So she spent some time thinking about it before she decided to phone it in. The call came from a pay phone at a gas station a couple blocks from here. There's only two reasons to call from there, if she heard the murder here. Either she doesn't have a phone, or she doesn't want to be ID'd."

Rolf gathered in his haunches and sat, giving Erin his full attention. He loved when his partner talked to him.

"Our caller's got to be Teresa Tommasino," Erin said. "Nobody else would've been close enough, even if Isabella screamed bloody murder. It was a cool morning. The windows were closed. You'd have to be either downstairs or within ten or fifteen feet of the building. And our caller just said she heard a scuffle, not a scream. But so what? She heard something? That wouldn't mean she could ID the killer unless..."

Erin paused, tapping her chin and thinking. Then she snapped her fingers. Rolf followed the movement of her hand with his eyes. His tail swept the floor.

"She lied," Erin said. "She saw the killer. She knows who it is. But she's scared of him. Teresa's the key to this. She can bury this guy."

For a moment, excitement overwhelmed Erin's fatigue. Then she sagged again. "But she's too scared to tell the truth. So we'd better see about physical evidence. *Fuss.*"

Rolf immediately went to his "heel" position at Erin's hip and followed her into the bedroom. CSU had been especially thorough in here. The body was gone, of course. The bed had been stripped. They'd even carted the mattress away. The evidence techs had gone over every inch of the room. A sheen of fine black fingerprint powder lay on every smooth surface. Several squares of carpet had been cut away and removed, presumably areas which had been stained with blood. Only the spatter on the walls indicated the crime that had been committed.

"They found her jewelry box," Erin said, remembering the report. "No signs of robbery. The killer only took the one ring off her finger."

Rolf sniffed at the bloodstained plaster and glanced at Erin. His tail waved uncertainly.

"Let's try this one more time," she said. She pointed to the blood. "*Such!*"

Rolf had followed this blood trail once before, but that didn't bother him. It just meant he already recognized the scent. He bounded eagerly forward, pulling out of the apartment and down the stairs. Erin went with him, flicking on her flashlight so she didn't stumble.

The K-9 led Erin on the same path as before, to the landing outside Teresa Tommasino's apartment, down the stairs and out of the brownstone, to the fire hydrant where the killer had been illegally parked.

Erin panned her flashlight up and down the gutter. She saw nothing. Rolf whined. He'd lost the trail, which wasn't his fault, but the dog was unhappy.

"Good job, kiddo," she said, giving his ears a rub. "Try again, will you? *Such.*"

Rolf gave it his best shot. He paced back and forth along the curb, trying to find a whiff of blood. Erin watched him, knowing it was long odds, but thinking about what she knew about anger. Isabella had been stabbed twenty-three times, according to Levine's disturbingly detailed report. Most of those had been completely unnecessary. Then the murderer had wrenched a ring off her finger hard enough to break it—at least, that was Erin's theory—and left. He'd been spattered with enough of the victim's blood to leave a trail, but that hadn't bothered him. Then he'd gotten into his car and left. But what had he done with the ring?

Rolf looked back at her with a mournful expression. He wasn't picking up on anything. She sighed.

"Nice try, kiddo," she said. "I guess when the sun comes up we'll hit the local jewelry places. Maybe if we're lucky the ring came from somewhere close by. You have any idea how many jewelry stores there are in Brooklyn?"

Rolf had no opinion on the subject.

"I don't either," she said. "Too many. Then I guess we lean on Ms. Tommasino and..."

She trailed off. Rolf had frozen in place, nostrils twitching. The dog was standing next to a bit of dense shrubbery. He turned abruptly and began snuffling around the base of the bushes, scratching with his claws.

Erin ran to meet him, the beam of her flashlight bouncing with every stride. She got there and shone the light into the underbrush.

For a long, breathless moment, she saw nothing. Then the light was caught and thrown back, glittering in the reflected facets of something small and shiny.

Erin yanked on a disposable glove from the roll she always kept in her pocket. Then she got down on her belly and reached in. She was just barely able to snag the thing with her fingertips. She drew it carefully out and held it close to the flashlight.

It was an engagement ring, and if that was a real diamond, it was a very valuable one, probably running several thousand dollars. The rock was held in an intricate setting, surrounded by a cluster of little side stones on a gold band. The band and gemstone were both speckled with little rust-red spots of dried blood.

The killer might've tucked it in a pocket. But he also might've made an angry gesture. He'd taken the time to write a nasty word on Isabella's wall. What if he'd flung the ring away? Erin remembered a scene from one of her favorite movies. The hero, having found out his wife is having an affair, moves out of the house in a huff. On the way out, he violently unplugs his TV set and takes it with him. But then, at a stoplight, he notices the TV. In a fit of rage, he kicks it out of his car onto the street.

Absurd? Maybe. Even funny, in a dark way. But it also rang true to Erin. A man who felt betrayed wouldn't care about the value of the thing. What man could stand to look at a ring that would remind him of the betrayal every time he saw it? A serial killer might keep a trophy, but she didn't think this was the work of a serial killer.

Rolf cocked his head again, watching his partner and waiting. He thought he'd done what she wanted, but wasn't quite sure.

Erin had remembered this time. She tucked her flashlight under her arm, reached into the pocket of her windbreaker, and took out Rolf's rubber Kong toy. She held it up. He stared at it, mesmerized.

"Good boy, Rolf," she said, dropping it into his waiting jaws. "*Sei brav. Sei brav.*"

*   *   *

Back behind the wheel of her car, Erin started working on her computer. Rolf, in his compartment, was happily chewing his rubber toy.

Most rings had the brand name of their jewelers engraved on them, usually on the inside of the band. It took some time, and a lot of squinting at the tiny marks on the metal, but she finally zeroed in on a Brooklyn jeweler just off Empire Boulevard. It wasn't open yet, of course.

"Got a couple hours to kill, partner," Erin told Rolf, settling in her seat and trying to get comfortable. "I'm going to close my eyes for a bit. Bark if a murderer shows up."

Rolf's jaws made a wet, squeaky sound on his Kong ball.

Two hours of uncomfortable dozing later, fortified by a fast-food sausage-and-egg biscuit and a cup of bad, lukewarm coffee, Erin pulled up to Kirschmann's Jewelry a few minutes before the store was scheduled to open. She climbed stiffly out of the Charger, unloaded Rolf, and took him for a brief walk. Then she went to the front door and knocked.

A very elderly gentleman wearing spectacles and an outdated suit, complete with bow tie, looked up. He shook his head and pointed to the clock.

Erin unclipped her gold shield from her belt and rapped it against the glass.

The man nodded and walked slowly to the door, leaning on a cane. He unhurriedly unlocked the door.

"Good morning, ma'am," he said, his English holding a hint of an accent, maybe Eastern European. "You are out early."

"Good morning," she said. "May I come in? I just have a few questions I need to ask you."

His gaze fell on Rolf and he flinched slightly. Erin saw the shadow of fear in his eyes.

"Rolf is a trained police K-9," she said. "You're in absolutely no danger from him."

"I am not overly fond of dogs," the man said, taking a shaky half-step backward. "Particularly his breed. Would it be a terrible bother if I asked you to leave him outside?"

"That's fine, sir," she said. "Just a moment." The air was cool enough that Rolf would be fine with a brief stay in her car, and his compartment would still run its air conditioning even with the engine off. She put him in the rear, from which he watched her with reproachful eyes as she returned to the store.

By the time she got back, the old man had an OPEN sign in his window and had shuffled behind his counter. He was seated on a padded stool, his cane clasped in both hands between his knees.

"I'm sorry to bother you, sir," she said. "My name is Erin O'Reilly. I'm a detective with Major Crimes."

"Solomon Kirschmann," the old man said, offering his hand. It was wrinkled, with knobby knuckles and liver spots, but his grip was firm. "I apologize for my mistrust of your dog. I am sure he is a fine animal."

"Did you have a bad experience with a dog?" she asked.

"A very long time ago," Kirschmann said. "Your dog is a German Shepherd, yes?"

"That's right," she said. "He was born and trained in Bavaria."

Kirschmann's mouth tightened and Erin felt that she'd made a misstep, though she didn't know what it was. "I thought so," he said quietly. "What is it you want, Detective?"

His tone had been pleasant at first, but now she was aware of a tightly-coiled hostility in him. This was something that went far beyond a dislike of dogs. If he didn't like her, he was unlikely to provide any useful information. Her mind raced. Kirschmann was old; how old? Upper seventies at least, maybe into his eighties. He'd been born in Europe, to judge from his voice. And his name; Solomon Kirschmann... a Jewish name.

The penny dropped. Erin understood. An Eastern European Jew who'd been born in the early '30s would have been a boy just getting into his teens during the Second World War. Any experience he'd had with German-trained police dogs would have come at the hands of the Nazis. No wonder he didn't like the look of Rolf.

"I don't know if you remember it," she said. "But a little over a year ago, there was an art theft from the Queens Museum. A Renaissance painting was stolen."

"Yes, I recall," Kirschmann said warily. "Detective, I deal only in jewelry, not paintings."

"I know," she said. "You might also remember that the painting turned out to belong to the family of a Holocaust survivor. And that it was recovered by a policewoman and returned to him."

"And her dog," Kirschmann said, nodding. "I read all about it when it happened. I had forgotten the officer's name, but now it comes to me. That was you, yes?"

"That was me," she said.

Kirschmann's wrinkled old face cracked into a smile. "Please forgive a foolish old man, Detective," he said. "I know the police here are not what they were during the War. But when a boy learns to fear certain things in his youth, it becomes difficult to shed those fears in later life. I would be delighted to offer you some coffee. I have a pot in my office, if you would care to step around the counter?"

"Thank you," she said, returning the smile.

Kirschmann led her into a small but comfortably furnished office. He directed her to a leather chair opposite his desk. Then, waving off her attempt to assist, he poured a cup of coffee for her and another for himself. He sat down behind his desk and clasped his hands in front of him.

"How is it?" he asked.

Erin took a sip. It was so far beyond the fast-food sludge she'd already drunk that it didn't even deserve the same name. "It's great," she said. "Thank you."

"You are from Long Island, yes?" he said.

"That's right. Queens."

He nodded. "I know by your voice. I am from Czechoslovakia... The Czech Republic, you call it now. I came over in 1949, after they let me out of the camp for displaced persons. Now I am here, with my family. How may I be of service?"

Erin produced the evidence bag in which she had sealed the ring. "I believe this was bought in your shop, sir," she said. "I was hoping you could tell me what you know about it. Please don't take it out of the bag."

Kirschmann took the ring. He bent over it and stared at it for a few moments.

"Excellent diamond," he said. "Almost two carats, very large for an engagement ring. I recognize it, yes. It comes from my shop. It is stained. I hope this stain is not what it looks to be."

"When did you sell it?" Erin asked.

"Five... no, six days ago."

"Who did you sell it to?"

"A young gentleman."

"How did he pay for it?"

"Cash."

"Wasn't that unusual? Don't most people use credit cards?"

Kirschmann shrugged. "Some do. Some pay cash. What do I care? One is as good as the other."

"Did you get his name?"

"No."

"What can you tell me about him?"

"He was young, younger even than you, ma'am. He had darker skin than you or I, but not like a *schvartser*."

"I'm sorry, a what?"

"I beg your pardon. I mean that he was not of African descent. I would say Mediterranean. Italian, maybe?"

"What else?"

"A very good-looking boy, no more than twenty-five, probably younger. Very polite, well-spoken. Good clothes. He dressed like a prosperous man twice his age. Very good shoes, black leather, well-polished. You can tell much about a man by how he cares for his shoes. He wore a gold watch on his wrist, a very fine one, very expensive."

"You've got a good eye, Mr. Kirschmann," Erin said. "And a good memory."

"In my business, one must pay attention to details," he said. "What has this young man done?"

"I can't say," she said. She called up an image on her phone, Gabriel Vitelli's mug shot. "Was this the man?"

He gave it only the briefest glance. "Yes," he said firmly.

"You're certain?"

"Positive. My body grows old, but my eyes are as clear as ever, and I hope my mind is still sharp."

Erin stood up. "Thank you, Mr. Kirschmann. You've been very helpful."

"I am glad," he said, getting gingerly to his feet and taking up his cane. "Please do convey my apologies to your hound. I hope he forgives an old man's folly."

"No need for an apology," she said. Then, curiosity getting the better of her, she went on. "Can I ask you something?"

"Certainly."

"How did you get here? To America, I mean."

Kirschmann smiled sadly. "I had an uncle in New York, in the diamond trade. My father's brother. He had made efforts to find my father and the rest of my family, but the war threw everything into chaos. He came to Europe to search for us. Unfortunately, by then I was the only one left. The Nazis shot my older brother. My mother finished in the camps, though I never learned what happened to her. She simply vanished, yes? Up in smoke, as the saying goes. Too true for her, I fear. And my father..."

He trailed away into silence.

"I'm sorry," Erin said awkwardly. "I didn't mean to bring up anything painful. You don't have to—"

"My father died for me," Kirschmann said, looking straight at Erin with eyes that, for all their age, were still bright and keen. "He was with me in the camps, always giving me food from his share, always protecting me. And in the end, when they marched us through the snow away from the Russians, he gave me the last of his strength, helping me to keep walking. He gave me everything, sacrificed his future for mine. You have children, yes?"

"No," she said. "But I've got a father."

Kirschmann nodded. "And he is a good man, your father?"

"The best."

"Then you know what he would do for you. Thank you for coming here, ma'am. I hope you find what you are seeking."

"We'll catch our guy," she said. "We usually do."

He smiled. "You have an early start on the day. That is a good sign, I think, the mark of a hard worker. As we said in the old country, *Pečení holubi nelítají do huby.*"

"I beg your pardon?"

"Roughly, it means, 'baked pigeons don't fly into your mouth.' It loses something in the translation, but you might interpret it as, 'if you want something good, you must work for it.'"

"I can't argue with that. It was very nice meeting you, Mr. Kirschmann."

"And you, ma'am. I wish you good fortune."

Chapter 14

Erin was halfway across the Brooklyn Bridge, on her way to Little Italy, when her phone buzzed. She hauled it out one-handed and saw the number of Carlyle's current burner phone.

"I'm sorry," were the first words out of her mouth, before he could say anything. "I should've let you know where I was. I was gone all night."

"You're a grown woman, darling," he said. "And the good Lord knows I've disappeared on you more than once. I was simply calling to make certain you hadn't fallen into bad company and gotten yourself another tattoo."

"I did that once," she said. "*Once.* And it wasn't bad company. Or if it was, it was the same company you keep, so you've got no right to complain. I can't believe I'm saying this, but Corky isn't so bad."

"Fair point, darling. All's well, I take it?"

"Well enough. I'm going to talk to a suspect."

"Grand. Would this be a lad involved with the unpleasantness with the Marshals, or the other business?"

"Ian filled you in on that?"

"Naturally."

"Both, I guess. It's Angel Face Vitelli."

There was a brief silence. Then Carlyle spoke slowly. "You're saying he killed the lass?"

"I don't know," she said. "But I do know he bought her an engagement ring. The same ring that was ripped off her finger and thrown away."

"And you're going to confront the lad with this information?"

"I'm going to talk to him."

"Be very careful, darling. Young Gabriel's no one of importance, but his da is the Oil Man's chief lieutenant."

"I know."

"You don't want to be getting on the wrong side of the Lucarellis just now."

"I know! You don't have to remind me. But I'm glad you called. Do you have any idea where Angel Face is right now?"

"I know where his da does business. It's a restaurant in Little Italy."

"I figured. I'm on my way there now. Which joint?"

"A place called Lucky's. Do you know it?"

"No, but I'll find it."

"It's a mite early, but if he's awake, you'll likely find him there."

"Thanks."

"Will you be coming home after?"

"No, I need to go to work."

"Please tell me you got at least a little sleep."

"I did. At least an hour, maybe two. That's not so bad. You know, your pal Ian once went—"

"Five days without sleeping. I know. Everyone's heard that story. He also went more than halfway mad in the process. Take care of yourself, darling."

"Always do. Bye."

*   *   *

Mob guys and seedy restaurants went together like bacon and eggs. When your business was crime, you didn't tend to rent downtown offices. The Mafia liked having a place where guys could hang out around a table, talk, and waste time without attracting undue attention. What better place than a small, out-of-the-way restaurant? They could sit for hours at a stretch, drinking, eating pasta, and shooting the shit, while New Yorkers with real jobs went to work. The lack of exercise and high-carb diet also explained why so many older mobsters were overweight.

Erin and Rolf walked into Lucky's and took a look around. It was exactly what Erin had expected. There was a small breakfast crowd of older Italians, all male, eating frittatas, pancakes, and some sort of sausage-and-egg concoction that looked like a heart attack on a platter to her. Not that she had any moral high ground, given what she'd eaten just a short while before. That fast-food biscuit sandwich was sitting awfully heavy on her stomach. She was also very conscious of the recording wire sewn into her bra. She'd activated the recorder before getting out of her car and the hidden microphone was picking up every sound around her.

"No pets, ma'am," said a heavyset, tired-looking waitress.

"Police K-9," Erin said, showing her shield. Rolf was wearing his official vest, not because Erin expected any particular trouble, but because a lot of people had been taking shots at each other the last couple of days. She was wearing her own body armor under her coat, just in case.

"What for?" the waitress demanded. "You think we got drugs here, or what? This is a restaurant. We serve food, that's it."

Erin only listened with half an ear. She was scanning the room, looking for familiar faces. In a back corner booth, sure enough, Valentino Vitelli was sitting. His son was beside him, pretty as ever.

"Thanks, ma'am," she said, brushing past the waitress. "I see who I'm looking for."

As she approached the table, she saw a pair of goons giving her the hairy eyeball. She met their eyes and saw the recognition in them. They knew exactly who she was. The knowledge didn't relax them. She was Junkyard O'Reilly, Cars Carlyle's personal attack dog. For all they knew, she might be here to whack their boss.

"Morning, gentlemen," she said to Valentino and Gabriel. She stood opposite them, careful to keep her hands in plain view and well away from her Glock. There was no point spoiling everyone's morning with a homicidal misunderstanding.

"Detective O'Reilly," Valentino said. The table, and his substantial bulk, prevented him getting all the way to his feet, but he bobbed slightly up from his seat in acknowledgment of her arrival. "What a fine surprise. Are you hungry? Please, sit down. Join us."

"Another time, maybe," she said. "I'm afraid I'm here on business."

"All the better," the old man said, extending a hand to indicate the seat on the opposite side of him from his son. "Business goes best with food. Simple meal, simple words. *Parla come mangi.*"

"Beg pardon?"

"Speak the way you eat," he translated.

"I actually came to talk with your son," she said, glancing at Gabriel, who hadn't moved or said a word. The younger Vitelli was as strikingly handsome as she remembered, but in the morning light, she could see shadows under his eyes. He didn't look happy.

"Very well," Valentino said. He was still smiling, though he looked slightly confused. "He's here, you're here, nothing could be simpler."

"I'd prefer to have this conversation in an official capacity, back at the station," she said.

Valentino's mouth continued to smile, but his eyes went dark and wary. "I hope you're not placing him under arrest."

"Of course not," she said smoothly. "I just need to ask him some questions about someone he knows."

"Ask your questions," Valentino said. "This is fine. We'll discuss this like civilized ladies and gentlemen."

Erin hesitated. She would have preferred to do this more formally, by the book, but she didn't want to spook either Vitelli. Besides, she'd still have the recording. She sat down.

"*Sitz,*" she told Rolf, who took up position next to her.

Valentino motioned to the waitress, who immediately came over.

"Another cup of coffee for me," he said. "What do you want, Detective?"

"I ate before coming over," Erin said.

"Nonsense," Valentino said. "You gotta try the ricotta pancakes. Fran, bring my friend here an order of ricotta pancakes, with some of those strawberries on top, and a coffee."

"Got it," the waitress said, and departed before Erin could think how to politely decline.

Out of nowhere, a movie misquote popped into her head. *I'm going to offer her some pancakes that she can't refuse.* She suppressed an entirely inappropriate giggle. Gabriel continued staring stonily at her.

"Gabriel," Valentino said. "You're being impolite."

"Good morning, ma'am," Gabriel said, taking his cue. "I hope you're well today." He didn't sound like he meant it.

"I'm good, thanks," Erin said. "And I appreciate you talking with me."

"Forget about it," he said. "How can I help you?"

"I understand you've been seeing Isabella Romano," she said. "For a few months, I think?"

"That's true," Gabriel said.

"How did you meet her?"

"Through a friend."

"Would you say you had a close relationship with Isabella?"

"I don't think I like what you're suggesting," Gabriel said. "I was always completely respectful of her."

"That's my boy," Valentino said proudly. "I brought him up good, taught him to treat a lady the right way."

"I didn't mean to imply anything improper," Erin said. "I just meant to ask whether it was a serious relationship."

"I was serious about it," Gabriel said. Erin noted that he'd followed her use of the past tense without any protest or confusion.

"Were you seeing anybody else?" she asked.

"No," Gabriel said flatly.

"You're a good-looking guy," she said. "You probably have lots of girls interested in you."

He shrugged. "I'm not interested in anything casual."

"What about her?"

"What about her?" he echoed.

"Was she seeing anyone else?"

Erin was looking for the flash of anger, hoping for it, but the depth of rage she saw in his eyes made her want to pull back and reach for her gun. His eyes had smoldered; now they blazed up, as if someone had poured gasoline on some inner fire.

"Not that I knew about," he said.

"Would it bother you to hear Isabella was dead?" Erin asked bluntly, deliberately pushing his buttons.

"Dead?" Valentino exclaimed. "Wait just a minute here!"

"Yeah, I heard about that," Gabriel said in icy tones. "It's a terrible thing."

"Where were you yesterday morning, between eight and noon?" Erin asked.

"He was with me," Valentino said. "Helping me with my business."

Erin looked into the old man's face and saw nothing there, only bland courtesy. She cursed inwardly. This was exactly the sort of thing she'd hoped to avoid. If she'd gotten Gabriel alone, his dad wouldn't have been able to lay down an instant alibi for him.

"Isabella was robbed and murdered," she said. "Somebody stabbed her to death, wrote a word on the wall over her bed, stole some of her jewelry, and left her lying there. It was a brutal killing of an innocent young woman."

"Innocent?" Gabriel repeated.

"You disagree?" Erin said.

"Listen, kid," Valentino said. "You know how cops are. Miss O'Reilly's one of the right kind, but she's still got her job to do, you gotta remember that. Don't say nothing out of line, don't get yourself in trouble."

"I know, Dad," Gabriel said. Then he looked back at Erin. "There's more than one kind of guilt."

"I know it," she said grimly. "What was she guilty of?"

"I don't want to talk about it," Gabriel said.

The waitress arrived with two cups of coffee and a plate of pancakes smothered in strawberries. Erin looked at them. The mass-produced sausage biscuit in her belly did a slow flip-flop. She poured cream into her coffee and sipped it gingerly.

"You speak Italian, don't you, Gabriel?" she asked suddenly.

"Of course," he said.

"Could you translate something for me?"

"I'd be happy to."

"What does *puta* mean?"

Valentino winced. "That's not a word we use in my house," he said. "It's rude."

Gabriel watched Erin without blinking. "It means a woman who sells herself," he said. "A cheap woman. A whore. A hooker. A slut. Is that what you want to know?"

"Was Isabella a *puta*?" Erin replied, matching his stare.

Valentino said something, but Erin wasn't listening to him and Gabriel didn't even seem to be aware of his dad. Angel Face was locked in his staring contest with Erin.

"Yes," Gabriel said. "That's exactly what she was, and that's why I'm done with her."

Erin blinked and sat back. The tension was broken. Valentino let out a slow breath. Rolf, who had been watching the proceedings, nudged Erin's hand under the table and laid his snout on her knee. She absently scratched his head.

"Go on," Valentino said. "Try the pancakes. You'll love them."

She picked up her fork and carved off a piece. It tasted a bit like strawberry cheesecake, only lighter and fluffier.

"It's good," she said, meaning it. "Thanks."

"Anything else you need to know?" Valentino asked. He sounded anxious now. He was worried.

"Not right now," she said. "I think I know what I need to know."

Chapter 15

"Where've you been, O'Reilly?" Webb asked. "You're late."

"Solving cases," Erin said. "And I'm not late. I'm early. I've been on the clock since... what day is it?"

"Thursday," Vic said. "I think."

"I didn't go home last night," she said.

"Where did you go?" Webb asked.

"Brooklyn first. Then Little Italy."

"And you solved the case?"

"More or less. I know who did it."

"That's promising," Webb said. "What's the catch?"

"No proof," Vic guessed.

"No proof," Erin agreed.

"Explain," Webb said.

"Coffee first," Erin said, angling for the break room. Rolf had already flopped down in his assigned spot by her desk and went immediately to sleep.

"Are you okay?" Vic asked, following her in.

"You tell me," she said. "This is my fourth cup of the day. The first one came from McDonald's. The second was given to me by a kindhearted old jeweler. The third was a present from a mob boss and it came with pancakes."

Vic whistled. "Busy morning. What'd you find out?"

"Angel Face killed Isabella," she said. "What's more, he wants me to know he did."

"I'm sorry, who?" Webb said from the doorway.

"Gabriel Vitelli," she said. "The boyfriend. Fiancé, actually." She pulled out the evidence bag with the ring and showed it to him.

"I thought you said you had no proof," Webb said.

"I don't," she sighed. "We can prove this is the victim's blood, and I've got the jeweler who sold the ring to Vitelli, so we can tie it to him, but that doesn't mean he yanked it off her finger. His lawyer could just say the killer stole the ring, but had second thoughts when he saw the blood on it and threw it away."

"Where'd you find it?" Vic asked. "Damn, that's a nice rock."

"Two carats, according to the jeweler," she said. "It was in the bushes near the apartment."

"That'll run at least seven grand," Webb said. "Maybe more, depending on the quality of the stone."

"You know jewelry, sir?" Vic asked, surprised.

"Two marriages," Webb reminded him. "That, and I worked robbery-homicide with the LAPD. Lots of jewelry robberies in LA. That's a hell of a thing to throw away. Even using a fence, and getting twenty or thirty percent, you could still clear a couple thousand."

"So tell us, Erin," Vic said. "What's going on?"

"Isabella was pregnant," she said.

"I know. We all read Levine's report."

"Vitelli hadn't been physically intimate with her."

"Come again?"

"He was offended when he thought I was implying they'd slept together," she said. "He was really sensitive on the subject."

"Oh, man," Vic said, putting a hand over his face. "Our pretty boy is going with this girl, he's in love, but he's old-fashioned, doesn't want to disgrace her before marriage. So he gets her a rock, gets down on one knee, does the whole thing. She says yes, of course she does, because she's staring at the biggest stone she's ever seen. Only problem is, this ain't a fairy tale, and she's already been knocked up by some other loser."

"Or she got knocked up after," Erin said. "While she was engaged to our pretty boy."

"Ouch," Vic said. "That's even worse. I like the way you think."

"Anyway," she said, "Angel Face finds out somehow. Maybe Isabella lets something slip. Or maybe Vitelli gets it from the other side, the guy who screwed around with her. According to her mom, Isabella was pretty fast and loose with the men in her life. It really doesn't matter how he found out."

"He confronts her," Vic said. "He probably doesn't go there meaning to kill her, or he'd have brought a weapon. But he loses his shit, grabs a kitchen knife, and goes all Norman Bates on her."

"Norman Bates thought he was his own mother," Webb said. "I don't think that's exactly the situation here."

"Hey, don't spoil the movie!" Vic protested.

"Spoil it?" Erin repeated. "Vic, that movie came out in 1960. It's a little late for spoilers. None of us were even born then. Except maybe you, sir."

"How old are you, anyway?" Vic asked Webb.

"I was born on November 26th in the year of none of your damn business," Webb said. "If you'd care to get back to explaining the crime?"

"Vitelli stabs her to death in a fit of jealous rage," Erin said. "After she's dead, he tears the ring off her finger."

"How do you know it was after she was dead?" Webb asked.

"Blood spatter on the gemstone. She was dead or dying."

"And he left fingerprints in the blood, right?" Vic said hopefully.

"Doesn't look like it," she said. "CSU can check, but it looks like the blood only hit the setting and the stone. Maybe he wiped the band clean."

"He'll still have his DNA on it," Webb said.

"Yeah, but his lawyer will just say it's from when he bought the ring," Erin said. "He won't deny it was originally his. But you know something interesting? When I talked to Gabriel, he didn't ask about the ring. A big, fancy rock he gave her, and he didn't even bother checking up on it."

"Nice," Vic said. "But then, he already knew what happened to it, didn't he?"

"Yeah," Erin said.

"So he writes a nasty word on the wall in his girl's blood, like any good, respectful young man would," Vic said. "Then he takes off."

"But he runs into someone on the way out," Erin said. "The downstairs neighbor."

"Hold on," Webb said. "How do you know that?"

"The blood on the landing," she said. "Ms. Tommasino was evasive when I talked to her. He paused on the landing long enough for blood to pool there."

"What do you think he was doing?" Webb asked.

"Probably deciding whether to kill her, too," Vic said.

"I think Vic's right," Erin said. "If she saw him, all covered with blood, that's testimony that would convince any jury. And he knows it. But he also respects women."

Vic snorted. "Yeah, he respected his girlfriend all over the goddamn room. Respected her twenty-three times, according to the report."

"Okay, he *believes* he respects women," Erin corrected herself. "He killed Isabella because she betrayed him, disrespected him. Ms. Tommasino is an innocent. He didn't want to kill her if he didn't have to."

"You think he paid her off?" Webb asked. "Or intimidated her?"

"I'm not sure," Erin said.

"Then you'd better make sure," Webb said. "She's the key to this case. Secure her testimony and we've got an indictment. You and Neshenko go down to Brooklyn and sort it out."

"She'll be at work now," Erin said. "She's a schoolteacher."

"Then she should be home by four, five at the latest," Webb said. "Stake out the place. In the meantime, O'Reilly, go lie down on the couch and close your eyes."

"I'm fine, sir," she said.

Webb shook his head. "You're misunderstanding me. That wasn't a suggestion; it was an order. Neshenko, how does O'Reilly look to you?"

"Like week-old roadkill on a hot day, sir."

"Thanks, Vic." Erin made a face. "That's what every girl hopes to hear."

"I'm serious," Webb said. "Get some rest now. You'll need to be sharp."

*   *   *

Erin tried to sleep, but four cups of coffee, the sunlight streaming through the break room's blinds, the scratchy fabric of the disreputable couch, and her own racing thoughts made it hopeless. She stuck it out almost half an hour. Then she gave up and got up.

Rolf was right where she'd left him, sleeping better than she'd managed to. His muzzle and front paws were twitching and he was making little yipping sounds. Vic was at his desk, looking like he'd rather be anywhere else. Webb was nowhere in sight.

"Where's the Lieutenant?" she asked.

"Smoke break," Vic said. "In case you're wondering, your beauty sleep didn't work. You're just as ugly as when you lay down."

Erin expressed her reply in the form of a single digit on her right hand.

"Geez, you're grumpy when you get out of bed," he said. "Feel any better?"

"Some," she lied. "Want to get out of the office?"

He was out of his chair before she'd finished the sentence. Rolf stopped yipping, raised his head, and glanced curiously at Vic to see what the commotion was about. The tip of his tongue had wandered out of his mouth while he was asleep and he hadn't noticed it yet, so it was still sticking out.

"Where are we going?" Vic asked. "Isn't your schoolteacher still in class?"

"We're not going to Brooklyn," she replied. "Not yet."

"Mysterious," he said. "Whatever. Get me out of here and you can take me to Newark, for all I care. I'm in. You can drive."

Erin left a Post-It on Webb's desk that they were following up a lead. Rolf was also eager to come and the three of them went down to the garage together. They piled into Erin's Charger and set out.

"You know, tired drivers cause as many accidents as drunks," Vic commented as Erin worked her way through the Manhattan traffic.

"You saying you don't feel safe with me driving?"

"I'm saying you might as well knock back a couple brews, while you're at it," he said. "It might not make a difference. Now spill. Where are we going?"

"To talk to a lawyer."

"Ugh. Turn the car around."

"It's the Madonna family's lawyer," she explained. "I need to ask him about Alfie."

"I don't get it," he said. "For a whole lot of reasons. One, that case has gone Federal, in case you didn't hear, so we're not working it anymore. Two, I thought you let this punk go, so what do you care what happens to him? Three, we've got another murder to solve. And four, even if you leave all that on the side, doesn't attorney-client bullshit privilege mean he won't tell you anything no matter what?"

"You're absolutely right."

"And don't give me any of that—" He paused. "Wait, what?"

"Everything you just said is true. But I'm going to talk to him anyway."

"I'm missing something here."

"So am I. How can you sleep on that damn couch? The upholstery itches and I swear one of the springs was poking me right in the back."

"Get tired enough and it gets comfy. Your point?"

"While I was trying to sleep, I was doing some thinking, and you know what? The Madonna thing makes no sense."

"Which part?"

"All of it. Alfie's a goldfish in the Mafia's shark tank. He's not important, he's not well-connected, he doesn't even have a big street rep. He doesn't know anything valuable. But Lucarellis have tried to kill him three times, maybe four, and every one was a high-risk operation. They tried to poison him in jail, then they worked a corrupt judge to get him sprung and had a guy dressed as a cop shoot at him outside the damn courthouse. Then they got in a car chase in the middle of Downtown. And after that, they sent a couple more gunmen to shoot it out with US Marshals! All over some kid nobody gives a shit about!"

"Okay, you got a point," Vic said. "So what're you thinking?"

"I'm thinking maybe this isn't about Alfie."

"And you think his lawyer knows something?"

"I'm hoping."

"It's still a Federal case. You planning on turning over whatever you get to the Feebies?"

"No."

"Why not?"

"Because I don't trust them. And the last time someone told the FBI something about Alfie Madonna, the next thing that happened was two Mob goons and one Marshal got shot."

"But you do trust me." He smiled. "Or you wouldn't have brought me along. That's kinda sweet."

"I brought you because there's a chance someone else might be gunning for the lawyer, too, if he does know something. You're an asshole, but you're a great guy to have watching my back when things go sideways."

"That's the nicest thing I think you've ever said to me."

"That, and there's a chance I've read this totally wrong," she added. "It could be the lawyer's the one gunning for Alfie. He was conveniently absent when the shooter went for Alfie at court, he might be tight with that judge I was talking about, and the bad guys were waiting outside his office. If that's the case, we might need to arrest him, and I wouldn't want you to miss out on the chance to cuff a defense attorney."

"That's my girl," Vic said. He was grinning widely now. "But wait a second. Should we be talking about this? I thought you thought your car might be bugged."

"I've been thinking about that," she said. "And I'm pretty sure it's not. At least, not by the Lucarellis. The moves they're making, they wouldn't bother if they had a line on me. If I'm wrong, I guess we're screwed."

"That's the spirit," he said.

Ayla Schultz was at her desk when they entered the law office. She gave Erin a bright smile and Vic a dubious look.

"Detective O'Reilly," she said. "How may I help you?"

"I need to talk to Mr. Schultz," Erin said. "Is he available?"

"I'm sure he'd be glad to speak with you," Ayla said. "Let me check if he's free."

She picked up her phone and punched a button. "Detective O'Reilly is here with one of her colleagues," she said into the handset. "Do you have a moment?"

She listened to the answer, then hung up. "Go on in," she said.

Kingston Schultz was on his feet to greet them, standing in front of his desk. He beamed at Erin and extended his hand.

"Detective!" he said. "It is so good to see you again. And who is your companion?"

"This is Vic Neshenko," Erin said, giving the hand a shake. "He's one of my partners. Vic, this is Kingston Schultz."

"My pleasure," Schultz said, offering his hand to Vic in turn.

"If you say so," Vic said. He took Schultz's hand and squeezed. Schultz wasn't a small man, but Vic had a few inches and quite a few pounds on him. Still, the lawyer gave as good as he got. Erin watched and waited while the two men worked out their machismo, smiling at one another while their arm muscles strained.

Finally, after fifteen long seconds, they let go by unspoken mutual agreement. Schultz was still smiling, though the lines around his eyes and mouth looked slightly more pronounced than before. Vic had one hell of a grip.

"Would you care for some coffee, either of you?" Schultz asked.

"None for me, thanks," Erin said. "I'm up to my eyeballs in coffee."

"I'm good," Vic said.

"Very well," Schultz said. "Let us sit down and talk."

He went around the desk to his leather chair and took a seat. Erin and Vic sat in the two chairs opposite. Rolf settled beside Erin and awaited developments.

"First, Detective O'Reilly, please accept my thanks," Schultz said. "It is my understanding that Alfredo would not be breathing if not for your intervention."

"It wasn't just me," Erin said.

"Of course not," Schultz said. "I will, of course, convey my thanks and good wishes to the fine members of the Marshals Service as well. I understand one of them was injured in the defense of my client. Do you know his condition?"

"I don't," Erin said. "He's alive last I heard, but he was shot up pretty badly."

"I would like to send something to his hospital room," Schultz said. "A nice floral arrangement, perhaps?"

Vic snorted. Schultz and Erin glanced at him. He unconvincingly cleared his throat and sniffled as if he'd sneezed.

"Thank you," Erin said. "Alfie told me if I needed to contact him, I ought to talk to you."

"What message do you wish to convey?" Schultz asked.

"I don't have any message at the moment," she said. "But remember, he's got a trial pending. He'll need to show up for his court date, and he can't leave the state. If he does, he'll wind up dealing with the Marshals again, but they won't be so friendly next time."

"I am a criminal attorney," Schultz reminded her gently. "I am well versed in legal proceedings. But I thank you for your concern. I assure you, Alfredo is safe for the moment. He is also under the impression that his continued safety is contingent upon the government being unaware of his precise whereabouts."

"I see," Erin said dryly. "That's pretty much what he told me the last time I saw him."

"Then we have an understanding," Schultz said. "But I can see by your face that you have other questions for me."

"Mr. Schultz," she said.

"Kingston, please," he said. "Or King, if you wish. My friends call me that, and after yesterday's events, I count you among them."

"All right, King," she said. "Someone's trying to kill Alfie. They're trying pretty hard."

"Agreed," Schultz said.

"We've been assuming it's Vincenzo Moreno," she said. "But what if it's not?"

Schultz interlaced his fingers and leaned forward. "An interesting idea," he said. "But if not him, then who? And why?"

"That's what I was hoping you could help with," she said. "I've been operating on the belief this was a standard Mob hit, the Mafia trying to silence witnesses. But Alfie's a pretty lousy witness. They've already caused more trouble trying to kill him than they'd have solved by permanently shutting his mouth. It's not that he's uncooperative; it's that he doesn't know enough to matter. That's not worth getting their guys killed over."

"What are you driving at?" he asked.

"We need to look at other motives," she said. "Vic, what are the usual motives for murder?"

"Money, sex, and revenge," Vic said without hesitation, sounding bored.

"Did Alfie have any romantic relationship you know of?" she asked Schultz.

"Nothing serious," Schultz said. "I understand he has been seeing a few young women from time to time, though I have made few inquiries on the subject."

"Are any of these women connected to major underworld figures? Wives, daughters, nieces?"

"Not to my knowledge."

"Okay. Did he piss anyone off?"

"Not badly enough to warrant this sort of response," Schultz said.

"Then it's money," Vic interjected. "Is he in deep to a loan shark?"

"I handle most of Alfredo's money," Schultz said. "At the request of his late father. He receives an allowance, but he cannot access the principal until he turns twenty-five, by stipulation of Matthew's will. He has substantial assets. I would be able to cover any reasonable debt he might have incurred."

"Besides, loan sharks don't kill their clients," Erin said. "You can't shake your vig out of a corpse. They'll take your fingers or your kneecaps, not your life."

"True," Schultz said.

"What are Alfie's assets?" Erin asked.

"Regrettably, I cannot disclose those to you in the absence of a court order," Schultz said with an apologetic smile. "It would go against my obligations as his attorney."

"I don't need to know how much money he has," she said. "I just need to know what happens to those assets if he dies."

"Alfredo has no living kin," Schultz said. "He is an only child and his father was his last relation."

"Does he have a will?"

"How many nineteen-year-olds of your acquaintance have made wills?"

"Teenagers think they're gonna live forever," Vic said. "Even the gangsters."

"Okay," Erin said. "So what happens if he dies?"

"His assets would revert to the State of New York, in the absence of heirs," Schultz said.

"Great," Vic muttered. "Now we've got a new suspect. Only problem is, it's the Governor."

"The Governor wouldn't get the money personally," Erin said. "Anyway, that would only be the assets the government knows about."

"Correct," Schultz said.

"King, is there anything off the books?" Erin asked. "Anything Alfie owns that wouldn't get turned over to the state because the state doesn't know about it?"

"Detective, you are asking me about illegal transactions," Schultz said. "Any answer I give that is not in the negative would admit complicity in criminal enterprise."

"Ask a lawyer, get a lawyer's answer," Vic said.

"Damn it, King, this is about Alfie's life," Erin said. "You know something."

Schultz thought it over. He gave Erin a long, slow stare. He tapped the tips of his index fingers together.

"We're wasting our time," Vic growled. He started to stand up.

"Theoretically speaking," Schultz said quietly, "I could imagine a situation in which a criminal organization might, to conceal its wealth, place a variety of holdings in the names of some of its lesser members. However, such an organization would be sensitive to the possibility of betrayal and internal theft. It might, therefore, have the idea to place said holdings under the joint names of, say, two of its members, as insurance against individual theft or betrayal."

"What sort of holdings might these be?" Erin asked. "Theoretically."

Schultz shrugged. "Real estate is particularly valuable in Manhattan, and it is a value which persists more reliably than, say, stocks and bonds. The names would be hidden behind shell companies, of course, to prevent the Internal Revenue Service being aware of their titular ownership."

"So, in this theoretical scenario," Erin said, "a given building might have its title in the name of a company representing somebody like Matthew Madonna, together with another member of his organization, such as..."

Another shrug from Schultz, as if he was pulling a name out of thin air. "Valentino Vitelli?"

"Mattie Madonna got murdered," Erin said. "His part of the title would be inherited by his son, right?"

"Correct."

"But if his son also dies, and the government isn't made aware of the joint ownership..."

"Then for all practical purposes, the property would belong to Mr. Vitelli alone," Schultz said. "And no one outside his organization would be the wiser. As I said, of course, this is a purely theoretical exercise."

"Of course," Erin said.

"Is there anything else with which I can assist you?" Schultz asked.

"Not at the moment," Erin said, getting to her feet. "Thanks for your time."

"For you, Erin O'Reilly, I will always make time," he said.

Chapter 16

"You believe him?" Vic asked.

"Yeah," Erin said. She steered the Charger through the Manhattan streets, heading for Long Island.

"You think he was using a random example, or..."

"No, it's Vitelli," she said. "And Schultz wants us to know it."

"What happened to that Sicilian code of silence? *Omerta*, or whatever it is."

"King isn't Sicilian. He's Jamaican."

"He's still Mafia."

"Yeah, but he feels responsible for Alfie. He's been the Madonna family lawyer his whole career, and before that, his dad worked with the same family, and so on, all the way back to Prohibition."

"The family business, huh? How touching."

"He couldn't admit to handling illegal assets," she went on. "And he doesn't want to tell us any specifics, but he still wants us to know who's out to get the kid."

"And we can't do anything with that information," Vic said. "If the titles are camouflaged behind shell companies, like the two of you suggested, there's no way we'll be able to figure out which properties he's talking about. Not without a forensic accountant and six months of work, and maybe not even then."

"Probably not," she agreed.

"There's one other thing I should probably remind you of."

"It's not our case?"

"It's not our case."

"But at least now we know what's going on," she said.

"I'm sure that'll be a great comfort when this bastard's hitmen put that little punk in the ground. So let me see if I've got this straight. Valentino Vitelli wants Alfie Madonna dead, so he can lay claim to some Mob real estate. Does his boss know about this?"

"I have no idea. But I'm guessing he does."

"How come?"

"Because it's the sort of thing that gets mobsters killed if they do it without permission."

"Okay. And while that's going on, this mope's son Garfield—"

"Gabriel."

"Whatever. His son the pretty boy is busy slicing up his girlfriend—"

"Fiancée. Sheesh, Vic, I'm the one who didn't get any sleep. What's with you?"

"Maybe I just don't care enough to remember this stuff."

"I don't buy it. You act like a dumb thug, but you're a sharp enough detective when you set your mind to it. What's eating you?"

Vic looked down at his hands. "I'm thinking about the ring," he muttered.

"Me too," she said. "Seven thousand dollars, and he chucked it away like it came out of a cereal box."

"Yeah, but it got me wondering. What if Zofia wants one?"

Erin shot him a sidelong look. "Vic, Zofia isn't expecting you to drop seven grand on a shiny rock. She knows what NYPD salaries are like."

"That's not what I mean. I don't care about the price. What if she wants a ring? Any ring?"

"Do you want to marry her?"

"I don't know. I hadn't given it much thought before this whole thing happened. But now we've got a kid on the way. You notice something about every single one of these jerks we haul off the street?"

"What's that, Vic?"

"They've all got daddy issues. Either their dad was a drunk who beat up on them, or he got thrown in prison, or killed, or ran out on them. It doesn't matter what kind of mom they've got. Every gangster's got a screwup for a dad."

"Not Alfie Madonna. His dad loved him."

"And his dad ate a bunch of bullets in some pissant dead-end bar in Little Italy and died in the back of an ambulance. Is that supposed to make me feel better?"

Then Erin understood. "You're not worried about marriage, Vic," she said, laying a hand on his and giving it a reassuring pat.

"I'm not?"

"No."

"Okay then, Doc O'Reilly. Psychoanalyze me. What am I worried about?"

"You're worried about being a good dad."

Vic snorted.

"Laugh if you want," she said. "But it's true. You just told me as much. You think if you don't do a good job, your kid's going to come out wrong and it'll be your fault. And you're afraid marriage is where that starts. You think if you don't put a ring on Zofia's finger, you'll wind up being some absentee deadbeat dad. Am I getting close?"

"Shit. Yeah, you're right. You're absolutely right. So what do I do?"

"For starters, stop putting the weight of the world on your damn shoulders. It's wrecking my car's suspension. Look, my dad worked long hours at one of the most stressful jobs in the world. The same job, by the way, that we're doing right now."

"He worked Patrol. He wasn't a detective."

"So what? He was out late, sometimes nights. He came home with bruises and cuts on him, and Mom was just glad he came home at all. My brothers and I grew up knowing Dad might be gone someday, not because he'd run off, but because some wino had stabbed him with a switchblade. You want to talk about growing up with a cop for a dad? That was my life, Vic."

"So what're you telling me? That you turned out fine, so I shouldn't worry?"

Erin raised her hand and gave Vic a light smack on the side of his head. "No. I'm telling you that Junior, Michael, Tommy, and I all knew Dad loved us. If he'd put his life on the line for strangers, he'd do *anything* for us. We were proud of him. I was so proud, I never wanted to do anything else. Just like your kid's going to be proud of you. Just like you're going to love your kid. *That's* why you shouldn't worry."

"Never mind that we're on our way to try to figure out how to bust the guy we think stabbed his pregnant fiancée."

Erin swallowed. "I hadn't realized how close to home this one was hitting you, Vic. I'm sorry."

"Forget about it," he said. "I'm a big boy. I can handle this. But I kinda want to wring that pretty boy's scrawny neck for doing what he did."

"Yeah, I get that. Just remember, you're not him. You're never going to be. You're already a better man on your worst day than he is on his best."

"Really? You must never have seen me on my worst day."

"What happened then?"

"You don't wanna know. Hell, I don't know myself. I was blackout drunk most of it. Woke up in a gas station bathroom in the Bronx, flat broke and wearing some other guy's shirt."

"Oh. Well, you didn't cut up any pregnant girls with butcher knives, so I think you're still a little ahead."

*　　*　　*

"If it wasn't for the NYPD, the takeout industry would collapse," Vic said.

Erin nodded and scooped another mouthful of fried rice out of the little white box in her lap. They were camped out in her car, across the street from Teresa Tommasino's apartment. They'd gotten Chinese from a restaurant along the way, and now they were just killing time until their witness came home. Rolf's head protruded between the seats. He wasn't begging, but twin streams of drool trailed down from his jowls at the smell of chicken and soy sauce.

"How do you want to do this, when she shows up?" Vic asked a few minutes later. "You gonna appeal to her sense of civic duty?"

"Is that very effective in your experience?" Erin replied. "Nobody cares about civic duty these days. I blame the politicians."

"You could slip her a couple twenties," he suggested. "That works on politicians, too. Hey, how come when people offer us money it's bribery, but when we offer it to them we're just developing sources of information?"

"We hold a position of public trust," she said.

"Public trust. Right. You've got no idea what you're gonna say to this girl, do you?"

"I'll have to see how she reacts," Erin said. "But mostly, I'm counting on her ultimately being willing to do the right thing."

Vic snorted a laugh. When she didn't join in, he stared at her. "Good God. You're serious."

"She's a schoolteacher at a public elementary," Erin said. "She's got a conscience and she believes in helping people. Because she sure as hell isn't in it for the money."

"Hey, you want to know your fortune?" Vic asked. He had a fortune cookie in his hands.

"Sure."

He cracked open the cookie and unfolded the little slip of paper from inside. "How about that," he said.

"I'm waiting," she said.

"It says you should buy the big, handsome beefcake in your car a case of Stoli."

"That's what it says, huh?"

"Well, it's in Chinese. You have to interpret. If I'm saying it right, which I'm not, it's 'tianshi.'"

"What's that really mean?"

"It means 'angel.' Y'know, that's actually a little freaky."

"The fortune's on the other side. That side's for learning Chinese."

"Right." Vic flipped the paper over. "Okay, it says, 'A woman will tell you everything you need to know.'"

"And we're back to making shit up."

"What it really says is, 'Worry about tomorrow tomorrow.'"

"Now that sounds more like Eastern philosophy."

"It's good advice. I think it's in the Bible, too."

"'Sufficient unto the day is the evil thereof?'"

"Yeah, that's the one."

Time passed slowly. Erin let Rolf lick up the leftovers of her fried rice, which he did with enthusiasm. Erin and Vic chatted about the sorts of things New York cops talked about on stakeouts: the Yankees, sleep deprivation, anecdotes from old cases, and the way the world was slowly but surely going straight down the toilet. Erin found herself yawning. The lack of sleep was really starting to hit her hard, now that the caffeine had worn off.

"Mountain Dew," Vic advised. "It's a lot more concentrated than coffee."

"So is crystal meth," Erin retorted. "Why don't we just go whole-hog and start mainlining speed?"

"They taught me to just say no in grade school," he said. "Speaking of which, I think we've got a schoolteacher inbound."

Erin stifled another yawn and looked where Vic was pointing. Sure enough, Teresa Tommasino was walking along the sidewalk, a cloth bag in her hand, a purse slung over her shoulder.

"She's kinda hot," Vic said. "Nice face, decent bod. In a 'girl next door' way."

"Really? You're going there? This is a murder witness we're talking about. And you've got a girlfriend. A *pregnant* girlfriend."

"Hey, a guy can look, can't he? It's hormonal. Every guy has schoolteacher fantasies when he's a teenager. Some of us never grow out of it."

Erin shook her head in disgust and got out of the car. Vic climbed out the passenger side. Erin unloaded Rolf and crossed the street, Vic trailing her.

"Ms. Tommasino?" Erin said when they were about ten yards away.

Teresa stopped short. She'd apparently been wrapped up in her own thoughts and hadn't noticed them. Her eyes went wide in a look of such sudden alarm that Erin involuntarily tensed, thinking the other woman meant to make a run for it.

"We just need to talk to you," Erin said. "It's okay. You remember me? Detective O'Reilly. We spoke earlier."

Teresa looked quickly up and down the street, as if she was afraid she was being followed. It was a guilty look. If she'd been a suspect, it would have only increased the detectives' suspicions.

"What do you want, Detective?" she asked in a low voice.

"Just to talk," Erin said again, keeping her own voice calm and reassuring. "You're not in any trouble. What do you say we get off the street?"

"Please," Teresa said quickly, casting another wild glance around the quiet neighborhood. Aside from a couple of pedestrians half a block away, there was nobody in view.

"Okay," Erin said. "We can talk in your apartment. Is that okay with you?" In her experience, asking permission was a good way to calm down a skittish interviewee. It made them feel more in control of the situation and less trapped.

"Yes, all right," Teresa said. She went up the brownstone's front steps at a fast walk, stumbling on the top step. She fumbled the keys as she tried to fish them out of her purse and Erin saw her hands were trembling. The woman was terrified.

Teresa managed to get the door open on the third try. She hurried upstairs to her apartment and somehow got it unlocked, too. Erin, Rolf, and Vic trooped in. Vic closed the door behind them and slid the deadbolt home. Then he stood in front of the door, trying to look solid and reassuring.

"All right, Ms. Tommasino," Erin said. "We're safe."

Teresa set her bag and purse down on an end table. She turned to face them, clutching her left elbow in her right hand. Vic was right; she was an attractive woman, a little heavier than the impossible Hollywood standard, but with a pleasant, round-cheeked face that made her look somewhat younger than she was. Her eyes were a little too wide, her lip quivering slightly. She might bolt at the slightest sign of a threat.

"Let's sit down," Erin suggested. The living room was neat and well-kept, obviously belonging to a single woman. There was a love seat, a pair of straight-backed wooden chairs with leather cushions, a glass-topped coffee table, and a small, old TV set.

Erin and Vic sat in the chairs, leaving the small couch for Teresa. The schoolteacher sat close to one end, huddled against the armrest, still holding her elbow.

"Do you like dogs?" Erin asked.

"What?" Teresa gave her a blank look.

"Dogs," Erin said, nodding to Rolf. "This is my K-9, Rolf."

"Oh," Teresa said. "Yes, I... I like dogs. I always wanted a puppy when I was little, but we didn't have room and the landlord wouldn't let us."

"Rolf, *geh voraus*," Erin said, giving him his "go ahead" command. The Shepherd obediently paced over and stood in front of Teresa, regarding her steadily.

"*Sitz*," Erin said, and Rolf sat. "You can pet him if you'd like. Just let him sniff your hand first."

Teresa offered her hand to Rolf, who gave it a businesslike inspection. Then he consented to her stroking his head.

Erin let Teresa and Rolf get acquainted for a few minutes without asking anything. She knew the value of a therapy animal, and while the K-9 wasn't specifically trained for that role, he was warm and furry, and that tapped into some primal human need for comfort. Dogs had a reassuring effect on frightened people, as long as the people weren't afraid of dogs.

Teresa looked into Rolf's face and kept stroking his fur. After a little while, she relaxed very slightly. She was still obviously spooked, but the edge of raw panic was blunted. Vic stayed in the background, watching and listening.

"I think you know why we're here," Erin said gently.

"Yes," Teresa said without taking her eyes off the dog.

"I know you're the one who called us, Teresa," Erin said, deliberately shifting to a first-name basis to try to build rapport.

Teresa nodded. "I thought so," she said. "You have a recording."

"We record all 911 calls," Erin said. "That's okay. You didn't do anything wrong."

Teresa bit her lip and said nothing. Rolf rested his chin on her knee and stared up at her with his big brown eyes. Erin silently blessed her dog.

"Teresa," she said quietly. "I know you saw him."

"Saw who?" Teresa asked. Her eyes darted up to meet Erin's for a second, then slid away again.

"The man who killed Isabella."

"How do you—" Teresa began. Then she stopped, aware she'd given herself away. She shook her head and shrank back. "I don't want to talk about it."

"You don't need to be afraid of him," Erin said. "He can't hurt you."

"Of course he can!" Teresa burst out suddenly, looking Erin full in the face. "You don't know. You didn't see!"

"I didn't see him," Erin agreed. "So help me understand. Tell me what you saw."

"I can't!"

"Why not?"

"Because he's one of them!"

"One of who?"

"*La Cosa Nostra*," Teresa whispered.

"The Mafia," Erin said. "How do you know he's one of them?"

She knew the Vitellis were in the Mob, but she wasn't sure how a grade-school teacher would know that.

"Isabella," Teresa said. "She told me his father was a big man in the Family."

"You know who he is," Erin said softly. "You didn't just see his face, you recognized him. You know his name."

Teresa nodded again.

"Listen to me, Teresa," Erin said. "I can help you, but I need to know what you know."

"I won't testify," Teresa said, trying to keep her voice steady and almost succeeding. "Not in court."

"Don't worry about that," Erin said, choosing her words carefully, not promising anything. "Nobody can force you to testify. Anything you can tell me will help. You'll feel better getting this out. Holding it in is just going to make you feel worse."

The other woman thought about that. Erin watched the internal struggle. One of the primary rules of interrogations was not to interrupt when the subject was talking. A corollary to that was not to interrupt when the subject was working up the nerve to speak.

"I was out getting groceries," Teresa said in a near-whisper. "Like I told you before. I was coming home. I'd just gotten to my door and unlocked it when I heard a sound. I looked up and I saw... him."

"Where was he?"

"At the top of the stairs."

"How did he look?"

"Bloody." Teresa shuddered. "He was wearing a suit. A nice suit. Not black. White. He... he had a red carnation in his... on his chest. And there was... blood... all over him. He was holding... a knife. Like in a horror movie. You know, the one with the man in the white mask?"

"*Halloween*," Vic supplied.

Teresa nodded. "I saw that movie in high school, at a slumber party. It gave me nightmares. I'm never going to watch it again."

"That must have been terrifying," Erin said.

"The strange thing was, he was crying," Teresa said, almost speaking to herself. "I remember tears running down his cheeks. My first thought was that he'd been hurt somehow, but then I saw his sleeves. He was... red... all the way to his elbows. And that knife..."

"What did you do?" Erin asked.

"I just stood there. I don't know how long. It felt like a long time. We looked at each other. He didn't move. And I couldn't. I felt cold, like my whole body had turned to ice."

"Did he say anything?"

"No. Neither did I. Then he started down the stairs toward me." Her voice died almost completely away. Erin and Vic leaned forward to catch her words.

"I've never been so scared. I unfroze, somehow. I ran inside and bolted the door. All three bolts. And I looked through the peephole and... he was standing right there. On the landing. Staring at my door and... and still crying. He raised one of his hands like he was going to knock, but then he wiped his face with it, like he was brushing away the tears, but his hand left a big red smear on his cheek."

"Then what?"

"He gave this little shake, like a dog that's come out of the rain. Then he turned and went away. Like he'd forgotten about me." Teresa shuddered again. "Is he crazy?"

"And then you called the police?"

"I stayed inside. For a while. Until I was sure he was gone. Then... I didn't want to get involved. So I went down the street. To a pay phone."

"Did you hear anything from upstairs, while you were waiting?"

"No. I guess Isabella was... was already..."

"Yes, she was," Erin said. "There was nothing you could have done for her. She was gone before you even knew anything had happened. If you were out shopping, you didn't get here until it was all over."

Teresa nodded. "I thought so. I didn't want to say anything, didn't want to do anything, but I couldn't just leave things that way. She... she might have... maybe nobody would have come... and I would have had to go to bed underneath, thinking about her... just over my head."

Rolf nudged her with his snout. She absently patted his head.

"Teresa?" Erin said. "What do you know about this guy?"

"Isabella was going to marry him. She showed me the ring. She was so... so happy." Teresa's own eyes filled with tears. "She was so proud of that ring."

"I need to know his name."

Teresa blinked several times, trying to clear her eyes. "You already know it."

"I need you to say it."

There was a long pause. Erin held her breath.

"Isabella called him Angel Face," Teresa finally said in a low voice. "Because he's so handsome. It's his nickname. His name is... Vitelli. Gabriel Vitelli."

Erin let out her breath. "You're sure?" she asked.

Teresa nodded. "You've seen him, haven't you?"

Erin nodded.

"Then you'd know him anywhere."

"Yeah," Erin said. "I would. He's got a distinctive face."

"My father told me about these men," Teresa said, biting her lip again and swallowing. "When he was a young boy, they ran his whole neighborhood. My grandfather taught him about them. The only way to be safe from them is not to be noticed. You live your life quietly, you don't cause trouble. If you call the police, they know and they will... kill you. My grandfather's best friend was killed by them, when he talked to a policeman. Back in the Forties."

"Teresa, things aren't like that anymore," Erin said, but at that moment she was thinking about Alfie Madonna. She wouldn't tell the FBI, she thought. There was no need for them to know. Then Teresa ought to be safe. "We can put you in Witness Protection, get you out of town."

"I don't *want* to go out of town!" Teresa burst out. "I live here! This is my home! I have a job, a family, a life!"

"I thought you weren't married," Vic said.

"I have parents," Teresa said. "And brothers and sisters. They all live in Brooklyn. Nieces and nephews, too. In-laws. Everybody. I can't just leave them. And my kids. My students, I mean. The school year just started, I'm just getting to know them. They need me."

Erin nodded sympathetically. "I know it's hard," she said. "Doing the right thing always is. But it would only be for a little while, until the trial. The Mafia doesn't retaliate against witnesses after it's all over, not these days. That's bad for business, and that's all they really care about."

"I'm scared," Teresa whispered.

"I know," Erin said. "But I promise, I won't let anyone hurt you."

"If Erin says she's got your back, she means it," Vic said. "She's the woman who saved the Civic Center last year. Remember that?"

Teresa nodded. Her jaw twitched, but she unclenched just a little.

"She's taken down Mob guys before," Vic went on. "They don't make 'em any tougher than her. There's nobody I'd rather have watching my tail."

Erin blinked. Vic had never said that about her before. She swallowed a sudden lump in her throat.

"Don't ask me to do this," Teresa said. "Please."

Being a detective could be a really nasty job sometimes. To get people to talk, you had to empathize with them, get emotionally close, open them up. And then you had to manipulate their emotions and use every dirty, underhanded trick in the book to get what you wanted from them. You told yourself it was for the greater good, for justice, to punish the guilty and protect the innocent. But here was a woman as innocent as any Erin had ever known, and she had to convince her to do something difficult and dangerous. This was the time to be a real bitch, and Erin hated it, but she'd do it anyway. Because she was a good detective.

"The kids you teach," Erin said. "They're what, nine years old?"

"Yes," Teresa said. "Third grade."

"I have a niece about that old," Erin said. "It's a great age, isn't it?"

"Yes. They're all so sweet, so eager to learn."

"What do you teach them?"

"Pretty much everything except math. They have another teacher for that, Mrs. Gambucci. I teach reading, writing, history, and social studies."

"What do you teach them about honesty?" Erin asked, suppressing a wave of self-disgust.

"I teach them to tell the truth," Teresa said, looking down at Rolf and caressing his head. "I try to teach them integrity."

"What do you think they'd want you to do?" Erin asked quietly.

"I know what the right thing to do is," Teresa said. "It's just so hard."

"The right thing usually is," Erin agreed. "The hardest thing there is."

"Oh God," Teresa whispered. "What am I going to do?"

And Erin knew they had her. She should have felt exhilarated, triumphant. But all she felt was tired and unhappy.

Chapter 17

"You'd better stay with her until the Marshals get here," Vic said. "The Lieutenant and I will go get Angel Eyes or whatever the hell he's called."

"Like hell you will!" Erin snapped. "This is my collar."

They were on the landing outside Teresa's apartment. They'd told her they needed to step out for a few moments to take care of some police business. What they'd meant was, they needed to have a discussion but didn't want to have it in front of a civilian. It was like parents not fighting where their kids could hear it; seeing disagreements between authority figures could undermine trust.

"I'm not trying to take credit for your bust," Vic said with uncharacteristic patience, speaking in an undertone. "Think about it. These Mob guys think you're watching out for them. How's it gonna look if you slap the cuffs on the son of a Mafia boss? I don't care what they think of me, and the Lieutenant doesn't give a damn. But you have to look out for your rep."

"We can have Patrol units watch the house," Erin said. It was weak and she knew it.

Vic threw her a contemptuous, almost pitying look. "Yeah, and we know the Lucarellis don't have eyes inside the Brooklyn precincts."

"You're right," she said heavily. "I just feel like I'm ducking out of my responsibilities."

"You kidding? We've got the easy job. These guys know better than to resist arrest when we roll up. But how do you know someone won't come round to shut this girl's mouth for good? Hell, for all I know, while I'm reading Pretty Boy Floyd his rights, you'll be swapping bullets with five of his buddies."

"Pretty Boy Floyd was a bank robber in the Depression," Erin said. "And Angel Eyes was the bad guy in an old Clint Eastwood movie."

"Do I look like I care? The only problem I have is, can you trust the Marshals?"

"Of course I trust them. They killed two Lucarellis yesterday, and one of their own is in the hospital. They'll be on the warpath."

"Yeah, but the bad guys heard about their last job."

"I know! That was the guy the Oil Man's got in the FBI."

"Are you sure one of the Marshals didn't leak it? Sure enough to bet this girl's life on it?"

Erin chewed the inside of her cheek. She was pretty sure, but not a hundred percent. Vic saw it in her face.

"Here's the problem," he said. "We've got plenty for an indictment, if we include her statement. But then somebody, somewhere, is gonna know about her. We can keep her involvement quiet for a while, and pray we get a grand jury that'll line up with us, but our case is weak without her and you know it. Besides, it's gonna come out anyway, on account of the discovery process."

Erin nodded. Vic was referring to the judicial proceeding in which the prosecution and defense were legally required to show their opposite numbers the evidence they had. In the real world, there were very few surprises at trials. All the surprises were worked out ahead of time, which made for bad drama but cleaner court cases.

"So we either hand her off to WitSec," Vic went on, "or we take care of it in-house. We can't trust our house on this, and from what's been happening, we can't trust the Feds either. I guess we've got a third choice."

"What's that?"

"We let the bastard walk."

"You know we can't do that."

Vic gave it a beat, looking at her. "Yeah, I know. But I wanted to hear it from you."

"What a mess," Erin said.

"Yeah," Vic said. "Times like this, I understand why the Lieutenant smokes so much. I haven't had a cigarette since I was sixteen, and right now I feel like I could use one."

"Is that why you chew toothpicks?"

He smiled. "Nah, that's just so I look like a badass. Nobody's impressed if you've got a mouthful of chewing gum, but a toothpick makes them think you're some sort of scary SOB."

"I shouldn't have pushed her so hard," Erin said.

"You mean that?"

Erin looked at her feet and said nothing.

"Hey," Vic said. "You gonna feed me that bullshit after you just told her how hard it was doing the right thing? You gonna be a hypocrite now? Because I was just starting to respect you a little."

"How do you do that?" Erin asked.

"Do what?"

"Act like an asshole and still make me want to like you."

"Years of practice."

"We have to bring some reinforcements in," she said. "Our squad doesn't have enough bodies to keep watch on her twenty-four seven. I still think the Marshals are our best bet. But if Valentino Vitelli was willing to have his guys shoot it out with them for money, what do you think he'll be willing to do for the sake of his son?"

"Oh yeah, if he hears about it, he'll come gunning," Vic said. "Absolutely. Look, we can hold off for a few days before we make the arrest. Maybe even a couple weeks, if it'll help."

"And give Angel Face the chance to slip out of the country for a nice, long stay somewhere warm, somewhere with no extradition treaty? No thanks. I appreciate you trying to find a way out of this, but sometimes, life serves you up a shit sandwich and there's nothing to do but take a nice, big bite."

"And swallow," he agreed. "So, it's got to be the Marshals?"

"Yeah. I don't have Calley or Boone's number, but I'll just call their office. That won't raise any suspicion. If I don't get one of them, I'll tell whoever I talk to that I'm checking up on Headley, which I should be doing anyway. Those two will understand the need for security."

"Copy that," Vic said. "You'll be okay on your own until they get here?"

"I won't be alone," she said, laying a hand on Rolf's head. "But the only car we've got is mine. I'd better keep it, just in case we need to move fast."

"No problem," he said. "I'll call a cab and expense it to the Department. Our tax dollars at work."

*   *   *

The Marshals office provided Erin with Calley and Boone's phone numbers. She tried Calley first, placing the call from Teresa's living room. Teresa was in the bedroom, thinking things over. Rolf lay at Erin's feet. He didn't understand the little boxes the humans liked to hold against their ears, but humans did a lot of things he didn't understand and he was used to it.

"Calley," the Marshal said by way of greeting.

"This is Erin O'Reilly," she said. "How's Headley doing?"

"Hanging in there," Calley said. "I'm at the hospital now, playing the waiting game. You know how it is."

"Yeah," she said. "I've been on both sides of it, too many times."

"They think he'll pull through," he said. "He's old-school tough. As they were wheeling him into surgery, I heard him ask one of the nurses what all the fuss was about. Said he didn't need an anesthesiologist, just a bottle of whiskey and a bullet to bite. They thought he was joking. I wasn't so sure."

"Where's Marshal Boone?" she asked.

"Home. You saw what he was like. Poor guy's a mess. I wouldn't be surprised if he hands in his star. I sent him home to get his head straight, and told him to give things a day or two before he does anything, so at least he won't make a snap decision."

"How about you?" Erin asked.

"What about me?"

"You holding up okay?"

"I'm doing my job." Calley sounded awfully calm for a man who'd been in a gunfight and literally held his boss's life in his hands only a few hours earlier.

"Glad to hear it. I've got another job for you."

"I don't work for the NYPD, Detective."

"It's witness protection."

"I'm listening."

"But this can't go through the FBI. Not this time. Not through anybody you can't personally vouch for."

"Are you saying what I think you're saying, Detective?" Calley asked sharply.

"Yeah. I am."

"That's a serious charge."

"If I was pressing charges, yeah. What I'm trying to do is save a woman's life. And before you tell me I'm being paranoid, think about what happened yesterday and why your boss is lying in a hospital bed."

There was a brief pause. Then Calley said, more softly, "Point taken. But doing this through back channels will be difficult. It'll take time to set everything up."

"How much time?"

"Two, three days. Could be as long as a week to get everything sorted."

"A week?" She didn't bother hiding her dismay.

"You'd better tell me the situation," Calley said. "Everything you can."

"I've got a witness who's agreed to ID a Mob killer," she said slowly. "But she's scared, and I've got reason to believe her fears are justified. She needs round-the-clock protection, and I can't use the NYPD. We're compromised."

Calley whistled softly. "Okay," he said. "We have a fair number of Marshals in the Southern District. I might be able to get a few of them detailed for short-term duty. It'll be irregular, but I can take it upstairs. I'll play it as close as I can. How soon do you need me and my guys?"

"As soon as possible. I'll be standing guard until you get here."

"I'll need the address. Can you send it, or is it secret?"

"I'll text you the address of the crime scene," she said. "Someone will meet you there." She didn't explain that the two addresses were in fact identical.

"Okay, send it now."

Erin did so.

"Got it," Calley said a moment later. "Give me ninety minutes. I'll be there with a couple other guys. Don't worry, they're solid."

"Thanks. I appreciate this."

"This one's not going to run out on us, is she?"

"No. She's pure civilian. You shouldn't have any trouble with her."

"Copy that. See you in an hour and a half." He hung up.

Erin walked around the apartment, checking sight lines from the windows. She checked her Glock and her backup snub-nosed .38 and made sure they had rounds chambered and ready. Then she went to the bedroom door and knocked.

"Come in," Teresa said.

Erin found her sitting on the bed, staring at the wall. The woman's eyes were puffy and bloodshot.

"It's going to be okay," Erin said. "A team of US Marshals is coming. They'll protect you. They'll need you to move to another location, most likely a hotel. You'd better pack clothing for a few days, along with anything else you'll need."

"I should call the school, let them know I won't be coming in."

Erin started to say that Teresa shouldn't call anybody, should be completely incommunicado. But then she realized that would probably raise more suspicion and attention than it would prevent. She nodded.

"Tell them you've got either a sudden illness or a family emergency," she said.

"How long will this go on?" Teresa asked.

"I don't know exactly," Erin said. "Probably a few months. It depends on how quickly the DA can get ready for trial."

"Will they give me a gun?"

"What?" Erin was startled. "Why?"

"For self-defense."

"Do you have any experience with firearms?"

Teresa shook her head. "None."

"Then you're in more danger if you have a gun than if you don't," Erin said. "Believe me, you're better off without. The Marshals will be armed. They'll protect you if anything happens, which it won't. We're going to fly under the radar. Nobody's going to shoot at you."

"You're carrying a gun," Teresa observed.

"I always carry a gun. It's part of my job."

"Have you ever shot anyone?"

"Yeah. I have."

"Oh." Teresa looked away. "I'm sorry. It's none of my business, really. I'm not used to all this. You must think I'm being silly."

"No," Erin said. "This isn't a world you're supposed to be part of. You stumbled into it by accident. There's nothing silly about what you're feeling. And you've got nothing to apologize for. I'm the one who should apologize."

"You're just doing your job," Teresa said. "I only wish..."

"What?" Erin asked after a moment.

"I wish I'd taken five minutes longer at the store," Teresa said. "Then I wouldn't have had to make a choice, because I wouldn't have seen anything. But I guess that's cowardly of me."

"It's sensible," Erin said. "There's plenty of awful stuff that happens all over the world. We don't see more than the tip of the iceberg. New York had a couple hundred murders this past year that you haven't witnessed. This would've just been another of those for you."

"But it's not," Teresa said with a sigh.

"No, it's not," Erin agreed.

"You're not going to leave me all alone here, are you?"

"I'll stay until the Marshals get here. You won't be alone, I promise."

"Am I doing the right thing?" Teresa asked in a small voice.

"You are," Erin said.

"Then why do I feel like I'm going to throw up?"

Erin smiled wryly. "Hey, if doing the right thing always felt good, nobody would ever do anything wrong. Then I'd be out of a job."

*   *   *

Erin had worked some security details back in her Patrol days, but those had been mostly a formality. She'd handled crowd control, making sure no crazies broke through a cordon to harass a politician or celebrity. Guarding a Mob witness was something else entirely. If people came after Teresa, they'd come with guns and the will to kill.

She told herself there was nothing to worry about. The only way anyone would even know Teresa had agreed to testify was if Calley or one of his guys was untrustworthy. And if Calley had been on Valentino Vitelli's payroll, he would've taken down Alfie Madonna. Everything was going to be fine. She just had to sit tight and wait for the cavalry.

Time slowed down. Teresa packed her suitcase. Erin and Rolf stayed near the front door, keeping their ears open for any sound of trouble. Every car on the street made them tense up, only to relax again a minute later as each vehicle passed by. Erin wondered about her car. The Charger was unmarked, but anyone in the Life would peg it as a police car from half a block away. Would it give Teresa away?

Of course not, Erin told herself. The top-floor apartment was a crime scene. Nothing was more natural than a police vehicle parked out front. She was just being paranoid again. She looked at the clock on the wall. More than an hour had passed. Calley should be arriving soon.

Her phone buzzed, making her jump halfway out of her shoes. Rolf gave her a startled look as she took out the phone and she gave her heart a second to get back in rhythm. Webb's name showed on the screen.

"O'Reilly," she said.

"We've got Gabriel Vitelli in custody," Webb said. "We're back at the Eightball now."

"I don't suppose he's confessed?" she asked without much hope.

"His dad lawyered him up before Neshenko even finished Mirandizing him," Webb said dryly. "The old man knows his way around our wonderful legal system. But the kid doesn't need to tell us anything."

"Who signed off on the warrant?" Erin asked.

"Judge Ferris."

"Good." Ferris was a solid ally of the Major Crimes squad, a crusty old judge who could be counted on to sign any reasonable piece of paper they put in front of him. "Any chance he'll post bail?"

"Not with what we've got on him," Webb said.

Erin felt a sudden chill. "Sir, we still need to get our witness under cover," she said. "If Vitelli's lawyer hears about her before then..."

"Relax, O'Reilly. Nobody's telling the courts anything yet. We don't have to charge him for forty-eight hours, remember? I'll be happy to run out the clock on him. Will that be enough time?"

"Yeah," she said. "Sorry. I just got shot at outside a courthouse, remember? I'm still a little tense."

"Understood. I don't blame you. Vitelli Senior was pretty upset. He stayed civil, but I believe if he'd had a gun in his hand, he would've murdered Neshenko and me on the spot when we slapped the cuffs on his boy."

"I believe it too," she said.

"You want me to send Neshenko down there to back you up? He offered."

"No thanks, sir. By the time he got here, we'd probably already be gone."

"Copy that. Take care, O'Reilly."

"Thank you, sir." Erin hung up and looked at the phone. That had been an uncharacteristic sign-off from Webb. Maybe he was worried, too.

Teresa came out into the living room. She was holding her suitcase in one hand, her purse over her other shoulder. She had a coat the color of robin's eggs draped over her arm. She was more composed than before, though she still had a slight tremor running just beneath the surface. It reminded Erin of high-voltage power lines. She could practically hear the humming if she stood close enough to the schoolteacher.

"Are we going yet?" Teresa asked. Her voice was thin and brittle.

"Pretty soon," Erin said.

The sound of another car was audible outside. This one slowed and stopped. Erin heard two doors open and close. The front door of the brownstone opened. Footsteps clattered on the stairs.

Erin held up a hand, motioning Teresa to stand back. Her other hand rested on the butt of her pistol.

The footsteps paused for a moment outside the apartment. Erin stepped forward and took a quick look through the peephole. She saw Marshal Calley on the landing. He was starting up toward the top floor.

Erin unlocked the door, one lock after another. She opened the door. Calley spun around, a man she didn't know at his side.

They were wearing plainclothes, but both men obviously had vests on under their coats. Calley had another vest in his hands. His partner, a very large man, was reaching for a gun.

"Whoa," Erin said. "Take it easy. It's me."

"Ready?" Calley asked.

"Yeah," Erin said.

"Then let's move," Calley said. "This is Marshal Hodges."

Hodges didn't even give Erin a second look. He was busy scanning the surroundings for any threat. He was a muscular man with a shaved head and no neck. He looked more like a football running back than a law-enforcement officer.

Erin nodded. "Come on in," she said. "Teresa, this is Marshal Calley and Marshal Hodges. Marshals, this is Teresa."

"Ma'am," Calley said, touching a hand to his forehead. If he'd been wearing a hat, he would've tipped it. "Put this on, please."

Teresa took the vest and nearly dropped it. "It's heavy," she said in surprise.

"It's Kevlar with ceramic ballistic plates," Calley explained. "It'll stop pistol bullets at any range, and some rifle rounds."

Teresa stared at him. "Do I need this?" she asked. "I thought... Detective O'Reilly said nobody would shoot at me."

"It's just a precaution, ma'am," Calley said. "Standard procedure. Now, if you're ready, we should get going."

"Where are we going?" Teresa asked as she clumsily fastened the Velcro straps on the cumbersome vest.

"The Hilton at JFK," Calley said. "Don't worry, it'll be safe."

Hodges led the way downstairs. Erin was fine with that. The man was so big, he qualified as portable cover. Then came Teresa, Erin, and Rolf, with Calley bringing up the rear. Hodges glanced out onto the street. A black SUV was idling at the curb, a third Marshal standing next to it. He nodded to Hodges.

"Back seat, ma'am," Calley said. Hodges opened the door for her. The other Marshal got behind the wheel. Calley circled to the far side of the SUV and got in back beside Teresa. Hodges climbed into the front seat. The vehicle was already moving as he pulled his door shut. The Marshals' car picked up speed and rolled around the next corner, out of sight.

Erin put a hand on Rolf's head. "Okay, kiddo," she said. "We did our job. Now we just have to trust them to do theirs."

Rolf leaned against her leg.

Chapter 18

Erin walked into the Barley Corner with Rolf beside her. The place was full to bursting. Erin was surprised, until she realized it was near suppertime. Her interrupted sleep cycle had left her with no good sense of the time. She'd seen the numbers on her clock, but they hadn't properly registered in her fogged-up brain.

Someone slapped her on the back in a friendly manner as she worked her way toward the bar. She saw Wayne McClernand, one of Corky's Teamsters buddies, and gave him a weary smile. For a gangster, smuggler, and convicted felon, Wayne was a pretty nice guy. He and Erin had done each other a few favors over the past months. He grinned cheerfully at her, showing gaps where he'd lost a couple of teeth.

She found Carlyle at the bar, James Corcoran seated beside him. Corky's patch of bar had four empty shot glasses lined up on it. Carlyle was nursing a pint of Guinness. When he saw her, he got to his feet.

"Evening, darling," he said. "We've been waiting for you."

"It doesn't look like you waited to start the drinking," she said, giving the empties a pointed look.

Corky laughed. "An Irishman can wait to take a maiden's virtue, or a drink of good whiskey, but he'd much prefer not to," he said. "I've some grand tidings for you."

"Okay, let's hear them," Erin said. "I could use some good news."

"Not here," Corky said.

"Are you serious?" Erin asked. The background noise was so loud, it would be next to impossible for anyone to eavesdrop on them.

"I'm never serious," Corky replied with a saucy wink. "But I do mean it."

Little alarm bells went off in the back of Erin's head, where her police instincts hadn't quite nodded off yet. Damn, but she was tired.

"We'd best step upstairs to my office, I'm thinking," Carlyle said.

Once they'd closed the apartment's reinforced door, climbed the stairs, and gone into Carlyle's wood-paneled office, Erin sank into one of the leather armchairs. Corky dropped into another, draping a leg carelessly over the armrest like a lazy teenager. Rolf settled at Erin's feet and tucked his snout beneath his tail. Carlyle remained standing, going behind his desk and fetching out a bottle of Glen Docherty-Kinlochewe whiskey and three glasses. He poured shots for the three of them, handed them out, and leaned against the front of his desk.

"Now then, lad," Carlyle said. "I can see Erin's carrying news of her own, but you've been waiting longer, and I can see you're fair bursting at the seams. Perhaps you'd best go first."

Corky took a long, slow drink of whiskey; the longest Erin had ever seen him take. He licked his lips in satisfaction. "All your troubles are over," he said. "Or they soon will be."

"I'm pleased to hear it," Carlyle said in a deadpan. "I don't suppose you've a bridge to sell me in Brooklyn while you're about it?"

"Not I," Corky said. "But if it's a bridge you're needing, I know a lad in the construction business."

"Not just now, Corks. What I'd most like is for you to explain yourself."

"I've been spending time with Maggie Callahan, as you well know," Corky said. "And she's carrying the whole of Evan O'Malley's business ledger about in that fine brain of hers."

"You've got the ledger?" Erin exclaimed, sitting forward. Some of her drink sloshed out of the glass. "If we've got that... then it can be over! Right now! We can haul the whole bunch of them in and—"

"Calm yourself, love," Corky said, patting her arm. "I'm not carrying a copy of the ledger—yet. What I've done is convinced the lass to write it all down, as an emergency backup. You see, I explained to her that she might have an accident, or be rendered otherwise unable to recall the information for dear Evan. So she's making a copy, which will be entrusted to a particularly trustworthy lad."

"Meaning you?" Erin asked, raising her eyebrows.

"You don't think I'm trustworthy?"

"I think you tried to sleep with my sister-in-law and nearly got her, my niece and nephew, Ian, and me all killed."

"There's that." Corky deflated slightly. Then he rallied. "But this is what you're needing, aye?"

"Aye," Carlyle agreed. "How soon will you have the ledger?"

"She'll have it done in a matter of days," Corky said. "And she'll put it in a safe-deposit box. This one." He pulled a ring of keys out of his pocket, selected a small one, and jingled it enticingly.

"Then we'll copy the copy," Erin said. "That way nobody will suspect anything. And we'll get it to the Captain."

"And once he's gone through it with a forensic accountant, and ensured it's all in order, we'll be ready to wrap this business up at last," Carlyle said. "But it won't happen all at once. That'll be taking some time, darling. We're not quite out of the woods yet."

"But the trees are thinning out nicely," Corky said. "That's my news, and well worth a glass of your best, Cars. Now, Erin, can you top that?"

"No," she said. "All I did today was bust Angel Face Vitelli."

Carlyle and Corky froze. They looked at one another, then back at Erin.

"You need to work on your delivery, love," Corky said. "I didn't know you were joking at first."

"I'm not," she said. "He's in a holding cell as we speak."

"Good Lord, why?" Corky asked.

"He's a career criminal," Erin said.

"So am I, but I'm not warming a cell!"

"He killed his fiancée," Erin said. "His *pregnant* fiancée. With a butcher knife."

Carlyle ran a hand over his face. "Erin, darling, I understand you need to take the lad in," he said. "But couldn't you have waited? Just a little longer?"

"I didn't know about Corky!" she retorted. "And I can't come in now, remember? You just reminded me it'll be weeks, maybe months, before we're ready to close down the O'Malleys. We can't let a murderer just wander around New York that long. Besides, I didn't arrest him personally. Vic and Webb took care of that. I made sure I wasn't there."

"Valentino Vitelli loves his lad," Carlyle said. "He'll not let Angel Face rot behind bars."

"He won't have a choice," she said grimly. "And after his goons put a Marshal in the hospital, I don't really give a damn what he wants."

"You're thinking like a copper, darling," Carlyle said.

"I *am* a copper, in case you forgot!" she snapped.

"Nay, you're a bent copper, at least in their eyes," he said gently. "And you need to preserve that illusion. Your safety, and mine, depends on these lads believing you're useful to them. You can't declare war on them. Not yet."

"So I'm supposed to just turn a blind eye when they carve up an innocent girl in her own bed?"

"I'm not defending the bastard," Carlyle said coldly. "You may recall, something similar happened to me once upon a time."

Erin flinched. Carlyle was referring to the murder of his wife and their unborn child, back in Ireland twenty years ago.

"I'm sorry," she said more quietly. "I didn't mean it that way."

"No harm done, darling," he said. "But I'm not your enemy, not in this, not ever."

"This is all very sweet," Corky said. "And I can't believe I'm the one to say this, but shouldn't we be thinking more along practical lines at the moment? What's she to do about this dog's breakfast?"

"That depends on the Italians, I'd imagine," Carlyle said. "And on what they know. I assume Valentino's apprised of the situation?"

"According to Vic, Gabriel's dad was there when he got arrested," Erin confirmed.

"Then we'll need to see what he does," Carlyle said, "and react accordingly."

Erin's phone buzzed, as if on cue. She looked at the screen and saw an unidentified number. "Just a second," she told the Irishmen, putting the phone to her ear. "O'Reilly."

"You know who this is," said a cold voice with a distinctive Brooklyn accent. "Come to Canarsie Cemetery. You got a meeting."

"I'm not on Long Island," Erin said sharply. "And I don't know who this is or what it's about."

"Yeah, you do," the voice replied. "It's about a mutual friend you've got. Be there in an hour. And come alone." The call disconnected.

Erin stared at the phone. "Shit," she said quietly.

"Vitelli?" Carlyle guessed.

"One of his guys," she said. "He wants to meet at Canarsie Cemetery in an hour. Just me."

"Why the cemetery?" Corky wondered.

"It'll be private," she said. "It's probably closed to visitors right now."

"He'll have one of the lads who works there on his payroll," Carlyle said. "It's a secluded spot where you'll not be disturbed, and it'll be simple to ensure you're by yourself. But I don't much like it."

"He's not going to whack a detective," she said.

"You said yourself he was willing to take on the Marshals," Carlyle said.

"Yeah, but they won't gain anything by taking me out," she said. "Gabriel will still be in jail and it'll just piss off the NYPD. Not to mention Vic. He'd friggin' kill them. Look, with rush hour traffic, I'd better get moving."

"I'll come with you," Carlyle said.

Erin shook her head. "He said alone. If they do try anything, remember there's a few thousand cops on Long Island. Backup's no more than a few minutes away. Besides, this is a chance to find out what they're thinking. Once we know what Vitelli wants, we'll have some idea what to do about him."

"Call me the second you're out of the meeting," Carlyle said.

"Sheesh," Erin said. "You meet with mobsters all the time. You're just mad the shoe's on the other foot now. If I can handle it, so can you."

"As I recall, you handled it last time by getting intoxicated and acquiring a tattoo," Carlyle observed.

Corky grinned. "Grand times," he said.

*   *   *

Traffic across the East River was awful. Erin ground her teeth and squeezed the steering wheel. She could've used the lights and siren, but this was supposed to be a covert meeting. The last thing she wanted was for some well-intentioned Patrol officer to follow her, thinking she might need backup. Better to be patient.

Erin O'Reilly hated being patient, particularly when something unpleasant loomed on the horizon. She knew Valentino was going to be mad. He probably wanted to either make her an offer or a threat. Maybe both. Until she knew what the offer was, it was hard to make plans. All she had was her wits, her guns, and her dog if things went bad. But those had been enough to get her out of plenty of tight spots in the past.

There was one thing she needed to do before she got to the cemetery. She fished out her spare phone, the one with only one contact in it, and placed a call.

"Everything okay?" Phil Stachowski asked, picking up on the second ring.

"Yeah, I'm fine," she said. "I just wanted to let you know I'm on my way to a meeting in Brooklyn. Canarsie Cemetery."

"With whom?" Erin's undercover handler asked.

"Valentino Vitelli."

"Do you expect trouble?"

"I always expect it these days."

"What do you need from me?"

"Right now? Nothing. We'll talk later."

"Okay. Let me know how it goes."

"Will do." She hung up, feeling a little less worried. Maybe there was a finite amount of worry in the world, she thought, and by spreading some of hers around, she lessened the burden on herself. That was a crazy theory, but an oddly comforting one.

Once she finally got across the river, the traffic eased up a little. Erin checked her clock. She still had time, but it'd be close. The cemetery was on the wrong damn side of Long Island. She went as fast as she dared. Valentino probably wouldn't make an issue of it if she was a few minutes late, but it was better not to piss him off more than necessary.

She turned off Remsen Avenue into the cemetery parking lot, passing between a pair of brick gateposts. The lot contained three cars: a pair of nondescript sedans and a big old Lincoln Continental, lovingly maintained.

Erin parked the Charger. She unfastened her seatbelt and adjusted her blouse. In the process, she squeezed the hidden wire in her bra, activating the recorder. The tape was good for an hour. She didn't think this meeting would take longer than that. Then she stepped out onto the pavement. She popped Rolf's compartment and the Shepherd hopped down to join her. She glanced around, seeing the funeral parlor, doors closed, lights off. The posted hours showed the cemetery had closed at four o'clock.

"Okay," she said. "Here we are. Where's the party?"

A man in a black suit and tie came around the corner of the building. He might be dressed like an undertaker, but Erin knew mob muscle when she saw it. The guy had an olive complexion, slicked-back black hair, and a jailhouse tattoo poking over the top of his starched white collar.

"Evening," she said levelly, watching his hands. Hands were the things that would hurt you. His were currently empty.

"You was supposed to come alone," he said with a Brooklyn accent thick enough to scoop up with a spoon.

"I don't see any other people around," she said.

"I'm talkin' about the dog."

"You're worried about the dog listening in?" She let him hear the skepticism in her voice. "I hate to disappoint you, but he only understands German, and not much of that."

Rolf kept his eyes on his partner, awaiting instructions. He figured he could take the guy if she wanted him to.

The man took a moment to think it over, deciding whether to make an issue of it. Erin decided this goon was definitely more brawn than brains.

"Your boss is the one who wanted this meeting," she said. "And you're the one keeping him waiting."

"Okay," he said at last. "Come on."

He motioned her to follow. They set out for a nice little evening stroll among the tombstones. The evening was cool but not chilly. A faint smell of autumn hung on the air. Erin scanned the area, looking for the other Mob guys who had to be there. With the cemetery officially closed, anybody hanging around was likely to be working for Vitelli. She felt very exposed, though the tombstones would offer decent cover if a firefight broke out. Her hand kept wanting to twitch toward her sidearm. She resisted the impulse.

The man led her toward the flagpole at the center of the cemetery. Three more men stood there. Two were obviously bodyguards, keeping a respectful distance from their mark. The third was Valentino Vitelli.

The old man was looking at a gravestone, a big statue of a weeping angel done in the old Victorian style. Vitelli was wearing a khaki trench coat and holding a fedora in one hand. In the other he held a bouquet of flowers. He didn't look up as Erin and her escort approached.

"Hey, boss," the goon with Erin said. He spoke in quiet, respectful tones. "She's here."

"Take a walk, Enzo," Vitelli said, waving his hand without taking his eyes from the grave. "And take these other two with you. Go on, scram. Stay where you can see me, but this is a private conversation."

"You got it, boss," Enzo said. He cocked his head meaningfully at the bodyguards. The three men moved off, glancing frequently back at Erin and Vitelli.

This hadn't been quite what Erin had expected. She came closer, stopping about four feet away from Vitelli. She turned and looked at the grave that so interested him.

"Rodolfo and Maria Vitelli," she read off the inscription. "Your parents?"

"That's right," Vitelli said. "They came over from Sicily way before your time. Not me. I was born right here in New York. They came after the war. 1946. Wasn't much left in Sicily after the Fascists and the US Army got done fighting over it, I gotta tell you. What my father said, the whole country looked like somebody dragged a rake over it, one end to the other. Your people came from Ireland, right?"

"Right," she said. "That was a long time ago."

"Yeah." Vitelli stooped and laid the bouquet on the grave. Then he stood back, ran a hand through his thin white hair, and put his hat back on. He finally turned to face Erin. "Family's important to me," he said.

"Me, too," she said.

"You got my boy."

"I heard he was arrested," she said carefully.

"By your people." Vitelli thrust a finger at her, stopping just short of poking her in the chest. "On your information."

"I work with a team of detectives," she said. "And I'm not the ranking officer. That's Lieutenant Webb."

Vitelli waved his hand dismissively. "Don't give me none of that crap. I work for another guy, too. I know what you are. You're just like me. You're a doer, not a planner. You see something that's gotta be done, bam! You do it. Whether your boss tells you to or not. And now my boy's locked up, and he's gonna go on trial. And for what?"

"He killed Isabella Romano," Erin said, keeping her voice as calm and neutral as possible.

"Says who?"

"Says all the evidence."

Vitelli waved his hand again. "Evidence!" he said scornfully. "Here's what you're gonna do. You're gonna find out all that evidence you've got don't mean nothing. And you're gonna let my boy go."

"It's not that simple, Mr. Vitelli," she said.

"It's exactly that simple!" he said. "I heard you're a reasonable woman, a businesswoman. Did I hear right?"

Erin had to be very careful now. The Lucarellis were allied with the O'Malleys. If she gave the wrong answer, it would get back to Evan O'Malley. It could give the whole game away.

"What do you need?" she asked, playing for time and information.

"I know the DNA don't mean nothing," Vitelli said. "And the fingerprints don't, neither. My boy was over there all the time, of course he left fingerprints. That's all circumstantial. Your guys don't have a case with that."

Erin waited. She knew her recorder was humming away, taking down everything that was being said. *Come on*, she thought. *Give yourself away.*

"You had to have something big," Vitelli said. "Something to make this a slam-dunk. And I know what it is. You got to the lady downstairs. She talked to you."

Erin fought to keep her poker face. She reminded herself that the Marshals had gotten Teresa out of the apartment in time. If the Mafia had gotten to Teresa, they wouldn't even be having this meeting. Teresa was safe.

"All this has to be about something that lady said she saw," Vitelli went on. "And that's a problem. Because you cops got all your fancy computer scans and blood tests, but everybody knows it's the witnesses the jury listen to. It's a human nature thing. We're all built to pay attention to other people."

Erin nodded, agreeing with the sentiment. That was a source of continuing frustration to prosecutors and cops alike. Witness statements carried disproportionate weight in the courtroom, even though they'd been proven to be among the least reliable types of evidence. Teresa's testimony would weld the bars on Gabriel Vitelli's jail cell nice and tight.

"I know she's gone," Vitelli went on. "I know she's hiding somewhere. And I know you know where she is."

A chill rippled down Erin's spine. Was he serious? "I don't know what you think you're doing," she said. "Your guys went after another guy in Witness Protection this week. They got in a gunfight with US Marshals! That was a crazy thing to do."

"I couldn't agree more," Vitelli said. "That was a terrible business, a real mess. It shoulda never happened. And I was real sorry to hear about that Marshal who got hurt. I sent him some flowers, anonymous of course. And I hope he gets better real soon."

"The thing is," Erin went on, "that incident's got the whole Marshal Service on edge now. *If* you're right about this, and *if* there's a witness in protective custody, then wherever they've got her is going to be a damn fortress. You'd never get a hitman in there. You might as well try to rob Fort Knox."

"I see your point," Vitelli said. "Okay, you're probably right. An outside guy can't get to her. But *you* can."

The chill had spread from her spine into her lower belly. Cold fingers seemed to be twisting her guts into knots. "Hold on," she said. "You're saying you want me to *murder a witness?!*"

"Did I say that?" Vitelli said, holding up his hands in a gesture of surprise and horror that fooled nobody. "I didn't say that. All I'm saying is, there's a lady who's telling stories about my son. She's trying to take his life away from him, get him thrown in jail forever. And that ain't right. So I'm doing what any good father would do, protecting his son. And I'm asking you to take care of this little problem. I was told you could handle this sort of thing. Was I told wrong?"

There it was, out in the open at last. Evan O'Malley believed Erin had killed two gangsters in cold blood: Caleb Carnahan and Mickey Connor. He'd paid her for taking down Mickey. Other mobsters had offered contracts to her, and now here was a Mafia boss explicitly telling her to kill an innocent woman.

Erin's first impulse was to pull her gun, slap the cuffs on Vitelli, and drag his sorry old ass back to the Eightball. She could throw him in the cell across from his kid and they could have a little father-son bonding. But she couldn't do that. For one thing, even with the recording, Vitelli was being very careful not to use exact words. His intent was clear to her, but would it be clear to a judge and jury? And for another, to do that would blow her carefully-constructed undercover role to pieces, just when they were about to win.

"You heard right," she said grimly. "But you're asking me to do something impossible. There's Marshals on this lady round the clock."

"You'll think of something," Vitelli said. "Like I told you, you're a doer. Get this done. You won't be sorry."

"How much?" she asked, hating herself for asking it but knowing she had to get this on tape.

"I don't wanna talk about money right now," Vitelli said.

"You're the one who said I'm a businesswoman," she reminded him. "And you're the one who wanted to talk business."

"Okay," Vitelli said. "If you make this problem go away, for good, you'll find fifty large coming your way. And that's on account of your reputation. On the street, this kinda thing goes for five, ten tops. Make it happen, Miss O'Reilly. You got forty-eight hours. We'll be watching."

Vitelli didn't offer a handshake. He just turned and walked away. Erin stared at his retreating figure, a deceptively harmless-looking white-haired man ambling through a graveyard.

She looked down and saw Rolf gazing back at her with his big brown eyes. He wagged his tail uncertainly. He had no idea what was going on, but he could tell she was worried. If it would help, he was perfectly willing to chase down the guy and bite him, but Rolf had the feeling that wasn't what was called for. So he just looked at his partner, putting all the trust and devotion he felt into his stare. She'd figure out what to do. He was absolutely sure of that.

Chapter 19

Even though she knew it wasn't going to happen, Erin half-expected a bullet in the back of her head all the way to her car. The hairs on her neck were standing on end, as if she'd been chewing high-voltage cables. Everyone knew dogs had hackles; now she knew how they must feel. She didn't even begin to relax until she was behind the wheel, a good three blocks from the cemetery. Then it was time to make a couple of phone calls.

"I'm okay," she said to Phil as soon as he answered.

"Good," he said. "Do you want to talk about it?"

"No, but we need to. Can we meet this evening?"

"Of course. Time and place?"

"How about the 9/11 Memorial? Say, eight o'clock?"

"I'll be there. Erin?"

"Yeah?"

"Are you sure you're all right? You sound a little funny."

"I'm fine," she lied. "See you there." Then she hung up and called Carlyle.

"Evening, darling," he said, calm on the surface. But she heard the undercurrent of relief.

"Hey," she said. "I'm coming home."

"What did he want?"

"We'll talk about it when I get there."

Carlyle didn't press her. One of the nice things about dating a mobster was that he appreciated the occasional need for temporary secrecy. All he said was, "I'll be upstairs. I love you, darling."

The northbound traffic wasn't nearly as bad. Most of the commuters went the other direction. Still, it was a little after seven by the time Erin parked in the garage opposite the Barley Corner, crossed the street, and went in. The place was full of guys eating and drinking at the end of their workday. The TVs were playing some sporting event or other; Erin didn't even register what it was. She and Rolf went straight to the back stairs and got a heavy steel-core door between them and the outside world.

"Hello," she called as she got to the top of the stairs.

"We're in the living room, darling," Carlyle replied.

We? Erin thought. She found Carlyle and Corky sitting next to each other on the couch. On Carlyle's coffee table sat what appeared to be the entire contents of his liquor cabinet, along with some extras from the bar downstairs. Corky was mixing cocktails.

"Come in, love," Corky said, holding up a glass filled with an orange-tinted concoction. "Sit yourself down and get this in your belly."

"What is it?" she asked.

"That spoils the adventure," Corky said.

"I've had enough adventure for one night. What is it?"

"Gin, applejack, and apricot liqueur," he said. "It's called an angel face."

Erin grimaced and made no move to take it. "That's in poor taste, don't you think?"

He shrugged and took a sip. "Tastes grand to me. Maybe a mite sweet for you, love."

"Do you want this to be a private conversation?" Carlyle asked her. He was looking closely at her. The man had marvelous instincts.

"Yeah," Erin said. Then she hesitated. "On the other hand, maybe Corky needs to hear this. It's his ass on the line, too."

"What did Vitelli want?" Carlyle asked. His tone remained calm, but his eyes went very sharp.

"He wants me to kill a witness."

"Jesus Christ on his bloody cross," Corky said. "That lot don't muck about, do they? Having a copper take out a contract takes some bloody nerve!"

"It's not exactly unprecedented," Carlyle said.

"Caracappa and Eppolito," Erin said, nodding. She was thinking of the notorious "Mafia Cops," a pair of detectives who had committed at least eight murders on behalf of the Mob in the '80s and '90s. They'd finally been brought to justice a few years ago and been thrown in federal prison for life.

"We knew this was bound to happen sooner or later," Carlyle said. "Have you told your superiors yet?"

"I've got a meeting with my handler in less than an hour. Christ, what am I going to tell him?" Erin grabbed a bottle at random from the collection on the table. She sank onto the vacant cushion on the couch, upended the bottle, and took a generous gulp.

It was the apricot liqueur. She made a face, but managed not to spit it across the room. She swallowed and put the bottle back on the table.

"You'll tell him it's over," Carlyle said. "Unless you can stall Vitelli and run out the clock on him."

"He gave me forty-eight hours," she said bleakly. "Maggie's not done copying down the ledger yet, and even if she was, there's no way we could close it out in two days. And if we start hauling in O'Malleys, Maggie probably won't ever write it all down. That's it. We're toast."

"Don't go talking like that," Corky said. "Not until we've considered all the options."

"Options?" she echoed. "What options?"

He shrugged. "This contract doesn't come from the Oil Man. It's straight from Vitelli."

"So?"

"If Vitelli isn't around anymore, it's rather a moot point, wouldn't you say?"

Erin stared at him. "Corky, we're not killing Valentino Vitelli."

"Very well," he said, unfazed. "Arrest him, then."

"And blow my cover?"

"Not for the hit contract," he said. "For sending his bully-boys after the Marshals."

"We can't prove that was him," she said. "And even if I wasn't personally involved, he'd still know I was behind it."

"You could botch the murder," he suggested.

"What do you mean?"

"Talk to the Marshals ahead of time, fire a few shots over the lass's head," Corky said. "Apologize to Vitelli, tell him you tried, but the security was just too tight."

"Won't answer, lad," Carlyle said. "Anything obvious enough to convince the Italians would force the Marshals to arrest Erin. Though I like the way you're thinking there. Perhaps something along those lines might serve."

"This sort of thinking requires more liquor," Corky said. "Whiskey this time, love?"

"That might be a good idea," Erin said.

"Perception," Carlyle said softly. "The important thing is what the Italians see, regardless of the truth."

"Go on," Erin said. She'd stood up and was pacing back and forth across the living room.

"I think you should kill Miss Tommasino," Carlyle said. "Just like Vitelli told you to."

Nobody laughed. Nobody had a snappy comeback. The three people stared at each other.

"Or," Carlyle amended, "that's what they need to see."

"Yes," Erin said. Then, louder, "Yes! That's it! But I'll need some help. Especially from you, Carlyle."

"What is it you're wanting me to do?"

"What you used to do best."

"That being?"

"I want you to build me a car bomb."

*   *   *

Phil Stachowski looked Erin over. His mild gaze traveled to Carlyle, at Erin's right, and Corky, at her left. The only sound was the water of the memorial, trickling quietly and endlessly into the gaping hole that marked the worst terrorist attack in American history. The four of them stood in a rough diamond shape next to the 9/11 memorial. The sun had gone down almost an hour earlier. The park was nearly deserted.

"It's risky, all of us meeting like this," Phil said mildly. He knew the two Irishmen had been flipped, and he'd met with all of them separately, but this was the first time all of them had been in the same place at the same time.

"Ian drove us here," Carlyle said. "The lad's got quite the eye. He's certain we're clean."

"Where is he now?" Phil asked.

"He'd call it perimeter duty," Carlyle said.

"If all three of you are here, something's happened," Phil said. "What's the situation?"

"Valentino Vitelli offered me fifty thousand to kill a woman," Erin said. "No, that's not quite it. He ordered me to kill a witness and he's giving me two days and fifty grand to do it. I can't say no without jeopardizing the operation."

"So we're done," Phil said.

"Not quite," Carlyle said.

"What do you mean?"

"The woman's a witness to a murder committed by Vitelli's son," Erin explained. "Gabriel Vitelli met a girl through his Mob buddies. Pretty, fun-loving, interested in him. He fell for her— hard. But his dad raised him to take girls and dating seriously, so he didn't just have a fling with her. He bought her a ring and proposed."

"Erin," Phil said. "This is very interesting, but—"

"She said yes," Erin went on. "There was just one little problem. She was already pregnant, and Gabriel hadn't slept with her. She had him over a couple mornings ago. I think she tried to seduce him, with the idea of playing off the kid as his. It wouldn't be the first time a girl tried that trick. Unfortunately for her, Gabriel had straight-laced, old-fashioned ideas about marriage and sex. He didn't go for it. Then, in the course of their conversation, he found out about the pregnancy. In a fit of rage at her betrayal, he grabbed a butcher knife from the kitchen and killed her. He left a label over the bed so everyone would know just what she was. Then he ripped the engagement ring off her finger and left."

Erin shook her head. "The victim's downstairs neighbor was just getting home with the groceries. Sheer bad timing. They saw one another, him all covered with blood and still carrying the knife. Literally red-handed. She got inside and locked her door. After she was sure he'd gone, she placed an anonymous call to the NYPD. Gabriel, meanwhile, ditched the ring outside, where Rolf found it. Either he realized having it would incriminate him, or he just couldn't stand having it with him. Then he took off. He got rid of the knife and the bloody clothes; mobsters are good at that sort of thing. And the only true proof we have of him at the scene is our witness."

"Why didn't he kill her?" Phil asked. "It would've been a lot less trouble to do it then and there."

"Gabriel thinks of himself as a gentleman," Erin said. "He'd never kill an innocent bystander, especially a woman."

"But he wants her dead now," Phil observed.

"No, his dad wants her dead," Erin corrected. "I doubt Gabriel knows anything about that. And the witness is in WitSec as we speak, protected by Marshals. The Marshals are extra twitchy because of that botched hit on another protectee the other day."

"So they want someone on the inside to do the job," Phil said. "In other words, you."

"Yeah."

"You've done a great job convincing me it's time to bring you in and shut things down," Phil said. "You can't keep playing this game. If it's too dangerous to refuse, you've got no choice."

"Of course I do. Relax, Phil," she said, cracking a weary smile. "I'm not going to kill Teresa. Except that I am."

"Perception's far more important than reality," Carlyle said. "What matters is that Vitelli thinks she's done as he wishes."

"You want to fake her death," Phil said. "And make it *look* like you killed her."

"It'll be tricky," she said. "And we'll need to bring a few more people in on the secret, which is risky, but they're good people. I need you to set up a meeting now. Tonight."

"With whom?" Phil asked.

"Captain Holliday, Sarah Levine the medical examiner, you, the three of us, and Skip Taylor from the Bomb Squad."

"The Bomb Squad?"

"Yeah," Erin said. "I've got a plan, but it'll need every one of us."

"I can get everybody in the same room," Phil said. "But I can't promise they'll go along with whatever you're planning. I hope you know what you're doing."

"So do I."

Chapter 20

"Nice place," Erin said. "So this is where you bring your girlfriends?"

Corky grinned. "If I'm wanting to impress them, aye. Are you impressed?"

"I like your other apartment better," she said. "It looks like someone actually lives there. This looks like a damn movie set."

After some discussion, Phil had agreed to Corky's suggestion that they meet at his spare apartment in Tribeca. Erin had heard about Corky's love nest, but this was the first time she'd seen it. She couldn't deny it was fancy, well-located, and expensively furnished, but it did feel artificial. The living room had an actual bar, an impressive sound system, and the largest projection screen she'd seen outside a commercial movie theater. Even Carlyle, with his expensive suit, didn't quite look like he belonged. Phil was hopelessly out of place. The Lieutenant was looking around, hands in the pockets of his threadbare coat, taking the whole thing in. Ian stood impassively by the door, watching and waiting. Rolf was sticking close to Erin.

"The others should be here any minute," Phil said. "Holliday is bringing Dr. Levine. Taylor is coming separately."

"They need to make sure they're not being followed," Erin said tensely.

"Your Captain will be careful, darling," Carlyle said. "And I can't think why anyone would be following Mr. Taylor. Most lads don't want to be in the same place as a bomb technician."

He had a point, Erin realized. Skip was a former Army EOD man who'd joined the NYPD because it was the only place he could use the unique skill set he'd picked up in the military. He was completely unconnected to organized crime. Nobody had any reason to tail him. In fact, the Lucarellis probably had no idea who he was.

"Sorry," she muttered. "It's just nerves."

"Reading these other folks into the case is chancy," Phil said. "I know they won't deliberately let anything slip, but everyone who knows is another chance for something to come out."

"I know!" Erin snapped. "But we need them. I'll explain once we're all here."

"Would anyone care for a drink?" Corky offered. "I've a grand selection of beverages."

Nobody replied.

"I'll just get one for myself, then," Corky said and poured himself a double whiskey.

"Incoming, sir," Ian said. He wasn't looking into the hallway. He was relying on his ears. Erin cocked an ear, but didn't hear anything. But thanks to his warning, she was unsurprised when there was a knock at the door. Ian sidestepped, gave a quick look through the peephole, and opened the door.

Captain Holliday stepped in, Sarah Levine behind him. The Captain was wearing a black topcoat. It was unbuttoned and his right hand hovered near his belt buckle, but he seemed calm enough. He gave a once-over to the assembled people, nodding politely to Erin. Levine, clad in a long black coat of her own, appeared completely disinterested in the proceedings. She wasn't even looking at the others.

"Welcome," Corky said cheerfully. "Let me take that, love."

Levine, a confused expression on her face, allowed him to take her coat and hang it in the closet. Underneath, she was wearing hospital scrubs.

"You'd be the famous Sarah Levine, I presume," Corky went on. "I'd heard one could find right lovely flowers amidst death and decay, but I'd no notion how right they were."

"That's true," Levine said. "Decomposition produces excellent fertilizer." Her hair was tied back in a plain ponytail and she was wearing no makeup. She did not look particularly floral.

Erin exchanged glances with Carlyle and smothered a smile. It was going to be interesting watching the contest between Corky's relentless flirtation and Levine's near-total lack of social awareness.

"I just got a call from Officer Taylor," Holliday said, selecting a hanger for his own jacket and revealing that he was wearing a pistol, an old Colt Detective Special. "He's right behind us."

Sure enough, Ian opened the door again before Holliday and Levine had gotten more than a few steps into the apartment. Skip Taylor's hand was raised to knock. He and Ian stared at one another.

"How's it going?" Skip asked. "You'd be… Thompson, right?"

"Affirmative," Ian said. "Taylor?"

"Ten-four," Skip said. "Where'd you serve?"

"Sandbox and the 'Stan," Ian said. "Marines. Scout Sniper. You?"

"Two tours in the sand," Skip said. "Army. EOD."

Ian nodded. Then he did something Erin had never seen him do. He extended his hand, unprompted. Skip gave it a brief shake.

"Looks like we're all here," Holliday said, once Skip had divested himself of his tattered leather jacket and joined them in the living room. "I suppose we should get down to business. This is an unusual meeting, Detective. You called it, and I've gone to some trouble to rearrange my schedule to accommodate you. Would you care to clue us in?"

Erin took a deep breath. She wished she'd taken Corky up on his offer. A stiff drink might have steadied her.

"As some of you already know," she began, "for the past several months, I've been infiltrating the O'Malley criminal organization, pretending to be a dirty cop."

"This is top-secret information that does not leave this room," Holliday said, quietly but forcefully.

"I've been assisted in this by Mr. Carlyle and Mr. Corcoran," Erin went on, indicating the two Irishmen. Corky raised his whiskey glass and winked. "Both of them are cooperating fully with the NYPD."

"And I thought *I* had a dangerous job," Skip muttered.

"As a result of several things that have happened, I've created the impression in some circles that I'm an assassin for hire," Erin said. "Unfortunately, that means I've been given a contract I can't turn down."

"Why am I here?" Levine asked abruptly. "Where's the dead guy?"

"Nobody's dead," Erin said.

"Not yet, at any rate," Corky added. "But if you're needing a body to examine..."

"I've asked you here because I need your help," Erin said. "I've been ordered to kill a witness by the name of Teresa Tommasino."

Holliday's jaw clenched. "Detective," he said. "You know what that means."

She held up a hand. "Please, sir, hear me out. Carlyle's told me, time after time, that what actually happens isn't nearly as important as what people *think* happens. Of course I'm not going to kill her. I need all of you to help me make it look like she's dead. We're going to fake an assassination."

"What sort of assassination?" Holliday asked.

"Ms. Tommasino is in Witness Protection," Erin said. "She's under twenty-four-hour guard by US Marshals. We can't clue them in on it, either."

"Why not?" Holliday asked.

"Because the Feds are infiltrated," she said. "So is the NYPD. I know of one FBI agent who's compromised for sure, and there's probably others."

Holliday said nothing, but his eyes went very cold and hard.

"We have to be able to fool not just the Mafia, but the NYPD and the Feds, too," Erin said. "And it can't be obvious to the government that I'm behind it."

"Otherwise they'd have to arrest you," Corky said. "And you'd likely keel over and die from the sheer irony of it."

"We'll tell the Marshals they've been made," Erin said. "They'll believe it. They've had one safehouse attacked already. We'll say we need to move our witness. I'll escort her to a vehicle. We'll load her in. A few seconds later, that vehicle will be destroyed by an explosive device, apparently killing her. My cover will be preserved, Ms. Tommasino will be safe, and we'll have a senior member of the Lucarellis dead to rights on conspiracy to commit murder, once he pays me for the hit."

She finished and looked around the room. Everybody was staring at her. Even Levine was paying attention now. Corky was grinning. Carlyle was thoughtful. Skip's mouth hung open. Holliday's face was as unreadable as a block of granite.

Twenty seconds passed. Nobody moved. Nobody spoke.

"I get it," Skip said at last. "At least, I get why I'm here. You need me to build you a fake bomb."

"Nay, lad," Carlyle said. "I'll build the bomb. It's rather in my line, I'm sure you'd agree."

"You're the guy who'll be investigating the bombing," Erin explained to Skip. "You'll need to say the right things in your report."

Skip snapped his fingers. "Gotcha."

"And we need Levine because of the issue of remains," Erin said. "Obviously, we're not actually killing anybody. But we need enough evidence to convince people there was a body in the car. I was thinking maybe she has some tissue samples we could sprinkle around the area."

"You want me to falsify a coroner's report," Levine said. "You want me to lie in an official report."

"Well, yeah," Erin said. "That's why you need to know ahead of time."

"No," Levine said flatly.

"Come now, love," Corky said. "Your honesty's admirable, to be sure, but this is for a grand cause. Surely you can make an exception."

"Science doesn't lie," Levine said. "I can't say something happened at a crime scene if it didn't happen."

"*This* is your plan, O'Reilly?" Holliday said. He started quietly, but as he went on, his voice got louder. "You want to falsify a major police investigation and willfully deceive the United States government by getting a known IRA terrorist to set off an explosive device to blow up a car in the middle of New York City? *My city?!*"

Erin bit back an angry retort and waited for him to finish. Now, more than ever, she needed to appear cool, collected, and controlled.

"Sir," she said when he ran out of breath. "I can show you a photograph of an FBI special agent having a clandestine meeting with Vincenzo Moreno at a donut shop in New Jersey. You can verify with the Marshals that the attack on their safehouse came less than twenty-four hours after they informed the FBI that they needed to borrow the use of the building. Vinnie has eyes and ears everywhere in this city. I can't guarantee Ms. Tommasino's safety any other way."

"No one will be hurt, Captain," Carlyle said. "I'll swear to it."

"And just how do you plan on ensuring that?" Holliday demanded.

"It won't be a real bomb," Carlyle said. "Not precisely. I've been thinking on it, and I think I've a good design in mind. Though I'd welcome your input, Mr. Taylor."

Skip, surprised but pleased, nodded.

"So you won't actually be blowing up a car?" Holliday asked.

"Nay, I fear the car will have to go," Carlyle said. "But I'll construct a device that will be more flash than substance, and what force it has will go upward. As long as Erin can keep folk at a distance, say, five meters, it should be safe enough."

"Except for the woman who'll be getting into the car," Holliday said. "What's your plan for her?"

"We'll have a change of clothes in back," Corky said. "A police jacket, say, and one of those fine copper's hats. She goes in one side, takes off her coat, puts on the other one, throws a hat on her head, and scampers out the other side looking like one of

New York's Finest. Anyone who sees her will simply assume she's part of the security detail."

"And what happens to her then?" Holliday asked.

"We spirit her out of the city," Corky said. "Someplace far away, where Vitelli's lads couldn't reach her even if they knew about her, which they won't. Clean out of the state."

"I can't send a protection detail out of state," Holliday said. "And she'd have to be gone weeks. Months, more likely."

"We can't use cops for it," Erin said. "The only ones I'd trust with this a hundred percent are Webb and Neshenko, and a Major Crimes detective going missing might tip the bad guys off."

"So she goes by herself?" Holliday asked, shaking his head. "That's even worse."

"I'll look after her," Corky said.

Holliday stared at him. "You? You're a gangster!"

"You?" Erin said almost in unison with her commander. "No way!"

"Technically, I'm a confidential informant," Corky said. "More to the point, I owe Erin a favor. I did something foolish some little while back and put an innocent woman in danger. This may be my best chance to balance my ledger. Let me do this, Erin. I'll not let you down, I swear by all that's holy."

Ian, who'd resumed his watch on the apartment door, turned and looked at Corky. Erin saw the surprise and grudging respect in the former Marine's eyes.

"Just where would you be taking her?" Holliday asked.

"I'm sorry, lad," Corky said. "I can't tell you. It's best if nobody knows."

"Good Lord," Holliday muttered. "I can't believe I'm listening to this."

"We'll bring her back for the trial," Erin said. "By then, we should be able to work out a good temporary defense to keep her safe in the city."

"It'll work," Carlyle said softly. "They'll fall for it. And you'll have them dead to rights."

"It's way too risky," Holliday said. "And even supposing everything does work, just the way you're saying, is it worth it to get one guy? There's got to be another way to nail this dirtbag."

"It'll make my reputation on the street," Erin said. "Evan O'Malley almost trusts me. This will get rid of any doubts as to which side of the law I'm on. I'll be all the way inside, both with the O'Malleys and the Lucarellis. I can tear the guts out of two organized crime families at one go."

"I understand that," Holliday said. "But maybe we should go back to the part where you're setting off a bomb on a city street."

"I think it could work, boss," Skip said. "I mean, it's not exactly a bomb. It's more of a fireworks show."

Holliday gave him a hard look. "Your job is to *stop* bombs from blowing up, Taylor."

"Or to make sure they go off harmlessly," Skip said. "I've studied Cars Carlyle, sir. He's a damn artist. Those garbage truck devices back in the '90s... perfect. Clean as they come."

"You've got a fan," Holliday observed sourly, turning to Carlyle.

"I believe the point the lad's making is that the bombs in question neither killed nor injured anyone," Carlyle said. "If we're thinking of the same devices, that is. It might be superfluous of me to point out that I was never charged, nor even arrested, in connection with the destruction of any garbage truck."

"And you've got immunity, in any case," Holliday said. "I saw the deal you signed with the DA. So leave the bullshit at the door."

"I'd like to think this is a chance to prove my good citizenship," Carlyle said.

"Why isn't Lieutenant Keane here?" Holliday asked abruptly. "This definitely concerns Internal Affairs and he's already read into the undercover operation."

"Frankly, sir, because I don't trust him with this," Erin said.

"Whether you trust him or not isn't the point, O'Reilly," Holliday shot back. "He has a right and a responsibility to know about this."

"Can you prove he isn't connected to Vinnie the Oil Man?" she asked.

"Of course I can't. How do you know I'm not? Or Taylor? Or Levine?"

"I don't know," Erin said. "Not for sure."

"That's the problem with a long-term undercover op," Phil said. "After a while, the lines get blurred. You don't know who to trust."

"You're here because I can't do this without permission, sir," Erin said to Holliday. "And Phil is my undercover liaison. The rest of you are strictly need-to-know, on the basis of your skills and positions. Keane doesn't need to know about this, so he doesn't."

"That sets a very dangerous precedent," Holliday said.

"Yes, sir."

The Captain looked at the carpet. He shook his head. "This is an extremely unusual situation," he said. "I've always tried to have my officers' backs, as long as their hearts are in the right place."

"Yes, sir." Erin didn't dare say anything else.

"If this goes sideways, I won't be able to protect you. If a civilian or an officer, either NYPD or Federal, gets injured or killed, you'll lose your shield. You'll probably face civil or even criminal charges."

"I know that, sir."

"You still think this is the best plan?"

"It's the only plan from where I'm standing, sir. If I don't do this, there's a good chance I'll be killed. If this goes wrong, I'll take full responsibility for it."

"No, you won't," Holliday said. "If this blows up, nobody walks away clean. We'll all get stained."

"So we're on?" Erin asked.

"I won't order you not to," he sighed. "But I'll tell you it had damned well better work exactly the way you say."

Erin nodded. "Thank you, sir." She turned to Levine. "Doc, I know how you feel about this."

"No you don't," Levine said. "It's physically impossible for one person to know what another person is feeling. Our nervous systems are not interconnected. Leaving that aside, feelings don't enter into this. I'm being completely logical. My job is the pursuit of facts through forensic analysis of human remains. If I falsify my reports, I'm not doing my job properly."

Erin stepped forward and laid a hand on Levine's arm. "Doc... Sarah, please," she said. "This is important."

"So is my work," Levine said. "I can't list a false cause of death."

"But nobody's dying!" Erin exclaimed. "There won't *be* a body!"

Levine blinked. "There has to be a body," she said. "Otherwise it wouldn't be a murder scene."

Erin stared at the other woman. "No, the whole point is that we're not killing her. We only need to make it look like we did."

"And for that you need a body," Levine said. "A car bomb isn't powerful enough to vaporize a corpse. There would be a large quantity of human remains. If you want verisimilitude, you need a human body in the vehicle."

"Which is why you're here," Erin said, speaking slowly, fighting a desperate battle with her own patience. "How would you make it look like a woman died in a car bomb? Hypothetically?"

Levine shrugged. "Hypothetically, the action most likely to produce a credible result would be to acquire a cadaver of the same sex and nearly identical height, weight, hair and eye color, and as many other congruent characteristics as possible. Then you'd destroy that body in place of the living woman."

"A cadaver," Erin said.

"Brilliant," Corky said. "Now we just need a dead colleen who looks like your Tommasino lass."

Captain Holliday's jaw worked. His mustache twitched. "This just keeps getting better," he said. "Now we're grave-robbers."

"Sarah," Erin said. "Didn't you go to medical school?"

"Correct," Levine said. "Johns Hopkins School of Medicine."

"When you graduated, you took the Hippocratic Oath, didn't you?"

"I took a comparable oath," Levine said. "It isn't the verbatim Oath of Hippocrates. For one thing, it wasn't in Greek."

"What did you swear?"

"I do solemnly swear, by that which I hold most sacred, that I will be fully committed to those I serve, and just, and loyal to the profession of medicine and its members; that I will lead my life, and practice my art, in uprightness and honor; that into whatsoever house I shall enter, it shall be for the good of the sick to the utmost of my power, holding myself aloof from wrong, from corruption, and from the tempting of others to vice; that I will exercise my art solely for the care of my patients, and will give no drug, and perform no operation, without justifiable purpose, nor ever suggest it; that whatsoever I shall see or hear of the lives of men and women which is not fitting to be spoken, I will keep inviolably secret. These things I do promise; and in proportion, as I am faithful to this my oath, may happiness and good repute be ever mine; the opposite, if I shall be forsworn."

Levine recited the lengthy promise calmly, clinically, the way she always talked. Still, Erin felt a lump in her throat. She remembered her own oath of service, which she'd taken at graduation from the Police Academy. The idea that promises really did matter to people, even in this modern age, was a strangely beautiful and touching one.

"You're going to be saving Teresa's life," Erin said quietly. "Along with Carlyle's. And mine."

Levine met her eye. In her gaze, Erin saw a softness she'd never suspected. "I'll fix the reports," the Medical Examiner said. "Afterward. I'll make up a set of accurate ones and keep them to one side, so I can correct the record."

"Of course," Erin said.

"The city morgue is the best place to look," Levine said briskly. Just like that, she was all business again. "They always have a number of unidentified cadavers. The usual procedure is to periodically inter them in mass graves on Hart's Island. These cadavers are placed in the custody of the Chief Medical Examiner."

"That'd be your chief?" Corky asked.

"Correct," Levine said. "However, these bodies are tracked and accounted for. I can't just divert one. I can, however, request a cadaver for examination. The paperwork would usually take two to four weeks to process, but I believe I can abbreviate that process. When do you need the body?"

"As soon as possible," Erin said. "Tomorrow night, or the day after at the latest."

"I'll need a physical description of the body type you're looking for," Levine said. "As precise as possible. An exact match will almost certainly not be available, but we can probably match basic ethnicity and size."

"That should be sufficient," Carlyle said. "This won't be a terribly violent explosion as such things go, but I imagine the mess will be considerable."

"I'll get her measurements to you," Erin said. "What else do you need?"

"A location to deliver the remains," Levine said. "And your personal assurance that this is necessary, and that you will treat the deceased with the respect she deserves."

"Absolutely," Erin said. On the tail of Levine's med-school vow, she was very conscious of what she was promising. In that room, words seemed to carry more weight than usual.

Chapter 21

The meeting broke up after that. Levine and Holliday left almost immediately, Levine to get started on procuring a suitable corpse, Holliday to go wherever NYPD Captains went when they weren't dealing with difficult subordinates. Erin suspected the Captain's evening plans included a very large bottle of antacid.

Skip hung around. He and Carlyle stepped off to one side and started talking explosives. Corky offered Phil a drink, which Phil politely declined. The Lieutenant came in close to Erin and spoke quietly, for her ears alone.

"This is a gamble," he said. "And it goes right up to the line. I just hope it doesn't cross it."

"It's okay, Phil," she said. "Really. This is worth the stretch."

"Can you trust her to that guy?" He didn't point at Corky, but his meaning was plain.

"Yeah," Erin said. "He's a shameless flirt, but he'll respect her. And if he says he'll protect her, he means it. He's been different ever since Mickey Connor. He's got something to prove, not just to me, but to himself. He's always seen himself as a hopeless screw-up. If he pulls this off, it'll be good for him."

"We're the NYPD, not a self-help therapy group," Phil murmured. "I can't understand how you can still see the best in people after all you've been through."

"It's either that or I end up like Sergeant Brown in Vice, thinking the whole world's a dumpster fire," she said. "That's no way to live. Besides, if Corky lets anything happen to her, he knows I'll kill him."

"I'd better not be involved with this part of the operation from here on out," Phil said. "I'd just get in the way. Be careful." He offered his hand.

Erin shook with him. "Copy that."

Phil nodded to the others, turned, and left the apartment. It made sense for them to stagger their departure times, just on the off-chance anyone was watching. Erin watched him go, then drifted over to see what Skip and Carlyle were talking about.

"They don't really want a lad like me for this sort of work," Carlyle was saying. "Nor you, come to that. You've the right of it, lad. This is fireworks, special effects. What you'd want is one of those Hollywood lads."

"We should have a special effects guy on the payroll," Skip agreed. "You're thinking black powder?"

"Aye," Carlyle said. "And gasoline. It burns clean and bright. You'll get a grand fireball, but it won't stick to things like fuel oil or napalm would. The worst anyone nearby will get is a bit of heat and a wee bit of concussion. And the blast won't create much in the way of shrapnel."

"Vertical blast," Skip said. "Pretty much straight up. Debris mortar?"

"That's what I'm thinking," Carlyle said. "A good length of stout pipe with a baseplate welded on. I've a shop in my cellar. I can throw it together in no time at all."

"Remember, we need to render the body unrecognizable," Skip said. "So it better have enough bang for that."

"I'll take out the seat and plant the device right under the poor lass," Carlyle said. "The body will take the full force."

"Careful of bone shrapnel," Skip said.

"Wait a second," Erin said, entering the conversation. "*Bone shrapnel?*"

"It's something we saw a lot with suicide bombers in Iraq," Skip explained. "When a guy's wearing a bomb vest, you don't have to worry about the squishy bits, but the bone can be dangerous. And don't get me started on teeth."

"Teeth?" Erin repeated weakly.

"You know how bad guys pack their bombs with ball bearings?" Skip said. "Teeth are the same way. They get going fast enough, those things can kill you. I've picked teeth out of corpses."

"Rolf knows all about high-speed tooth delivery," she said, trying to make a joke to cover a sudden surge of nausea. "But maybe not quite the same way."

"The point the lad's making is that we don't want to damage anyone with bits of the dear departed," Carlyle said. "It's a legitimate concern. We're more than flesh and bone, darling, but not less."

"Sounds like you've got the situation under control," Erin said.

"I'll be needing a car to destroy," he said. "And a few hours in which to install the device, free from interruptions."

"Right," Erin said. "I'll see what I can turn up."

"Corky could provide one."

"No. Nobody's stealing a car just so we have one to blow up. The car needs to be clean, legally obtained. I'll get the vehicle. Holliday can get me one that we've confiscated."

"Government-sanctioned theft. Even better." Carlyle smiled. "You could be quite the criminal mastermind, darling, if once you set your mind to it. I think all the necessary pieces are falling in place."

"Except one," Erin said. "The hardest part."

"What's that, darling?"

"I need to tell Teresa."

*   *   *

Erin was already thinking about going to the hotel, and what she'd say to Teresa once she got there, when she had a rush of common sense. It was after eleven o'clock; Teresa was a civilian and, though she might still be awake, she was probably in bed. Also, Erin herself had been awake for two days straight with only a short nap in the middle. She wasn't in any condition to have a delicate conversation with a scared schoolteacher.

"Let's go home," she told Carlyle.

"You heard her, lad," Carlyle said to Ian, who aimed the Mercedes toward the Barley Corner. Carlyle was riding up front. Erin was in back with Rolf. The dog was lying down, his head in her lap. She was rubbing his ears.

"I can't believe Corky volunteered for this," she told Carlyle.

"To rescue a damsel in distress?" he replied. "Surely you're joking."

"If he sleeps with her, I'll cut his balls off," she growled.

"Fair enough. You're the one who vouched for him to your Captain."

"It made sense. He's already part of the case, so there's no extra security risk. He doesn't have any family or firm attachments here. But I don't know how he'll square it with Evan."

"Let Corky worry about that. I imagine he's already thought up a story."

"God, I'm tired," Erin said. "But I don't know if I'll be able to sleep. This whole thing's probably going down tomorrow night. We'd better do it under cover of darkness, and Vitelli said I had forty-eight hours. That gives us one more night."

"All the more reason to rest while you can."

"We had a saying in the Corps," Ian said without turning around. "When they stop shooting, start sleeping."

"This from the guy who stayed up five days straight," Erin said, smiling.

"No choice," he replied. "Didn't have anyone watching my back. Only guy with me was hurt too bad. You've got a different situation. Got a safe base of operations, good security. Don't have to worry about getting popped in your sleep."

"That's true, I guess," she said.

"Not guessing," Ian said. "I'll stay on duty, on perimeter. Nobody's getting near you."

"You don't have to do that for me."

"Part of the job." He caught himself before he could add his customary "ma'am." Erin had been very firm about that.

Once they were back at Carlyle's apartment, Erin did feel a little better, but not much. The problem was, she wasn't worried for her own sake. She was thinking of the completely innocent woman she'd dragged into this mess. She was the one who'd convinced Teresa to tell what she knew.

"I'll be in the cellar," Carlyle said. "In my shop. I've a bomb to build."

"Be careful," she said. "I like your hands just the way they are, with ten fingers."

"This is child's play, darling," he said. "Black powder's safe enough, as long as you keep it out of the threads of a pipe bomb. It's not as if I'm sculpting nitroglycerin."

"You haven't built one of these things in a while," she said. Then she paused. "Have you?"

"Nay," he chuckled. "Not since the alleged truck bombings on Long Island, and that's near twenty years gone. But it's like riding a bicycle. It's not something a lad forgets how to do."

"How often does the bicycle explode?"

"You never can tell," he said. "I grew up in Belfast, remember? Bombs exploding on my street weren't entirely unheard-of. Don't fret yourself, darling."

"I think I'm more bothered by the fact that you've got a bomb lab in the basement. I've been sleeping here!"

"It's a workshop, darling, nothing more. I don't keep explosives on the premises. I'll have to send out for the powder. Sleep well."

He kissed her and went downstairs. Erin got ready for bed. She lay back on Carlyle's fine silk sheets. Her head throbbed with exhaustion and unwelcome thoughts. The knowledge that her lover was two floors below, building a homemade explosive device, wasn't exactly comforting. She told herself he'd be fine. He was careful and competent. He'd never accidentally blown himself up. Then again, that was the sort of mistake a bomb-maker only tended to make once.

"Rolf," she called quietly. "*Hupf!*"

The K-9 leaped easily up onto the bed. Erin patted the sheets next to her. He circled once and lay down, curling his snout under his bushy tail. Erin wrapped an arm around his furry, reassuring bulk.

Teresa would've been in trouble no matter what, Erin said to herself. The moment they arrested Gabriel Vitelli, he would've remembered the woman on the landing. He would've assumed she'd talked. That was almost certainly what had made Old Man Vitelli take out the contract in the first place. Whatever Erin might have done, the only way they wouldn't have ended up in this situation would have been to let Angel Face go.

Angel Face, she thought groggily. What an odd name for a gangster. She thought of Carlyle's staunch Catholicism and the weird religious faith possessed by a lot of Mob guys. How could they possibly believe they were on the side of the angels? She remembered Gabriel talking about Isabella, the girl he'd murdered.

"I was always respectful of her."

He had a very strange way of showing respect. Thank God Carlyle wasn't like that. He was more angelic than Gabriel, Erin thought. Like that angel statue over the graves of Valentino's parents; solid, watchful, beautiful.

Erin, her thoughts wandering, one arm still resting on her dog, wasn't aware of falling asleep.

*   *   *

She woke up feeling a strange mix of refreshed and tense. Rolf had gotten up sometime during the night, as dogs tended to do. He was lying on the floor in front of the closet. There was no sign of Carlyle.

Erin got out of bed and got dressed in her running clothes. Rolf was instantly up and ready, wagging eagerly. Time was tight, but she had to do something about her nerves. A quick jog would be just the thing.

It was a little before six in the morning. The Barley Corner was quiet and empty. The pub served breakfast, but didn't open until six-thirty. Erin was pretty sure an explosion would've woken her up, but she decided to check the basement and make sure Carlyle hadn't electrocuted himself or something. The cellar door was locked, but Carlyle had given her a full set of keys. She opened the door and went down the stairs.

"It's me," she called, not wanting to startle him. It was a bad idea sneaking up on a bomb-maker.

"In here, darling," he replied.

She found him in his workshop, a place she hadn't previously had much occasion to go. It was a well-appointed room, stocked with all sorts of tools, both hand-operated and electrical. Carlyle was at his workbench. His coat hung on a peg on the far side of the room, along with his necktie. His shirtsleeves were rolled up. He was dirty, smudged, and dusted with something shiny and metallic. He turned to face her, showing a pair of safety glasses.

"Is that glitter?" she asked, pointing to his face.

"Steel dust," he replied. "I've been cutting and welding a fair deal of metal."

"How's it coming?"

"Nearly done." He showed her what he'd made. It was a squat tube of steel pipe, reinforced by bands of metal that had been welded around it. It pointed straight up, resting atop a flat piece of plate steel with holes drilled in the corners.

"It looks like a cannon," Erin said.

"That's effectively what it is," Carlyle said. "The charge loads from the top. It fires the same way, up and out. It'll make quite the light show. I hope to make the charge the proper force to blow a fine great hole in the top of the automobile."

"Why?"

"So the blast won't go out the sides. We don't want window-glass flying too far. Car safety glass shatters into wee pebbles, rather than the jagged shards you'd get from plate glass, but someone could still get hurt."

"How will you set it off?"

"Remote detonation. I'll use a blasting cap in the bottom, wired to a cheap cellular phone. Another advantage of black powder and gasoline; they ignite rather easily. Are you off for a run?"

"Yeah."

"Take Ian with you. You'll be wanting him about you more than I will. I've the rest of my ingredients ready to hand. All I'm needing now is the car we'll be using, and two or three hours to put it all together."

"Great. I'll let you know."

She found Ian in the security room next to the restrooms, watching the monitor. The Barley Corner had cameras at both entrances and in the main room. Though he'd obviously been up all night, Ian showed no sign of fatigue.

"Care to come for a run with me?" she asked.

"Affirmative," he said. "Can you give me five to get changed? I've got PT gear here." He nodded to a duffel bag under the desk.

"Is there anything you're *not* prepared for?" she asked.

He thought it over as if it had been a serious question. "Plenty," he decided. "But I'm good at improvising."

Ian drove them to Central Park in Carlyle's Mercedes. Rolf kept poking his head between the seats to see where they were going. Ian steered through the early-morning New York traffic with his usual outward calm.

"How do you feel about all this?" Erin asked.

"All what?" he replied, keeping his eyes on the road.

"Changing sides."

"Haven't changed sides."

"That's your only stake in this business? Carlyle?"

"That's how it was at the start," he said. "Then mission creep set in."

"How do you mean?"

"Mission creep is when you start with one objective," he explained. "But then the brass comes in and says you've got to do this other thing, too. Then another, and another. Goalposts keep moving. Pretty soon the mission's changed so much, not even the planners know what it was supposed to look like."

"I bet that happened to you a lot in the Marines."

"All the time."

"What does the mission creep look like here?"

"Started out looking after Mr. Carlyle. Not a problem. Then you. No big deal, you can pretty much take care of yourself."

"Thanks."

"Just stating facts. Then the thing with Ms. Finneran happened. Complication. After that, wasn't just a security gig. More like a covert op. Had to add information security to physical security. Then your people got pulled in. Your brother's wife and kids. Now? This is a pretty simple op, compared to what we've been doing. Single objective, fixed target."

"Okay, I get that," she said. "But how do you *feel* about it? Do you think you're doing the right thing?"

"Didn't used to worry about that. Most of the time, nobody cares if you're doing the right thing or not. Didn't care myself until that thing that happened in the Sandbox."

Ian was referring to the woman and baby he'd mistakenly shot in Fallujah. Erin swallowed. That was one hell of a thing to carry around with you.

"And now?" she asked.

"Now? First time in a long time, pretty sure I'm doing the right thing. You say this is how we save this lady? I'm in, do what I can. Wish I was doing more."

They got out of the car, stretched, and started their run. The air felt unusually heavy for September, thick and moist. A low layer of fog hugged the grass. The sun came up around six-thirty, but the light failed to burn off the moisture.

"Storm coming," Ian said between breaths.

"Great," Erin muttered. "That's just what we need."

"It's a good thing," he replied. "Whole point of this op is misdirection. Rain and darkness should help."

Erin hoped he was right. But weather was just one of the many variables she couldn't control, so she tried to put it out of her mind. The thick, wet air stuck in her throat and made it hard to breathe. Sweat poured down her. Rolf, trotting beside her, was panting. His tongue, looking twice as large as usual, hung halfway to the ground. But they stuck it out and finished their loop.

After returning to grab a quick shower and change of clothes, Erin headed to the Eightball. There was a lot to do and only a few daylight hours to do it in. Neither Webb nor Vic had arrived yet, which was just as well.

Her first stop was Captain Holliday's office. The Captain was behind his desk. He looked tired.

"O'Reilly," he said in the tone of a man facing an inevitable and unpleasant meeting. "Come in."

Erin closed the door behind her. She didn't waste time. "We need a car. One the Department won't want back."

"I figured that was coming," Holliday said. "I already started the ball rolling. If you go to Impounds, they ought to have something for you. There'll be a paper trail, but that's fine. If there wasn't, people might wonder how you came by the car."

"Thank you, sir."

"Has the principal been notified?"

"She'll be my next stop after this. I need to get the car first, so we'll have time for the, uh, modifications."

Holliday nodded. "Anything else you need from my office?"

"This is going to make one hell of a stink," Erin said. "I'd appreciate any PR cover you can provide. And don't let Angel Face out of jail. We still have to hold him for trial. Is there any way we can file the witness statement with his lawyer today?"

"Why?" Holliday asked.

"There's no reason not to, sir. And this way, when our witness gets blown up, we'll already have her information on the books. That way, when the trial rolls around..."

"We can produce her on the witness stand, because her testimony was part of discovery," Holliday said. He cracked a weary smile. "Sneaky. I didn't know you thought like a shady lawyer."

"Under the circumstances, I'll take that as a compliment, sir."

"You're welcome."

"And is there any way we can make sure Judge Barberis isn't hearing this case?"

"Not without tampering with judicial process," Holliday said. "Why not him?"

"Because I'm about ninety-five percent sure he's on the Lucarelli payroll."

"A New York City judge in the pocket of the Mafia," Holliday said quietly. "It's like the 1930s all over again. All I can do is talk to the DA. But without proof, that sort of accusation can do more harm than good. I'll have to be circumspect."

"I appreciate anything you can do, sir."

"Anything else I should know about?"

Erin shook her head. "I just wanted to say thank you, sir. For trusting me and having my back."

"You're one of mine," Holliday said. "The day I stop going to bat for my officers is the day I hand in my shield. I don't need your thanks, O'Reilly. Just prove me right. Give me results."

Erin drew herself to attention and snapped off the best parade-ground salute she knew how to do. "Yes, sir."

Chapter 22

Erin needed to get to the Impound lot next, which presented a slight logistical problem. If she was going to drive a vehicle away from the site, what was she supposed to do with her own car?

The solution presented itself in the form of a surly Russian. Vic dragged himself into Major Crimes just as Erin was leaving Holliday's office.

"Vic!" she said. "Glad to see you. We've got an errand to run."

"Goodie," he muttered. "Where are we going?"

"Impound lot," she said. "I'm picking up a car."

"What for?"

She hadn't wanted to explain this, but it was inevitable, and she'd been thinking of a plausible cover that had the advantage of being almost completely true. "We may need to move our witness on short notice. I want an unmarked, non-police vehicle, just in case."

"Really? I thought she was the Marshals' problem now."

"You trust the Feds?"

"As a general rule? No. In this case? Yeah, I kinda do."

"This is just a precaution. I cleared it with the Captain. But I need you, because we'll end up with two cars."

"Okay. Beats doing paperwork, I guess. We'll take my Taurus."

The parking garage was staffed by overweight, under-motivated police officers. Most of the cops Erin encountered took physical fitness halfway seriously, because they knew their lives might depend on being able to outrun or outfight a perp; Lieutenant Webb was an exception, but he was getting close to retirement and didn't mix it up on the street anymore. Not so the guy she met at the Impound lot. He actually had a box of donuts right there in his gatehouse with him, and it was already half-empty even though the day had just started.

"Detective O'Reilly," she said, sliding her shield through the hole in the booth's window. "This is Detective Neshenko. We're from the Eight. Captain Holliday put in a request for a car."

"Oh, yeah," the officer said. "Rush order, wasn't it? Came in overnight, said you needed it ASAP. What for?"

"Major Crimes operation," she said, which was essentially true. "What've you got for me?"

"Vern can take you to it." The cop turned and shouted, "Hey, Vern! Got that Major Crimes gold shield up front!"

Vern ambled out. He was, if anything, bigger than the gate guard. He wore a gun, but was carrying a clipboard. He gave Erin an unhurried, appreciative look that started at her legs and worked its way up, but she was used to it and didn't let it bother her.

"Okay," he said. "C'mon back. Got a pretty sweet ride for you."

"What is it?"

"Black Chevy Suburban, modified."

"How so?"

Vern grinned. "Have a look."

They went around a corner and Erin saw a big, black SUV.

"Wow," Vic said. "That car was definitely bought by some guy with a really tiny dick."

"That looks like what the FBI ride around in," she said.

"Like I said," Vic said. "Really tiny dick."

Vern guffawed. "We grabbed it off a gang boss," he said. "Punk was worried about other bad guys gunning for him, so it's got bulletproof glass, tinted past the legal limit of course, and armored door panels. It's basically a tank. Gets shitty gas mileage, but anybody wants to stop you, they'll need a damn rocket launcher to do it."

"It doesn't have machine-guns behind the headlights, does it?" Erin joked.

"Nah, but I heard they found an Uzi in the glove compartment."

"What do you guys usually do with something like this?"

"We sell most of the confiscated vehicles at auction," Vern said. "But we can't sell this one. You think we want some joker running around New York in a friggin' armored car? The ones we can't sell, we send to a recycling plant on Long Island. They shred 'em into scrap metal. Give it a week, this would've gone down there. How long you need it for?"

Erin hadn't thought about that. She buried a sudden mad impulse to tell him she only needed it for a day, after which the Long Island plant wouldn't have to bother. It'd be scrap metal no matter what.

"A week should be plenty," she said.

"Sure. Just sign these forms." He handed her the clipboard and a pen. She signed.

"Keys?" she asked.

"Here." He produced a key ring and handed it over. "You wanna be a little careful when you start driving her. She corners kinda funny, probably on account of all that extra weight in the door panels."

"I always wanted one of these," Vic said, looking the massive vehicle over in much the same way Vern had ogled Erin.

"Because you've got a tiny dick?" Erin asked innocently.

"My dick is none of your business."

"Thank God for small favors."

"I see what you did there."

"Did you need a magnifying glass to see it?"

"Okay, okay. Where are you going with this thing? Back to the Eightball?"

"I've got a place to stash it. I'll meet you back at the station."

Vern was right. After driving her Charger with its eight-cylinder police engine, the armored Suburban handled like an overloaded oil tanker. Erin drove carefully, leaving wide margins. Rolf sat in the shotgun seat, enjoying a rare opportunity to ride up front. His tongue hung out and he watched the New York streets with great interest.

Erin called Carlyle on the way. "I've got the car," she reported. "Where do you want it?"

"Corky knows a mechanic just down the street," he said. "Take it to O'Leary's Body Shop. I'll be waiting."

"Will Mr. O'Leary be discreet?"

"He works with Corky all the time. He knows to keep his mouth shut."

Mr. O'Leary was a grizzled man with a salt-and-pepper beard, several missing teeth, and only three fingers on his right hand. When Erin carefully drove the Suburban into the shop, he was standing watching her, hands on his hips, another mechanic next to him. Both men wore grease-stained overalls and work shirts.

Erin did a double-take. The other man was Carlyle, less dressed-up than she'd ever seen him. He smiled and gave her a wink he'd doubtless learned from Corky. O'Leary grunted and walked away.

"I've paid him to take the rest of the day off," Carlyle explained. "In the meantime, I've the run of the place."

"That sounds expensive," she said.

"Not compared to some of the things I've done."

"I've never seen you so... disheveled."

"You'd hardly expect me to wear a suit while disassembling an automobile," he said. "What am I working with here?"

She explained. Carlyle listened, nodding and rubbing his chin.

"The armor's a fine thing," he said. "It'll contain the blast and focus it upward. You ought to be able to stand within three to five meters. No closer than three, though. It'll be safe, but noisy. Now I'd best get to work."

"I'll need to pick it up sometime this evening," she said. "When will it be ready?"

"Any time after five ought to do."

"Thanks," she said, giving him a quick kiss and handing him the keys. Then she frowned. "Damn!"

"What?"

"I have to get back to the Eightball. My car's there."

"I'll ask Ian to drop you off."

"You know he's been up all night, right? He may not be at his best."

"Oh aye, but just try telling the lad to go home. Not to worry, Ian tired is worth three ordinary well-rested lads. He's sticking around until this business is resolved. He does worry about the two of us."

She smiled. "He's right to worry. We do have a way of getting in trouble."

"And out of it again," he said. "Ta, darling. Do remember to leave time for acquiring our... additional passenger."

"I'll get to that. See you this evening."

Ian got Erin and Rolf back to the Eightball without incident. Erin went straight to the garage, got into her Charger, and headed for the Hilton at JFK Airport. This required yet another trip across the East River. The airport was just a few miles from Canarsie Cemetery. If she'd had this plan a little earlier, she could have combined the trips. As it was, she was running up the mileage on her car.

Rolf didn't care. He got to go for another car ride with his favorite person in the world. As far as he was concerned, this was the best of all possible plans.

Erin kept reflexively checking her rearview mirrors, looking for a tail. That was ridiculous. Even if the Mafia were following her around, it didn't matter now. She was working for them. So what if they found out where Teresa was? The witness was only a few hours from apparent death. If the Mob knew Erin was going to see her, it would just seem like she was casing the joint and getting ready to make the hit. It would strengthen the illusion.

She still checked the mirrors. If Mafia thugs were on her ass, she'd rather know about it. She didn't see anyone suspicious, but that didn't make her feel much better. She had an unpleasant crawly feeling on her spine. The weather was playing hell with her nerves. She wished it would go ahead and rain. That might break the tension. But the clouds just kept piling up and getting darker.

She got to the airport hotel and parked. Then she remembered she didn't know which room the Marshals were in. Nor did she have a direct line to them. So she had to call the main office and get patched through to Calley.

"Calley," the Marshal said.

"This is O'Reilly," she said. "I need to talk to your protectee."

"Okay, I'll get her on the line."

"No, face to face."

There was a pause. Then Calley said, "Why?" He didn't sound happy.

"Some stuff about her testimony and the case. I'm in the parking lot. Don't worry, I wasn't followed."

"You're sure about that?"

"I've dealt with Mob guys before, Calley. Yeah, I'm sure. I just need the room number and I'll be right up."

"This isn't good procedure, O'Reilly. You shouldn't be here unless it's an emergency."

"I'm hoping it won't become one. Look, I'm already here. What do you want me to do?"

He sighed. "Okay, room 519. Geez. I've never had this much trouble with protection details."

Erin saw nothing out of the ordinary at the hotel. She didn't like taking the elevator—Ian's influence—but she did it anyway, knowing that the only gunmen in the building would be guys wearing stars. She and Rolf rode up to the fifth floor, got off, and walked to room 519. After a quick glance up and down the hallway, which was empty, she knocked.

The door opened a crack, showing the chain lock and the massive shape of Marshal Hodges. He looked at her, grunted, and unfastened the chain.

The Marshals had gotten two adjoining rooms. The connecting door stood open. Hodges and the Marshal who'd driven away from Teresa's apartment were in 519. Calley and Teresa were in 517. Teresa was sitting on the edge of the bed, looking tense. When she saw Erin, she sprang to her feet and stared at her.

"If I could have the room for a few minutes, Marshal?" Erin asked Calley.

"Sure," he said. Then, to Teresa, "We'll be right next door, ma'am." He joined his comrades in the other room.

Erin closed the connecting door and turned to face Teresa. "Ms. Tommasino, we need to talk about something important," she said.

"What? What is it?" Teresa was wringing her hands nervously. "What's happened now?"

Erin knew she had to handle this carefully. If she said the wrong thing, the woman might panic. Teresa might faint, or even worse, bolt.

"Teresa, you need to listen to me very carefully," she said, laying a hand on Teresa's shoulder. "I'm going to keep you safe. I promise. No matter what. As long as you do what I say, you'll be okay."

"You said I was safe before," Teresa said. "That's why I'm here, not at home."

"But you can't stay here," Erin said. "I've got contacts on the street. Valentino Vitelli knows his son saw you. His son wouldn't have hurt you, but the old man will do anything to protect his boy. Do you understand? Anything. We've been lucky so far. We got you out of your apartment just in time. But they're looking for you. If they find you, they will kill you. But that's not going to happen."

Teresa's flesh was trembling violently under Erin's hand. Her eyes were very big and wide. "Oh God," she whispered. "What am I going to do?"

"There's only one way they'll stop looking for you," Erin went on. "They have to believe you're not a threat."

"Then I won't testify," Teresa said. "I'll... I'll sign something that swears I didn't see anything!"

Erin shook her head. "That's not how the Mafia operates," she said. "The only way you're not a threat to them is if you're not alive. So we're going to get you out of town. Tonight. And we're going to do it in a way that makes it look like you've been killed."

"I don't understand."

"This evening, if we're lucky, it'll be raining. In any case, it'll be dark. I'll come back and tell the Marshals they've been compromised. I'll have a car. You'll go out to the car with me. Do you still have that light-blue coat you were wearing earlier?"

"Yes, of course," Teresa said, bewildered. "What does that have to do with anything?"

"That's good. It's bright and conspicuous. You'll wear that. You'll get into the car when I tell you to. Inside, there'll be another jacket for you, a police jacket. And a hat. You'll change into those as quickly as you can. There'll also be a body in the back seat with you."

"A... body?" Teresa repeated.

"Yes," Erin said. "We'll be doing a switch. Just leave your blue coat on the seat next to it. Once you've got the police jacket and hat on, you'll slide across to the other side of the car and get out. Close the door and walk away from the car. Don't run, walk. One of my people will be waiting for you nearby. I'll tell you where he'll be, and what sort of car he'll be driving. When you're a little ways away from the other car, it'll explode."

Teresa just stared at her, mouth open.

"It'll be loud and it'll be scary," Erin said. "When that happens, you'll want to run. *Don't.* Walk briskly. Don't look around, don't look back. The rest of us will be fine. Get in the car I'll tell you to. My friend's name is James. He's skinny, redheaded, and smiles a lot. He'll be watching for you. Once you get in that car, he'll take care of the rest. He'll look after you. You'll be fine, Teresa, just fine. It'll look like a car bombing killed you. Nobody will know different. Do you have any questions?"

Erin saw whole volumes of questions in Teresa's eyes, but it took the schoolteacher a few moments to gather her wits.

"How… how big an explosion?" Teresa asked.

"Big enough. It'll look and sound worse than it is. We've got our best explosives guys working on it. You won't be in any danger." Erin truly hoped that was true.

"Can I call my mother? To let her know I'm okay?"

"No. Absolutely not. You can't call anyone, can't talk to anyone. James will get you clean out of New York. Nobody else will know exactly where you are, and only a few people will know you're still alive. That's the best way we can guarantee your safety. But if your parents find out, they won't be able to keep it a secret. Next thing you know, the Mafia will hear about it, and we'll be in the same position as before, or worse."

"But… but Mom will think I'm… dead. My whole family…"

Erin nodded patiently. "Yes, that's the point. I'm sorry, Teresa. I know it'll hurt them. But it won't be forever. You've just got to look down the road to when you get to see them again. It'll be like a miracle then."

"How long?" Teresa asked in a very small voice.

"I don't know exactly. That depends on the District Attorney. He'll put the case together as fast as he can, but it'll be a few months, I'm afraid."

"*Months?!*" Teresa said in a strangled voice.

Erin nodded again. "I'm sorry," she said. It was always an inadequate thing to say, but it felt especially pitiful now.

Teresa started to cry. Erin put out an arm and awkwardly held her. The woman's shoulders shook with half-suppressed sobs.

"I… I should have… kept… kept… my mouth… shut," Teresa gasped out. "Like my… my father… told me."

"It would've come out the same," Erin said. "As soon we arrested Angel Face and he told his dad you'd seen him with the bloody knife, they would've come after you. And if you hadn't talked to us, you wouldn't have us to protect you. Then your parents would be burying their daughter for real, instead of pretend. You'd probably already be dead."

"Is this really the only way?"

"It's the best way we could think of," Erin said. "And you can't tell the Marshals, either. They need to have a genuine reaction, and they don't need to know. You need to act normal. It's fine to be a little scared and tense, that's normal for a woman in your position."

"That won't be too hard," Teresa said, managing a weak and watery smile.

"It'll be fine," Erin said for what felt like the hundredth time. She wondered if it was even remotely true.

Her phone buzzed. She pulled it out and, unsurprised, saw an unknown number.

"Excuse me," she said to Teresa. Then she answered the phone. "O'Reilly."

"Hello, love," Corky Corcoran said. "I'm thinking you and I need to have a wee meeting."

"Yeah," Erin said. "I think we do."

Chapter 23

"Erin, love, let me say how very honored I am that you've trusted me with this important job," Corky said.

Erin glanced around the Laughing Man Café in Tribeca where Corky had suggested they meet. It was a few blocks from his love nest. The only people in sight were well-to-do New Yorkers, and not many of those. The two of them were sitting outdoors in spite of the looming thunderclouds, which had earned them a funny look from the waitress, but made it very unlikely anyone would be able to eavesdrop on them. Rolf was under the table, chin between his paws.

"I appreciate it," she said. "Why'd you want to meet?"

"To go over the plan, of course," he said. "We've information to exchange."

"We could've done that over the phone."

He grinned. "Ah, but then we'd miss the fine people-watching afforded by this excellent establishment, not to mention their unparalleled coffee."

"What people-watching?" Erin took a sip of what was, indeed, excellent coffee.

His smile didn't falter. "They're staying indoors, I'd imagine, on account of the weather. The rain should be starting any moment now, and it'll keep up most of the night, so they say."

"Have you got a car?" Erin asked.

"One? Think bigger, love. I've all manner of automobiles lined up for the festivities."

"Do any of them actually belong to you? Never mind, don't answer that. I don't want to know."

"Every vehicle I'm borrowing will be returned to its owner, none the worse for wear," he said. "I'll be changing rides, naturally, after plucking our damsel off the street. Can't be too careful."

"I didn't think I'd ever hear you say that," Erin said. "I've given her your description and first name. What'll you be driving at the hotel?"

He sighed theatrically. "The least romantic getaway vehicle one can imagine. It's a gray Corolla. I still can't believe I'll be driving it. If you'd rather, I could take my convertible."

"The yellow BMW? Oh yeah, that'd be nice and inconspicuous. And a convertible? In a thunderstorm? I think we'd better stick with the Toyota."

"As you say, love. Now, about the lass I'll be transporting. Have you a picture about you?"

"No, but she'll be hard to miss. She'll be wearing an NYPD windbreaker and hat and she'll be moving away from the blast. All the real cops will be looking at it. She's about the same height as me, slightly heavier build, mid-thirties. Black hair, brown eyes, kind of a round face. Italian-American, obviously."

"I'll be needing her measurements," he said.

"Corky! Don't you ever think about anything else?"

"Come off it, love," he said impatiently. "You're the one who's thinking improper thoughts. She won't have her luggage, will she? So I'll be needing to provide her with additional clothing."

"Oh, right." Erin felt slightly abashed. "Sorry. I don't know her measurements."

"You've a copper's eye, and you're a woman. I'd wager you can make a fair guess."

Erin thought about it. "I'd say she's about a thirty-eight, thirty-four, thirty-six," she said.

"Cup size?"

"Corky!"

He held up a hand. "I promise I'll not purchase any slinky negligees or lingerie. I just want the lass's clothes to fit her properly."

"Okay, okay. Call her a 'D,' I guess."

He nodded. His face stayed serious, but his eyes twinkled. "I think I'll get along just fine with this lass."

She pointed a finger at his face. "Don't even think about it. This woman's counting on you for her safety. Her life is in your hands. If you jump in bed with her, you'd better pray the Lucarellis find you before I do. I swear, if I hear one word about you stepping out of line, she'll be the last woman you ever screw around with."

Corky's eyes grew somber. "She'll come to no harm if it's in my power to prevent it," he said. "I know what you think of me, Erin. I'm going to do this one thing right, even if nothing else in my whole, wayward life. Let me be the hero, just this once. I'd swear to God I'll do it right, but He and I aren't precisely on the best of terms at the moment. I've no family hereabouts. So I'll swear it on Morton Carlyle, the best lad I've ever known, and a man both of us love. Though not in quite the same way, thank the good Lord."

He extended his hand across the table. Erin looked at it, then at him.

"Oh, for God's sake, shake it already," Corky said. "Don't leave me hanging. I feel silly enough as it stands."

Erin slowly took Corky's hand. "I'm counting on you," she said. "And so is she."

"If she doesn't come back alive, neither will I," he said. Then, unable to hold the serious demeanor any longer, his face cracked and his familiar boyish grin shone through. "Not that it'll come to that. We'll simply disappear. Like smoke on the wind, that's the plan."

"Do you have everything you need?" Erin asked.

"Oh aye, you needn't fret about that. Remember, I've a particular talent for moving things about without attracting notice."

"You're a professional smuggler."

"That's what I said. I've even laid hands on a copper's outfit, just so I can blend in at the scene."

"Corky, impersonating a cop is a felony."

"So is blowing up a car. I'll not tell anyone I'm a copper. Besides, it's not precisely a regulation uniform."

Suspicion pricked the corners of Erin's mind. "Just what sort of uniform is this?" she asked.

"One might say it's better than what you wore when you drove a blue-and-white, love."

"How so?"

"It's equipped with handy bits of Velcro so it's easy to change out of in a hurry."

"Oh, God," Erin said, putting a hand over her face. "You got a fake uniform from a stripper, didn't you."

"I know a lad in that line of work, aye, and he's about my size. In the important parts of him, that is."

"Keep it low-key," she said. "And for the love of all that's holy, don't take your clothes off in the middle of this."

"Erin, you're a lovely lass, and Carlyle's the luckiest lad in New York, but has anyone ever told you, you worry too much?" He stood up, leaned across the table, and planted a kiss on her cheek before she could react. "What time should I be there?"

"Eight o'clock sharp," she said.

"I'll be there at quarter to," he promised. "Come hell, high water, or both. Relax, love. It'll be fun."

"I've had fun before. It didn't feel like this."

"Ah, you're only saying that because you've never had me." He winked. "Changes your whole outlook, love."

"I haven't forgotten you tried to screw my sister-in-law," Erin said.

"I'm not asking you to forget it," Corky said. "But perhaps, once all's done, you'll forgive it. I'll see you in a few hours, love. Try not to miss me till then."

*   *   *

The last piece of the puzzle was the acquisition of a suitable decoy. Accordingly, Erin pulled up to the city morgue in the midafternoon. The sky was heavy and gray, leaving Manhattan brooding in a sullen half-light. It struck Erin as appropriate. You didn't want to visit a morgue on a sunny day.

Erin had called Levine after meeting Corky to check on her progress and had received a typically terse response.

"Got the body," Levine had said.

"Where?"

"City morgue."

"I'll meet you there."

"Okay."

So now here she was, leaving another nice, wide paper trail. There was no good way around it; she had to sign in and present her ID before they'd let her in. If anyone asked, she'd have to say she'd been looking for Levine with questions about the Romano case.

The place was cold and antiseptic, all tile, metal, and fluorescent lights. The clack of Erin's shoes on the floor was loud, the echoes following her, the sort of sound that made her want to keep glancing over her shoulder to make sure nobody was sneaking up behind. She'd left Rolf in the car and now wished she hadn't. Even to a professional cop who'd been around more than her share of dead bodies, morgues were creepy. They were a sort of in-between place, inhabited by both the living and the dead. She suppressed a shiver and kept walking, making for the vault where they kept the unidentified corpses.

A storm brewing outside; a basement full of anonymous bodies; a woman walking alone. Erin wished she hadn't watched this sort of movie as a teenager. She told herself to stop being stupid. She had enough real monsters to handle without populating her imagination with fake ones.

She pushed through a double-hinged door and found herself in the inner vault with Sarah Levine and a body bag on a slab. The bag was black plastic and disturbingly lumpy.

"Is that her?" Erin asked, nodding to the bag.

"Jane Doe," Levine said, looking at the paperwork in her hand. "Found in a public restroom, August Fifth. Cause of death: ruptured aneurysm, natural causes. Age estimated at forty-three. Height: one hundred sixty-five centimeters. Weight: Fifty-nine kilograms. Ethnicity: Hispanic. No identifying documents found in her personal effects. No phone. Fingerprints not on file. No matching missing person report."

"Wow," Erin said. "Lucky break. For us, I mean. That's nearly a perfect match."

Levine shrugged. "Approximately forty thousand unknown bodies currently reside in the United States," she said. "New

York is the largest city in the country. Our odds of finding an approximate match were reasonable."

"And we're sure nobody's looking for her?"

"There's no way I can know that," Levine said. "All I know is that the city has failed to identify her and her remains are scheduled for anonymous burial on Hart's Island."

"So can I just... take her?" Erin asked.

"The body has been released to me," Levine said. "You need my permission."

Erin looked at her. Levine looked back.

Erin sighed. "Okay, can I have your permission?"

"Yes," Levine said. "Sign here. The body is well-preserved. It was found before severe decomposition had set in and has been refrigerated. However, there is some putrescence."

"So it'd be a good idea not to open the bag," Erin said.

"How long will it be before the body is explosively dismembered?" Levine asked matter-of-factly.

"Jesus Christ," Erin muttered. "You've got a hell of a way with words. It'll happen around eight o'clock. Four hours?"

"You'll need to keep the remains cool as long as possible," Levine said.

"Got it," Erin said. "I guess we can't take the meat wagon."

"That would require additional paperwork," Levine said. "It's possible, but time-consuming. It would also require the use of a qualified driver."

"Which would be Hank or Ernie," Erin said. "No, thanks. I'll put her in the trunk of my car. Can you give me a hand?"

They loaded the body onto a gurney and wheeled it to the elevator. Levine had all the necessary forms, so they were able to work their way out of the morgue through the loading dock. Erin left Levine there, fetched her car, and backed it up to the dock. She popped the trunk. As Rolf watched from his compartment, the two women hoisted the heavy bag into the trunk.

"This must be how a hitman feels," Erin said quietly. "Sneaking a body into a car."

"You didn't kill her," Levine said. "Neither did I."

"Thanks for doing this," Erin said, swinging the trunk shut with an awful, final-sounding clang. "I owe you one."

"One what?"

"Never mind," Erin said. "Just remember, you need to identify the remains as Teresa Tommasino."

"I'll be writing two reports," Levine said. "One for public consumption, the other one with the truth."

"Okay, but you can't show that other one to anyone. And you've got to keep it secure. I'm talking locked safe, password, the works. We can't have people come sniffing around for it."

"I use unscented paper," Levine said. "And I've never had anyone question my reports."

"You're right," Erin said. She shook her head. "I'm just tired. Sorry."

"Why are we still talking?" Levine asked. "If you don't want to be seen here, this is counterproductive."

"Right. Thanks again." Erin got into her car, started the engine, and drove away.

She only went a couple of blocks. Then she parked again and went into a convenience store. She angled straight for the freezer aisle and grabbed four big bags of ice, two in each hand.

"That's a lot of ice, ma'am," the guy behind the counter said. "You having a party tonight?"

Actually, I have a corpse in the trunk and if it thaws out too much, it'll start stinking, Erin thought. "It's going to be a blast," was what she said.

"You need anything else?" he asked. "Soda? Chips? Salsa?"

"I'm good, thanks," Erin said, opening her wallet and pulling out some bills. Then she went out to the Charger, gave a quick look around just in case anyone was watching, and placed two bags of ice on either side of the body bag. It was the best she could do for the moment.

When she got back in the car, Rolf was sitting facing the back of the vehicle. Usually he greeted her with a wagging tail and an outthrust snout, but this time, he whined and scratched at the floor of his compartment.

"You okay, kiddo?" she asked.

Rolf whined again and wagged anxiously.

Then she understood. He was a trained search-and-rescue dog. He was alerting her to the presence of human remains. Erin couldn't smell anything, thank God, but her K-9 could.

"It's fine," she told him. "I know."

Rolf cocked his head at her. In his experience, dead bodies were a big deal. He didn't understand why his partner wasn't interested in this one. He barked, in case she hadn't gotten the message.

"Okay, okay," she said. "You found her. Good boy. *Sei brav.*" She tossed his rubber Kong ball into the back.

Rolf snagged it in midair. Then he plopped down on the floor and started chewing. He'd done what he was supposed to. As far as he was concerned, everything was exactly the way it was meant to be. The rest was up to the humans.

Erin wished she shared his optimism. She started the car and drove toward O'Leary's Body Shop.

"God," she said, suddenly getting the awful, unintentional pun. "Body shop. I don't believe it. I'm taking a body to the body shop."

As Erin O'Reilly chauffeured a corpse toward its rendezvous with a homemade bomb, she started laughing. She couldn't help it.

Chapter 24

Erin drover her Charger up to the entrance to O'Leary's. She got out and opened the door. The place was dark and very quiet. She saw the black bulk of the Suburban in the workshop. Its dome light was on and she could see somebody moving inside.

She felt alarm and irritation. Carlyle wasn't a trained police officer, but he'd been in the IRA, for God's sake! Didn't he understand basic security precautions? Anybody could just walk right in and see what he was doing.

Then she smiled, feeling foolish. Without turning around, she said, "How's it going, Ian?"

"Proceeding on-mission," he said from somewhere behind and to her right. "Sitrep?"

"Everything's under control." Then she did turn. There he was, in a shadowed alcove from which he could cover the door. "You know, people like you are the reason the instructors yell at us to check our corners when we practice room-clearing."

"Glad to help," he said.

"Can you open the garage door?" she asked. "I need to back my car in."

"Affirmative."

Erin steered the Charger in. Ian shut the door immediately afterward. Erin backed up close to the Suburban and climbed out, leaving Rolf inside. The K-9 peered at her from his compartment, head cocked to one side, trying to figure out what the humans were up to.

Carlyle poked his head out of the back seat of the SUV. He was unkempt and grease-stained, but he smiled when he saw her. He climbed out, wiped his hands and forehead on a handkerchief, and came to meet her.

"Everything's ready, darling," he said. "I was just putting the seat in place. Here, I'll show you."

He indicated the back seat of the Suburban, which looked no different than when it had rolled off the factory assembly line. Carlyle reached in and patted the middle seat.

"Here's where you'll want to be putting your decoy. The force of the blast will come straight up through the seat. It won't carry far, but at close range, it'll be quite spectacular."

"Okay," Erin said. "Do you have a big freezer or something here?"

"There's one of those in the office," Carlyle said. "For ice cream and the like. What is it you're needing... ah. I see. Of course. We'll need to empty it out, but that's no great difficulty. You're right, we'll want to be keeping her cool until the last possible moment, and we can't exactly pack the rear of this auto with ice. It'd spoil the illusion. We'll just have to make certain we don't freeze the poor lass solid."

The freezer in O'Leary's office was big enough, once they'd cleaned it out. After making sure the blinds were pulled down tight, Ian came over to help Erin move the body. They carried the bag into the office and laid it on the floor next to the freezer.

"You'd best unpack her now," Carlyle advised. "So we can get her dressed. She may stiffen up a wee bit from the cold."

"Dress her up?" Erin repeated.

"Bodies in the morgue are generally nude, aye?" Carlyle said.

Erin mentally slapped herself. "Oh, shit. You're right. I forgot! And I don't have any of Teresa's clothes."

"Not to worry," Carlyle said. "Surely you've time to run to a department store and fetch a few things."

"But we need shoes, too," Erin said. "Everything! I wasn't thinking. And I don't know her size."

Carlyle laid a hand on her arm. "I've been to the scenes of a few bombings," he said gently. "So I've some notion what they look like. It's common for the victims to be blown clear out of their shoes, sometimes their clothes as well. Just find a pair of shoes of about the right size. So long as they're close, they'll serve. I don't think anyone's likely to be reenacting *Cinderella*, you ken?"

"Right," she said. She checked the time. It was getting close to five. "We've got three hours to get down to the Hilton at JFK with everything ready to go. It'll take a half hour to drive there, but we'd better allow an extra fifteen minutes in case of delays. That leaves us two hours and forty-five minutes. What needs to happen between now and then?"

"The vehicle's ready," Carlyle said. "So is the device. I've the remote here. Freshly purchased and clean. Untraceable." He took out a burner cell phone.

"You'll need to be able to see the car to know when to trigger it," she said. "Where will you be?"

"I'll be in the lot out front of the hotel," he said. "I'll be well within range."

"Are you sure you'll be able to see? It'll be dark. What if it's raining?"

"Erin, darling, I've never blown up anything, nor anyone, I didn't intend to."

She made a face. "Thanks, I guess. I'd better get some clothes. I'll be back in a few minutes."

After the quickest—and definitely the strangest—shopping trip she'd ever been on, Erin returned with a button-down blouse, a pair of loose-fitting jeans, a pair of cheap sneakers that roughly resembled the ones Erin recalled seeing on Teresa's feet, and a pair of socks and underwear. Then, as Ian stood watch, she and Carlyle went about the curious and sad business of arraying the body of Jane Doe for her unorthodox cremation.

In Erin's experience, life was what gave human beings their individuality. Dead bodies all had a sameness about them. Erin's mom had once said, after the open-casket funeral of Erin's great-uncle, that you only needed to see one dead body of a person you'd known in life to convince you that souls existed. She understood what her mom had meant. A corpse was an empty shell. It wasn't a person. The person was already gone. And that was what was so terribly sad about them. Whoever Jane Doe had been, now all that was left of her was this cold lump of meat, smelling faintly of death and the morgue.

Carlyle and Erin worked as respectfully as they could, slowly and carefully dressing the body. Erin buttoned the blouse over the ghastly Y-incision left by the autopsy.

"Is that going to be a problem?" she asked.

"That's why your Medical Examiner's a part of our wee conspiracy," he said. "But I'm thinking the lass's body's going to be in no condition for it to matter."

"Okay, that does it," Erin said. They lifted Jane Doe and laid her gently in the freezer. The dead woman's face looked waxy and unreal, like a sculpture of a person. It was a good thing the Suburban had tinted windows, Erin thought.

"Now we've time for a spot of supper," Carlyle said.

Erin shuddered. "I'm not hungry," she said. She could smell formaldehyde on her hands. "I think I'll head to the Eightball. I'd better check in with the Lieutenant. I'll be back here no later than seven to get the car. And her."

"I'll be waiting, darling."

*　　*　　*

"Where have you been all day?" Webb asked.

"Dealing with Lucarelli stuff," Erin said. "Trying to take care of the tail end of the Vitelli case."

"Good work on that," Webb said. "Getting the witness to talk. I don't know if we would've had enough to charge him without her."

"Yeah," Erin said. "Where's Vic?"

"Doing something with the SNEU squad from the Five," Webb said. "Something about a hot tip from an informant. He left about ten minutes ago. I was about to call it a day."

"Anything you need me to do here, sir?"

"Just make sure all your paperwork is squared away on Vitelli," he said. "I don't want some weasel of an attorney getting him off on a technicality."

"That's not going to happen, sir. Did the arraignment go okay?"

"Neshenko and I were there," Webb said. "It went about like usual. Neshenko fell asleep."

"Say, who's the judge on the case?" Erin asked with feigned nonchalance.

"Funny you should ask," Webb said. "Our old friend Ferris. According to the DA, there was some behind-the-scenes maneuvering on that one. It was going to be Barberis, but Ferris got swapped in at the last minute. Judicial horse-trading, I guess. Why?"

"No reason. I was just wondering if it was the same judge that'd worked the Madonna case. Barberis seemed a little lenient when he set bail on Alfie."

"Right." Webb nodded. "Well, Ferris is a lot of things, but nobody would accuse him of leniency."

"No, sir."

"Good night, O'Reilly. Try not to get in any trouble in your downtime."

Erin tried not to wince. "Good night, sir."

*   *   *

Now that everything was ready, time slowed down. Erin tried to think what she was forgetting. She knew she was leaving a wide paper trail, so everything had to look aboveboard. It was better to make things look right than to try to completely conceal them. So she wrote up a report about requesting a spare vehicle from Impounds, on the basis of a threat she'd heard from a CI regarding Teresa. Fortunately, her underworld contacts were well enough known to Webb that he'd be likely to accept an anonymous tip at face value.

What she really wanted to do was talk to someone, but that was the one thing she couldn't do. The only people she could discuss this with were Holliday, Carlyle, Corky, Skip, and Levine, and all of them were either busy with other things or ought not to be disturbed.

"Conspiracies suck," she confided to Rolf. "You think you're part of a team, but you end up even lonelier than if you work alone."

Rolf licked her cheek.

Erin killed time doing pointless paperwork. She got a Diet Coke and a bag of chips from the vending machines, then couldn't force herself to eat the chips. Was this how criminals felt before pulling heists? If so, how come they weren't all in the hospital with stomach ulcers? She'd have to ask Carlyle about that.

A little after six, she called it quits. She drove back to the Barley Corner, then took Rolf around the block to work out a little nervous tension. She went into the pub by the back way and slipped upstairs with her dog. She filled his food bowl and set the kibble in front of him.

Rolf stared at the food. Then he stared back at her. He didn't move.

"Go on, kiddo," she said. "Eat it."

The Shepherd didn't budge. He just looked at her with reproachful eyes. She didn't know how he knew, but he did, and he wasn't being shy about his feelings.

"You're staying here," she told him. "You can't come. Not on this job. You're too good. You'd sniff out the bomb, or the body, or both, and then we'd be toast. You could blow the whole operation, and you'd think you were doing the right thing."

Rolf answered her with his eyes.

"Sorry," she said. She double-checked that his water bowl was full. "I'll be back, but not till late. This is going to be a long night."

He lay down on the kitchen floor and heaved a great sigh. Erin left him there and went into her closet to get some of her old Patrol gear. The NYPD windbreaker would be very tight on Teresa's larger frame, but there wasn't much she could do about that. The other woman wouldn't have to wear it more than a few moments. Erin also grabbed her Patrol hat. She stuffed both of these into a plastic bag and took it with her.

She left the apartment, followed by Rolf's accusing gaze, knowing she'd probably find him staring at the door when she came back. At times like this, faithfulness and unconditional love were an awfully heavy burden to bear.

*   *   *

O'Leary's was within walking distance of the Corner, which was a good thing. She didn't want to leave her car there. The sky was dark with a premature twilight. As she walked, she heard a distant rumbling. The air was heavy and humid. It was hard to take a full breath. Just before she reached the body shop, she felt a big, fat raindrop splash against her cheek.

She found Carlyle and Ian waiting. Carlyle was reading a magazine. Ian was standing, feet slightly apart, apparently relaxed. Erin knew better.

"Showtime," she said.

Carlyle handed her the car keys. Then he and Ian opened the ice chest and removed Jane Doe. The body was cold, but hadn't had time to freeze. Erin held the back door of the SUV and the two men maneuvered the corpse into the rear seat. Carlyle carefully positioned the body upright. Then he buckled the seatbelt.

Safety first, Erin thought. She fought down a borderline-hysterical giggle. The seatbelt made good sense. She couldn't have Jane Doe sliding all over the inside of the car, and this way they could be sure the body was in the right place. She took the windbreaker and hat out of the plastic bag and set them on the seat next to the body.

"I wish we knew who she was," Carlyle said quietly.

"Me, too," Erin said. "But if we did, we couldn't do this. I guess it's like being an organ donor. We're using her body to save another life."

"That's a grand way to think of it," he said. He kissed her cheek. "It's probably best if we don't travel precisely together. You won't see me again until this is over. Best of luck, darling."

"If it comes down to luck, we've screwed up," Erin said.

"It always comes down to luck," Ian said.

"Fortune favors the prepared," Carlyle said.

There was no point waiting around anymore. It was time to get moving. Erin got behind the wheel of the Suburban and twisted the key. The engine coughed to life. She flinched involuntarily, knowing she was driving a car with an armed explosive under the back seat. She suddenly wondered what would happen if she got rear-ended. Ian opened the garage door and Erin steered the heavy vehicle out onto the Manhattan streets. Just one more trip to Long Island and this part of the mission would be over.

Out of old habit, she glanced in the rearview mirror at the back seat. But instead of the reassuring furry shape of her K-9, a weeks-old corpse stared back at her. The sunken eyes seemed to be measuring her, asking if she was up for this.

"Erin O'Reilly, chauffeur for the dead," she muttered. At least she understood Hank and Ernie, the Coroner's collection crew, a little better. Dark humor was more than a help in this sort of job; it was a necessity. Otherwise you would go crazy.

Traffic was heavy. She'd caught the tail end of rush hour. That was okay; she'd been running a little ahead of schedule. The lack of sleep the night before scarcely mattered now. Her nerves were stretched as tight as violin strings. She wondered what she'd do if a Patrol officer happened to glance in her window at the corpse. Could she just show her shield and explain she was a detective on official business?

Getting across the Brooklyn Bridge was agonizingly slow. Erin started to wonder whether she'd left enough time after all, then reminded herself that nothing was going to happen until she got there. Corky would wait, and Carlyle would be dealing with the same traffic she was. Little flashes of lightning rippled through the clouds overhead. More raindrops began to fall, spattering the windshield. She turned on the wipers and willed the cars to move.

Finally, after what felt like half a lifetime of waiting, she broke free of the gridlock and began making her way across Brooklyn. She'd covered less than a quarter of the distance, but more than half her driving time was behind her. The movement of the vehicle made her feel a little better.

Her phone vibrated against her hip. Startled, she swerved slightly, recovered, and fished it out. To her surprise, she saw Vic's name on the caller ID.

"O'Reilly," she said.

"Erin!" Vic said loudly. She heard road noise over the line and realized he was driving, too. "Where the hell are you?"

"What do you mean? I left work more than an hour ago."

"I know that! Where are you?"

"Long Island. I've got something to take care of."

"It can wait," he said. "Listen, I just talked to Firelli. We've got a problem."

She sucked in a sharp breath. "Vic, I'm a little busy right now," she said. "Whatever it is, it can wait."

"No, it can't," he said. "Firelli's got contacts in the Mob. He just gave me a tip from a guy he knows. Something's going down with the Lucarellis. He thinks somebody's gonna pop our star witness."

Erin smiled in the darkness. Ian was right. A lot of things did come down to luck, and sometimes, luck was on the side of the angels. This was perfect.

"Yeah, I was afraid that might happen," she said. "I've been hearing some stuff about that, too."

There was a brief pause. "Were you planning on doing anything with that information?" he replied. "Like, maybe telling somebody?"

"I'm going to move her. Right now."

"Erin, you're not making any sense. You need to talk to the Marshals about this. She's in WitSec, not under NYPD protection."

"We can't trust the Feds, Vic. You know that. She's my responsibility and I'm going to take care of her."

"And just how are you planning on doing that?"

"It's better if I don't discuss the details," she said. "Even with you. Thanks for the heads-up, Vic. I appreciate it."

"Wait a second!" he said. "I'll come back you up. I'm already—"

"I've got this," she interrupted, hanging up on him mid-sentence. She didn't want Vic getting involved. Anything he did, however well-intentioned, could throw off the delicate ballet they'd set in motion.

Her phone buzzed again. It was Vic, calling her back. She let it roll to voicemail. He tried twice more before giving up.

The rain started really pelting down as she approached the airport. Even with the wipers on their highest setting, the windshield was a blur of streetlights, headlights, and water. Erin cursed quietly. Would Carlyle be close enough to see? How would he judge the right moment to set off the bomb? And just how safe was the device? He hadn't built a car bomb in years. It wasn't the sort of thing you could afford to get almost right.

She saw the sign for the Hilton and put on her turn signal. The big, armor-plated Suburban slewed to one side, throwing up a curtain of spray from the gutter. She drove up under the awning in front of the main entrance and parked. Then, with a final deep breath, she opened the door and got out.

Chapter 25

The front door of the Hilton stood under a glass-roofed arched awning supported by stainless-steel pillars. In front of that, a fountain bubbled pointlessly under the pouring rain. The ground was red brick instead of asphalt. It was dry here, but outside the awning's protection it would be slippery.

Erin left the SUV with its cargo of death and walked briskly to the front door. She passed between a pair of reinforced posts that had, she realized with dark amusement, been put there to prevent someone driving a car bomb into the lobby.

"Ma'am, you can't leave your car there," the clerk at the front desk said. "I know it's raining, but—"

Erin held up her gold shield. "NYPD," she said without slowing down. "Official police business."

She hit the button for the elevator and rode it up to the fifth floor. On the way, her phone buzzed yet again, informing her that she had another missed call from Vic.

"Sorry," she muttered. The doors slid open and she stepped into the hallway. It was deserted. She felt a surge of uncertainty. This plan was crazy. It would never work. Somebody was going to get hurt. Teresa would panic and do something stupid. There were so many ways it could go wrong.

Erin remembered something Rolf liked to do. When the Shepherd got tense, he'd shake himself. It seemed to help. She loosened her shoulders and shook her head from side to side as vigorously as she dared. She did feel a little better. Then, before her second thoughts could catch up with her, she went to the Marshals' door and knocked.

"Open up, guys," she called. "This is O'Reilly."

There was a brief pause. Then Calley said, "What's happened, Detective?"

"We don't have much time," Erin said. "I'm the only one out here. Open the door."

The bolt slid back and the chain-lock disengaged. Calley opened the door, but Erin saw the wariness in his eyes. She also saw that his sidearm was in his hand, though it was pointed at the floor.

"Jesus, Calley, it's me," she said. "Careful there."

He didn't smile. "What's up?" he asked.

"I got word from a guy I know on the street," she said. "Vitelli's heard about Teresa. He knows where she is."

"Bullshit," Calley growled. "Nobody knows we're here. I kept this under tight wraps."

Erin shook her head. "They know."

"Then you were followed when you came here earlier," Marshal Hodges said.

"I don't think so," Erin said. "But it doesn't matter how they know. They're planning something. It's going to go down soon. I can get her out, but she has to go right now."

"Are they coming for me?" Teresa asked from the connecting doorway. The schoolteacher was wide-eyed and obviously scared half out of her mind. Her voice trembled slightly.

"Our best bet is to bunker up here," Calley said. "And call for backup."

"This hotel's full of civilians," Erin said. "If there's a shootout, people are going to get hit. These guys have access to military weapons, Calley. Remember what happened with Alfie Madonna? This'll be worse."

Indecision crept into the Marshal's face. He wasn't used to commanding a detail; that was Headley's job. But Headley was in the hospital. Calley hesitated.

"I don't like it," he said. "She's my responsibility."

"Mine, too," Erin said. "I got her into this. I'll get her out of it."

"You're taking her out of WitSec?"

Erin nodded. "We're getting out of town right now, tonight," she said. "I know a place she can lie low while we sort out all these damn security leaks."

"Okay," Calley said, making up his mind. "We'll come with you."

"Just as far as the front door," she said. "The more guys we have, the greater the chance we'll be noticed. And it's better if none of your people know where we're going."

"What're you implying?" Hodges demanded, bristling.

"All I know is, info about witnesses keeps getting out," Erin said. "We can't take chances. Get your coat and shoes, Teresa."

Teresa wordlessly nodded and disappeared into the adjoining room.

"I'm sorry about this," Erin said to Calley.

He shook his head. "I think we should trail you, just to be on the safe side," he said.

"Okay," she said, improvising. "Send one of your guys down to get your car. I'm parked out front. I got a special vehicle from Impounds. It's unmarked and it's bulletproof. Chevy Suburban, black."

"Got it," Calley said. "Monson, go get the car. Hodges, you and I will go down with O'Reilly and the principal."

The third Marshal nodded and hurried out of the room. Erin swallowed her nervousness and impatience. She reminded herself that the Marshals had to feel involved. They'd go along with it much more easily if they were.

Teresa emerged, sliding her robin's-egg coat over her shoulders. Under it, Erin saw the bulky bulletproof vest. She was holding her purse in one shaking hand.

"Ms. Tommasino?" Erin said.

"Yes?" Teresa said.

"It's time to go. Are you ready?"

Teresa looked around the room, as if she was taking inventory. She'd brought very little with her. The suitcase would be coming, but it wouldn't be leaving the car.

"Let's go," Erin said.

"We'll go first," Calley said. He nodded to Hodges. "Get the elevator. I'm right behind you."

The big guy left the room. Calley followed. Erin gave them a few seconds' lead.

"You clear on the plan?" Erin asked Teresa in a low voice.

"I think so," Teresa said.

"Hey, it's going to be okay," Erin said. Then, in a very soft whisper, "You'll go out to the car, just like we discussed, get in the back seat, make the change, and get out the other side. There'll be a gray Corolla waiting in the lot, just a few yards from you. Don't stop, don't look, and *don't run*. Got it?"

Teresa nodded. Her jaw was very tight.

"Okay," Erin said more loudly, for Calley's ears as well as Teresa's. "The rain will help. It'll make it harder for anyone watching. Let's do this."

The elevator seemed to take forever to reach the ground floor. Calley had his hand inside his coat, but Erin knew he was holding his gun. Nobody said anything. As the elevator slowed and stopped, Erin realized her own hand was instinctively resting on the grip of her Glock.

The lobby was empty except for the clerk behind the desk. He gave Erin an odd look, his eyebrows raised. She ignored him.

At the main doors, Teresa started to pull up her jacket's hood.

"No," Erin said quietly, motioning with her hand. For the sake of witness statements, it was important that Teresa be seen to leave the hotel. There had to be no doubt.

The Suburban waited under the rain-streaked awning, black and ominous. Outside the halo of the hotel's lights, only the driving rain was visible. Erin felt a swell of panic. She couldn't see a gray car. Hell, she couldn't even see the rest of the parking lot. Why hadn't she double-checked for it when she'd first arrived? What if Corky wasn't there? What if Carlyle wasn't in position to set off the bomb? Their clever plan was going to fall apart if even one piece failed.

A black Lincoln pulled up behind the SUV. That'd be the Marshals' car. Calley and Hodges split off, Hodges going to the front of the Suburban and Calley to the rear corner. Teresa hesitated, staring at the Chevy.

"Keep moving," Erin said softly. She reached out and, without thinking, opened the back door.

The SUV's dome light didn't come on. Belatedly, Erin recalled that it hadn't lit up when she'd gotten in and out previously. Carlyle, bless his clever heart, must have thought to disable the light. The interior of the Suburban was dark, the corpse cloaked in shadows.

Teresa swallowed, tucked her coat around her legs, and got in. Erin closed the door behind her, turned to Calley, and nodded.

There was a short pause. Erin started around the back of the SUV. She saw the driver of the Lincoln watching her. He'd be in a perfect position to see Teresa get out of the vehicle. Erin turned to face him, remembering something she'd learned on a previous case, a trick of stage magic. The key to doing a magic trick wasn't to hide what you were doing; it was to make the viewer think you were doing something else. Cops were trained to watch hands. Magicians showed you the wrong hand. She needed a distraction.

At that moment, as if in answer to her prayers, she saw a silhouette. It was a man, a big one, coming up behind the Marshals' car. She couldn't make out his features through the driving rain, but the guy was running toward them.

"Calley!" she shouted, pointing. "Six o'clock!"

Calley and the other Marshals reacted instantly, as they'd been trained. Calley's hands came up, gripping his pistol. Hodges was moving down the passenger side of the Suburban, his own gun in hand. Erin shifted to the driver's side of the Lincoln and started toward the rear of the car. She was screening the Suburban from the Lincoln driver's view and she'd bet he was watching his rearview mirror. She was also getting a little distance from the Suburban. It could go at any second.

The noise of the rain on the awning was loud, a continuous drumming. Had Teresa changed clothes yet? Had she gotten out of the car? Erin didn't dare look.

"Stop!" Calley shouted. He was pointing his gun at the newcomer. Then he yelled, "Gun!"

The dark figure brought up its hands. Erin caught a glint of silver from the rain-soaked barrel of a pistol. The man was very large and strong-looking. And his face was familiar, from the buzz-cut hair to the twice-broken nose.

"Freeze!" the man shouted back.

"US Marshal!" Calley shouted. His finger went inside the trigger guard of his pistol.

"Wait!" Erin screamed. "Vic—!"

The night turned brilliant red-gold. Intense, almost liquid heat rippled across Erin's back and shoulders. There was a tremendous noise and a giant, invisible hand shoved her away from the Chevy. Every pane of glass in the hotel's awning shattered at once. Erin turned halfway around as she fell, landing heavily on her hip. She saw a rolling ball of fire burst through the skeleton frame of the awning, hurling shards of broken glass up and out. Sparkling fragments hung in the air like new constellations. Then they began to plummet to earth, raining down all around her. Something else was falling, too, solid pieces of something that had once been human.

Erin curled into a ball and wrapped her arms around her head. Glass tinkled off her upraised arms, accompanied by rain, falling through the ruined awning. Raindrops hissed like a chorus of devils as the water struck the blazing vehicle.

She risked opening an eye and raising her head slightly. The Suburban was a black cauldron, open on top. Flames and smoke boiled out of the shattered vehicle. A car alarm was shrieking plaintively from somewhere in the parking lot. Somebody screamed.

The rain was cool on Erin's face. Her exposed flesh felt flushed, as if she'd gotten a bad sunburn. She smelled the thick odor of gasoline and spent gunpowder, along with a roasted-pork scent that was all too familiar. She lay on the brickwork, in no hurry to get up.

The thought of one of her father's favorite movies came to her. Sean O'Reilly was a big Paul Newman and Robert Redford fan, and he loved *Butch Cassidy and the Sundance Kid*. She remembered a scene where the bandits were trying to blow up a safe during a train robbery:

Redford manages to blow up the whole train car, destroying the safe, the money, and just about everything else. Newman turns to him and says, "Well, that oughta do it, Sundance Kid."

Redford replies, "Think ya used enough dynamite there, Butch?"

"Think ya used enough dynamite there?" Erin muttered. That crazy urge to laugh was on her again.

Dimly, she heard men yelling at each other. Calley was telling somebody to stay back. Vic was shouting over him.

"Listen, buddy!" Vic yelled. "You don't get outta my way, your jurisdiction's going up your ass and out your goddamn nose! She's NYPD, and she's one of mine! Move it!"

Then Vic was there, standing over her, large as life. He had his phone at his ear and was talking to Dispatch, speaking very fast.

"Repeat, we've got a 10-13!" he said. "Officer down! Looks like a car bomb! Send everybody you got, right now! Hilton Hotel at JFK!"

"Hey, Vic," Erin said. "What're you doing?"

"Take it easy," Vic said, dropping to one knee beside her. "Don't try to move. You might have broken bones."

"I'm okay," she said. Her ears were ringing, but besides that and the weird flushed sensation on her cheeks and the back of her neck, she felt pretty much fine. Just tired; really, really tired. She almost felt like she could go to sleep right there on the wet parking lot.

Then Calley stepped up to face Vic. "Step back, sir," he said. He'd gotten a handle on himself, but he was shaking with a combination of adrenaline and intense emotion.

"Screw you," Vic retorted without sparing him a glance. "I'm NYPD and this is my partner."

"This is an active Federal crime scene," Calley said. "I'm ordering you to back off."

Then Vic did look at him. "I'm starting to want you to try and make me," he said.

"He's okay, Calley," Erin said, reluctantly sitting up. Her arm sent a jolt of pain from her wrist. She must have landed on it badly. It might be sprained. "I know him."

Sirens were audible through the downpour. Blue and red lights came dimly into view, converging from two sides at once. In the lurid light, Calley and the detectives stared at one another.

"Christ," Calley said. "What a goddamn mess."

Chapter 26

Vic wouldn't let Erin stand up until the paramedics arrived on scene. It was immediately obvious that the passenger in the Suburban was in no need of medical attention, and nobody else was hurt, so the EMTs went straight for Erin. After a few minutes, during which Vic hovered annoyingly, one of the medics pronounced her basically okay. Her wrist was mildly sprained, and she had some minor flash-burns, but they weren't even blistering.

"You're a very lucky woman," he said. "I can't believe you were standing that close. You ought to be dead."

"The car was customized," Erin said dully. "Armored door panels and windows." Her head and wrist ached. What she really wanted was to find a quiet place to lie down, hopefully for a week or two.

Vic looked at the smoldering wreckage. "Still," he said. "You were, like, ten feet away. That's the sort of thing they need two or three body bags for. Or maybe a bunch of Tupperware."

"You've got a clean bill of health, ma'am," the EMT said. "Just take a few aspirin for any aches and pains. You'll probably be sore in the morning."

"Thanks," Erin said, starting to get to her feet. Vic, seeing her movement, put out a hand and helped her up.

Cops were all over the place, standing around and getting wet, but nobody seemed to be doing much of anything useful. All they'd managed was to set up a perimeter around the blast site. A couple of officers were stringing yellow police tape. The Marshals had retreated to the doorway of the hotel, where a metal overhang shielded them from the worst of the rain. Calley was on the phone, talking to his boss. He didn't look happy.

"How're your ears?" Vic asked.

"Fine," Erin said. "Ringing a little, that's all."

"I don't get it," he said. "This is the second time you've been blown up, right?"

"I've never been blown up, Vic," she said.

"You know what I mean. Last time a car blew up near you, you couldn't hardly hear for ten, fifteen minutes. And you were a lot farther away." He looked at the Suburban. "I guess this was a smaller bomb. That other one, practically the only thing left was the chassis."

"Vic," she said. "What the hell are you doing here? How'd you even know where I was?"

"Pinged your phone," he said matter-of-factly. "You told me you were going to Long Island, so I booked it down here. I figured you were getting in trouble, what with all the Mob shit you've been dealing with. You had my back with that Russian thing last year, without even being asked, so I owed you one. So here I am."

"You almost got shot by the Marshals!"

He shrugged. "You think I can't handle a couple pencil-dick cowboys? Look, let's get outta the rain while we wait for the Bomb Squad. You want to go inside, or wait in my car? I guess your ride doesn't keep the rain out so good anymore."

"Sure," Erin said. "I don't want your car to get wet, though."

"It's a police car," he said. "Guys throw up in the back seat all the time. A little rainwater won't make a bit of difference. C'mon, let's go. You're gonna get hypothermia or something out here."

They crossed the parking lot and climbed into Vic's Taurus. Vic started the engine to get the heater running. The police radio was full of chatter about the bombing. Vic turned it off. They sat there, listening to the rumble of the Taurus's engine and the patter of the rain on the windshield and roof. They could see the flames of the burning Suburban through the rain. Somebody was spraying a fire extinguisher on it. This would wreck evidence, but Erin thought this was a good idea for two reasons: firstly, she actually *wanted* evidence to be compromised this once; secondly, the SUV's gas tank hadn't blown up yet, and if it did, there was an excellent chance it would kill a few of the cops that were still milling around like spooked cattle.

"They almost got you that time, huh?" Vic finally asked.

"What?" Erin hadn't been expecting him to start the conversation that way.

"The friggin' Mob. They almost took you out."

She stared at him. His face was hard to make out in the darkened car. "Vic, I wasn't the target."

"Yeah, I know," he said. "They got your witness, though."

"Looks like it."

"What happened? Look, I called you as soon as I heard from Firelli. He got the word from a guy he knows in the old neighborhood. You know, he's got connections in the Lucarellis, and—"

"Vic, I'm not blaming you. Whatever happened here, it's more my fault than anybody's."

"Shit, Erin, don't go blaming yourself. How many times have you talked to victims who think it was their fault? You almost got killed! I just wish I could've got here faster."

"There's nothing you could've done, Vic."

"Yeah," he said morosely. "Well, there goes our case against Angel Face. That pretty bastard's gonna walk. Hell, the DA will probably drop the charges. Not to mention what happened to that poor girl. What was her name again?"

"Isabella Romano."

"No, not her. The witness. The one who just got blown up."

"Oh. Teresa. Teresa Tommasino."

"Geez, Erin, you sure you're okay? You're not thinking straight. You think maybe the explosion scrambled you a little? On account of that concussion you got from Mickey Connor?"

"I don't think so. But how would I know?"

"Erin?"

"Yeah?"

"How come you hung up on me?"

He was studying her face. She wondered how much he could see in the dark. She tried to keep her expression neutral and to tell him as much of the truth as she could.

"I was busy, Vic. I was trying to figure out how to get Teresa somewhere safe."

"Do you think the bomb was already under the car? Or did they plant it at the hotel?"

"I was only inside for a few minutes," she said. "But I guess the hotel's got a security camera watching the front door. If anyone messed with the car, it might be on tape."

"Yeah," he said. "But that means somebody knew what you were gonna use the car for. Who signed off on the vehicle?"

"Captain Holliday. But if you're suggesting he's dirty—"

"Nah, Holliday's about as dirty as my Sig." Vic patted the butt of his pistol. He took excellent care of his guns. Erin knew if she looked at his Sig-Sauer automatic, it would be as bright and clean as if it'd just come off the assembly line. "But someone *knew*," he repeated.

"I guess so," she said.

"You guess? Erin, you're the one who's supposed to be good at figuring this shit out. I'm just the meathead they bring in to scare the hell out of the bad guys. You don't guess. You see stuff. And there's something I can't figure in this thing."

"What's that?"

He was still looking at her. "Where's the mutt?"

Erin blinked. "What?"

"Your other half. And I don't mean that slick Irish prick. I'm taking about your K-9. Where is he?"

"He's at home."

"You left him at home? You came down here to transport a witness to a Mob killing, a woman you knew bad guys wanted to kill, and you left your bomb dog at home? Bullshit."

"It's the truth, Vic." She bristled slightly. "I was in a hurry, and—"

He cut her off with an impatient gesture. "Don't give me that crap. You're as likely to forget him as you are to leave your gun on your night table. I've seen you and him. He wouldn't let you forget him. And you know how useful he is. Hell, if he'd been in the car with you, he'd have smelled the damn bomb before it went off! Then none of this would've happened!"

There was a pause. Little points of reflected light shone in Vic's eyes like distant stars. Erin, looking at him, knew she wasn't the only one who was telling lies. Vic was a lot more than just a thug, whatever he said. He was a first-class detective, when he wasn't being intellectually lazy. Once he got on the right path, he usually knew how to follow it.

"Erin," he said quietly. "Remember when we found out about your boyfriend? Remember what I told you?"

"Which part?" she replied. "I remember a lot of swearing."

"I said you'd screwed with the Department and you'd screwed with me. And you promised you'd tell me the truth from then on."

"Yeah, I remember."

"So tell me. You're hiding something. What is it?"

She shook her head. "Vic, look. I'm not going to lie to you. But there's plenty of things I haven't told you, especially about what I'm doing with the Irish. You know that. You're not cleared for that operation."

"This hasn't got anything to do with the Irish," he said. "This is the Mafia we're talking about here. Okay, I'll tell you what I know. I know you got the Captain to sign off on a special vehicle. I know you drove it down here, without your bomb-sniffing dog, with what was obviously a bomb hidden inside. I know you yanked your witness away from the Marshals, who were doing just fine protecting her, and now she's a big bowl of chunky spaghetti sauce in the Hilton's driveway. I also know you're sleeping with a guy in the O'Malleys who used to be in the IRA. Specifically, he used to build car bombs for the IRA. Now that's one hell of a coincidence."

Erin said nothing.

"So here's how I figure it," Vic said. "The Lucarellis want this witness out of the picture, so their golden boy can skate on his murder rap. But they couldn't get to the Marshals, on account of the way they botched that hit on the Madonna punk. But they could get to you and your boyfriend. And you could get to this Tommasino chick. Jesus Christ, Erin, you killed an innocent fucking woman!"

She was already shaking her head before he finished. "No, Vic, you're wrong," she said.

"Your boy Carlyle built a bomb for you," he went on. "Now, maybe he could've put it in the car without you knowing it, but then you'd have had your dog along, and he would've sniffed it out. So you had to know about it. Erin, I don't want to believe this, but you're not giving me a whole lot of choice here."

Erin saw Vic's hand was still resting on his gun. His fingers were now curled around the pistol grip. He honestly thought he might have to draw on her. She felt sick to her stomach, not from fear, but from disappointment and disgust.

"I didn't kill her," Erin said. "I swear, Vic, I didn't."

"Then who the hell did? You gonna split hairs, like Tom Cruise in *Collateral*? 'I didn't kill him. I shot him. Bullets and the fall killed him.' Seriously?"

"I didn't kill her!" she insisted.

"Who did?" he repeated. "Carlyle? Your other pal, Corcoran?"

"Nobody!"

"What the hell do you mean, nobody?" He was shouting now, his left hand clenched around the steering wheel, his right still clutching his pistol.

"She's not dead!"

Vic froze. His mouth hung open at the sheer absurdity of what she'd just said. "Bullshit," was all he could manage.

Erin was horrified at what had just come out of her own mouth. She hadn't meant to say it. This wasn't the plan. Vic wasn't supposed to know. She'd just spoiled everything, all the careful planning, the sleight-of-hand, all of it. She'd never thought Vic would figure things out so quickly, and all because she'd left Rolf at home.

It's the little things that screw it all up, she thought. Big cases broke on small details. How many times had her dad told her that?

"There's pieces of a dead woman out there right now," Vic said, speaking slowly and deceptively softly. "I stepped on her hand when I was coming to check on you. Her friggin' *hand!* And

I know it was a woman, 'cause it had nail polish on the fingers. Red nail polish."

Erin couldn't think of a single thing to say, so she kept her mouth shut. She'd done enough damage with her words already.

"Wait a second," Vic said. "That Tommasino girl, she wasn't wearing nail polish. I saw her hands when we were talking to her. What in the hell is going on here? You telling me that was somebody else's hand? You blew up somebody else?"

Erin chewed the inside of her lip.

"Holy shit," Vic said in tones of quiet wonder. "You blew up a decoy. A damn *decoy*! You weren't kidding. Our witness isn't dead. But somebody else is. That's no mannequin out there."

Erin didn't see the point in hiding any longer. It was time to come clean. What Vic didn't know mattered a lot less than what he did. "It's a Jane Doe," she said. "From the city morgue."

"You stole a corpse?"

"I had permission. Levine's in on it."

"I guess she'd have to be," Vic said. "Otherwise she'd figure it even faster than I did. She'd know for sure the body was already dead when it got nuked. Who else knows?"

"Skip Taylor from the Bomb Squad. Carlyle. The Captain. My undercover handler. And the guy who's looking after Teresa." Erin didn't tell him that was Corky. She was a little afraid Vic might have a stroke right there on the spot if she told him that little tidbit.

"Not the Marshals?"

"No."

"Or Webb?"

"Not him either."

"Internal Affairs?"

"Nope."

"Jesus," he said. "You're crazy, Erin. You're absolutely crazy. Why would you do that? There's ways we could've protected her. Sheesh, the Mafia isn't what it used to be. They're not everywhere, damn it!"

"They gave me the contract," she said. "This is how I get Angel Face's dad. He told me to take care of this personally."

Vic pursed his lips. He whistled. "You get him on tape?"

"Yeah. He was careful, but I have him telling me to take care of the problem. Now that I've done it, I'm going to talk to him again. He'll give me the cash and everything else I need to bury him."

"These mopes think you're the real deal, huh? A dirty cop, a gun for hire?"

"They will now."

"Damn, girl. You got a pair on you like billiard balls."

She made a face. "Thanks, I guess."

"So, just to be clear, you didn't actually murder anybody tonight?"

"No, damn it! How many times do I have to say it?"

"And the Bomb Squad and the Medical Examiner are gonna back you up?"

"Yeah. But Vic, you can't talk about this. Not to them, not to Webb, not to anybody."

"How come IAB doesn't know?"

"Because I don't trust them."

"Nobody trusts them. But if they ever find out, they're gonna rip you up one side and down the other. They'll tear your shield right off your chest so hard it'll leave a permanent scar."

"The Captain's got my back."

Vic nodded slowly. "Yeah, okay. And so do I. But don't scare me like that ever again, okay? First I thought you were dead. Then I thought you were a stone killer. Now I don't know what the hell to think. I need a drink."

"How about an angel face?" she suggested wryly.

"Sounds like some weak-ass hipster cocktail. What's in it?"

"Apricot liqueur."

"Hell no. I get home, I'm drinking Stoli straight from the bottle." Vic cocked his head. "Looks like the Bomb Squad just got here. Nice response time. Almost like they were expecting some shit to go down tonight."

"They didn't know exactly where," Erin said. "And you have to act like you don't know what's going on. This is important, Vic."

"That won't be hard. I act like that every damn day. Because I *don't* know what's going on. Because nobody will tell me!"

Chapter 27

Skip Taylor was a cheerful, upbeat guy who didn't worry much. However, when it came to his work, he was careful and competent. Disarming explosives was like brain surgery; when you did it wrong, people died. The main difference was, the bomb surgeon was the one who ended up dead or crippled.

Therefore, even though he'd been warned about this bomb ahead of time, had even discussed its composition with Carlyle in person, Skip still operated with extreme caution. Bombs were unpredictable and tricky. For all he knew, some of the charge might not have detonated properly. The gas tank might have gotten superheated and be ready to explode at any moment.

With these considerations in mind, the bomb tech moved slowly and methodically. He was getting drenched, but he didn't seem to care, or even notice. He examined the wreckage, not touching anything. The other officers gave him plenty of room. The Bomb Squad was a unit best observed from a respectful distance.

Erin and Vic rejoined the cops on scene. They watched Skip and didn't say much. More police arrived.

"Does Webb know about this?" Erin asked after a few minutes.

"Yeah," Vic said. "I dropped him a text when I got here. He'll have heard about the bombing. I expect he'll show up pretty soon."

"Goody. I can hardly wait."

"You've been hanging around me too long," he said. "My sarcasm's rubbing off."

A beat-up old station wagon chugged into the parking lot and stopped in the midst of the squad cars. A familiar trench-coated figure climbed out of the driver's seat and stalked toward them. Lieutenant Webb looked cold, wet, and tired.

"O'Reilly," he said.

"Yes, sir," she said, trying to stiffen her spine to some semblance of attention. She really was tired.

"We lost our witness?"

"Looks that way."

"Care to tell me what happened?"

"I got a tip from one of my street sources of an imminent threat," Erin said. She'd learned a lot from Carlyle, particularly the importance of technical truth. The key to successful lying was to not actually lie. You just told misleading truths and let your listener's assumptions lead them into the tall grass.

"And what? You ran down here all by yourself to play white knight?" Webb asked.

"Not exactly, sir. I thought we might have to move Teresa on short notice, and I wanted it to be low-profile, so I asked the Captain if I could borrow an impounded vehicle. Then—"

"I got a tipoff from SNEU," Vic broke in smoothly. "And I passed it on to Erin. She was closer than I was, but I got here as fast as I could. I was just in time to see the blast."

"How did the bomb get under the car?" Webb asked.

"Skip Taylor's looking into it right now," Erin said, indicating the bomb tech, who was still studying the wreck.

"And Ms. Tommasino is dead?"

"There's body parts all over the place," Vic said. "That doesn't look survivable to me."

Erin managed to avoid looking impressed. Vic had also figured out the trick of lying by omission.

Webb clenched his fists. "Damn," he said. "That poor woman. Are you okay, O'Reilly?"

"Yes, sir. Just a little shaken up."

"She was standing a few yards from the car when it blew," Vic said. "She was about to get in, but she saw me coming. I was running, and I didn't know quite what to expect, so I had my gun out. I guess she didn't know it was me right away, so she and the Marshals threw down on me. That was when the car went up. Who knows? Maybe if I hadn't shown up right then, she would've gotten in and she'd be all over the place just like our victim. Maybe we got lucky."

He said it straight, no hint of irony in his voice. Erin realized that even after working with him for better than a year, she was still underestimating Vic Neshenko. "Maybe," Webb said. "Is this a Federal case, or NYPD?"

"I think it's us, sir," Erin said. "Teresa was under my protection when it happened. The Marshals were present, but only as an escort."

"All right," Webb said. "We'll need you to give a statement, in that case. I guess I'm in charge of this *meshuganeh.*"

"Look at you," Vic said. "You're finally a New Yorker, boss. You can't go back to LA now that you're tossing the Yiddish around."

"There's plenty of Jews in LA," Webb said. "They practically built Hollywood. Haven't you ever heard of Samuel Goldwyn? Stanley Kubrick? Woody Allen, for God's sake?"

"Woody Allen doesn't count," Vic said. "He's a transplanted New Yorker."

"Can I just give my statement, please?" Erin said. "I'm not feeling so good, and I think I should get home."

"I agree," Webb said. "I think it's best if Neshenko and I handle the primary investigative work on this one, since you were one of the intended victims. Your judgment may not be a hundred percent."

"If you say so, sir," she said.

He looked surprised at her lack of resistance, but didn't press his luck.

By the time Erin was done giving her Lieutenant a doctored version of what had happened, the Coroner's van had arrived. Sarah Levine collected everything she could find of Jane Doe's mortal remains, a lengthy and messy job. Carlyle's bomb had been spectacularly successful at rendering the body unrecognizable.

"I think that should do it for now," Webb said. "I'll need yours, too, Neshenko."

"Can't I just say 'ditto' to everything she said?" Vic asked.

Webb looked at him.

"Okay," Vic said. "Fine."

"Go home, O'Reilly," Webb said. "Get some rest."

"I can't, sir."

"What now?" he asked.

"My ride got blown up."

"Oh. Right. Well, I need Neshenko here. Call a cab and expense it."

* * *

Erin sent Carlyle the briefest of text messages: "I'm fine, coming home now." Then she sat in the back of the taxi for the ride to Manhattan. Fortunately, with the hotel so close to the airport, she hadn't had to wait long for the cab.

"Rough night out there, huh?" the cabbie said.

"Rough night," she agreed.

"What's all that stuff with the police at the Hilton?" he asked.

"There was some sort of explosion," she said. "I'm sure it'll be in the papers."

Her phone buzzed with Carlyle's reply. It was even shorter than hers, only two words: "Thank God."

After all the subterfuge and misdirection, it felt very odd to have the taxi pull up right outside the Barley Corner. The pub was an island of warm light and cheerful hubbub in the midst of the rain-drenched concrete. Erin resisted the call of the front door and went around the back way, wanting to avoid attention. She slipped in as quietly as she could, squelching in her soaked shoes, leaving wet footprints on the floor.

Ian was standing in the doorway of his security office. He nodded to her.

"Thanks for the help," she said.

"Help with what?" he replied, wearing a perfect poker face.

She mustered up a weary smile and trudged past him, dragging herself up the stairs. Rolf was lying on the landing, nose protruding over the top step. She couldn't see his tail, but she could hear it swishing back and forth on the floor.

"Hey, kiddo," she said. She knelt on the steps and put her face up close to his. "How're you doing?"

Rolf was not, as a rule, a demonstrative dog, but cops, as a rule, didn't blow up cars either. There was a time and place to break the rules. He extended his tongue and licked her cheek. Then he kept doing it, giving her a vigorous slurping.

"Darling," Carlyle said from the living room doorway. There he was, immaculate in one of his expensive gray suits, necktie neatly knotted. But his face was very pale, his eyes hollow.

Erin stood up. "Hey," she said. "I'm back. Jesus, you look awful, like you're the one who nearly got blown up."

He came to her and took hold of her hands in a surprisingly tight grip. "What were you thinking, Erin?" he burst out.

"Huh? What do you mean?" she replied, startled and confused.

"I told you the bomb would go up," he said. "*Up!* And then you went and parked under a bloody great sheet of plate glass! Good God, darling, I could've killed you! And for what? So you could stay out of the bloody rain?"

She pulled her hands free. "Knock it off!" she snapped. "I'm the one who nearly got killed!"

"And if you'd had your head taken off by a chunk of glass, I'd have been the one who killed you!" he shot back. "God damn it, Erin, have you any notion how near a thing that was?"

"I've got three weeks' explosives training," she said. "So no, I don't. You're the damn expert! If it was so close, why'd you set it off?"

"I didn't see any choice," he said bitterly. "Ian got us close enough that we could see you fairly well. I watched the lass get in and out the back, right enough, but the bloody Marshals were all over the place. And then your mate Neshenko showed up out of nowhere. I'd a very small window of opportunity, in which nobody was particularly close to the vehicle, but your lad was on his way in. For all I could tell, your lot were about to have a bloody committee meeting right next to the bomb. I couldn't chance anyone getting closer than they were. And I couldn't very well *not* do it! Then you'd be left with a corpse in the back seat, a missing witness, and a cover story in bloody tatters!"

He paused for breath and leaned against the doorframe. "I nearly killed you," he repeated dully.

Erin's anger drained out of her. She knew he wasn't really mad at her; he was deeply scared, because he loved her. She laid a hand on his arm.

"It's okay," she said. "I'm fine. Really. I mean, I'm soaked to the bone and I got a little crispy on the backside, but other than that, I'm just fine."

"Of course," he said, his gentleman's instincts immediately asserting themselves. "Forgive me. You'll be wanting to get out of your wet things and into the shower. Can I fetch you anything in the meantime? Food? A hot drink?"

"Some of that Irish stew from downstairs would be great," she said. "And a whiskey. Or two. But hold on a sec. What about Teresa? Did you hear from Corky?"

Carlyle's drawn features cracked into a smile. "Aye, the lad gave me a call. No fear, it was burner to burner, both phones clean. He said he'd be out of town on business for the foreseeable and not to fret."

"He didn't mention her?"

"Of course not, darling. That's implied. You might not think it, but Corky understands operational security. The lad used to be in the Brigades, remember."

"So they're gone," Erin said. She walked toward the bathroom as she talked, stripping off her dripping clothes. Rolf trailed at her hip, staying within six inches of her. He wasn't about to be left behind again.

"Aye, they're gone. Out of New York by now, if all's gone to plan. No fear, Corky's got it all planned out, to the extent he plans anything. While I've no specifics as to his location, I know he'll be taking her somewhere warm and sunny. It ought to make for a fine vacation for the lass. He's plenty of money, a reliable vehicle, and two sets of false papers."

"False papers?" Erin repeated. She stopped in the bathroom and turned to face him. "How'd he manage that?"

"He knows a lad who works with the City," Carlyle said. "That lad got copies of the lass's identification photos and whatnot to him. Then he went to another lad he knows, one who specializes in illicit documents. It was a rush job, but Miss Tommasino can pass under another name, even to the point of leaving the country if she's a notion."

"Good enough," Erin said. "And you can get in touch with him?"

"Not exactly. He'll call once a week or so, to let me know all's well. That way, we can tell him when it's safe for her to come back."

"Okay," she said. "I'll get clean and dry, and then I'd better get in touch with Vitelli. Collect my blood money."

"Not tonight," he said firmly. "He'll not expect it. He'll be thinking you'll be lying low, or dealing with police matters. And you need a good night's sleep if you're to be dealing with the likes of him. You've done enough for one day. I'll see about your supper. I'm sorry I raised my voice, darling."

"I forgive you," she said. "I'm sorry about the glass."

"No fear," he said. "I don't imagine you'll do anything of the sort again."

"Not much chance of that," she said. "We were crazy to try it once."

"Ah, but we got away with it," he said.

"Not yet," she replied. "Most of the cops bought it, I think, but Vic figured it out. I thought he was going to arrest me, or maybe shoot me."

"Then the illusion held," he said.

"So far. But Vic's not the only detective with two brain cells, and we still need to deal with the Mob."

"They're no match for you, darling."

"Easy for you to say. You're not the one who'll be talking to them."

"I could always blow them up, if you'd rather."

"Don't tempt me."

"I'm rather good at it, you ken."

"Yeah," she said. "I noticed. Oh, it slipped my mind with everything that's been going on, but we've got a dinner invitation."

"Really? With whom?"

"The Vitelli family."

Carlyle smiled. "That's grand. Will we be taking him up on it?"

"I don't know." Her face twisted wryly. "I have trouble eating with these guys."

"They'll not poison you."

"That's not the point. It feels... wrong. But maybe we should do it. For the look of the thing."

"It'd help, aye. If you can play cards with Evan O'Malley, you can break bread with Valentino Vitelli."

"That's a good point." She finished peeling off her wet clothes, leaving them in a sodden pile on the bathroom floor. "Now, are you going to stand there staring at me, or get me something to eat?"

He smiled. "It's a grand view, darling, but I'll not keep you waiting. I'll be back directly."

Chapter 28

The *Times* trumpeted the news on the front page. The words MOB WITNESS SLAIN IN CAR BOMBING marched in big, all-caps letters across the top of the paper. Beneath the headline was a photograph taken by some enterprising reporter. The picture was a weird, impressionistic blur of fire and rain and police flashers, like a snapshot from an old gumshoe's nightmares. It would probably win a Pulitzer, Erin thought sourly. She laid down the paper on Carlyle's dining table and flipped it upside down.

Somebody had leaked Teresa's name to the press; that had probably been Holliday's doing, or at least had been done with his knowledge and permission. The whole point, after all, was to tell the world that Teresa Tommasino was dead. But that would be awfully hard on the poor woman's family. Maybe Webb and Vic had managed to get to them with a victim notification ahead of time. It wasn't much consolation.

Erin decided not to bother with her morning run. She still felt tired and dragged out. She'd just take Rolf for a short walk, she thought, and figure out what to do next. Carlyle was still in the bedroom, asleep. He'd had as stressful a night as she had; in some ways, worse.

Rolf nosed her hand and wagged his tail. He'd had a quiet, boring evening. It was time for some excitement.

Her phone buzzed with a text message from Webb:

"You're on modified assignment until we get the report from the Bomb Squad. Enjoy your paid vacation."

"Thanks for nothing, sir," she muttered. While she was still staring at the phone, it lit up with an incoming call from an unknown number. Having a guess as to what it might be, she activated her recording app before answering.

"O'Reilly," she said.

"Come to the restaurant. The boss wants to buy you breakfast."

"Which restaurant?" she asked. "Which boss?"

She was talking to a dead phone line.

"Typical," she said to Rolf. "At least that answers the question of what I'm eating right now."

She stood up and went into the bedroom. Carlyle stirred and opened his eyes.

"You're a fine sight on a September morning," he said with a sleepy smile.

Erin snorted. She was wearing an old T-shirt and NYPD sweatpants. Her hair was a mess. But it was the thought that counted.

"I guess I've got my meeting with Vitelli," she said.

"Oh?" He sat up. "When?"

"Now. He invited me to breakfast. He didn't say where, so I assume it's at Lucky's, like last time."

"I'll have Ian drive you."

"Don't bother. I can get myself there."

He wasn't smiling any longer. "I wasn't making a suggestion, Erin. I'd feel much better if you'd a stout lad close to hand."

"Vitelli's not going to try anything."

"Probably not," he agreed. "And having Ian Thompson at your back makes it even less likely. You'll find the lad downstairs."

Erin had been fighting too many battles lately. This was one she chose not to fight. She just nodded and set about getting dressed. Rolf bounced slightly, tail wagging more enthusiastically. This looked promising to him.

She went with a dark ensemble; black slacks and a midnight blouse. It seemed appropriate. She also took a few moments to apply some lipstick and mascara. Normally she wouldn't have bothered, but she was trying to look like a crooked cop, someone who valued appearances more than Erin actually did. She did what she could with her hair on short notice. Then she buckled on her shield and her guns, leashed up Rolf, and headed downstairs.

She found Ian still in the security station. He had one of his Berettas on the desk in front of him, disassembled, and was cleaning it. He glanced up at her, no surprise on his face. He'd probably heard her coming from halfway down the hall.

"Need something?" he asked.

"Yeah. I need to get to Lucky's in Little Italy," she said. "Carlyle said to have you give me a lift."

"Affirmative," he said. Without looking at his hands, he reassembled the pistol in a matter of seconds. He finished by slipping the magazine into the butt, pulling the slide back to chamber a round, and holstering it under his jacket.

"Wow," she said. "You can do that blindfolded, I bet."

"Affirmative," he said again. "You don't always have enough light to see what you're doing. You ready?"

"Yeah. Are you?"

"Yes, ma—" he started out of force of habit, cutting himself off at the last moment.

"Ian, how long since you had any sleep?"

"I'm about to go off duty," he said. "Catch some sleep then."

"Have you been up for two straight nights?"

"Give or take."

She decided this was another fight not to wage. "Just remember, sleepy drivers cause as many accidents as drunks," she said.

"I'll watch out for both," he said.

*　　*　　*

Despite his lack of sleep, Ian drove with his usual skill, getting the Mercedes to Little Italy without incident. Erin made a halfhearted effort to get him to stay in the car, but she knew she wouldn't succeed. So she walked into Lucky's Restaurant flanked by a ninety-pound K-9 on her left and a former Marine Scout Sniper on her right. It occurred to her that as a show of force, it wasn't half bad.

Valentino Vitelli was in the same booth as last time. He had a pair of slab-faced goons two tables over, watching Erin's approach with stony expressions. Erin nodded to Ian and cocked her head toward the thugs' table. Ian split off from her and walked over to the two meatheads.

"Mind if I sit, sir?" he politely asked one of the thugs.

The Mafia soldier glanced at his boss, who nodded. He shrugged. "It's a free country, buddy," he said.

Ian sat, sliding his chair back from the table so he could keep an eye on both the bodyguards and Vitelli. His jacket hung open and his right hand lay in his lap, comfortable but ready.

"Miss O'Reilly," Vitelli said, standing up and extending a hand. "I'm so glad you could join me. Please, sit down."

Erin shook hands with the old man and took a seat. "*Sitz*," she instructed Rolf, who sat just outside the booth and watched her.

A waitress came to take their order, as if she'd been waiting for Erin. Maybe she had been, on Vitelli's instructions.

"You remember the pancakes?" Vitelli asked. "You gotta have the pancakes again. My friend here wants the strawberry pancakes and coffee. Same for me. How about your buddy over there? What's he want? I'm buying."

"Nothing for me, thank you, sir," Ian said.

"Not even coffee?" Vitelli said. He waved his hand dismissively. "A cup of coffee for my friend there."

The waitress departed. Erin looked at Vitelli. He seemed friendly and pleasant enough. He had a copy of the *Times* on the table, front page up. She didn't think that was a coincidence.

"You done good, Erin," Vitelli said. "Can I call you that? Erin?"

"Of course you can, Mr. Vitelli," she said. It was good to get the names on tape. Her recorder was listening.

"Real good," he said. "But my boy's still behind bars."

"Without their star witness, they're going to have a lot of trouble making the charges stick," she said.

"Yeah, but they got the wrong judge on the case," Vitelli said. "The guy they got's a real hardass. Old-school, like they used to have out west. You know, the kind who just wants to string 'em up? But what can you do?"

"I did my part," Erin said. "I took care of the witness, just like you asked."

He patted the back of her hand. Erin saw his hand coming and schooled herself not to flinch.

"Yeah, you did," he said. "Beautiful. And I'm glad she didn't suffer none, didn't know it was coming. That poor girl, just in the wrong place, wrong time. Terrible thing."

"It's a little late to feel bad about it," she said.

"Yeah, you're right," Vitelli said. He sighed. "It's a hell of a world we live in, and we gotta leave it to our kids. It's better they don't know what we do for them, isn't it? If they knew, they'd either be guilty or they'd be spoiled. We want them to be better. But nine times out of ten, they grow up just like us. We got a saying where I come from: *La mela non cade mai lontana dall'albero.*"

"What's that mean?" she asked.

"The apple don't ever fall far from the tree," Vitelli said. "That's the worst part of it. You ever have kids, you'll know what I mean."

"We've got a business arrangement, Mr. Vitelli," she said quietly. "I assume that's why you asked me to come here."

"Yeah, sure," he said. "Al over there, he's got something for you. Al, you want to give this nice lady what you got?"

One of the goons got to his feet and lumbered over, pulling a manila envelope out of the inside of his jacket. It was a very thick envelope. He handed it to Erinwith a nod of professional respect and returned to his seat.

Erin bent the fastener on the envelope and popped it open. She glanced inside. It looked to be full of large-denomination bills; lots and lots of them, tied in neat bundles. She made no effort to count the cash, knowing that would be rude and would also take a while and raise some eyebrows. She didn't think many women counted out fifty grand on the table in this restaurant. Then again, maybe some of them did.

"It's all here?" she asked. "Fifty grand?"

"Every cent," Vitelli said. "You earned it."

He patted her hand again. "You're one of us now, Erin," he said. "You can't get made, of course, on account of you're not Italian. But anybody needs me to, I'll vouch for you. You got a friend in me, and if you ever need anything, you just give me a call."

"I'll remember that," she said.

"And we may have more work for you, down the road," he said. "You did so good with this one. I bet I know where you learned it, too. Everybody knows about Cars and what he done in the old days. I guess he still knows his old tricks."

"You can't teach an old dog new tricks," Erin said, pasting a smile on her face. "But he doesn't forget the ones he knew."

The waitress came to the table. She distributed the plates. Rolf watched with interest, but without much hope. In his experience, professional food-service workers rarely dropped things.

"Come on," Vitelli said to Erin. "Eat up."

The ricotta pancakes were delicious, but the lump in Erin's throat made it hard to swallow. The taste of victory, she'd learned, could be bittersweet.

* * *

"Interesting place for a meeting," Phil Stachowski said. "Appropriate, I guess. How did things go?"

He was sitting in the pew just behind Erin in the sanctuary of Carlyle's church. Morning Mass had already ended and the room was empty. Up in the loft, a woman was practicing a requiem. The high, sweet soprano tones echoed from the rafters. Phil and Erin faced forward, as if they were just two ordinary parishioners who'd come in off the street to pray. Rolf was lying at Erin's feet, chin on his paws.

"Everything went more or less according to plan," Erin said. "I mean, my boyfriend almost killed me, my partner wanted to arrest me, and the Hilton's going to be making one hell of an insurance claim, but besides that, it went great."

"Was anybody hurt?" Phil asked.

"No. Except Jane Doe, but she was already dead, so I don't think she counts."

"And your witness?"

"Safe and on her way to an undisclosed location," she said. "With a hopeless womanizer. What the hell was I thinking, Phil? This was a terrible idea."

"It worked," he said. "You saved an innocent woman's life and you got in deeper with the Mob. Have you heard from them yet?"

"Yeah." Erin dropped the manila envelope to the floor, planted her foot on top of it, and slid it back under the pew. Phil stooped and picked it up.

"Is this what I think it is?" he asked.

"Fifty thousand in there," she said. "To the dime. I counted it after. I didn't disrespect Vitelli by counting it in front of him. And I got him on the wire. We've got him dead to rights for conspiracy to commit first-degree murder. Of course, we can't arrest him yet. We'll build a file and nail him the moment we close down the undercover operation. Take down all the bad guys at once."

"Good work, Erin."

She knew it was bad tradecraft, but she twisted her head around to look at him. "If it was such good work, why do I feel like shit?" she demanded.

"You're spending time with murderers and thieves," he said gently. "You're lying about who you are. You're looking at the worst side of humanity and being forced to smile at it. You just accepted money for what they think was the vicious murder of an ordinary woman. This is supposed to feel bad, Erin. If you felt good about this, I'd be worried about you."

"They're still people, Phil," she said. "That's what gets me. These jerks aren't a hundred percent bad. I mostly hate them, but not all the way. I mean, Carlyle is one of them, and I love him."

"Carlyle made his own choices," Phil said. "Including, in the end, the right ones. These others have the same choices to make. It's not up to you."

"I know that," she said, turning back to face the altar. "It's just… I used to think it was black and white. Cops and robbers. Angels and devils. But it's not that simple. There's angels on their side, and a few devils on ours. And you know something? Every devil used to be an angel."

"As long as you can tell the difference, you'll be okay," he said. "Is that what's bothering you?"

"We had to go outside the rules," she said. "If what we did had gone sideways, we'd be the criminals. I would've taken the responsibility, but all of us would've been in the wrong. Holliday warned me about that. And… geez. This wasn't business, it was personal."

"What do you mean?"

"This whole thing was about fathers and sons," she said. "Alfie Madonna wants to get back at the Lucarellis for what happened to his dad. Valentino Vitelli was just trying to look out for his son. Yeah, I get it, you can't murder people, not even for the sake of your family, but at least I understand why he was doing it. Did you ever notice that every gangster has daddy issues?"

"I think every boy has daddy issues," Phil said. "Every girl, too, come to that."

"My dad was a cop," Erin said. "Is that why I always wanted to be one? What if he'd been a gangster? Would I be just like Alfie?"

"There's no way to know," he said. "But I believe, when you get down to it, no matter where we come from or what's happened to us, we all choose what we do and who we are. That's what tells us which face we'll see in the mirror; the angel or the demon."

"All I see when I look in the mirror is a woman who sleeps too little and drinks too much," she said sourly.

"It's hard to keep a sense of perspective when you're in the middle of something," Phil said. "You need to look at it from the outside."

"Maybe," she said. "From where I'm standing, the people I ended up trusting this time were on both sides, gangsters and cops. Levine and Skip, Corky and Carlyle."

"No, they weren't," Phil said. "Everybody was on the same side: yours."

"Is that supposed to make me feel better?"

"Doesn't it? You brought out the best in a couple of men most would've given up on. You made a plan, a risky one, but it worked. And our team won this round. You may not feel like it at the moment, but we won."

"Is it worth it?"

Erin wasn't looking at Phil as she asked the question. She was looking at the stained-glass windows that lined the sanctuary. Those angels and saints had golden halos. It was always easy to tell what they were.

"I can't answer that for you," he said. "But I can say this. Sure, your dad might've been a gangster, and then maybe you would've grown up to be a gangster girl. But he wasn't, and you didn't. What was your dad?"

"A cop," Erin said quietly.

"And what are you?"

"A cop," she said more firmly.

"That's what I thought." He put a hand on her shoulder and squeezed. "And for what it's worth, I think you're a damned good one. Hold on to that."

Phil got up and left the sanctuary, the echo of his footfalls fading away. Erin stayed where she was. She looked down at her hands. A cold, wet nose brushed her knee. Rolf stared up at her, head cocked.

"That's what we are," she told the K-9. "We're cops, right?"

Rolf watched and listened. He wanted her to know that he was on her side, no matter what.

She scratched behind his ears. "Good boy, Rolf. We've got this. And next time, I'll bring you along. I promise."

Rolf laid his chin on her leg and wagged his tail.

Watch for

Tequila Sunrise

*A romantic thriller featuring
Corky Corcoran and Teresa Tommasino*

Coming February 2023

To get a reminder,
sign up at clickworkspress.com/eor

Here's a sneak peek from Book 19: Italian Stallion

Coming 3/27/2023

"You know, normal couples go out dancing," Erin O'Reilly said. "They eat out at fancy restaurants. They buy each other flowers and chocolates."

"That so?" Vic Neshenko replied. "I always wondered what normal people did." He shifted his rifle to his left hand and used his other hand to adjust his Kevlar vest. The vest was black, emblazoned with big white letters that read POLICE.

"Quit squirming around," Zofia Piekarski said. The petite blonde shot Vic an elbow. "We don't have enough room in here."

"I can't help it," Vic grumbled. "This damn thing is chafing me. I'm gonna get blisters."

"Better than catching bullets," Erin said. "Look at Rolf. He's wearing a vest and he's not complaining."

"He never complains," Vic said. "Because he can't talk."

"Of course he can," Erin said, bending down to give Rolf an affectionate scratch behind the ears. "It's not his fault you don't know how to listen."

The German Shepherd tilted his head sideways to give Erin better access. His tongue was hanging out and he was panting, but it wasn't on account of his K-9 body armor or the crowded, stuffy van. Rolf was excited. He knew action was coming and he couldn't wait to get in on it.

"*Platz,*" Erin told him, giving him his command to lie down in his native tongue. Rolf obediently laid his head between his paws, but his tail would not be restrained. It was whipping back and forth across the floor.

As Erin sat back and tried to get comfortable, she had to admit Piekarski had a point. The surveillance van was very crowded with Street Narcotics Enforcement Unit cops. Officer Firelli and Sergeant Logan were the lucky ones; they got to ride up front, where there were actual seats and headrests. The others—Erin, Vic, Rolf, Janovich, and Piekarski—were in back, stuffed in among SNEU's snooper equipment, weapons, and other gear.

The van itself was more than a decade old, painted a shade of brown that reminded Erin of clogged toilets in subway restrooms. A few months back, the van had taken a few rounds during a shootout. Some cheapskate mechanic had slapped sheet metal over the holes without even trying to match the color. If the intention had been to create an inconspicuous vehicle, Erin thought, they'd failed. This was the sort of van you wouldn't just remember. If you liked cars, it would follow you into your nightmares.

"So tell me more, Erin," Vic said, twisting his shoulders awkwardly. He was a big guy and there really wasn't enough room for him. "What else do these normal people do? Do they go to bars?"

"Yeah," Erin said.

"How about strip clubs?" Janovich asked.

"Those, too," Erin said, looking directly at Vic. "Especially for the bachelor party."

"I don't think that's a good idea," Vic said.

"You don't want a bachelor party?" Janovich asked.

"We're not even engaged!" Vic protested.

"Choose your next words very carefully," Piekarski advised.

"I'm not talking about bachelor parties," Vic said. "I'm talking booze. We're sitting here, bored out of our minds, armed to the friggin' teeth. Now imagine if we were all hammered. Next thing you know, we're monkeying with our guns and we've got half the wedding party in the hospital with GSWs. That's if we were getting married, which we're not."

Everyone shut up for a few moments. Erin tried to avoid looking at Piekarski's midsection. The other woman wasn't showing yet, and it'd be hard to tell under her clothes in any case, but Piekarski and Vic were facing an unavoidable biological deadline.

"Hey, Sarge?" Piekarski called, banging on the thin metal wall that separated the front of the van and putting her face up to the little mesh-covered window in it. "Anything going on yet?"

"Not yet," Logan replied. "But don't fall asleep back there. This was a good tip."

"I hope so," Vic muttered.

"Firelli has his ear to the street," Piekarski assured him. "If he says there's a delivery going down, he's right."

"Thanks for bringing us along," Erin said. "Vic was getting bored. So was Rolf."

"Yeah," Piekarski said, patting Vic's cheek. "I know how he gets. All work and no play."

"We haven't taken down a perp in two weeks," Vic growled. "Another day or two and I was gonna have Erin put on the bite sleeve."

"You help with Rolf's training?" Piekarski asked.

"Sometimes, yeah. But I was gonna be the one chewing on her arm."

"How sweet," Erin said. To tell the truth, she was just as happy as Vic and her K-9 to get out of the office. The last major incident they'd been involved in, a bomb blast which had destroyed a car and apparently killed the only eyewitness to a murder, had resulted in the entire Major Crimes squad being temporarily benched.

Captain Holliday had explained it as a question of optics. Internal Affairs had cleared Erin of any culpability in the explosion, but the result had still been a serious dent in the state's case against the son of a prominent Mafia boss. A slap on the wrist was both inevitable and necessary.

The whole thing was absurd, of course, for three reasons. Erin had been culpable in the bomb; in fact, she'd set it up with her boyfriend's help. Morton "Cars" Carlyle might be retired from the IRA, but he hadn't forgotten how to build a car bomb. However, the bombing had been a fake-out. They'd swapped out their witness for an unidentified cadaver at the last moment. That witness was somewhere safe and warm right now, probably sitting on a beach sipping cocktails with Carlyle's best friend. Erin's only concern for the woman's wellbeing was that Corky Corcoran was bound to be hitting on her, in spite of Erin's specific instructions. That was just Corky being Corky.

Last, but not least, Captain Holliday himself had been in on the scheme and had personally approved it. And Vic hadn't even been involved; he'd shown up at the last minute, just in time to see the fireworks. So for the two of them to be punished by being placed on the dreaded "modified assignment" was deeply unfair. But there was no point whining about it. Sometimes you just had to take your lumps, even when you didn't deserve them. It was part of the Job.

Two weeks was a long time for cops like Erin and Vic to shuffle paperwork, and it was particularly hard on Rolf, who'd been completely innocent. The Shepherd's sad brown eyes had remorselessly tracked Erin every hour of those endless days.

Thus, when Piekarski asked Vic if he wanted to ride along on an SNEU stakeout of a suspected heroin dealer, Erin had seized the opportunity to accompany them. Now they were in the back of SNEU's van in a back alley in Little Italy. They were still bored, but at least there was the promise of action in the near future.

"These guys aren't Lucarellis, are they?" was the only concern Erin had expressed when she'd climbed into the van.

"Nah," Firelli had said. "These are freelancers, just setting up shop. Hell, we're probably doing the Oil Man a favor by taking them off the street. We're eliminating his competition."

Erin didn't like the idea of helping Vinnie "The Oil Man" Moreno, but the head of the Lucarellis thought Erin was a crooked cop, so for now, it suited her purposes. So she'd nodded and kept her mouth shut.

"We should've brought a deck of cards," Janovich said.

"Like you know how to play poker," Piekarski said.

"I'm a great poker player," Janovich said. "I'm just unlucky."

"He blew five grand in Atlantic City once," Piekarski told Vic.

"*Really* unlucky," Janovich said. Like the rest of the SNEU squad, he was in plainclothes, wearing his shield on a chain around his neck. Erin, Vic, and Rolf were the only ones wearing vests over their clothes. The others' armor was concealed under their coats.

"If you've got consistently bad luck, it's not luck," Erin said.

"Hey guys, put a sock in it," Logan said through the screen. "We got company."

The squad immediately quieted down, becoming all business. SNEU had a reputation as reckless cowboys, but they were trained professionals at heart. Vic hefted his rifle. The rest of the team drew their sidearms. Erin press-checked her Glock, racking the slide just far enough to confirm a round was chambered.

"We've got a white panel truck," Firelli reported. "Two guys up front. They're backing into the alley across the street. Looks like they're going to the loading dock."

"Wait until they park," Logan said. "We need to confirm their destination."

"Where do we think they're going?" Erin asked quietly.

"The White Stallion Nightclub," Piekarski said. "Firelli's guy says it's a front. Under new management as of last week."

"How many guys we dealing with?" Vic asked. "Besides the two in the truck."

"Don't know," Janovich said. "At least one, maybe more."

"We should have backup," Erin said.

"Why do you think we brought you folks along?" Piekarski asked. "This is how we roll in SNEU."

"Okay," Logan said. "They stopped. They're getting out of the truck. Showtime."

The van's engine coughed reluctantly to life, sputtering and vibrating unhappily. The smell of exhaust filled the interior.

"You guys gotta get a new ride," Vic groaned.

"Hey, you wanted to be here," Erin reminded him as Firelli put the van in gear. The rustbucket lumbered across the street. Firelli wasn't driving quickly, not yet. The whole point of the van was that it didn't look like a police vehicle. He'd try to get as close as possible without spooking their targets.

In back, Erin clenched her jaw and waited. It was all she could do. She couldn't even see out of the van. She hoped Logan knew what he was doing.

The van lurched to one side as Firelli clipped the curb. Erin's head smacked into the metal paneling and she winced. Then the van swung diagonally and came to an abrupt stop.

"Take 'em at the dock," Logan said. "Go!"

Janovich twisted the handle on the back door of the van, swinging it open. He jumped down and went around the vehicle. Vic and Erin were right behind him, Piekarski bringing up the rear. Rolf scrambled beside Erin, claws scrabbling in his eagerness.

The alley was narrow and Firelli had parked at an angle, blocking it almost completely. The officers darted through the narrow gap at the van's back corner and rushed toward the dock, weapons ready. Behind them, Logan was getting out of the passenger seat. Firelli stayed behind the wheel, ready to drive if they had to run down an escapee.

Erin saw an unmarked white truck at a concrete loading dock. Two men were standing on the dock, staring at them. One was bent over, gripping the bottom of the sliding door, getting ready to pull it open. He stayed that way, frozen, a comical look of surprise stamped on his face. The other was upright, but also caught totally off guard.

It was a textbook bust, Erin thought. They had these guys cold. Everything was going exactly the way it was supposed to. She felt the old thrill of action, the spike of hot adrenaline. It felt so damn good to be out on the street, making moves.

Then somebody shouted "Gun!" and everything went straight to hell.

A pistol went off, three quick shots, the echoes bouncing off the brickwork on both sides of the alley. Erin couldn't see any muzzle flash, had no idea where the shots were coming from. The guy standing on the dock went down in a heap. The other man screamed and dropped flat on the concrete. More shots were fired.

"Hold fire!" Logan shouted. "God damn it, hold—"

"I didn't shoot!" Janovich shouted back.

"Nobody did!" Piekarski yelled, which made no sense at all.

Then a man in a white shirt came out the back door of the nightclub. He had a pump shotgun in his hands. Two more shots went off. Erin took aim at him and slid her finger inside the trigger guard. She was uncomfortably aware that the alley had very little cover. If the gunman raised the weapon and pointed it at her or any of the other cops, she'd have no choice but to shoot.

"NYPD!" several of the squad shouted, voices overlapping.

The gunman turned, but he turned away. He wasn't even looking at Erin or her comrades. He was staring at something on the far side of the truck, something she couldn't see.

"Drop it!" Logan and Vic shouted in perfect unison.

Several guns fired, the echoes of the shots rolling across Erin's ears in a continuous cacophony. Chips of brick and clouds of dust exploded around the gunman, who convulsed violently as at least one bullet hit home. Erin saw blood blossom on the white fabric over his back. The man fell, twisting with the impact, and the muzzle of his gun swung toward the SNEU squad as he lost his grip with his left hand. The shotgun went off with a roar. The man slumped against the wall and dropped the gun, which clattered to the loading dock.

"Taking fire!" Piekarski yelled.

Erin's head was spinning. There were other shooters behind the truck. A rival gang? Lucarelli muscle, maybe? She had no idea.

"Vic!" she screamed.

Vic had dropped to one knee beside the alley wall, his M4 at his shoulder, looking for targets. He glanced Erin's way. "What?" he called back.

She pointed with her leash hand. "Active shooters!"

He nodded, got his feet under him, and rushed toward her. Rolf, at Erin's side, barked excitedly. His tail whipped back and forth, but he stayed with her, waiting for instructions.

Erin ran to the front of the truck, keeping low. A lot of people thought a car's bodywork would stop bullets. They were wrong. Modern cars were flimsy, made of plastic and thin sheet metal. Even a handgun could punch right through. But the engine block was solid. Erin crouched behind it and got ready. She could hear the SNEU officers all talking and shouting at once. Sirens wailed in the background, punctuated by still more gunfire. Backup would be there in seconds, seconds they didn't have.

Vic joined her, dropping down beside her. "Ready?" he asked.

"Yeah," she said. "Rolf, *platz*. On three?"

He nodded. "One... two... three!"

The two detectives came up side by side, bringing their guns in line. Erin didn't know what to expect; a bunch of bad-attitude gunmen seemed the most likely. What she saw was a trio of men with pistols, aiming and firing at the loading dock, holding the guns in two-handed grips. They were wearing ordinary street clothes, but they clearly knew what they were doing with their weapons. The guy in the middle had on a pair of sunglasses.

"Drop your guns!" she shouted, taking aim at the guy in the middle.

The middle guy's head turned her way. With the glasses screening his eyes, she couldn't tell what his expression was. He held up his left hand, palm toward her, but his right was still holding the pistol and it was pointed at her.

A shotgun blast came from Erin's left, followed by a volley of pistol fire at her back. At least, that was what she thought. Her ears were ringing from the echoes and she was having trouble placing the gunfire. But the man in her sights wasn't currently shooting, so she hesitated, finger tight on her trigger.

One of the gunmen behind Sunglasses Man saw Erin and Vic. He swung toward them, drawing a bead with his pistol, and snapped off a shot. The bullet ricocheted off the hood of the truck and tumbled between the two detectives.

Vic fired. The M4 was a powerful, accurate rifle, very similar to the so-called civilian AR-15. Vic was an excellent shot and the range was less than twenty yards. He might as well have been standing right in front of his target. The rifle round struck the man high up on the chest and went straight through, exiting in a fine spray of blood.

The third man cursed and fired twice at Vic, before Vic's target even had time to fall down. Erin, operating on reflex and training, shifted aim and pulled the trigger. Her Glock barked. A brass casing spun out the back. The slide snapped forward, chambering another round, and she fired again. Both rounds slammed home, perfect center-of-mass shots. The man toppled backward as if she'd slugged him with a baseball bat. His gun spun out of his hand.

Sunglasses Man let go of his pistol, letting it clatter to the pavement. He had his hands up now. Both his buddies were on the ground, writhing in pain.

"Cover me," Erin snapped to Vic. Keeping her Glock trained on the unwounded man, she walked quickly around the front fender of the truck. Rolf kept pace, his eyes on Erin in spite of the noise and confusion.

"Get down on the ground!" Erin snapped at the man. "On your stomach!"

"Hold it!" Sunglasses Man said. "You don't understand!"

"On the ground, or I'll put you there!" she shouted. "Now! Or I will shoot you!"

Her absolute sincerity was written on her face. He did the only smart thing and dropped to his knees, then flat on his belly. He laced his fingers behind his neck in a gesture which showed he knew how this sort of thing went.

Erin looped her leash around her wrist and took out her cuffs, dimly aware that the shooting had stopped. Someone was screaming. It sounded like a woman.

"Vic, we need a bus!" Erin called without taking her eyes from her prisoner. "And a first-aid kit!"

Vic made no reply. Erin stood over her target and got ready to cuff him. Rolf watched the man balefully, hoping he'd try something.

"Officer, you're making a huge mistake," Sunglasses Man said. He started to twist his head toward her.

"Don't look at me!" she ordered. She'd heard it all before, and there was too much going on to take any notice of a criminal's bullshit. They had multiple gunshot casualties in the alley, not to mention an unknown number of living perps and unsecured weapons.

"Vic!" she said again. "Call Dispatch!"

There was still no response. The female voice kept screaming.

A thought penetrated the adrenaline-soaked fog of Erin's brain. As far as she knew, there were only two women in the alley, and she was one of them. If another woman was screaming, that could only be...

"Piekarski," Erin gasped. She glanced toward the truck. Vic was nowhere in sight.

"Shit," she muttered. "Shit, shit, shit." She holstered her gun and quickly cuffed the man at her feet, leaving him on the ground. Then she tried to think.

Backup would be there any minute. The sirens were very close. She couldn't do anything for Piekarski that Vic wouldn't already be doing. Her job was to guard these three shooters and make sure they didn't escape or die before the Patrol units arrived.

"Rolf!" she said. *"Pass auf!"*

That wasn't one of his more usual commands, but Rolf knew what it meant. He immediately went stiff-legged and attentive, staring fixedly at the man on the ground. He'd stand guard until she told him otherwise, and if any of the perps tried anything, he'd make them sorry they had.

"You stupid bitch," Sunglasses Man said.

"Shut up," Erin said absentmindedly. "Stay right there. Don't move an inch." She went toward the man Vic had shot. This guy had been writhing around at first, but now he was lying still, which wasn't a good sign. A pool of blood was spreading out around him.

"You stupid bitch," Sunglasses Man said again. "We're cops, you idiot. You just shot two of your own."

Erin went suddenly very cold inside. She dropped to her knees beside the wounded man and pulled his jacket open. Under the leather coat was a black Kevlar vest. Contrary to popular opinion, it wasn't bulletproof; just bullet-resistant. Against Vic's high-powered rifle at close range, it had been about as useful as tissue paper. On a chain around the man's neck hung a gold NYPD shield.

"Oh my God," she whispered. Erin O'Reilly was a tough woman. She'd seen plenty of violence and death in her twelve years on the street. But now her vision went gray. Nausea curled inside her like a sickening snake. She put out a hand to brace herself on the pavement, or she would've fallen over.

Dimly, as if from the bottom of a very deep hole, she heard Sergeant Logan. He was shouting something, but to her ears it was very faint.

"Officer down! We've got an officer down!"

Ready for more?

Join Steven Henry's author email list
for the latest on new releases, upcoming books and
series, behind-the-scenes details, events, and more.

Be the first to know about new releases in the Erin
O'Reilly Mysteries by signing up at
tinyurl.com/StevenHenryEmail

About the Author

Steven Henry learned how to read almost before he learned how to walk. Ever since he began reading stories, he wanted to put his own on the page. He lives a very quiet and ordinary life in Minnesota with his wife and dog.

Also by Steven Henry

Fathers
A Modern Christmas Story

When you strip away everything else, what's left is the truth

Life taught Joe Davidson not to believe in miracles. A blue-collar wood-worker, Joe is trying to build a future. His father drank himself to death and his mother succumbed to cancer, leaving a broken, struggling family. He and his brother and sisters are faced with failed marriages, growing pains, and lingering trauma.

Then a chance meeting at his local diner brings Mary Elizabeth Reynolds

into his life. Suddenly, Joe finds himself reaching for something more, a dream of happiness. The wood-worker and the poor girl from a trailer park connect and fall in love, and for a little while, everything is right with their world.

But suddenly Joe is confronted with a situation he never imagined. What do you do if your fiancée is expecting a child you know isn't yours? Torn between betrayal and love, trying to do the right thing when nothing seems right anymore, Joe has to strip life down to its truth and learn that, in spite of the pain, love can be the greatest miracle of all.

Learn more at clickworkspress.com/fathers.

Tequila Sunrise

A James Corcoran Story

A steamy romantic thriller set in the world of the Erin O'Reilly Mysteries

Teresa Tommasino has always avoided trouble. Never married, she's gone through life quietly, content to be a Brooklyn schoolteacher. She knows the Mafia run her neighborhood, but as long as she keeps her head down, she figures she'll be safe.

But trouble has a way of slipping into even the most peaceful life. After witnessing a terrible crime, Teresa is drawn into a world of gangsters, fear, and deception. With a contract out on her life, she agrees to a desperate plan: a car bomb, a faked death, and an escape from New York.

Now Teresa is on the run through a world bigger and more frightening than she ever imagined, her only protection an enigmatic Irishman. James Corcoran seems to be everything she needs: charming, resourceful, and brave. But he, too, is running from something, and he has secrets of his own.

Drawn to James, Teresa will have to balance her survival with her slowly awakening desire. Will the terrified witness and the repentant criminal find their way to a future together, or will their pasts destroy them?

Learn more at clickworkspress.com/corky01.

More great titles from Clickworks Press

www.clickworkspress.com

The Altered Wake

Megan Morgan

Amid growing unrest, a family secret and an ancient laboratory unleash long-hidden superhuman abilities. Now newly-promoted Sentinel Cameron Kardell must chase down a rogue superhuman who holds the key to the powers' origin: the greatest threat Cotarion has seen in centuries – and Cam's best friend.

"Incredible. Starts out gripping and keeps getting better."

Learn more at clickworkspress.com/sentinel1.

Hubris Towers: The Complete First Season

Ben Y. Faroe & Bill Hoard

Comedy of manners meets comedy of errors in a new series for fans of Fawlty Towers and P. G. Wodehouse.

"So funny and endearing"

"Had me laughing so hard that I had to put it down to catch my breath"

"Astoundingly, outrageously funny!"

Learn more at clickworkspress.com/hts01.

Death's Dream Kingdom
Gabriel Blanchard

A young woman of Victorian London has been transformed into a vampire. Can she survive the world of the immortal dead— or perhaps, escape it?

"The wit and humor are as Victorian as the setting... a winsomely vulnerable and tremendously crafted work of art."

"A dramatic, engaging novel which explores themes of death, love, damnation, and redemption."

Learn more at clickworkspress.com/ddk.

Share the love!

Join our microlending team at
kiva.org/team/clickworkspress.

Keep in touch!

Join the Clickworks Press email list
and get freebies, production updates, special deals,
behind-the-scenes sneak peeks, and more.

Sign up today at clickworkspress.com/join.

www.ingramcontent.com/pod-product-compliance
Lightning Source LLC
Chambersburg PA
CBHW021219310726
48971CB00006B/1621